Dear Reader,

Camera Shy is a very special story to me. This book helped free me from a writing slump. Yes, it is a romance story and I hope you enjoy all the spice, but I hope you also find a story about demanding respect, kindness, and loyalty from all the relationships in your life—romantic, friendship, and family.

I think too often we tolerate bad behavior from those closest to us because of that age-old saying: you hurt the ones you love. **It's time to change that narrative.**

Don't let the insecurities, fears, and toxicity that others are battling seep into your life and rattle your self-worth. If the people you love are hurting you, cut the dead weight. Let's champion and support the relationships that mean most to us, instead of trampling all over them out of jealousy and carelessness.

For every single woman in the world who is suffering from self-doubt, and painful insecurities, I hope the message you'll take from this story is that: **You are beautiful. You are worthy.** You are already a queen and deserve to be treated as such. As Finn will say in this story ahead, you should be **earned** every day of your life.

So, put down this book for a moment and go compliment a friend who treats you well; tell them they are amazing. Go hug your significant other and tell them how much you treasure their love. Get in front of the mirror, then tell yourself how *lucky* you are to be you because you're beautifully unique and should be celebrated just the way you are.

Then, pick this book back up and enjoy the sassy, sexy journey to Avery and Finn's HEA!

Happy Reading!
Kay

CAMERA
SHY

KAY COVE

PAGE
&
VINE

Page & Vine
An Imprint of Meredith Wild LLC

Paperback ISBN: 979-8-9895288-4-4

Chapter 1

Avery

I scour Mason's face for any glint of a tell as the waitress sets a colossal slice of chocolate cake in front of us.

"Happy birthday," she says with a wide, toothy smile.

"Thank you." I rub my hands together then straighten the single, pink-striped candle that was starting to tilt. "It's my thirtieth today."

"Oh, hey," she chirps, her eyes lighting up, "it's your golden birthday."

"My what?"

"It's April thirtieth, and you're turning thirty." She twirls her wrist. "Hence, your golden birthday. You only get one. I'm June first, so mine was wasted before I even knew what a birthday was." She pokes out her tongue playfully. "But your golden birthday kicks off your golden year—which means thirty will be the best year of your life."

"I like the sound of that." I look back into my boyfriend's deep-brown eyes. "Cheers to my *golden birthday*." I hold up my champagne flute and tilt the rim towards the waitress. "And thank you for being so wonderful tonight. The steak was superb. You were lovely. This is officially the best birthday meal I've ever had."

Mason chuckles as he leans back in his seat and tugs on the sleeves of his navy sports coat. "That's my girlfriend's subtle way of telling me to leave you a generous tip this evening."

I glance between them as they exchange a quick, knowing look.

Oh, it's happening.

She knows something.

There is most definitely a hidden surprise in this slice of cake.

"Would you like me to bring out the staff to sing?"

I open my mouth, but Mason answers for me. "Please God, no." He embarrasses so easily, but I don't mind the singing. It's fun and silly. These days we've hardly had time for fun and silly. Our business together is booming, which means we're working nearly fourteen-hour days. My birthday celebration dinner is the first time we've gotten dressed up and gone out in months. Hell, I think tonight is worth singing about.

Our waitress lights my single pink candle and flashes me one more genuine smile. "I'll leave you to it."

"Damn." Mason lets out a whisper of a chuckle as soon as she's out of earshot. "Did we order a slice or a whole damn cake?" The rich triple-fudge frosting matches the hue of his irises, and the dense devil's food cake is the same color as his furrowed brows.

With a devious smile, and much to Mason's horror, I dive in with both of my forefingers, using them as chopsticks as I massacre the dessert.

Searching... Where the hell is it?

Leave it to Mason to do something tacky as all hell like hiding an engagement ring in a slice of birthday cake.

Thirty. I'm freaking thirty years old today. The moment is here, and that damn ring better be somewhere in this massive piece of chocolatey goodness.

I found the ring about six months ago in our upstairs closet, hardly hidden. It was careless of Mason, really. We've been dating for over four years. We've lived together for two. He should be well aware by now that once the winter weather hits, I am religious about folding my summer tank tops and flowy skirts into tidy, color-coordinated piles and stacking them neatly on the top shelf of the closet. Of course I noticed the lonely ring box on the top shelf. He probably tossed it up there in a hurry to hide it, unaware that when someone's standing on a small step stool, eye level with the highest shelf, the tufted black jewelry box is impossible to miss.

I'm a good girlfriend, though. I didn't even peek. Sliding the box about a foot to the left, I went about my business and pretended I didn't notice. I've never rushed Mason. It took him exactly ten dates before he officially asked me to be his girlfriend. We waited an entire year before he introduced me to his family. Another year after that we moved in together. Mason is slow and steady like a turtle. My reliable, loving, sweet turtle whose last name I can't wait to share. I can be patient for him...

Or, at least that's what I told myself six months ago.

I didn't expect him to propose at his parents' fortieth wedding anniversary reception...although I'd hoped. It was such a beautiful night. It was a tad chilly on the California beach in October. Mason draped his suit coat over me like the gentleman he is. We all sat barefoot on the beach as we watched his parents dance right at twilight, listening to the low hiss of the waves crashing against the tide. It would've been the perfect time to tell me that it's exactly what he wanted for us in forty-some years.

But the night came and went. I get it. It was his parents' night, not ours.

Then there was Thanksgiving—okay, I didn't have high hopes for that one. We both looked like potbellied pigs after three Thanksgiving dinners—his parents, my mom, and my dad's family. I was so swollen from the sodium- and sugar-induced coma, he would've had extreme difficulty sliding a ring on my finger. It was not exactly romantic.

Christmas was—again—*hectic*. Three separate families crammed into one day. Once again, it was a no-go on the proposal. On New Year's Eve, I fell asleep early. I was so certain he was going to pop the question that in my giddy delight, I knocked back an entire bottle of champagne and passed out in Mason's lap by ten o'clock. I kicked myself for weeks after, wondering if I foiled his big plans.

Valentine's Day was another bust. The evening started wonderfully. He bought me the most beautiful flowers, and his card nearly had me in tears. We were in the car, on the way to the Italian restaurant to make our seven o'clock reservation, when some idiot riding our ass hit us from behind. We were okay, but Mason's bumper and right taillight were destroyed. The airbags deployed, meaning we were all but urged to go to the emergency room as a precaution. Needless to say, our moods, as well as our evening, were ruined.

Since then, it's been quiet. About once a week, I grab my little step stool and check the top of the closet, hoping the box has moved. It hadn't budged. It lay in the same spot to the left of my neat piles of clothes...

Until tonight.

Oh, you bet your ass I checked before tonight. *My thirtieth birthday.* As of eight o'clock this morning, the ring box was removed from the closet, which was why I wore my classiest black dress with the slit up to my knee, was extra thorough curling my hair, and spent an obnoxious amount of time on my smoky eye makeup. I could've given Thomas Kinkaid a run for his money the way I painted on light and shadows, contouring and highlighting my round face into the angles of a sleek antelope.

Tonight is my goddamn night.

And I will take a picture to document this monumental moment. *I swear.* Yes, I'm camera-shy. Yes, I duck and run anytime someone pulls out the selfie stick. I'm comfortable in my body, but I'm not exactly proud of it. I'm healthy. I'm just not a model. Let the beautiful people be beautiful. I'll cheer them on from the sidelines. I don't need to be a trophy. I'm treasured...by this man.

"What are you doing?" Mason asks with wide-open, bewildered eyes as I pinch apart the last remnants of cake. There is a crumbly chocolate graveyard in front of me...but no ring. I murdered this dessert, and now it's time to confess.

"*Enough,*" I grumble when I realize I'm left without a proposal for the umpteenth time. "I *know*, Mason." Grabbing the linen off my lap, I wipe off my fingers one by one. "Just ask already. If you're nervous, don't be. Of course I'll say yes."

I give him a warm, bless-his-heart smile, but instead of relief, I'm met with his petrified expression.

"Ask what?" His face flushes, and he looks incredibly nervous.

I tent my clean but still chocolate-smelling fingers over my nose and mouth. "*Oh. My. God.*" The horror floods through me as I imagine all the *other* things that could fit in a small square ring box. A crumpled-up necklace. Earrings. A key...to a safe...where I could stash my egregious embarrassment and lock it away forever. I should've opened the damn box before I let my expectations run rampant. "It wasn't a ring? *Shit*. I am so stupid...I...I thought—"

Mason holds up both of his hands in surrender, like he's trying to dissuade an approaching grizzly bear. "Avery, calm down. Are you talking about the black box on the top shelf of our bedroom closet?"

I nod sheepishly.

"Honey, it's a ring." He pats his sports coat on top of the breast pocket. "An *engagement* ring."

I let loose the breath I didn't realize I was holding. "Oh, thank God."

"You knew? How long?"

I grimace as I shrug my shoulders. "About six months."

"*Six months?*" he squalls. Clearing his throat, he leans forward. "Six months?" he asks again in a lower voice, far more collected. "And you didn't say anything? You never even asked..."

Reaching over the table, I place my fingers over his tenderly, trying to show him how I feel with just a touch. "I didn't want to be demanding or steal your moment. I know you're careful with all your decisions, and I admire you for it. You're my rock, honey." I squeeze the tips of his fingers. "When you're sure, *I'm sure.*"

Mason reaches into the inside pocket of his sleek sports coat. "You thought I put the ring in the cake?"

Hanging my head, I nod.

"And you knew about this ring for half a year and didn't badger me for a proposal?" He pulls out the familiar little black box with the thin golden lines around the seams and sets it on the table between us. At this point, I know what's coming, but there's no controlling the nervous tingles dancing furiously around in my chest.

"I wanted you to ask me because you wanted to, not because you felt you had to."

Mason's eyes begin to well and his complexion grows blotchy. His thumb knocks nervously on the table. It's an odd response, but this is a big moment for both of us. Finally, after all the familiarity of our very tame, even-keeled relationship, at least his behavior is...new?

"How long would you have waited?"

I answer his odd question with a tepid smile. "When our finish line is forever, what's the rush?"

"You're too good of a woman." He says it like an admission instead of admiration. "You're too good to me."

I shake my head, my hair falling into my face. "No, I'm not—"

"You are." His tone is so matter-of-fact that I have to study his strained expression. It's in this moment I realize he won't return my gaze. He's looking in my direction but over my shoulder. I glance behind me, trying to see what's caught his attention, but there's nothing but an elderly couple silently enjoying their steak dinner behind us.

"Is everything okay?" My eyes toggle between the box on the table and Mason's wandering gaze. Instead of answering, he covers both of his eyes with his hand. My full stomach drops ten floors as the nerves shift from excitement to dread.

"Open it," Mason says, nodding to the little box. He's normally such a gentleman. I thought when I saw the ring for the first time, it'd be between his fingers as he was down on one knee. Mason's avoiding the box like it's on fire. "Please."

I pry the box open. It's reluctant, like a clamshell unwilling to lose its pearl, but the prize inside...holy hell. "Oh my God," I mumble as I free the ring from its resting place nestled inside the tiny plush velvet pillow. "Mason, this is too much...this is what? Two carats? It's stunning. So elegant."

It's a simple platinum band with a brilliant round diamond. The cut and clarity seem flawless. I know it's far more than he can afford. Mason and I share everything—a home, a business—so I know he stretched the limits with a ring like this. I slide the ring over my finger, and it halts at my knuckle. Ignoring the pain, willing my finger to instantly slim, I force the ring over the thickest part of my finger.

"Oh, wait!" I palm my forehead. "Honey, I'm so sorry. You didn't even ask yet." I try to pull the ring off, but it's useless. It might as well be superglued on. "Shit. It's stuck." I chuckle and shrug helplessly. *That's okay. I'm never taking it off.* "It'd probably be a good time to ask me to marry you now."

He doesn't match my humor. A tear dribbles down his cheek. Mason's not cold and callous, but he certainly isn't one for public displays of affection...or unguarded emotion.

"Mason, what's—"

"I can't do this." His breath is ragged as a single tear turns into a small stream. Wiping the wetness from his cheeks with the back of his thumb, he adds, "I'm—I'm so sorry, Avery. I love you so much, but I... I really was going to ask...but...seeing it..." His eyes lock on the ring choking my finger. "Not like this. I'm so sorry." He covers his face, hiding his tormented expression. "I'm so, so sorry."

The hairs on the back of my neck rise like an animal that senses danger. "What's wrong?" I try to reach for his hand. "If you're not ready, we don't have to rush."

He quickly places his hands in his lap, safe from my clutches.

"I think we're over." He closes his eyes and braces like he's paused at the top of a rollercoaster. "I want to break up."

The world stops. Everybody in this fancy steakhouse freezes in place. The sound of thunder roars around us. Lightning strikes, splitting the ground, and from the crack, fire emerges. Or maybe that's only in my head. For now, I just focus on breathing. *In and out.* One breath at a time.

Mason watches my stunned eyes and tries to fill the silence. "I...I really do love you...I just...we're..."

I'm having trouble making sense of the moment. His stammering sounds garbled in my head. I'm wearing a ring...but we're over? *What the fuck?... It's my birthday... I can't breathe.*

"We're what?" I force the words out in a staccato. "Tell me."

"Can we go home?" Rotating his head, he takes in a cursory glance around the fancy steakhouse, ensuring no one's listening. "Please?"

"No." I shake my head and deliver my message clearly and curtly. "Start talking."

He shrugs his shoulders and holds up his palms to the ceiling. "Our sex life is..." He shakes his head, his grim expression saying everything he can't.

I quickly defend myself. "I've tried. You're the one who's always tired."

He drags both hands over his red, splotchy face. "Lately, I haven't *wanted* to have sex with you." His words are like an uppercut to my ego then a follow-up sucker punch to my heart. "Please," he says again, studying my face as intently as I was scouring his earlier.

"Please what?"

"Can we leave? Can we at least just talk in the car?"

My throat is dry, so I reach for my water, but my hand doesn't cooperate. My limbs are numb. Everything is heavy, even my eyelids. Blinking becomes a chore. Ignoring his request, I ask, "Did you cheat on me?"

He buries his face in his hands. "No," he mumbles.

I nod in relief. I don't know why it makes it better, but at least—

"But I wanted to."

My eyes snap back to Mason, who hangs his head.

"I'm sorry. If I'm being honest...there's someone else I'm interested in. *Nothing happened.*"

"Yet," I whisper, feeling the burn in my chest like I just took a straight swig of Jameson. "You're leaving me for *someone*?"

"This is about us, Avery. I'm trying to be truthful. We have a business together, we live together, and I don't want to string you along. Yes, there's someone I'm interested in, but I would never ever cheat on you. She's not important."

"Yet," I whisper again.

My demeanor is eerily calm. Mason looks concerned at my collectedness. I should be crying, blubbering...maybe throwing something at his head. But for some reason, I'm very interested in the logistics at the moment.

"What's her name?" I ask.

Mason has the audacity to roll his eyes at me. "Do you really want to do this? It's only going to hurt your feelings."

"You brought her up," I hiss. "You've just humiliated me and broken my heart on my birthday. The least you could do is answer my questions."

His eyes shift uncomfortably. "Maura."

"Where'd you meet her? And when?"

"I, uh..." His pleading eyes beg me to stop my interrogation, but when I raise my brows at him, he answers. "She's a trainer. I met her at the gym."

Of course he did. Mason and I live together, work together, eat together, and sleep together. The only time we're not attached at the hip is when he's killing himself at the gym. I always thought we were a good balance. My face is soft and a little round. Mason's jaw is chiseled and cut in clean angles. I love the feel of his strong arm against the soft slopes of my curves as I nestle into his hard stomach and muscular chest. I like how it feels when he holds me at night. I thought he liked the way I feel too.

I realize it's been a while since we've had sex, but we built a brand-management business from the ground up. We scored our first major contract with a Fortune 500 company. We're overloaded, overwhelmed, and have had more instant success than we could've dreamed of. *I thought we were just tired.*

"When did you meet her?"

His eyes stay locked on his lap. "Right after I bought that ring. Avery, I'm sorry. But honestly, are you happy? Are you excited about the idea of a future together or tolerating it?"

"Tolerating?" *That's what you've been doing with our relationship? Tolerating it?*

I ignore the twisting and writhing in my gut, telling me I don't want to dig deeper. No more truths tonight—I can't handle it. But I ignore my instincts. "Are you not attracted to me?"

"You are the *perfect* woman in every single way..." He ducks his head, ashamed. "Except the way that matters to me the most. I tried to get past it. You were always on the cusp of being beautiful, but then the business started and I handled my stress by working out and you handled it by..."

Eating. It's the word he wants to say. But while he already dug his grave, I don't think he's dumb enough to crawl into the open casket.

I narrow my eyes. "I gained eight pounds, Mason." *Fuck you.*

"It's not just the weight. It's how you dress...or don't. You never put on makeup. We live off of garbage takeout food. We're sloppy. There's nothing sexy or appealing about the way we are around each other, and I couldn't say anything without sounding like an ass. I know how this all sounds, but I can't help how I feel. I was panicking about committing to our lifestyle forever. It wouldn't last. We'd end up divorced in a few years, and isn't that worse than this?"

I raise my voice, incredulous. *"Worse than pretending like you loved me for four years?"*

He blows out a breath and checks over his shoulder, seeing if my loud response has attracted any attention. "I wasn't pretending. I loved y—*I love you.* I just don't think we're meant for each other. Avery, I never wanted to hurt you." He actually looks sincere, which makes this entire conversation ten times worse. "But I'd rather waste four years of your life than leave a marriage. I... um...I'm trying to do the right thing."

"It's my birthday." I let out a bizarre, raspy chuckle. "You chose to do this on my *birthday*?"

"No," he says, shaking his head adamantly. "I didn't choose

anything... I had every intention of proposing tonight. I really did. I just saw that ring on your finger, and I couldn't deny the truth anymore." He holds up his hands, showing me his palms across the table. "I'm so sorry. I hate myself for this. I wish I could just change how I feel."

Taking in a deep breath, I stare right at the shriveled-looking man across the table, who not five minutes ago looked like the man of my dreams.

"Please," he says.

"Please what?" I hiss as the dull background noise of the restaurant resumes. The earth slowly but surely begins to rotate again as my racing heartbeat calms.

He clasps his hands together like he's praying desperately. "Can we talk about this at home? We don't have to do anything right away. We have a two-bedroom apartment. We can take some space...figure out the business. This can all be amicable."

I glare at him. "You want this to be amicable?" My words are cool, but there's fire in my eyes, and he's about to burn.

"Or I can stay at a friend's house for a while and give you your space until we figure out the next steps. However you want to handle this, Avery...I want to be supportive."

"A friend's house?" I laugh. "You condescending piece of shit." Why do I have a sneaking suspicion I know exactly what friend he'd like to stay with. "You did cheat on me, didn't you?"

He shakes his head. "No, I said I *wanted* to, but I would never. I respect you too much."

"Seriously? That's your grand gesture?" I widen my eyes. "Well, *thank you* for only *wanting* to cheat on me. Congratulations on your self-restraint."

He looks left and right, clearly uncomfortable having this conversation in public, but my limbs still aren't working and I'm glued to this chair, so I'll have to wait out the shock here a bit longer.

I'll admit, our sex life has been lackluster. I thought it was a mixture of the honeymoon phase ending, the stress of our business, and the aftermath of getting really comfortable with someone. I thought his lack of sex drive was odd, but I didn't realize it wasn't the drive that was the problem... It was apparently the vehicle.

"Whatever you need to say...say it. I deserve it." He stupidly holds his hand out.

I'm not touching that.

"I'm sorry. And I'll say it a thousand times again. I really wanted this to end up differently."

Is he tearing up?

My head is spinning. He's trying to be apologetic, but everything he says slices me in a new spot. He is implying I'm big, but it's funny—at the moment, I've never felt smaller in my life. So small, in fact, I could slip right through the wooden floorboards of this luxury steakhouse, never to be seen again.

I yank again on the ring on my finger. It still won't budge, but at least my limbs seem operable again. "It's fucking stuck," I mumble.

"Keep it," he says quickly.

"What?" I screw up my face.

His brows are furrowed in anguish. "I don't...know how else to apologize."

I don't even recognize him. How quickly a man can go from the love of your life to a complete stranger.

He actually looks relieved as I push away my plate of chocolate cake crumbles and scoot out my chair. I don't exactly have a plan, but I collect my clutch and rise. When I walked in tonight, I felt like a goddamn piece. A knockout. A total ten. I'm leaving in ugly, fat humiliation...alone. How could this man's perception of me so quickly change my own view of myself?

I pause by Mason and watch his face shrivel up in concern when he realizes I'm leaving without him.

"Are you going to call for a ride home?" he asks, looking me up and down.

"What home?" I whisper. I clear my throat and enunciate. "*We* no longer have a home."

He catches my hand as I try to pass him. "Aver—"

I rip out of his grip. His hands feel cold and clammy, and I don't want them anywhere near me. "Don't you dare follow me."

I flee to the restaurant entrance, maneuvering between handsomely dressed waiters carrying large trays of fancy dishes. I dart past our waitress on the way out and force a small smile as I say thank you and good evening. She'll clue in once she sees Mason alone at the table, waiting for the bill.

I burst through the glass doors and into the crisp night air feeling like a free bird with clipped wings. I laugh to myself as I think about how abruptly the sky fell on such a pleasant evening. I never saw it coming. I didn't suspect a damn thing.

Golden birthday...golden year...

My ass.

Chapter 2

Finn

"Mrs. Mattley," I call out from across the room, "can you arch your back and stick your butt out a little more, or will that be bothersome for your arthritis?"

My assistant, Lennox, blinks at me as I lower my Canon, peeling my eyes away from the LCD screen. I roll my eyes at her. "Yeah, I heard it," I mutter under my breath.

"Weird sentence, man. Just *weird*." Lennox lets out a breathy chuckle.

There is a seventy-year-old woman kneeling next to a large wooden-framed bed, trying her best to squeeze her breasts together and form some semblance of cleavage. I groan.

This isn't working.

"She looks so uncomfortable," Lennox says as she bumps her elbow against mine. "I feel bad for her. We need to start putting an age cap on these photo shoots."

"*Hush.* She's elderly, not deaf," I say in a low tone. "This is really fucking brave of her. Be supportive and hope you're this cool when you're in your seventies." I shoot her a warning look. "Go get me the really big red pillows from the main living room."

Lennox stalls, her brows furrowing. She staged this set meticulously, down to the antique jewelry box sitting on the mirrored dresser. She even sanded and stained the wooden saloon doors because they weren't the exact right shade for the photo shoot.

This set is the only reason my business is somewhat afloat.

Not every woman wants their boudoir photographer to be male, which I understand. I really think I'm the best in the business. I know how to make a woman feel comfortable, respected, and championed, but they have to take a chance and actually hire me to understand that. But the Western set Lennox designed sways enough business our way. We have a lot riding on the fact that apparently every woman wants to be photographed as a sexy cowgirl.

Lennox is very particular about the set, and I just asked her to bring in impromptu props that she did not approve. *Tough. Deal with it.* I'm the boss. She designed the set, but I run the shoot. I handle the clients when it matters most. It takes a very special personality to run a boudoir photography business—zero snark, snickers, and judgment allowed. "Hustle, girl." Shooing Lennox off the set, I grab a mini bottle of water off the break table toward the back of the room.

"Here you go, Mrs. Mattley." I hand her the water bottle after I twist off the cap. "You're doing really great. How about a little break?" Holding her elbow firmly, I help her off her knees and guide her to sit. "There. Better?"

She nods and rubs her aching knees.

Poor thing. I really didn't take into consideration how difficult some of these positions could be on her body. Even the tops of her bare feet are red from pressing against the wooden floorboards for so long. I can touch up the photos and remove the angry red pigment, but while I'll mess with lighting and background blurring all day, I try not to touch up the models too much and disturb their authentic beauty. That's the point of all this. *Natural.*

Sitting down next to her, I rest my back against the bed's wooden footboard.

"They don't look good, do they? The pictures? Can I see?"

Turning my head, I look into her steel-blue eyes with wrinkles around the corners. Even at seventy, I recognize the vulnerability. Most of the women I shoot are at least topless. Some, fully nude. Of course, not Mrs. Mattley. She's more on the modest side, so the sexiest outfit we planned for her was a cap sleeve leather catsuit with a very low-cut V-neck for a little edge.

"You know the rules." I give her a little wink. I never let my clients see their photos until the shoot is over. Insecurity is evil. It creeps into their minds and poisons the entire shoot. They either become too shy or overcompensate by contorting their bodies into weird positions, trying to hide the bits they're most ashamed of. The secret to this kind of photography is bold confidence. They can see the photos after I've worked my magic. "But for your peace of mind, you are by far the most beautiful woman I've photographed on this set." I give her a dashing smile, and she snorts out loud.

Patting my cheek with her dainty hand that's a little too cool to the touch, she says, "Finn, sweetheart, you are such a sweet young boy...and so fucking full of shit."

Now I snort in laughter. "Mrs. Mattley! Language," I say, pretending to clutch my pearls. "I thought you were a classy broad. But I mean it. You look great." I pat her knee reassuringly.

She shoots me a teasing smile. "My goodness, Finn. Are you flirting with me?"

Sucking in my lips, I level a stare right into her eyes. "Now, we both know Mr. Mattley would descend from above and kick my sorry ass for making a move on his lovely widow." I wink.

Mrs. Mattley presses against her chest like her cackling hurts. "Ascend, honey."

"What's that?"

"*Ascend*." She points down. "It's sweet that you think Mr. Mattley is in heaven. That old grumpy fart is looking up at us as we speak."

I can't help but join in her playful laughter.

"But he was *my* grumpy man. His entire company hated him for being such a hard-ass, but he treated me like a princess. I was his soft spot."

Mrs. Mattley booked the luxury package. Her late husband was a very successful investment banker, so she has all kinds of money she doesn't know what to do with. So, for eight thousand dollars, over the course of three months, we've spent ample time together as we measured for her wardrobes for three different sets and had numerous meetings about her vision for the photographs. We hand-picked the final packaging—which for Mrs. Mattley will be a custom, white, Italian leather-bound photo book and three giant canvases. It's been a genuine pleasure getting to know her over the past few months. I'd go as far as calling her a friend at this point. It's nice. I never knew my grandmother. I sincerely hope she was half as delightful as Mrs. Mattley.

"What do you think he'd say about all this?"

She's quiet for a moment, a touch of sadness coating her eyes. I can't imagine how lonely she is. Her only daughter lives in New York. Mrs. Mattley is terrified of flying, so seeing her daughter Rose and her granddaughter is a rare treat when she can pull herself away from the office and fly out to Las Vegas.

She squeezes my shoulder, and her lips spread into a devilish smile. "He'd tell me to take my top off."

We both burst into laughter as Lennox walks back into the room holding two red velvet pillows, so large, they nearly hide her entire body.

"There we go!" I hop to my feet to relieve Lennox of one pillow.

"What are we laughing about?" Lennox asks.

"Oh, Mrs. Mattley was just telling me she'd like to try the second half of the shoot topless."

Lennox's jaw drops and she turns beet red.

Still laughing like a loon, Mrs. Mattley waves her hand in our direction. "Oh, calm down, honey." She winks at Lennox. "If I took my top off, Finny here wouldn't be able to control himself, and it's very unprofessional to get randy with your boudoir photographer." She blows a kiss in my direction as I salute her.

"That's right. Duty first. All professional here."

Lennox chuckles. "I think you're in the clear, Mrs. Mattley." Lennox flashes me a half smile with a conniving expression. "He can't have sex."

"What?" Mrs. Mattley asks as I pat the floor, instructing her to lie down. I prop her elbow up on one of the red pillows and fluff her white hair that has been fixed into soft, full waves. "You're celibate? I thought that was a tradition that's dying with my generation."

Rolling my eyes, I grumble, "I'm not celibate. I'm abstinent. Here, slide your elbow forward just a bit."

She adjusts, and I'm satisfied.

"Good. Where do you feel the tension?"

"My back."

I grab the other pillow from Lennox and tuck it behind her back. "How's that feel?"

She sighs with a smile. "So comfortable, I could take a nap."

"Good. You look great." In this position, Mrs. Mattley looks relaxed, meaning her face won't be pinched in torture as I take pictures. "Now pop that back knee up for me, and let's get back to it."

"Wait, wait," Mrs. Mattley protests. "Why are you abstinent? That won't do. You're ruining my whole plan, Finny. I was trying to set you up with my daughter when she comes to visit next month. Do you like kids?"

I screw up my face as I adjust my camera settings. Distracted, I ask, "Isn't your daughter married?"

"Separated. Soon to be divorced."

"Ah, I'm sorry to hear that."

Mrs. Mattley scoffs. "I'm not. Her husband, like mine, is a grumpy asshole, except he has no soft spot. He treats my Rosie like garbage. If he didn't treat my grandbaby so well, I'd fly out there and beat him with a crowbar myself."

"So you'd finally brave a flight to beat a man up?"

She curls up her lips in a snarl. "Desperate times, desperate measures."

I laugh at her feistiness. "Well, I sincerely hope the best for Rose and your granddaughter. What's her name?"

"Arielle."

"Pretty name," I say. "And I do like children, but I'm taking a break from dating at the moment."

"Why's that?"

I pull my eyes from my camera settings to blink at Mrs. Mattley. "Well, isn't someone a nosy little bird today?"

She shrugs. "I'm seventy-four, Finny. I'm allowed to be nosy."

Much to my annoyance, Lennox jumps in on my behalf to explain. "Finn had a psycho ex—super controlling, jealous, and"—she glances at my irritated expression—"I'm just going to say it—rageful. Anyway, they had an extremely toxic, volatile relationship for a long time, and when he finally broke it off about eight months ago, he went a little buck wild."

"Buck wild?" Mrs. Mattley asks as I flush in embarrassment.

Lennox, ignoring my red cheeks, continues, "One morning he was late for a shoot, and when I checked on him, I found not one, but two naked women in his bed."

"Oh my." Mrs. Mattley covers her mouth.

Lennox's smile grows wider if it's even possible. "Oh, but he wasn't in bed, Mrs. Mattley. He was in the shower...with the third woman who spent the night."

"Lennox!" I snap in irritation. I hold up one palm in a what-the-fuck motion. "For the love of God."

"What?" She shrugs innocently. "She asked."

Lennox is my assistant, but she's also my cousin and my best friend since childhood, so basically, she lives to give me shit.

"What she's trying to say," I explain, still glaring at Lennox, "is that I felt a little lost after my breakup and admittedly had a little too much *fun*, so I'm taking a break. Like a palate cleanser if you will."

It's the absolute most tame way to explain myself. After Nora and I broke up, I'd lose myself for days at a time. All the things she accused me of while we were together, *that I never did*—I dove right into out of spite. I live just off the Las Vegas Strip, and I took full advantage. I went on benders for days straight. I partied, binge-drank, and fucked. I fucked so much, I stopped feeling my orgasms. The only real evidence of my climax was the mess I'd leave behind. I was numb. My heart was *completely* numb.

It had to stop. After months of pressing the self-destruct button, I needed to stop.

"Finn, honey," Mrs. Mattley says, pressing her palm against my cheek. "May I give you some advice, dear? From your elder."

I nod into her hand. "Of course you can."

"You are young, dashingly handsome, and have a body fit enough to captain a ship."

I glance at Lennox from the corner of my eye. Her perplexed expression tells me I'm not the only one who finds that compliment odd.

Mrs. Mattley continues, "You're going to blink and be an old, withered mess like me. So, while you have the stamina that you do"—she flashes me a devilish smile—"stick your thing in everything you want. I mean, use a condom for goodness' sake, but have fun, Finny."

Lennox bursts out laughing. She wraps her arms around her ribs to try to control her heaving.

My dry mouth falls open. "Mrs. Mattley—"

"I'm serious, Finn. As long as you're safe, what's wrong with making as many connections as you can? You only get one life."

Nothing, I suppose. But what happens when sex no longer feels like connecting?

"You know, I think I've learned more about you in this one session than I've learned in months of knowing you."

Mrs. Mattley flicks her hair with sass, causing Lennox to fall into a fit of laughter, tears beginning to form at the corner of her eyes. "I...love...her..." she says between gasping chuckles.

"This is what happens when you put me in skintight leather," she explains. "You get the devil."

"All right, you randy little minx, save some of that energy, would you?" Rising, I tap my camera *gently*. This camera is worth half a year of car payments. I squint at the LCD display to confirm we still have the perfect lighting pouring in from the large windowpanes to the right of the studio. Then I get bossy. "All right, tilt your chin like I showed you—ah! No, stop that."

"Stop what?" Mrs. Mattley freezes in place, startled, like I told her there was a giant spider on her head.

"What are you doing with your mouth?" I ask, watching her try to pucker her thin lips awkwardly.

"I'm told it's called duckface. It's supposed to be flattering."

Palming my forehead, I shake my head adamantly. "It is not and stop that. *Natural*," I remind her. "That's what looks best. Don't try so hard."

"Well, are you going to fix these pictures with all your Photoshop magic when I look like a wilted, decrepit, old widow?"

Groaning, I abandon my perfect positioning and squat down so I'm level with her eyes. Without looking, I jut my thumb over my shoulder at the giant sign on the back of the studio wall. "Read it."

Mrs. Mattley blinks at me, unimpressed.

"Out loud," I demand. The sign is an eight-by-four-foot white canvas, with simple words scrawled in black calligraphy. It's mounted to the back of the studio wall so that no matter where you are on the set, the client can read it clear as day. A constant reminder...

"You're beautiful. You're worthy," she mumbles.

"Mmhmm," I say, looking into her blue eyes. "Nowhere on that sign does it say 'wilted,' and I'm certain I've never uttered the word 'decrepit' in here." I brush my thumb against her cheek that's tinted with a perfect blush, thanks to the makeup artist who was here not two hours ago. "You are beautiful. You are worthy. So act like it, Mrs. Mattley." Standing again, I back away a few paces and raise my camera once more. "Just stare over my shoulder at that sign and give me a simple smile."

Once her shoulder relaxes and she's mastering the flattering poses without distorting her body, the camera becomes obsessed. I click away furiously, capturing her energy that's growing bolder by the minute.

This is the reason I work so hard at my job. The reward is seeing a woman believe in her own magic. *This* certainly isn't sex... But it's most definitely connecting.

Chapter 3

Avery

"Oh, babe, this is not a good look." My best friend, Palmer, bursts through the front door of her apartment, mercilessly flicking on the overhead light of my bedroom. And by "my bedroom," I mean her living room couch, which has been my primary domain for the past few days since the night of my birthday.

Palmer drops a large cardboard box on her living room coffee table, which has become my desk, my dresser, and my dining table. I eye the slinky black dress lying at the top of the box.

Sitting up, I give Palmer my most unamused side glance. "I said pick up some *comfy* clothes. My little"—well, technically *not so little*—"black dress is not comfortable."

Palmer gets in my face so her nose is barely an inch from my own. Her makeup is flawless as usual. She should be giving lessons on contouring. Makeup tutorials might pay better than her lackluster acting career. The ironic part is while Palmer is phenomenal at makeup, she doesn't need it. Her tone is perfectly even, her skin looks like she has no pores, and her bright baby blue eyes don't need adornment. They are striking all by themselves. What's more—Palmer's platinum, almost white-blond hair is completely natural. Some women were just born in the light.

"You don't need comfortable. You need a sexy black dress and to get laid."

I resist rolling my eyes at her ridiculous statement. "Are you offering?"

She scrunches up her nose like I smell. "Maybe...if you shower first." She peels away a piece of my hair that was glued to my cheek from dried drool.

Snorting in laughter, I plant my palm against her forehead and push her away.

"I did pick up some of your sweatpants, though, so you're welcome."

"I love you." I give her a half smile.

Palmer, my savior. My best—no, more accurately, my only— friend in the world right now. It's not because it's hard for me to make friends. It's just hard for me to maintain them. I love to work. I *love* my job. My job as a brand consultant is very social. I spend a lot of my waking hours behind the scenes, researching and designing, but client meetings are still a huge chunk of my calendar. Virtual or not, it's still *social*. I also study people and their behavior all day. Researching what makes people click, buy, and review. My job is creating connections, so my tolerance for social interaction outside of work is relatively low. But Palmer doesn't let me go into the lonely cave. Every time I bury myself in manic obsessive work, she straps on a harness and dives into the depths to yank me out of the dark pits of my solitary confinement. She forces me to see sunshine.

Mason calls us uncomfortably symbiotic and needy. Maybe he's right... I need Palmer to tell me I should own at least one pair of shoes that don't have the word "comfort" in their brand name, and Palmer needs me to tell her car wash bikini model is not a real job and will never allow her to plan for retirement.

Mason... Fuck. I even flinch when I say his name in my head.

I nod toward the box. "How's he doing?"

Palmer spins around and glares at me from her kitchen. She slams two bottles of water onto her kitchen countertop. "We don't care how Mason is doing right now."

"Palmer." I narrow my eyes. "How does he look?"

Her hand trails down the taut line of her slim waist and lands on the slight curve of her hip. "Like shit."

Funny. He dumped me. Shouldn't he look relieved?

Since I walked out on Mason at the restaurant, we've had no contact outside of work. We have an unspoken agreement to stay cordial through work emails. We're not in the process of onboarding any new clients and are mostly just maintaining current contracts. It doesn't require a lot of intra-office communication. Outside of a few forwarded messages from clients asking for SEO analytics and metric reports, Mason and I don't have anything pertinent to say to each other workwise.

But *personally* has been an entirely different story.

He's called a few times, but I don't answer. He's texted me to ask how I'm doing, which I find more patronizing than kind. I could block him. But I don't. I like for the phone to ring so he knows I'm here...just out of reach. He knows I'm staying with Palmer, but he's smart enough not to come here. Palmer once threatened to chop Mason's dick off with gardening shears if he ever broke my heart. Who knows what she's capable of now that we're living the reality.

"Aves." Palmer's tone is drastically serious. Devoid of sass, she says, "It's time to get up. Let's go for a walk and get some sunshine. Block him. You're not *this* weak."

I sigh as I smooth back my flyaways and pull my thick hair into a low, side-swept ponytail. "Do you remember the time I had to pick you up from the border because your car was confiscated when you tried to sneak in like fifty bottles of cheap tequila from Tijuana?"

"Yes," she says in a huff.

"Remember how you didn't even have money to pay for gas for the return trip?"

She rolls her eyes. "Yeah."

"And remember the time I had to drive to Las Vegas and pick you up because you were drunk and got locked in what can only be described as some type of stripper birdcage contraption? They wouldn't let you out until you paid your massive bar tab—that you couldn't afford?"

She sucks in air against her teeth. "Vaguely."

"Mmhmm, and who covered the bill?"

"You did," she mumbles.

"And remember when—"

"Oookay, what's your point, Aves? That I'm a fuckup and you're way more put together than I am?"

I purse my lips. "No, honey. *No.*" I press my fingertips against my closed eyelids and feel the cool metal on my ring finger against my cheek. "What I'm trying to say is I've had your back through every situation—your highs and lows. I am your biggest cheerleader. I'm the one who told you smuggling cheap tequila over the border was just savvy shopping, that you can't take your money to your grave so why hold on to it so hard, and that anyone with a blood alcohol level of point-one would of course willingly crawl into a stripper cage—you've got nothing to be ashamed of."

Her eyes hit the ceiling. "And you believe none of that."

I force out a breath and shake my head fervently. "Not a damn word. But I love you. And my job as your best friend is to support you and let you come through things in your own time and your own way. Right now, I need you to do the same."

Her eyes lock on to the ring on my finger. *Why am I still wearing this thing?* Maybe I'm pretending. In my mind, I found the damn thing in the cake, wiped it clean, slipped it on my finger to see Mason on his knee, asking me to marry him...not dumping me.

"Did he actually ask you?"

"What?" I squint at her odd question.

"You're wearing the ring. He said he didn't officially ask you... to marry him."

What a freaking odd thing to say. "You guys talked about it?"

I sent Palmer to get me some clothes and toiletries. I didn't realize she'd sit down to have a heart-to-heart with Mason.

"No." She shrugs. "Briefly," she adds. "Obviously, we crossed paths, and as I was leaving, I asked him why the hell he would propose to you, just to break up with you five seconds later. When he said he didn't ask, I asked if he wanted the ring back..."

I narrow my eyes at her. *That's not your place to ask, Palmer.* "He told me to keep it."

"Odd."

"Indeed. I now own a guilty conscience, non-engagement ring." *Which is worse than no ring at all.* I stare at my finger, knowing I'm going to need a vat of Vaseline to get this off. Why would Mason buy this in a ring size too small? Maybe it was wishful thinking. Maybe he thought a proposal would shrink me and by some miracle I'd squeeze into his standards. The ass.

She points at me, her sparkly gold nail polish catching a glint of sun pouring in through the shades. "You should pawn it."

Rising, I stretch my arms overhead and crack my fingers. My muscles resist like they are permanently frozen in the sit and lie position. Standing...moving... It all feels like a foreign concept, and my body protests. I've lost four days of my life, moping. It's time to get the blood flowing again. "I'm going for a coffee. Can I get you something?" I grab my purse from the floor and sling it around my shoulder.

Palmer's eyes turn to slits. "You better not be going to see him. I won't let my best friend beg her ex to take her back. He doesn't deserve you."

I love her with my whole heart, but her bossiness triggers me. I'm already torn and tormented, and right now I don't need anyone telling me what I am or am not allowed to do. My heart is bleeding, my jealousy is on fire, and my head is exploding... I'm already juggling too many emotions.

"Palmer, *please.* I'm thirty years old. You have to let me breathe. I said I'm going to get coffee, but if and when I choose to talk to Mason, I won't be asking for your permission."

"Well, you're staying here indefinitely, right? I thought my job was to protect you from yourself?" Her lips press into a hard line. Her whole demeanor is overly agitated. I'm not proud to say this, but right now I kind of wish I had a friend to tell me that if I wanted to salvage my relationship, it was an option. Maybe it's a long, hard, broken road, but if I wanted to win him back, the path is still an option.

The truth is Mason could've cheated and gotten away with this. I would've been none the wiser. I trusted him so much, I never suspected a damn thing. If he was really a pig, he could've just lied... But he told the truth. He wasn't happy. Is he wrong for not wanting to commit to a life of lackluster sex? Did I play a role in the demise of our relationship? I never knew he wanted the sexy girl. I thought loyalty, kindness, patience, and intelligence were enough. Am I dumb for thinking our situation was enough to make him happy?

And the biggest question—was I happy? Or was I just goal-focused? Am I even ready to ask that question that will unravel the past four years of my life?

No.

I want some peace and quiet.

I want to not pick at the wound while it's so fresh.

I want to stop feeling so broken, weak, and insecure.

I want an overpriced fancy coffee.

"Iced skinny caramel macchiato with no drizzle?" I ask Palmer, making my intentions clear. *I'm going where I want, whether you like it or not.*

She nods reluctantly. "Thank you."

I blow her a kiss as I pass the kitchen to make my way to the front door.

"Wait, you're going right now?"

"Yes?" I scrunch up my face, confused at her surprise.

"Looking like that?" She eyes me up and down.

Fucking geez, Palmer. I mean, she's not wrong. My pajama shorts are frayed a little at the bottom. My baggie beige T-shirt looks like it came from a Goodwill's reject pile. But for the love of God, I'm in my mourning phase of the breakup. *Let me mourn.*

"I'm going through the drive-through," I say haughtily and slip out the door before she can say another damn word.

* * *

The normally obnoxiously long line at the Starbucks drive-through is quick today. So quick, in fact, that after picking up a hot latte for myself and Palmer's iced drink, I circle back to the parking lot, roll my windows down, and grant myself a moment of quiet.

I'm still agitated at our interaction and am in no hurry to run back to her apartment. I can't go home. It's clear I can't keep holing away at my friend's place unless I develop rubber skin so her bossy, passive-aggressive jabs can bounce right off of me. I forgive her because Palmer has the best intentions and she's the only friend I have who would immediately drop what she's doing, scoop me up from a restaurant on the opposite side of town, and hold me all night while I cried on her shoulder. She's also the friend who thinks vodka is a perfectly appropriate way to start the morning. That's exactly the energy I need right now after having my boyfriend of four years tell me that instead of marrying me, he wants to sample his other options.

I promised myself I wouldn't look her up.

But dammit, it'd be so easy.

Maura...from the gym...who is a trainer. I bet I could go to Edge Fitness's website right now, scroll to the staff page, and see her beautiful face and perfectly shaped body. There's no doubt in my mind this woman is stunning. I bet in comparison, I look like a bump on a pickle. I just didn't know Mason was *looking*. I know I shouldn't check her out. It's only going to drive me absolutely insane. The next two years of my life will be a comparison game to this woman who will become a beauty beacon in my mind. What's the point? Why torture myself?

Curiosity...that's why.

I let my fingers dance over the keyboard letters...www-dot-edge—

My phone rings, startling me and yanking me away from temptation. By now I just assume it's Mason, so I instinctively move to hit the decline button. Instead, Dexter Hessler flashes across the screen—one of my favorite long-term clients. I slap a perky smile on my face even though he can't see me.

"Hello?"

"Avery. Helloooo." Dex's cheery voice is so loud through the car's Bluetooth, I have to lunge for the volume button to turn his energy down. *Whew.* "Sorry to call you on a Saturday. I hate being *that* client."

"No problem at all, Dex. How are you?"

"Fuckin' great! This is a happy call, by the way, where I tell you that the egregious amount of money I paid you and Mason was well worth it and I earned it back tenfold."

I chuckle. "Glad to hear it. Care to share the specifics?"

"We booked the entire summer for guided tours. Every single slot is filled, and the trip is more than funded. Not to mention the entire line of the new Aqualung fins and wetsuits are sold out. The gear hasn't even shipped yet. My mind is blown."

Dive and surf shops are wildly competitive. Dex needed an edge to make his little business competitive. Mason and I loved working on developing the Best Fishes brand. Dex didn't even have a real logo, and his marketing package was messy. I invented a brand new look, defined a color palette, and curated entirely new brand messaging. While I worked with Dex to increase his social media presence by making one-minute educational videos of gear care, emergency preparation, and the different types of scuba certifications, Mason dove into SEO. If you Google scuba shops in the state of California, Best Fishes now shows up on the first page, which was a nearly impossible feat for a company based in Las Vegas, over five hours away from the California beaches where they certify their students.

"Dex, I'm so happy to hear it. Where are you starting the guided tours?"

"Cozumel. Then off to the Cayman Islands."

"Incredible."

"Hey, I have an idea. Do you want to come on one trip? Just pay your way in travel, and I've got you covered for the tour, gear, and everything else. It's going to be beautiful."

Sharks? Me in a skintight wet suit? Both comparable threats.

"No, thanks. I'm not a big water person."

"Yet you live in California?"

"Anyway..." I take a long sip from my hot coffee. Why I'm drinking hot coffee in the eighty-degree weather, I don't know. It's a thing of mine. To me, coffee was meant to be brewed *and* served hot. I would sip on a piping hot latte in the flames of hell. "You enjoy your trip. Just make sure your content manager stays consistent with posting. Mason and I will handle the web traffic and make sure we're staying on top of the search results competition. But right now, social is what's really going to continue to drive sales— brand presence. So don't let your social guy slack, okay? You can always call me if you need a helping hand while you guys are traveling."

"You're amazing, Avery. You're due for a raise—"

"You pay us plenty."

"Thank you. I feel like I can go into this summer worry-free. You've handled everything. Well, almost..." He trails off.

I wait for a moment, as it's obvious he's texting. When he doesn't continue, I jump back in. "Is there something else I can help you with, Dex?"

"Sorry," he mutters distractedly. He sounds far away, like he pulled the phone away from his ear. "Another one bites the dust." He grumbles in agitation. Giving me his full attention again, he says, "You wouldn't happen to know anyone who doesn't already have summer plans and needs a job, would you?"

"Do you need another assistant for the scuba tours?" It's not my typical job, but I'm happy to research anything for Dex. He's such a good client and always in a good mood. I'm sure it has something to do with his family money and wanting for nothing. While he desperately needed help with his business, he works because he likes to, not because he has to. "We could do a listing for a summer assistant job, but you'd probably have to include travel expenses and meals for perks."

He laughs. "Oh no, I have enough hands on deck for the tours and enough mouths to feed. I need a pet sitter for the summer."

"You have a pet?" That's odd. Dex travels so much. His life mission is to explore every inch of every sea and ocean in the world. He's going to be brain-dead by the time he's fifty from all the time he spends breathing from an oxygen tank and living in the pressurized depths of the world below.

"Sort of. More of a *house* sitter," he explains. "I have a guy who maintains my aquariums, but I need someone there to feed my saltwater fish daily. They are a little high-maintenance. Auto feeders are good for maybe a week or two, but not the whole summer. This is the longest I'll be away from home, and I can't risk losing my fish, nor do I want to get slapped with all these HOA fines."

"You travel all the time. Who normally feeds your fish?"

"Employees from the dive shop. Or my next-door neighbor is always willing to lend a hand. But that's for a couple of days here and there. Maintaining tropical saltwater fish and tanks is way more involved than just feeding them, and I can't take over his entire summer. Not to mention there was that one time he poisoned my Damselfish with Fruit Loops. I question his ability to handle this."

I balk. "Your neighbor tried to kill your fish?"

"*Not on purpose.* He couldn't find more fish food and didn't want them to go hungry."

I snicker to myself as I perk up in my seat, tasting my reckless words before they fall out of my mouth. "Just for the summer?" *Just enough time for me to figure out my next steps.*

"Yeah. I've asked around, but so far, the only people who are interested are wild-ass college students on break who just want a free house to host orgies after getting shit-faced on the Strip."

"I'll do it."

"What?"

"I'll stay at your place for the summer, feed your fish, and make sure everything you need gets done. I most definitely don't do orgies, and after three years of working together, let's hope you already know you can trust me."

"Are you serious? How much would you charge?"

"Free." *You're doing me a favor.*

"You're kidding. Mason would be okay with moving for the summer?"

I grumble as I take another sip of my white chocolate mocha. "Okay, one cost. It'd just be me, and you can't ask me why or about Mason. Deal?"

"Deal." I can tell by his tone he has questions, but as instructed, he sidesteps his concern. "Okay, well, great! Damn, Avery, you're really saving my ass here. I'll text you all the details. I have a really nice place. I swear you'll love it. I'll have it professionally cleaned, and I'll clear out my drawers and stuff so you can take over the master bedroom if you want. And the Las Vegas Strip is only like fifteen minutes from my place when you feel like going out."

I glance down at my baggy white T-shirt. *Highly unlikely.* I want to use Dex's place as a hideout while I collect my thoughts. *Out* requires talking to people. *In* is what I'm aiming for. "When do you need me?"

"The sooner the better, actually. If I had your help, I might be able to squeeze in a dive to Cancun for just my girlfriend and me before the summer craziness starts. How soon is too soon? Do you need to get things sorted with work first?"

I can work from anywhere. Las Vegas is a five-hour drive from the outskirts of L.A. I'd need exactly eight hours—one to sneak into my apartment and collect a few things, one to get my oil changed at the Oil Express up the road, one hour to explain myself to Palmer, and then five for the drive. But I'm not trying to come off *that* desperate. I stare at the ring still wedged onto my left finger. In a fit of excitement, or maybe rage, I finally rip it off my finger, which seems to have shrunk the tenth of an inch necessary to relieve me of this diamond burden.

"How's next Thursday? Gives you time to show me the ropes and take off before the weekend?"

"Perfect," Dex says. "I'll make the arrangements. Avery, *thank you.* You're my lifesaver in all things now."

No, no, Dex...
Thank you.

Chapter 4

Finn

Sweat is dripping down my face. I do my best to mop it up with the back of my hand as I jog the last few meters to my driveway. But after a few more strides, the sweat mixed with my sunblock moves down my forehead and seeps into my eyes. I stop in my tracks in front of Dex's driveway as I try to blink away the burn. If I were wearing a shirt, I'd try to soak up my stinging tears, but it's Las Vegas in May. It's already scorching, so I'm running shirtless.

Hooonk!

The sound of a glaring horn causes me to jump in place.

Whipping my head to the right, I notice the gray Jeep Cherokee on the street with a blinker on, trying to turn into the driveway I'm standing in front of. The woman in the driver's seat is a brunette with her hair pulled up into a sloppy ponytail. The woman in the passenger seat is a platinum blonde whose sunglasses are so big they take up the majority of her face. Most notably, though, neither of these women is Dex's girlfriend, Leah.

Strange. No way Dex and Leah broke up. These must be family members...or contractors...or maybe people who work at his dive shop?

I obediently take a step backward on the sidewalk and gesture for them to pass in front of me. I hold my hands up in an apology. The brunette rolls the window down and pokes her head out of the car. "I am so sorry," she calls out. "Please excuse the honking. It was"—she throws a glare toward the passenger side of the car—"*very rude.*"

I chuckle, understanding that she wasn't the one to honk the horn. I can't see her eyes clearly, but the blonde's face is fixed in my direction, and I get the feeling that she's thoroughly checking me out. I'm not sure why this is immediately off-putting. I don't mind when women notice me.

But not like this.

Not like I'm property and she's considering putting in a bid.

"It would've been far more rude to hit me," I call back. "So the heads-up is appreciated." I flash her a wide smile.

"Pedestrians first." The brunette gestures me past with her hand. "Please." She slides back into the car, but I can see her full cheeks bunch as she smiles through the windshield. I wish she'd take off her dark sunglasses. The little jolt in my chest tells me she's pretty. And not in the obvious, thirsty-for-attention way her friend is coming off, but in the subtle mystery way that is kicking up all kinds of curiosity in my male brain.

Somewhat reluctantly, I hold up my palm and jog past Dex's driveway. I laugh at the loud whistle behind me, knowing one of them, probably the blonde, is commenting on the view of my ass.

I'm barely through my front door when I see the disaster that is my normally tidy sitting room. It's the very first thing you see when you walk into my rancher. I try to keep it pristine—first impressions and all. At the present moment, you can barely see the floors amidst the bags upon bags from Hobby Lobby and Michaels. I step out of my running shoes and call out, knowing exactly who the culprit of this mess is.

"Lennox!"

She appears immediately from the hallway, a steaming mug in her hand, looking dog-eared and a little crazed. She's completely changed her look in the last forty-eight hours since I've seen her. Her hair is dyed black with violet streaks in multiple shades. Her bangs are cut in a straight line. I have a feeling the shopping bag graveyard that is now my living room is the aftermath of this new edgy look.

"What the fresh hell is all this?"

She touches the corner of her eye and then points to me. "I am a visionary."

Oh, Christ. "Why are you a visionary?"

"We are more than sexy cowgirls, Finn. We can do better than that."

I blink, trying to absorb her odd remark. I consider asking her what the hell she's talking about but decide to side-step it instead. "Your hair is cool." I pat her shoulder as I walk past her to the kitchen to grab a cold bottle of water. Soft footsteps trail behind me. "How'd you get here?" I ask Lennox as I twist off the cap. Still struggling to cool down, I'm tempted to dump this cold bottle of water all over my face and chest. "I didn't see your car."

"I pulled into your garage."

I raise an eyebrow at her. "You're really at home here, aren't you?"

Lennox and I don't technically live together, but we might as well. My photography studio is in my basement. It only works because it's a walk-out basement, meaning there's plenty of natural light I need for headshots and family portraits. I think my lower level was originally built as a mother-in-law suite. It has a private access door through the back gate. You can access the studio without needing to access my home. Lennox knows this but also knows no boundaries. My entire house has become her domain.

She shows me her teeth through a snarky grin and holds up her mug. "You want coffee?"

Pressing my palm flat against my chest, I check my still-racing heart. "Not at the moment. The run was grueling. I'm one sip of caffeine away from cardiac arrest."

Lennox's eyes drop to my knees, and she scrunches her face in confusion. "What's wrong with your knees?" She points to the kinesiology tape wrapped around both of my knees, tracing my quads, and outlining my kneecaps.

"It's for extra support. I've logged thirty miles this week on concrete sidewalks. I'm trying to avoid my tendonitis flaring up."

She twists her lips in that familiar way that tells me she's about to say something sassy.

"What?" I begrudgingly ask.

"Wouldn't it be easier to just start having sex again than trying to physically outrun your testosterone?" She cackles.

"Ha." She's not wrong.

"How long has it been?"

I roll my eyes at her. "A couple months." Three months, twelve days. Or, in other words, about one hundred body-punishing runs.

"How long is this going to go on?"

"I don't know. Until I feel like it." *Until I stop seeing the worst in women.* I'm not exactly open about it, but Nora did a number on me. After what we went through, now all I see are red flags in women. I remember one night after Nora and I ended things, I brought home a new girl I actually liked. She was a bit of a wallflower—polite and soft-spoken. Maybe I liked that she was my ex's polar opposite. I had high hopes. But the morning after, when she thought I was sleeping, I caught her checking my phone. I didn't say anything. I just pretended to sleep and let her scroll through my messages, my apps, and my pictures. I had absolutely nothing to hide, but I was not about to put myself through that shit again. *Deal breaker.* I never called her again.

I want a woman confident enough to ask me questions and believe my answers. If she's wondering if I'm sleeping with multiple women at the same time—just ask. The answer is no. If she's interested in something serious—just tell me. Maybe she'd be surprised to know that I am too. I'm twenty-eight. By now, I'm sick of the mind games, paranoia, and jealous fights over nothing. I want a woman who is honest, earnest, and trusts me enough to just be real...

And I am thoroughly convinced this woman doesn't exist in Las Vegas. It's kind of why I gave up. Once I was single again, I started being exactly the manwhore bachelor all these women assumed I was, until even that got old.

"So, why are you a visionary?" I throw my thumb over my shoulder, reminding her of the mess she made in my living room.

"Noir," she says with a bright-eyed eager expression.

"Yeah...I'm going to need a little more of an explanation than that."

"*Film* noir. With a touch of bondage."

I take a few glugs of my water. "What?"

She squints one eye. "You know, like handcuffs...*toys*...lots of leather..."

An uncomfortable realization sinks in. "Is my living room full of women's sex toys right now?"

"*Nooooo.*" Lennox laughs awkwardly then widens her eyes and nods empathically. "And I found some of these cool black roses at the craft store. I'm thinking all black and white. Black flowers, white sheets, a torn white wedding dress that's ink-stained draped over a chair. Wedding lingerie in the same style."

"Are we staging a boudoir set or a murder scene?"

She laughs. "Bold sexuality is in. I really think this could be a big moneymaker. In fact, we've gotten requests through the website for something more *dramatic*. We have to adapt to the market, Finn." Lennox grimaces. "Business is not...great."

She's right again. Photography is an ebb-and-flow business. Everyone with the newest iPhone these days can take professional-looking photographs, so you have to bring more value to the table than pictures. I try to help women love their bodies and appreciate their unique beauty. No matter what size, color, or shape—every single woman is beautiful. They have to look at themselves through the right lens. Somehow through my noble plight, I also have to find a way to pay the bills. Lately, it's been getting more difficult to find clients.

"You're a woman... Explain this to me."

Lennox follows as I make my way into my front living room and pull a pair of fuzzy black handcuffs from a plastic shopping bag.

"Why is bondage sexy? I want to help build confidence, not tie up women and put them on display like roast chickens."

Lennox squints one eye at me. "I think we can be more tasteful than roast chickens." Furrowing my brows, I return a skeptical look, so she continues, "I'm not suggesting we go dark dungeon or anything like that, but we can just tease the idea. We'll have edgier costumes but have them wear their hair in soft waves. We'll do the entire shoot in a moody black and white, but they can smile in some pictures. It'll be very floral but dark colors. Handcuffs—"

"But fuzzy," I finish for her.

"Exactly." Lennox pops her shoulders like she's pleased with herself. She really has an eye for stage design. One day, she is going to move to Hollywood and become an acclaimed set director. I'm sure of it. For now, I'm grateful to have her help. I take great pictures, my editing is unrivaled, but without the set, I'm a fish in a barrel. I need Lennox.

"You really think it'll bring in more business?"

She widens her eyes and nods slowly. "At this point, we have to try anything. It's either edgy or topless clowns."

"*What?*"

"Don't ask." She shoots me a wink, but her smile is less than innocent. I don't want to know what websites Lennox visits. My cousin is not shy about her quirky taste. Let's leave it at that.

"So the idea is bold but feminine," I muse.

"Right." She nods as she points to my forehead. "That's what we should call it. Boldly feminine. Give me a week or so to build the set, and then why don't we do a test run? We can offer a free photo shoot to someone and put new pictures up on the website. Let's just see who bites. If it's a bust, we'll go back to the drawing board." She looks around the room. "We've got to try something, Finn... Our calendar is pretty much empty. I don't think it's the service. It's a good time to be in boudoir. It's just no one knows we exist, and it's a tough business for word-of-mouth marketing."

I nod in agreement. "And I basically have no budget for paid marketing."

"Right—so anything that can capture people's attention..."

"Okay, I'm sold. No harm in trying it out." I smile at her. "Good work, Lennox."

She crosses her legs and bows. "Lovely. Now go take a shower. You stink."

"Roger that." I finish off my water then turn toward my bedroom.

"Hey, by the way, do you want to go out tonight? There's a foam party at Ultimate. Invite only. I hung out with the bouncer last week, and he gave me an extra ticket. There's going to be a surprise celebrity DJ—rumor is it's Khalid."

"A foam party on the Vegas Strip? That sounds like a lot of drunk, wet women running around."

Lennox taps her nose twice. "Exactly. Have some fun. All you've been doing for months is working and"—she points to my knees—"running. It's been a year. When are you going to be done being sad?"

"I'm not sad." I don't think the look I'm giving her is convincing because Lennox puckers her bottom lip.

"I don't believe you. I'm *proud* of you. But I don't believe you. Look, Finn...Nora was—"

I hold up my hand to interrupt her. "I'm okay. But thank you, little cousin." I close the space between us and drape my arm around her shoulders, pulling her into a sweaty hug.

"Gross," she complains.

"You're sweet to worry about me. But don't. Have fun at your foam party." I release her.

"What are you going to do tonight?"

On cue, my muscles start to ache and tense. I pushed it a little too much today. I could use some relief. "I'll probably just bring Dex a six-pack of beer and sneak into his hot tub."

Dex never uses his in-ground hot tub. Leah, his girlfriend, does very rarely. If it were portable, I'd just buy it from him and move it to my patio. Instead, we put in a gate between our yards so I am free to access his tub whenever I like. In exchange, I bring him beer and pay for the monthly maintenance. I could not have asked for a better neighbor. Not to mention he's richer than God, so the neighborhood barbeques he hosts are top-tier. Who buys ribeye steaks for an entire block of people?

"Want me to stay in? Keep you company?"

"Uh, no. The only thing sadder than staying in on a Saturday night to hot tub alone is staying in on a Saturday night to hot tub with your cousin."

Lennox bursts out in laughter and bobs her head in agreement.

"Just call me if you need a ride home, and please be smart. I don't want to have to rescue you and kick someone's ass."

She salutes me. "All right. Oh, and hey, ask Dex which wet suit he's packing for Cozumel. I think he said a shortie, but I run cold, so I think I'm going to bring my long-sleeved one."

I forgot Lennox is taking a week off next month to go on a dive trip he's leading. She, Dex, and Leah instantly bonded over their love of scuba.

"Can't you text him?"

"He's so damn flaky and disorganized with his phone. Great dive instructor, but I don't know how his business isn't in flames."

"All right, I'll try to remember," I say as I head down the hallway. I tap my temple firmly like I can push a reminder right through the side of my head. That's two things I need to ask Dex now. Lennox's wet suit...

And who the hell is the pretty brunette who stopped by his place.

Chapter 5

Avery

"Dibs," Palmer says as she drops her purse on Dex's marble kitchen counter. "And holy shit, this place is amazing." Her face twists into a wicked smile. "How serious are Dex and his girlfriend?"

I flatten my stare at her. "Soul mates, ride or die, Bonnie and Clyde serious. Don't even think about—"

"*Jesus,*" she grumbles as she spins in place, looking up, taking in the high ceilings and exposed beams. "I'm kidding obviously."

"Homewrecking," I mutter under my breath. "Hilarious."

I'm torn between grateful and annoyed that Palmer is here. She insisted on helping me drive out and get settled, but she had an audition yesterday. Waiting on Palmer meant me missing Dex before he left. He texted me instructions and left a key under the mat for me. Apparently, the fish guy will be here on Monday to teach me how to feed the fish. I mean, it's fish in tanks... I'm fully capable of sprinkling flakes into water, but whatever makes Dex feel more comfortable, I'm happy to oblige.

"The 'dibs' wasn't about Dex, by the way." Palmer immediately finds and opens the hidden fridge that matches the sleek black cabinetry with gold handles. She pulls out two beers, but I shake my head.

"It's ten in the morning on a Friday." I grab one beer and then place it back into the beverage compartment of the fancy fridge. "And I need to get a little work done this afternoon."

"Ugh," she responds, rolling her eyes. "How come you work

for yourself, from home in your pajamas most days, but you still have that stick wedged firmly up your asshole? If I made the money you do, with the schedule you have, I'd be enjoying my life thoroughly."

"Yeah, and how do you think that money is earned, Palmer? I work in my pajamas because not worrying about getting fixed up for the day gives me an extra hour of work time in front of the screen before my brain melts."

She twists the cap off her beer. It's a foreign label I don't recognize, but it certainly looks upmarket. I knew Dex was well-off... I didn't know he was *this* well-off. Of course he drinks lavish beer. "I'm a small business owner too, yet I still find a way to have fun."

Palmer's a part-time influencer, part-time makeup artist, and full-time desperately-want-to-be-famous, struggling actress. It's not quite the same. And maybe that's the problem. Maybe I'm not fun. Maybe that's part of the reason Mason saw our relationship as a duty and a chore.

Fuck. Mason.

It's been a little over a week since my birthday. I am trying to be numb. I would rather be numb than collapse. I am trying not to let the demons in my mind sneak up on me and tell me that somehow the man I loved for almost half a decade lost his way because I wasn't doing my part in the relationship.

It's not just the weight. It's how you dress...or don't. You never put on makeup. We live off of garbage takeout food. We're sloppy. There's nothing sexy or appealing about the way we are around each other...

I can't stop replaying that night in my head. Over and over. Mason is an ass... He's a no-good shallow ass...a fucking worthless asshole...

But did I play a part?

Did I push him to be the worst version of himself?

Stop. Don't go there. Stay numb.

"What were you saying about a dibs?"

She takes another swig from her beer and sets the glass bottle down on the counter too hard. The loud clink makes me flinch.

"Be careful," I hiss. "This is not my home." I place her bottle in the large trough sink before running my fingers over the kitchen island granite, worried Palmer chipped it.

Paying me no mind, she says, "The runner from before. Whoever that is—*dibs*."

A ripple of annoyance flows through me. Palmer gets every man she wants, and once she sets her sights on something, I know better than to try and compete. I noticed him too. I've never seen a man that good-looking in my life. Tall, tan, strong jawline, with perfectly styled jet-black hair. But when I close my eyes, all I see is the smile he flashed me. It looked so sweet and innocent. It didn't match his body, which screamed dirty lust. Perhaps because his pecs and six-pack were glistening with sweat while he stood in the near-blinding sunlight.

Beautiful people. I swear they glow even when they aren't trying to.

"Palmer, you can't *dibs* him. He's not the front seat of a car or the first pick from a litter of golden doodles."

She cocks one eyebrow. "How do I put this delicately?" Rolling her wrist, she says, "I want that man to wear me like a condom that's one size too small and let me choke the life out of his dick."

"*Wow.*"

"Unless you're"—with her palm facing up, she points her index finger at me—"interested?"

I shake my head aggressively and laugh. "No. Definitely not."

"Um, do you have eyes?" she asks.

I exhale. "I didn't say he wasn't attractive. I said I'm not interested. I'm a realist. He's a little too hot for me, don't you think?"

She finds the curve of her hip with her hand. "Excuse me?"

Uh-oh. Palmer's a lot of things. A hot mess. A mooch. The person who reminds me that I should probably get a pedicure more than once a year and that my favorite bra gives me major uniboob. But she's the only person who can say it because she loves me. She protects me. She does not tolerate when I'm self-deprecating.

She's stoic as she glares at me, so I continue, "Oh, *come on*. Be realistic. That man we saw jogging is ten times sexier than Mason, and I can't even keep the one I have interested." I suck in a breath as the pang in my chest gets dangerously close to the wall I've built around my heart. *Stop it. I am numb.* "Had. I mean *had*."

Palmer lowers her voice. "Avery Leigh Scott." She narrows her eyes. "You are beautiful. Yes, you need new clothes, new shoes, and for the love of God, let me teach you how to contour your face properly, but you are a *fucking ten* inside and out and could pull any man you want." She closes the space between us and yanks me into what can only be called an aggressive hug. "I love you."

"I know," I mumble into a mouthful of her hair.

She sniffles as she pulls away and looks directly into my eyes. I fight the urge to look away from her intense stare. "I know you agreed to stay here to run away from me."

"Palmer..." I let out an exasperated sigh. She's half right. Why lie? "I need a summer to find myself."

"I'm your best friend," she says with a disingenuous smile. "You can't find yourself around me?"

"I need space to figure out..." *What do I need to figure out?* It's really hard to solve a problem when you refuse to let yourself face it.

"Please, please, tell me you're not considering trying to get him back. This isn't even about your feminine power, okay? You guys aren't—" She buries her face in both hands and shakes her head in frustration. Taking a deep breath, she drops her arms to her side and pleads with me. "You deserve better. You deserve a man who doesn't think being with you is settling."

Her words sting. This is why I needed to spend my summer here, away from it all. I need a break from the truth Mason shoved down my throat. The worst part is he *almost* went through with it. Apparently, I'm good enough to marry, but not intriguing enough to fuck. I wish it didn't bother me, but it does...

So much.

What woman doesn't want to be treated as beautiful, desirable, and tempting? Part of intimacy is sex. How is it possible I'm so good at one but lacking miserably at the other?

"What I deserve is the time and space to get through this in my own way."

She nods, albeit reluctantly. "Okay—"

Her phone ringing interrupts us. Palmer scrambles for her phone, all jittery and twitchy like she's about to wiggle out of her own skin. She's always like this after auditions, and I don't want to see the heartbreak in her eyes if it's bad news. Excusing myself from the kitchen, I explore Dex's main living room.

There are two large fish tanks that seem to be built into the walls. I don't even understand how to access them. Does the wall come apart? What the fuck? How do the fish eat? How does the aquarium guy clean this tank?

From what I understand, the higher maintenance fish are in the saltwater tanks, which are upstairs. Those are the ones that need careful tending to. The fish down here live off of auto feeders and nutrient-enriched water. They are beautiful swimming around in their little enclosures, none the wiser that the world is so much bigger than these glass walls. But maybe it's better—they can't get hurt in here. I know some people think aquariums are cruel and that fish should swim in the ocean...

But at least they won't be shark food in here. Is that such a bad life? Cared for, cleaned, fed, and admired? Or is running and hiding for life daily a fair price to pay for freedom?

I follow the tiniest fish in the largest tank darting back and forth in a tizzy. It's cherry-colored. Not quite red, not quite pink, right in the middle and slightly iridescent. How strange. It looks like it forgot something and it's struggling to remember exactly what it's doing.

"I got an audition," Palmer says right behind me, making me jump and smack my palm against the fish tank.

Cherry, as I've dubbed my little fish friend, is stunned. It's staring right at me like I just caused an earthquake in its little paradise. I cringe. Dex did warn me never to tap the glass. It's cruelly disorienting for the fish. *Sorry, Cherry.*

Spinning around, I face Palmer. "When's the callback?"

"Not that audition." She grimaces. "That was a bust. They're going with some baby-faced coed because Chase Ford likes them young." She grunts in frustration.

Anytime Palmer doesn't land an audition, the casting directors and the movie stars they've cast become the ultimate enemy. Apparently, Hollywood heartthrob Chase Ford is no exception.

"I'm pretty positive he's married." I swear I saw him and his new wife on a magazine cover. "She's not an actress. She's an artist or something. Noa—"

"Like marriage stops these Hollywood fuckboys from cheating. *Please.* Anyway, moving on. My agent got me an audition for a lead in a new pilot. The main actress dropped out last minute for some reason." Her eyes widen. "It's a big deal. It's like the next *Breaking Bad* or something."

"Palmer, that's amazing! When is it?"

"They want me to read for them by tonight. They have to make a decision ASAP."

"Let's go." I nod over my shoulder. "I'll drive you home." My back is still a little stiff from the five-hour drive out here, but good God, this could finally be her big break.

"It's not in L.A., Aves. It's in New Mexico. Albuquerque." She shrugs. "I don't know if—"

"Take my car."

Her big eyes grow even larger. "What? And leave you stranded here?"

I waltz past her to fetch my keys from my purse. I lay them on the counter and pull up Google Maps on my phone. "You've got at least an eight-hour drive, and that's if traffic behaves. *Go.* Hell, your suitcase is still in the car. It was meant to be."

"Aves, I..."

I wink at her. "I know. You can call me from the road to tell me how amazing I am. But seriously, *go*. This is your moment, Palmer. Finally. I really believe it, and I believe in you. Just drive safe. Do not try to read lines on the highway."

She nods, her smile growing. "Okay." She grabs the keys from where I placed them and wraps her arm around my neck, pulling me into one more quick hug. "Do you need anything out of the car?" she asks as she fetches her purse from the other side of the kitchen island.

"Nope. I brought everything of mine in."

"Okay," she says again, blowing out a quick breath. Spinning on her heel, she hustles toward the front door. "Thank you, Aves," she calls without turning around.

"Oh wait, only eighty-seven and up for the Jeep," I call after her. "Don't put cheap gas in—"

Bang.

The front door slams and she's out of earshot.

* * *

Thirteen days.

Thirteen days is how long it takes for my self-restraint to crumble and for me to go to Edge Fitness's website and find Maura Montoya. Suspicions confirmed—she's a total fucking knockout. This woman outshines even Palmer, and that's really hard to do. Her body is flawless. She's muscular, yet with feminine curves. Her stomach is so flat that if she lay down, you could set a wineglass on it without worrying it'd spill. Her shoulder-length hair is a richer brown than mine, and she's at least three shades tanner than me. She looks sun-kissed, like she's not afraid to show off her body on the beach. But enough rambling...

A simpler way to sum up Maura is that she is quite literally my polar opposite.

I dove headfirst into the rabbit hole. Within twenty minutes,

I found Maura's Facebook page, Instagram profile, and watched several of her videos on TikTok about proper form when deadlifting. I really want to hate her, but what did she do wrong besides exist?

It's been nearly two weeks...

I wonder if Mason has asked her out yet.

It'd be a little easier if she had resting bitch face, but not only is she stunning, she's also charming. I bet her client list is booked solid. I teach the business owners, Dex included, about this effect. Charisma. When you market a great personality, you could sell salt to a slug with ease. People want personable, relatable, and authentic. Those are the three magic ingredients to brand loyalty.

As if his ears are burning, an incoming phone call from Mason halts my social media stalking. I could send him to voicemail, but seeing as I've already been internet stalking his potential new girlfriend, I'm embracing my current masochist mentality.

"What?" I answer in the flattest monotone I can muster.

"You answered," Mason says, sounding surprised.

"You called," I snap.

He huffs through the phone, encouraging my frustration. "Avery, can we please be civil? We have a business together. Remember when people told us not to start a fifty-fifty LLC together? Remember how we told them we worked really well together and we would never let our relationship interfere with what we created?"

Remember when I thought you loved me and we were going to be together forever?

But he's right.

We do work well together, and the only relationship I had that rivaled mine and Mason's was my relationship with work. I'll be damned if I lose both this year.

My chest rises high then falls. *Is this allowed? Can we just be civil?* "What's going on, Mason?"

"Maynard Realty referred us for a major contract. *Major.* I didn't even want to entertain the idea without talking to you first."

Maynard Commercial Realty is our biggest client, not to mention the best-paying. But the research is devastatingly boring. Real estate is a lot of basic design and antiquated marketing strategies. It's simple color schemes, basic fonts, polished, professional, pristine, and absolutely no creativity. I'm not sure if I want to take on their referral. It's mind-numbing work.

"What kind of contract? And more importantly, with whom?"

He pauses for seemingly dramatic effect. I'm not amused. I put my phone on speaker and place it face up on Dex's coffee table. I nestle backward into the oversize navy sectional and watch Cherry dart around. The tank's dimmers are on an automatic schedule, so she's swimming in what she probably assumes is moonlight.

"Legacy Resorts."

My mouth falls open. "As in Sandals' biggest competitor?"

"That's the one."

I'm familiar with Legacy Resorts. I helped my dad and his new wife plan an anniversary trip with Legacy once. He's computer illiterate and nearly paid an upcharge of thirty percent to book through a travel agent. I had to swoop in and save him from getting swindled. I spent quite a bit of time on that website. Their branding is spectacular.

"What do they need help with?"

"From what I understand so far, they need help relaunching some of their larger properties as kid friendly. Right now, they are doing very well in the adult-only vacation space, but to stay competitive, they're learning they have to be family friendly, meaning—"

"They are going up against companies like Disney."

"And if Disney doesn't hand their ass to them, you've got Airbnb, VRBO, direct rentals—"

"All the more budget-friendly options that are making fancy all-inclusives obsolete for the middle class." I nod along as I keep my eyes on Cherry, who seems to be slowing down.

"Exactly." Mason clears his throat. "It's more than just

consulting. They want long-term strategists. They're looking for a five-year commitment."

"*Five years?*" My stomach twists. Normally, our contracts are on a six-month basis. We're consultants. We do the research, develop a strategy, help implement the strategy, and then hand over the baton. Never did we plan to work with a specific client for five years. Plus, this isn't just a five-year commitment to a client. It's a five-year commitment to Mason. I haven't even thought that far ahead... How in the hell can we keep working together in our current situation?

"I know, but, Aves, it's a seven-figure contract. And there's room for negotiation."

"Seven figures?" I lean forward, smacking my elbows against my knees. "Are you kidding me?"

"One million, at minimum. But I think we could ask for more if you can come up with a killer presentation."

"Holy shit, Mason."

"I know," he says through breathy huffs. "I was in shock. I'm not trying to put the cart before the horse. We still have to earn the contract, but we should be fucking proud we even get to have these conversations. I'm so proud of you."

"Proud of me?" I grab the phone off the table, take it off speakerphone, and press it against my cheek. Mason's voice becomes much clearer in my ear.

"You are who they're impressed with. They specifically asked for you after Maynard Realty told them all you did for them. It's you, Aves. I've said it from day one. I'm just the numbers guy. You're the talent. It's your way with people."

Every wall I built instantly crumbles.

The tears fall as fast as they form, and I have to mute the phone to hide my sudden outburst of hysteria. We should be hugging. We should be dancing in celebration. We should be so excited that we have the best sex of our lives.

We should not be having this conversation over the phone because we're broken up.

We're not spending our lives together.
Mason doesn't want me.
I'm alone.
I. Was. Dumped.

"Aves? You still there?"

I sniffle hard and then suck in a deep breath and hold it for a moment, collecting myself. Unmuting the phone, I say, "What do we need to do?"

"For now, preliminary research. But if you're interested in moving forward, we'll get in touch with their head of marketing. They'll probably want an official proposal."

"Okay," I grunt, trying desperately to save face. "I can do that."

"So...we're...interested?"

I'm numb. I'm numb. I'm numb.

So why does it hurt so fucking much?

"Yeah, Mason, I'm interested. Set it up. I'll start the industry research right away."

"Okay, great. I'll do that. I'll email you all the details."

The line is silent between us for a moment. It's easy to talk business. It's all we've been talking about for months now, apparently. How do we sign off? How do I say goodbye to the man who ripped my heart to pieces but apparently still has the power to put it back together?

"Thanks for calling—"

"Hey, Ave—"

We both try to speak at the same time.

"Go ahead," I say.

He pauses for a moment more before he says, "I, um, I just wanted to let you know that I'll take care of the rent here while you're in Vegas."

I clear my throat as it catches. "You don't have to do that—"

"No, it's only right. You're not living here. You shouldn't have to pay for it. As for the furniture and stuff—"

"Mason?" I interrupt.

"Yeah?"

I decide to acknowledge the hurt for the first time since my birthday dinner. It's taken almost two weeks, but I finally let my heart shatter. "I don't want to talk about all that right now. I'm still hurting over everything. Can we deal with *furniture* after the summer?"

"Of course."

"Okay, good night—"

"Avery," he interrupts.

"What?" I ask in exasperation. *Let me go so I can melt.*

"I don't know if I'm allowed to say this...but I'm hurting too. I don't want you to think I don't miss you every day."

And that does it. I hang up the phone and become a puddle of hysterical, blubbering tears. Curling up into a ball on the couch and clenching my eyes shut, I see her face. Her shiny rich brunette waves, her tan skin, flawless smile, flat stomach, and the perfect curve of her ass.

The woman he wants.

The woman I'm not.

Chapter 6

Finn

I charge through the gate separating my yard from Dex's. I'm not angry. The damn springs have too much tension. You have to rip through it, or it'll snap back and smack you in the face. I learned that lesson the tough way.

Innocent or not, me barreling through the gate like a bull startles the woman who is already in the hot tub. Her eyes bulge in surprise as her arm instinctively flies across her chest, sending a spray of water in my direction. I recognize her immediately from outside of Dex's driveway today.

Neither of us says anything.

She's frozen with a look of terror like I'm about to mug her.

Her green-gray eyes gleaming under the overhead deck lights stun me a little. Maybe just gray? I don't know. They are so light they almost look ghostly. They are hauntingly enthralling.

"Who are you?" she finally asks. "And why are you smiling like that?"

Because I love when my hunches are right. I knew you were pretty. I drag my hand over my mouth and wipe the smug smirk off my face.

"I'm Finn." I nod over my shoulder while holding out the six-pack of Alaskan Amber. "I'm Dex's neighbor. Who are you?"

She tightens her forearm around her chest and sinks an inch lower under the water line. "You just barge into your neighbor's private residence at nine o'clock at night, uninvited?"

Fair point. It takes me a moment to realize why she's holding herself so tightly and her entire demeanor is so defensive. I try to hold in my chuckle. "You know Dex has a very serious girlfriend, right?"

"Yes." She squints at me.

"Just making sure, seeing as you're topless in his hot tub."

She looks down at the bubbling water. "You can see me?" Her cheeks go from pink to red, once warm from the steam, now burning with embarrassment.

"No." I shake my head to reassure her. "Not with the jets on, but you've got no straps and you're holding your breasts like they might fall off, so I just assumed." I shrug.

To my utter pleasant surprise, she bursts out in a laugh. A rich, melodic laugh, punctuated with an adorably dorky snort.

"What's so funny?"

She timidly raises her shoulders, ensuring all the important parts of her body stay covered under the water line. "Today has just been the weirdest fucking day. Of course it ends like this."

"Like what?" I take one step forward.

"With the hot runner catching me skinny dipping in the hot tub."

Hot runner, huh? I'll take it.

With her free hand that doesn't have her full tits wrapped in a death lock, she points to the three sides of the eight-foot privacy fence. "I made sure no one could see me. I didn't anticipate anyone coming through the gate. Dex failed to mention you'd be stopping by."

"He didn't know. He lets me use his hot tub whenever I want." I take another step forward and hold out the six-pack. "In exchange, I bring him beer. What're you doing here?" I have a clear view of her doll-like face, now. Her striking eyes were easy to notice from three paces back. But I can appreciate her full cheeks and pink pouty lips much better from up close.

"I'm pet sitting"—she cocks her head to the side—"or more like fish sitting for Dex this summer. He's guiding scuba tours for the next couple of months straight."

"*Oh.*" Makes sense. Dex has a weird obsession with his fish. He has about seven tanks in his home. I always expect his place to smell fishy, but it's surprisingly fresh every time I've been over. "He didn't tell me you were staying here or I wouldn't have barged in on you like this. I can go..." I say it as a statement, but I mean it as a question.

Of course I'll give her back her privacy, but I'm really hoping she's in the mood for company. It's not just that my aching lower back and stiff quads really could use a long soak, but it's been a long time since I've been this curious about a woman before I even know her name.

She points to the six-pack in my hand. "That's a really good beer."

My smile spreads wide. "You know Alaskan Amber? I feel like everyone I meet is a die-hard Killian's fan."

She scrunches her face and shakes her head. "Alaskan is so much smoother. Plus, I like the company's back story better."

"Back story?"

"I'm a brand strategist." She rolls her wrist in the air. "I pay attention to a company's origin story as a part of their branding package—" She abruptly stops and rolls her eyes. "Sorry, not interesting. It's Friday night. Who wants to talk about work?"

I nod, but I actually don't find it uninteresting at all. "Hey, what's your name?"

"Oh, sorry." She instinctively rises with her hand extended, until apparently, she remembers she's topless and immediately slams back into the tub to hide her body, causing the water to splash out onto the deck on all sides.

This time I openly laugh. I've seen so many sets of tits between my work life and my sex life, I'm immune. But her shyness is endearing. "I didn't see anything," I say between hearty huffs of laughter.

"I'm Avery," she mumbles, looking up at the pergola strung with lights above us, refusing to look at me. "Avery Scott."

"Well, Avery Scott, I'll let you enjoy your evening." I take a step backward as a test.

"Wait!"

Thankfully, she passes.

Her smile reminds me of the one before, from the car this morning. Genuine. Sincere. She must be starting to relax. Especially now that she's probably aware I'm not here to rob her. "Don't be silly. You clearly wanted to use the hot tub. I'm pretty much done."

I nod at her. It's a bit of a reach, but I take my shot. "Or maybe we both stay? Do you want some company? I can share my beer," I say, raising one brow. "I'd love to find out what the hell a brand strategist is."

To my great surprise, she slowly nods. I really thought she was going to take the out. "Sure. Sounds good. But could you turn around first and close your eyes so I can grab my towel? I'll put on a swimsuit and come back."

I set my six-pack down on the deck where I'm standing and walk over to fetch the fluffy green towel draped over the patio chair behind us. Squatting down near the edge of the tub, I offer her the towel. With my other hand, I point to the far side of the hot tub. "I can just stay on my side. I told you, I can't see anything." I force myself to lock onto her peculiarly light eyes and don't dare let my gaze scour what it wants to.

"Thank you," she says, matching my stare with a clipped smile. "But it's not so much that I'm topless... It's that I'm not wearing any bottoms either." Avery points to the deck, where I should leave the towel, and then rotates her finger in the air. I rise then obediently follow directions and spin around. I even cover my eyes.

I hear the water falling off her and splashing into the tub as she must be climbing out in a hurry.

"Okay, I'm decent."

I spin back around to see Avery secured in the oversize green fluffy towel. She's a little shorter than I was picturing. I'm barely over six-foot, yet I really tower over her.

"I'll be right back."

She makes her way through the glass sliding door, leaving me alone with the tub, my beer, and a whole lot of anticipation for a night that just got far more interesting.

Avery

"Want one more?" Finn asks, removing the last two bottles of Alaskan Amber from the cardboard six-pack. Using the bottle opener he brought, he pops both lids.

"Why not? No one's driving tonight. We can be sloppy."

He smirks. "Two beers get you sloppy?" He rises and crosses no man's land, finding me on the opposite side of the hot tub. He holds out one bottle. I take it, but this time he stays on my side. I don't blame him. We've basically been shouting at each other across the tub for the past twenty minutes. It's hard to make conversation over the loud rumble of the jets.

"Nope, but three might," I say before taking a swig of the fresh beer. *Mmm.* It's crisp. I took too long to finish my last bottle and did not appreciate the bitter, flat end, warmed by the steam of the tub.

"Cheers to sloppy, then." Finn points over my shoulder to Dex's house. "Your commute home seems manageable." He shoots me a little wink, and I purposely ignore the flutter in my chest.

Finn is easily the sexiest man I've ever seen in person. I'm thoroughly convinced he accidentally wandered out of some woman's fantasy and got stuck here in reality. He's even fitter than I realized this morning. Runners are usually lean. The way he had his legs secured with athletic tape, I assumed he's a serious runner, but up close it's clear that his exercise routine includes far more than cardio.

His entire left arm is tatted as well. I've seen a lot of tribal sleeves but never something like this. I can't make out all the pictures with his arm bobbing in and out of the water, but the image starting on his broad, muscular shoulder is a ghost pirate ship. The sails are tattered, and there's half a skull on one of the main sails. The intricate designs show off some seriously impressive artistic ability. I've never seen a tattoo like this, which should be slapped on a canvas and hung in a museum.

It really adds to Finn's already peak-level attractiveness.

Which actually makes it much easier to talk to him.

I am not one bit nervous about sharing a beer and a conversation with the Adonis next to me in the bubbling hot tub. The reason is simple. He's so damn hot that I've friend-zoned the shit out of him. He's in the no-touch zone, locked in a box, key flung into the ocean, because there is no way on God's green earth that I can handle an unrequited crush situation right now. He's so far out of my league, it hurts. But he's also funny and smiley, and our conversation is a welcome distraction from the fact that I'll be spending the night alone.

The first night by myself. I left my home and moved immediately onto Palmer's couch. This will be the first night I'm truly by myself and have to face the music that this is my new reality. *Alone.*

"So what exactly does a brand strategist do?" Finn asks as his baby blue eyes lock on mine. Obviously, he has pretty eyes and dark lashes that accentuate them. Because all Grecian gods have sexy eyes that can stun you into oblivion.

I take a quick swig of my beer. "The simplest way to explain it is I evaluate brands and provide them with guidance on how to adjust their marketing to monetize and scale."

He blinks at me. "That's the vaguest response I think I've ever heard."

I laugh. "Okay, how about this? I help brands come up with a game plan to be visible and competitive. So I do a lot of industry research and help companies plan their branding image. I consult on everything from logos and print material to blueprints for product packaging if they sell tangible products. I do web design and help develop a pricing strategy." I raise my brows at Finn. "I could continue..."

He squints one eye at me. "All that stuff is necessary for a business to bring in money?"

I clench my eyes closed and nod. "Definitely. Eighty percent of being profitable is being visible. Yes, having a good product or service is important, but it really doesn't matter unless customers know you exist. Most businesses fail not because they aren't competitive. It's just because people don't know about them."

Finn points at me. "That's *exactly* what I'm dealing with right now." He takes another long swig of his beer before setting it on the deck behind him. "I'm having the hardest time finding clients."

"What do you work in?"

He hesitates for a brief moment then says with confidence, "Photography."

"Ah, that's a tricky one. Unless you have a niche, the market is saturated. Not to mention there are really no barriers to entry. Anyone can be a photographer, and the prestige of names like Ansel Adams is a thing of the past. Not to mention, video content is superior these days."

He blinks at me in surprise.

"Oh, I'm sorry. I don't mean to be discouraging. I just meant you're probably a great photographer, but it's a hard business to sustain."

"I couldn't agree more." He braces against the deck and hoists himself out of the tub. Sitting on the edge of the deck, his legs dangle two inches from my shoulder. "I'm hot. Are you hot? I need a break."

I shrug as I turn my head. "I'm not too—" I choke on my spit when I realize I'm at eye level with his crotch. His trunks are soaked and are melded to the outline of his dick, which is in-your-face massive.

"Whoa, you okay?" He pats my shoulder, likely because he's unable to reach my back pressed against the hot tub wall.

"Beer...wrong pipe..." I manage to say through sputtering, but I notice his eyes dart from me to the beer resting on the deck behind me, which I haven't touched in at least a minute.

"What?"

"Okay, fine," I mumble then clear my throat one more time. "You're..." I twist my wrist. "You know...kind of on display."

His eyes fall to his lap. "Oh, sorry." Finn immediately unties his trunks as he spreads his legs into a wide V. He slips his hand underneath his waistband, grabs his dick, and tucks it out of sight. How that's possible, I don't know. His penis could probably be spotted from outer space. I'd like to say I have more self-control, but no, I watched the entire fiasco with my mouth wide open. "Better?" he asks, completely unashamed.

"Mmhmm," I mumble. I grab my beer and chug just to have something to do.

"I guess we're even now," he says with a chuckle.

"Excuse me?"

Finn shrugs nonchalantly like we're talking about what we had for lunch. "I saw your tits earlier."

I gawk. Caught off guard, I do the most childish thing I can think of and throw a handful of water at his face. "You said you couldn't see anything."

Laughing, he holds up his hands in surrender as I cup my hand to prepare another water grenade. "I couldn't in the hot tub, but you dropped your towel when you got into the living room. You must've forgotten about the windows in there." He points to the left side of the deck, where Dex's living room is in clear sight through enormous clear glass panes. So clear in fact, I can see that Cherry has finally finished swimming around in a frenzy and is nowhere in sight.

Fuck me. I dropped my towel right in front of the damn fish tank. Of course he saw everything.

I was in such a hurry to get dressed, I threw on my bra, tank top, and underwear where I'd left them earlier on Dex's navy sectional. When I decided to hot tub naked this evening, it wasn't because I was trying to be sensual. It was because I didn't bring a swimsuit. Because I don't like getting into swimsuits. I *hate* the beach. I don't like being photographed half naked, unlike the millions of other Californians who go to the beach for selfie photo shoots. How nice it must be to have a body you don't mind documented.

I'm not even really a hot tub kind of girl, but I got a massive headache from all the hysteric crying after I got off the phone with Mason. I couldn't find any painkillers in Dex's home, and I'm stranded without my car. A relaxing hot soak seemed like an interim remedy for my throbbing head.

I scowl at Finn. "And you looked?"

His shoulders shake as he lets out a soundless laugh. "I didn't look. It just happened right in front of my eyes. If it makes you feel better, the back of the couch blocked everything from the waist down."

I bury my face in my hands, breathing in the strong chlorine aroma. "I'm so sorry."

"What?"

I let out a defeated laugh, or more like a grumble. Maybe something in-between. "Sorry you had to see that." I assume the baby raccoon protective position. If I can't see Finn, he can't see me...

But I hear him.

There's a little splash as he slides back into the hot tub.

And I feel him.

Large hands gently peel mine from my face. His baby blues are two inches from my face. "Avery, did you just apologize to me because I saw you half naked?"

I don't feel like this is the kind of question that needs a response. The way he's looking at me is intimidating. He looks almost agitated. Standing this close to me, I realize how much larger he is than me. I never feel like the petite woman in the room, but Finn is making me feel really small at the moment.

"I see this all the time at my job," he continues as he keeps his hands loosely locked around my wrists. He must know the second he releases them, they'll snap right back to my face so I can hide again. "Apologizing about your body is ridiculous. Please don't ever do that for me or for anyone else, okay?"

His intense stare is making me wildly uncomfortable, yet at the same time, I'm relieved he can read my mind. "Your job?" I wriggle my wrists in his grip, and he immediately releases me.

"I run a boudoir photography studio." He settles back into his seat in the corner of the hot tub.

"Oh. That's definitely niche...yet you're having trouble finding clients?"

"It's not like I can really advertise some of my best work."

"You shoot nudes?"

Finn shrugs. "Occasionally." For the first time since he graced this deck with his presence, I see him flush, just slightly. "It's not what you think. It's all very tasteful."

I cross my arms as my mind wanders. From what I understand, boudoir photography is trending. I think I remember reading some sort of statistic about how "boudoir" is one of the highest-searched photography keywords next to wedding. "How's your website health? Click traffic? Is it mobile optimized?"

My questions seem to surprise him. "Are you about to go all brand strategist on me?"

I shoot him a glib smile. "Yup," I say, popping the P at the end of my response.

He shrinks a bit in his seat, sinking half an inch lower into the water. "It's okay, I think."

I give him a mischievous smile. "What's your business name?"

"It's just Finn Harvey Photography."

"So...let me guess, finn-harvey-photography-dot-com? Two Ns?"

He nods slowly, and then his forehead crinkles as he watches my teasing smile spread. "Oh, no."

"Oh, yes. It's audit time, buddy. Let's check your work."

He lunges for me, but I'm shockingly too quick. With far more grace than I could pray for, I pop my ass out of the water onto the deck, swivel my legs around, and dart to my phone lying by Dex's fancy built-in grill.

Finn is right behind me. We're soaking the deck with chlorinated hot tub water. I shake my hands off before unlocking my phone. He wraps one arm around my rib cage from behind and tries to snatch my phone out of my hand as he chuckles against my ear.

"Not fair. I haven't put in the marketing effort I probably should've. I'm totally unprepared for an audit."

I laugh and hold my phone as far above my head as I can. He could easily take it from me as his reach far surpasses mine, but I get the feeling his arm is wrapped around me simply because he wants to touch me...

Is this...no...wait. Is he flirting?

He squeezes my rib cage gently, and I nearly keel over from the ticklish feeling.

Holy shit. Is this flirting?

I almost ask him, until my phone vibrates in my hand. The notification banner preview shocks me so much I nearly throw up in my mouth.

I pull at Finn's arm. He takes the cue and releases me. My whole demeanor changes in an instant, and Finn looks concerned.

"Hey, are you okay?"

I ignore him, unable to speak as I open my text messages.

> **Mason: I want to see you tonight. It's been over a month. I need that sweet pussy in my mouth again.**

I might as well be in a movie. The entire set stills, and I'm sure the camera would zone in on my dismal facial expression with suspenseful music. My heart is pounding so hard, I bet Finn can feel it from two steps away from me.

This text message wasn't for me. I know because Mason doesn't do *that* for me.

Maybe once or twice in our entire four years together has he put his head between my thighs. He told me it's just not his style. He also would never speak to me that way. Never once in our entire relationship has he said the word pussy to me or around me.

But that word certainly isn't the most shocking from the message. It's the over a *month*, and the again part that's making me feel sick.

The fucking bastard lied.

The cogs start spinning in my mind. *He lied.* He cheated on me. *He's* been *cheating* on me. When? How is that possible? All he does is work...*with me.* Then it hits me. That's why he wants this breakup to be amicable. He needs me for this contract. He's known about Legacy Resorts for far longer than he's led on. *He's using me.*

Holy shit. I feel nearly nauseated and woozy, like my knees are going to give out. I watch the steam rising from the top of the hot tub and try to slip away with it.

Just float. Just disappear. Just rise...

"Avery, are you okay?" Finn's low, honey-sweet tone is alluring enough that it pulls me back to reality.

Dammit. I was so close to just drifting away right back to *numb.*

"Hey, I, um..." I take a few steps backward toward my towel. "I think I'm going to call it a night."

He scours my face. "Okay?" His lips twitch. "Is my website *that* bad?" He forces a chuckle, but his eyes are narrowed with concern.

"I didn't look," I mumble absentmindedly. I text Mason back before I can change my mind. I want him to know he's caught.

> **Avery: Funny. I thought you hated doing that. Just with me, huh?**

The minute my message says delivered, Mason calls me. He's

panicking, I'm sure. I would be too. Right now, I'm the key to unlocking a million dollars. If I were him, I'd be scared shitless.

I silence his call. *Let him sweat.* I hope he's distracted as all hell when he's fucking Maura tonight.

"Sorry, Finn," I say, trying to refocus on the man in front of me, but all I can see is Mason's face. His blotchy, anguished red face from the restaurant when he told me he loved me and would never cheat on me... "I need to get to bed, but don't feel like you have to rush out. Would you mind turning the hot tub off and covering it back up when you're done?"

"Okay," he says.

I can tell he wants to ask more, but he doesn't. *Thank you, Finn.* Thank God this man knows exactly what I need right now. Privacy. So I can shatter into a million tiny pieces.

"Have a good night."

I freeze, trying to hold back the tears for a moment longer. *Don't fucking cry, Avery. This is embarrassing enough. Don't be that girl. This is just icing on the shit cake. You and Mason are already over...*

Except maybe I didn't believe that. Maybe I thought time and space would heal all. Maybe I thought Mason would miss me enough to come to his senses.

Maybe I'm the dumbest girl on the planet.

"Good night, Finn," I say over my shoulder as I slip through the sliding glass doors into the house.

Chapter 7

Finn

"I can assure you this isn't mine," I say to the grocery delivery man standing on my doorstep. He looks agitated, like I'm the last delivery of the day...except I didn't order any groceries.

"I don't know what to tell you, man. The order says 297 Fisher Street." He steps back and points to the house numbers on my side paneling. "This is 297 Fisher Street." He holds two plastic grocery bags out insistently. "Are you sure you didn't just forget you ordered something?"

Sighing in exasperation, I take the bag from his left hand. I peek inside and see a blue box of tampons, a small tube of scented sensual lubricant, and a brown eyebrow pencil. "I live alone, man. I don't have a need for tampons."

"I guess I could just take them back, but we don't do refunds."

The eyebrow pencil is a shade nearly identical to Avery's hair. "Just leave them. I think I know where they're supposed to go."

He shrugs and then hands me the other bag. Without further question, he flees down the driveway, cranks his car, and the blaring sound of Latin rap fills the street. I close my front door and head out into the warm evening air to Dex's house.

Our houses are similar in design, except Dex has at least an extra fifteen hundred square feet. I have paneling. He has stucco. His landscaping makes my little rose bushes out front look like a joke. Everything about Dex's house screams money, but my favorite part about the guy is he's so down to earth. Dex is a good friend, and I would've happily checked in on his fish over the summer. I wonder why he didn't just ask me for help. He probably assumed I had more interesting plans than excessive runs in the torturous Las Vegas heat. Not to mention there was that one time I fed his fish cereal, but I stand by it. There was no fish food left, and I couldn't let them starve.

Then again, I'm not complaining because meeting Avery was a pleasant surprise. Until she freaked out and ditched me in the backyard last week, I was really enjoying the conversation. It's been a long time since I've felt at ease around a girl.

I chuckle to myself, remembering she put on a tank top to get in the hot tub with me. It's been a while since a girl has been that modest around me, too. I wonder if she'd be put off knowing that her ample tits have popped into my mind a time or two since I accidentally saw her undress.

I debated asking her out, but she's only here for the summer. She has fling written all over her, and that's exactly what I'm trying not to do with my life right now. The irony. The first interesting woman I've met in months is, of course, not an actual resident of Las Vegas.

Holding both plastic bags in one hand, I ring Dex's doorbell. After waiting a full minute, I raise my finger to ring once more, but in perfect timing, Avery rips the door open.

Good God.

She looks like a mess.

Avery's hair is in a high sloppy ponytail. Her oversize T-shirt looks like it was once a dog's chewing toy. It's also stained with what I pray is pizza sauce or something.

"You." She rolls her eyes when she sees me and grumbles, "Would you consider showing up unannounced when I'm *not* naked or wildly unpresentable?"

"Wow." I can't help but smile at her unamused pout. "That's a rude way to greet the man who comes bearing gifts." I hold up the grocery bags. "By gifts I mean tampons, of course."

She hangs her head. "They got delivered to you?"

I nod in response and watch her gaze snap up to mine.

"*Wait.* You went through my groceries?" She's trying to sound cross, but her cheeks are bunched in that cute smile.

"I had to confirm they weren't my tampons...or lube."

There's an audible smack when her hands hit her face. "Kill me now," she mumbles through her fingers as I fall into heaves of laughter. "It's not what you're thinking."

"I didn't ask." I hold out the bags to her. "Feels like there's something cold in here."

"Ice cream," she admits.

"You might want to pop it into the freezer."

She takes the bags. "Thank you. I must've fat-fingered the delivery address. Sorry they bothered you."

I shrug. "Not at all. It was a good excuse to come over and make sure you were okay." But is she? Now that I'm only an arm's length away from her, I notice her swollen eyes and the red tip of her nose. It's a clear sign that she's been crying. "Are you...okay?"

"Nope." She peers into one of the plastic bags. "But a little better now that my dinner's here...which is melting, so I better—" She throws her head back, gesturing inside.

I can take a hint, so I nod and turn to leave...

But something stops me. *Dammit, Finn.* It's not your business. *But fuck.* When a woman cries like that, I usually know the reason. And if I can help, shouldn't I?

"Avery, are you only eating ice cream for dinner?"

She purses her lips. "Well, it's a quart of rocky road, so believe me, I'm hitting the calorie count."

I snort. "Dex keeps a stockpile of grass-fed, organic ribeye steaks in the chest freezer in his garage. They are worth like thirty bucks a piece. Knowing Dex, he probably told you to help yourself to whatever, right?"

She nods. "But I don't really know how to cook a steak, so it's a moot point."

I move toward her, stalling halfway through the door. "Well, I do. Want some company?"

She shifts, just slightly. Angling her shoulders and hips, she allows just enough room for me to squeeze past her into Dex's house.

I hear her soft footsteps behind me as I head toward the kitchen.

"But I can still eat my ice cream, too, right?"

* * *

"Finn Harvey, you are a man of many talents." Avery arches her back, purposely protruding her belly before she pats it. "I'm assuming, at least. I haven't seen your photographs, but you sure as hell grill a mean steak."

"You sure?" I ask from across the couch. "You barely touched your food."

I nod toward the dining table that still holds the remnants of our dinner. We found a bag of salad to pair with our steaks. My plate is nearly cleared. Avery poked a few lettuce leaves and took maybe three bites of meat.

She widens her eyes at me. "No, it was superb. My appetite is just a little off."

Pointing to the grocery bag holding the box of tampons still on the kitchen island, I raise my brows at her. "Lady stuff?"

Her head knocks back against the soft couch as she laughs. "No, *lady stuff* tends to have the opposite effect," she says with a smirk. "What I have is a cheating bastard of an ex-boyfriend... *stuff.*"

I really think she meant it as a joke, but her eyes immediately fill with tears. I'm getting a feeling she's a smile-through-the-pain kind of girl. She nestles deeper into the couch and grabs a square throw pillow. Hugging it tightly to her chest, she draws her knees in, curling herself into a ball, like she's trying to make herself as tiny as possible.

Her eyes are glued on one of Dex's built-in aquariums, and I seem to lose her to her thoughts again. I break the silence and try bringing her back. "Do you want to talk about it?"

She answers with her eyes still fixed on the fish tank. "I just found out, the other night when you were over, so the wound is still pretty fresh. My best and only friend in the world landed a lead role on a big deal TV pilot. It could be her big break, and I don't want to distract her right now. My parents don't know Mason and I broke up, and I moved out here for the summer. I literally have no one to talk to." She turns her head, looking at me, and I finally pinpoint the color of her eyes. Hazy. Light. A little more green than blue. They are seafoam green. "So don't offer unless you mean it."

"Hmm," I say, rising.

She looks immediately horrified, misinterpreting my actions and probably thinking I'm trying to excuse myself. I feel her eyes on me as I head to the kitchen and scour Dex's fridge. Pulling out a bottle of white wine, I check the label. Pinot Gris? Not my favorite, but it's not for me. After finding a clean wineglass, I pour a generous amount for Avery and join her back on the couch.

"Thank you?" she asks.

I plop down right beside her. "I'm all ears. Lay it on me."

She takes a small sip and makes a face. "I'm more of a beer kind of girl."

My kind of girl. I take the glass from her hand and set it on the coffee table.

"And I don't know where to start."

"How about with the fact that this Mason guy sounds like a little bitch."

That earns me a little laugh. "He didn't use to be. Up until about three weeks ago, he was actually a decent guy. I wanted to marry him."

I reach out to pat her knee and then decide against it. Boundaries. This woman is hurting, and the last thing she needs is to be led on. Even if Avery did live here, I sure as hell am not ready for another relationship at the moment. I still can't see straight after Nora. I tried to date in every way possible after we broke up. I hooked up. I took women out to nice restaurants. When that led nowhere, I even dabbled in a couple of threesomes. One foursome. Everything felt chaotic. Things got so much better when I took a little break from it all. But I'd be lying if I said breaks weren't lonely.

"What happened?" I ask.

"On my thirtieth birthday, he gave me a ring." My eyes instinctually search for her left hand, but it's hidden under the pillow. "Then, after seeing it on my finger, he panicked and told me there was no way he could commit to our unsatisfying sex life for the rest of his life."

My jaw clenches. I have a growing urge to break her ex's nose. "He said that to you?"

"More or less."

"What a piece of—"

"I think I would've gotten through it. I mean, we were together for four years, so I know I needed time. We own a business together, so it's not like we can completely sever ties. I think I was okay with eventually being amicable until..."

"The other night?" I ask.

She hugs her knees to her chest again. "He meant to text another woman but accidentally texted me. He let the cat out of the bag that he was screwing someone else...for a while, apparently."

"Shit, Avery, I'm sorry." *Ah, screw it.* I pat her knee tenderly, and she smiles at me.

"Thanks."

"Want me to send him a threatening text?" I ask, and she giggles. "I'm completely serious," I say with a laugh. "Am I bigger than he is?"

"Yes." Her eyes immediately land on my crotch. She flushes and diverts her gaze when she notices me noticing, and I can't help but howl in laughter.

"I meant"—I gesture to my pecs—"muscles-wise."

She smirks. "Also yes."

Goddamn, she's cute. And funny. She's good at flirting and doesn't even realize it. It's so refreshing to talk to a woman without needing to be on guard. Shit, why not? Maybe we should just sleep together. Lennox is right. If I keep working out my feelings by logging miles on hard pavement, I really will break my knees. I remember Mrs. Mattley's advice about connecting when I can. *This feels like connecting.* She's hurting. I'm hurting. I have a feeling a night wrapped up in the sheets could be a good stress relief for both of us. The image of her full tits and thick, dark nipples fills my mind.

Oh, sue me. I can't un-see them. Nor would I want to.

"You know what the shitty part is?" Avery asks, interrupting my thoughts about her topless. "It's not like I was exactly satisfied myself, but I would've never considered cheating to be a solution. Have you ever been cheated on?"

I shrug. "Not exactly. But in a way. I can empathize, though."

"How long have you been single?" she asks.

"Why do you assume I'm single?"

Avery clears her throat and turns toward me, her knee knocking against my thigh. "Because you just had dinner with me, and while I realize I'm not exactly a threat to another woman, no way your girlfriend would let you out of her sight on a Friday night. Not a man like you."

Not a threat? What? "What kind of man am I?"

"Don't make me say it out loud," she mutters before she rises, leaving me behind on the couch. She grabs the quart of ice cream from the fridge and returns to me with two spoons. "You don't exactly have a body that screams *I love ice cream* or anything, but I'm more than happy to share." She gives me a sheepish smile before popping off the lid. She balances the container in her lap.

"You're making a lot of assumptions about me, Avery," I say as I take a spoon from her. I stab the cold dessert with the side of my spoon and scoop out a generous bite. "I don't appreciate it." I give her a knowing look before putting the spoon in my mouth.

"I'm sorry." She shrivels in her seat.

I nudge her shoulder with mine, finding any excuse to touch her. "I'm just teasing you."

I squeeze her knee again, and this time leave my hand there to see if she'll take the bait. Maybe she knows that making me work for it is the best way to turn me on. I don't even mind her raggedy shirt and faded cloth pajama shorts. I like her chirpy personality, even when she's upset. How easy it is to talk to her. That she seems to say whatever is on her mind.

"I am indeed single, though."

"I figured. You know, you made quite the impression on my friend Palmer."

Huh? My hand is on her knee, and I'm doing that thing where I rub little circles against her skin with my thumb. Yet she wants to talk about her friend? "The blonde who was in your car last week?"

"Yeah. She's a spitfire. You'd like her. She's more on your level."

"My level?" I drag my hand an inch farther up her thigh. She shifts in her seat, and I seriously can't tell if she's uncomfortable or intrigued. *Maybe one more inch higher will give me answers?*

"Yes. She's a ten. You're a ten. Actually, you're a ten and a half." She laughs.

"Well, thank you, but I don't know her." By now my hand is on the inside of her upper thigh, pressed against the carton of ice cream teetering in her lap as she squirms. My breathing slows into heavy, drawn-out inhales and exhales. I pull the ice cream off her lap and set it on the coffee table. I watch her eyes, purposely making my stare as intense and asking as possible. Maybe now I have her attention.

"She'll be back to return my Jeep, eventually. I could introduce you two."

I grumble in annoyance and grab a handful of her fleshy thigh. Goddamn, that feels good. *I really like how she feels.* "Avery, no offense, but I don't give a fuck about your friend. I'm hitting on you. Am I not being clear enough?" I rub her thigh where I squeezed. "Or are you not interested?"

Avery

Every single cell in my body is on fire. If I'm playing this cool, it's because I'm the best actress in the world. Clearly, I'm nailing performance under pressure, and by performance, I mean managing not to melt under Finn's touch.

Am I interested? *Yes. On a different planet. In a different world. Where you don't look like you, or maybe I don't look like me.* I could come up with a million different excuses to dissuade him. I love the feel of his hand on my thigh, and I'm more aroused right now than I've ever been, but we can't happen. And I should probably be honest about why.

"I'm interested," I say clearly. A satisfied smile spreads across his face. The kind of smile a man gets right before he knows he's going to get laid. It's filled with eagerness and relief, and now I need to give this man a reality check. "But please stop touching me."

He immediately complies. Ripping his hand away from my lap, he leans backward. "I'm sorry," he says.

"Don't be. It was nice. You're nice. This whole evening was really nice. I needed it," I admit. "I had a really crappy day."

"So you must not hook up. That's okay."

I furrow my brows. "Is it? Or is this night kind of over now?"

"Of course not," he says with unconvincing enthusiasm. "I like talking to you. You don't have to have sex with me to hang out. I have no plans tonight. Let's watch a movie. Or play a board game," he says as he watches my blank expression. "Or you can tell me more about your job. I made some tweaks to my website. I think I'm ready for that audit."

I swallow the lump in my throat as we sit in silence for a moment. *Oh, shit. Here we go.* I'm about to embarrass the hell out of myself. I suck in a deep breath and hold it as long as I can until I exhale my confession.

"Finn, if I had ten minutes left alive, my dying wish would

be for you to fuck me. Not have sex with me...*fuck me*. But my boyfriend, whom I share a home and a business with, just dumped me. Don't you get it?"

He's watching my lips. "Get what?" His brain must've gone fuzzy after I told him I wanted him to fuck me. But he only wants me because I'm the easiest target that's right in front of him.

"The man I've loved for *four years* all but told me that even though we're great together in every other way, he couldn't bear the idea of having sex with me for the rest of his life. I am shattered. I am humiliated. My ego isn't wounded—it's completely gone. I am *never* getting naked in front of another man again. I am never sharing my body with another man ever again. Especially not with a man who looks like he fucks like a porn star."

I didn't expect to be so dramatic. I didn't expect the end of my rant to come through in breathy sniffles as tears stream down my face. I certainly didn't expect Finn to half pull me into his lap and into an all-encompassing hug.

For fuck's sake, he smells amazing.

I try to wiggle backward so my weight is on the couch and not his legs, but he doesn't let me go. He just hugs me so tightly that I have no choice but to calm my hysteria and steady my breath.

"Shh, shh," he says unnecessarily. I've already quieted down. "Is this your first major breakup?"

I nod into the crook of his neck.

"Yeah...this is how it feels...like death. Like the world stopped spinning and it'll never pick up again. It sucks even worse when you finally get through it, think you're invincible, and then it happens again."

"How many times for you?" I ask as I pull my face away from the warm nook between his neck and shoulder.

"Three and counting. My most recent relationship was a fucking mess. It's probably the reason I just made a move on you on Dex's couch, instead of asking you out like a gentleman should. Avery, I'm working through my shit, and I'm still not ready for anything serious. But I don't want you to think that has anything to do with you. I happen to think you're incredibly sexy."

I scoff. "Let's just be honest."

"Okay?" he asks as his brows furrow with confusion.

"I know this is Mason's fault. I know I deserve better. Yada, yada." I roll my eyes. "But it's not like I can shrug off the insecurities. The pain and shame have seeped into every pore. I'm terrified for the rest of my life, every time I look in the mirror, I'm just going to hate what I see."

He wipes the loose hairs away from my forehead and tucks them behind my ear. "Men need to be more careful with the women they love." He tilts his head, his expression full of pity. "They have no idea the damage they can do."

"Thank you for listening." I push against his arms and then crawl off his lap. Standing to face Finn, I rest my hands on my hips. "And that completes tonight's total humiliation session. I'm going to need a five-minute heads-up moving forward every time you plan to use the hot tub so I can hide somewhere. Deal?"

He laughs. "You have nothing to be embarrassed about."

I cover my eyes. "I'm going to do the raccoon thing where I pretend you can't see me. If you could just see yourself out." I point somewhere in the direction of the front door, but I'm not positive. I've really committed to the eyes closed bit I'm putting on.

"You need baby steps," Finn says softly.

"What?" I drop my hands and watch his pointed expression.

"When I have clients who want to be a little more daring in the studio, but they're so uncomfortable and embarrassed, we have to work our way up. We start with just flattering poses in jeans and a T-shirt. Then, we move on to shorts, maybe a tank top. When they're ready, lingerie. Then we take off the bra...sometimes more. The more they force themselves to step out of their comfort zones, the more natural confidence begins to feel. But it usually happens in baby steps."

"Your *actual* job is photographing naked women?"

He presses his lips in a flat line. His agitation is briefly apparent before it disappears. "I'm really good at helping women find their confidence." Finn extends a hand to me. "Do you trust me?"

"Who? You? As in the stranger I've met all but three times who watched me undress through the window."

He narrows his eyes at me.

"I'm kidding," I add. "I trust you." It's the truth. Finn somehow toggles the line between making me feel unnervingly embarrassed and yet comfortable at the same time.

I take his hand, and he leads me toward the staircase. I stop in my tracks and snatch back my hand. "Everything else aside, I'm actually on my period, Finn. Hence the need for more tampons. I'm not having sex with you tonight." *If nothing else I've said has scared him off, that certainly should do the trick.*

He grabs my hand demandingly. "Calm down, we're not having sex. Come on." He tugs me up the stairs, ignoring my begrudging footsteps. "Are you staying in the master?"

"Yes."

Finn knows his way around Dex's home. They must be closer than I realized. "I don't know how you sleep with that giant fish tank in your face."

Dex's bed and the sitting area in his master are divided by a partition, which is one giant fish tank. It's one of the most magnificent things I've ever seen. "I find it comforting. It makes me feel like I'm not alone in the bedroom at night."

"Dear God, woman, you really do need to get laid," he mutters under his breath. I debate telling him I heard that, but I don't think he was trying to be subtle about it.

We waltz right through Dex's bedroom and into his enormous master closet. It's so large, it could easily be another bedroom. A sizeable nursery. That's what I'd do with this room if I could ever afford a house like this. But as we weave past the counter in the center of the room, it's obvious where Finn is taking me, and I crumble inside. The floor-to-ceiling mirror in the back corner. It's humongous. There are fluorescent lights surrounding the frame. It hides nothing. It'll spit your insecurities right back in your face.

"Finn, no," I protest.

"Hush," he says, spinning around to face me. He drops my hand and holds five fingers in my face. "Five. Just give me five minutes. No arguing, no hesitating, no silly jokes. For five minutes, let me talk you through this."

"Talk me through what?"

"Your first baby step."

"To what?"

He sighs. "Good sex, Avery. You said you were never going to share your body with a man ever again. That's no way to live. First step is to let a man see you naked and believe him when he tells you how beautiful you are."

I freeze in place, the nerves prickling every centimeter of my skin. *See. Me. Naked. Under this fluorescent lighting?* Hell no. "That's not a baby step. That's a fucking leap to the moon, Finn."

He laughs. "I promise you, you need this. *Trust me.* And if it makes you feel bad, I won't bother you for the rest of the summer. I won't go near the hot tub. We'll never talk about it again. You'll go back to California, and all this will become a distant memory."

I cringe when he mentions home. I forgot that my summer hideaway will eventually end. The part of me that believed Mason and I would be back together by fall is long gone. So what am I really going home to? If Palmer's pilot gets picked up and this becomes a series, she'll end up in New Mexico permanently. All that's waiting for me at home is the constant reminder of the withering messy version of myself I now can't stand. I can't go back to that.

I won't.

Finn's right.

I need to reinvent myself, and I have exactly one summer to do it.

"Five minutes." My voice is small, so I force myself to exhale and, with a little more bravado, say, "No hesitating."

"Good." There's a little glint of excitement in his eyes. Taking me by the shoulders, Finn positions me directly in front of the mirror. He takes his place behind me, watching me through the mirror. I instinctively smooth my sloppy hair that's so unruly it looks more like a messy bun than a ponytail. *Jesus.* What am I wearing? What the hell is on my shirt? Is that sauce from the pizza pockets from *yesterday*? How do I let myself exist like this? Finn, noticing my squirming, pulls my ponytail holder out. He runs his hands over my hair from my scalp down my back.

"You have the most gorgeous eyes I've ever seen. It took me forever to figure out the color. It's called seafoam green. Did you know that?"

"Only sometimes. In direct sunlight, they look—"

Reaching around, Finn presses his finger against my lips. "My bad. That was misleading," Finn says. He's purposely changed his tone. His cheery tenor is gone. He's all but growling in my ear.

Finn's talking to me like...

Stop. It's ridiculous. There's no way.

Like he's hungry for me.

His breath against my neck stuns me. I freeze like a deer in the woods after the sound of a twig snapping breaks the eerie silence. *He's too close.* The hairs on the back of my neck rise, and I try to decide whether I should bolt or just succumb to my fate.

He continues, "I technically did ask a question, but here's how the next five minutes are going to go. You're not going to speak. I'm going to talk to you. I'm going to strip you down and point out all the things I love about your body. For five minutes, you are going to just enjoy a man, who you think fucks like a porn star, worshiping you. How's that sound?"

I open my mouth then clamp it shut. I don't answer his question. I don't say anything at all. I just nod.

"Okay, good. Arms up," Finn says as he cups my elbows and guides them upward.

It's taking every ounce of strength in me to keep myself steady enough to stand. The pangs of nerves flood my body, but I hold my breath to combat the trembling.

I force myself to follow his command as I fully extend my

arms. He immediately reaches for the hem of my T-shirt.

"There you go," he mutters. "Good girl."

Chapter 8

Avery

"Will you please hurry up?"

I feel Finn's light, breathy chuckle against my neck. My shirt is off and tossed aside. I'm shivering, but it has nothing to do with the temperature in the closet. *Why did I agree to this? What was I thinking?* The mirror is taunting me with every loose, wobbly part of my torso. I want to run and hide—but I can't. Finn's large body is behind me, steadying me, locking me in place. There's no retreat.

"What did I tell you about talking?" he grumbles from behind me.

"But you're moving at a snail's pace." I wish he'd just undress me already. Rip it off, like a Band-Aid. Maybe it'll be less painful that way.

"Yeah, Avery. That's what you do when you're savoring something..." He blows on my naked shoulder, causing a sea of goose bumps to pebble my skin. *"You...go...slow,"* he whispers into my ear.

In this moment, I understand three very important things.

One, Finn is very good at this. He's overwhelmingly sensual. He's taking my literal worst nightmare and somehow making it sexy. Enjoyable, even.

Two, Finn knows exactly what he's doing to me. Every time I shudder and flinch, he smiles. Just moments ago, when his fingers grazed across my belly and chest as he pulled off my T-shirt, I nearly lost composure. When he rubbed the back of my bare arms to warm me up in an already sweltering room, I wanted to scream.

Three, and probably the most shocking revelation is...

Finn likes this.

This man must be desperate, blind, or high as a kite, because he's looking at me like I'm the first woman he's ever laid eyes on. Like I'm a prize he's won.

My gulp is audible as he pulls my left bra strap down over my shoulder.

"Breathe," he instructs, "and keep your eyes on the mirror." He pulls down the right. "Let me explain what I see."

I'm fear frozen. My limbs no longer answer the alarming commands from my brain.

I give myself major credit for at least giving this a try. I'm not the girl who wants to beg her cheating ex to take her back. I'm also not the girl who knows how to throw my ex the bird and seduce the hottest guy in the bar for rebound sex. I'm something in-between. *This.* Finn touching me and talking me through this seems *in-between.*

He unclasps my bra, and it falls to the floor. My heavy breasts drop an inch. My mind whirls, and I immediately attack myself mentally with criticisms. My breasts aren't perky enough, my waist isn't slim enough, my skin isn't taut and tight, and my hips are too wide. The silver lines against my skin from puberty where my body grew too fast mock me. *You're marked.*

Maura is flawless. I bet her skin has never overstretched a day in her life.

I am marked. I am—

"Goddamn," Finn says, interrupting my silently spoken assault. Watching his eyes through the mirror, I see they're bouncing between my breasts. "Your tits are unbelievable."

"You're just—"

"Ah, ah. *Hush.*" He clasps his large hands around my shoulders. "Your breasts are perfection. They are full in all the right places, and your nipples are my favorite shade of brown. So sexy. Thank God you're not a client, Avery. These tits would make me act unprofessional in the studio. We wouldn't want that, would we?"

I meet his eyes in the mirror. "Finn, did you just ask me another question I'm not allowed to answer?"

"Smart-ass." He smirks.

"I really like your smile," I say. The words fall out before I can stop them. He smiles wider, his perfect teeth and deep dimples on display in the mirror. The nerves begin to settle and I suddenly have the urge to reach behind me and feel his stubble. It's clear Finn shaved this morning, but by nine at night, his five o'clock shadow is tempting. I bet it feels like ultra-fine sandpaper. Not enough to scratch me, but just enough to agitate my skin until it's sensitive. It'd heighten my senses and make my skin so tender to his touch. I wonder how his cheek would feel against my thigh.

I wonder if Finn does *that*. Maybe he likes what Mason hates. He's certainly looking at me in a way Mason never did.

"I *really* like your smile too," he replies. He winks into the mirror. "And your tits." Reaching around my body again, Finn trails his thumbnail between my breasts and down my stomach before he sinks his thumb into my belly button. My knees buckle, but I don't fall because he immediately wraps his other arm around my ribs, securing me. "Whoops, you're really ticklish. Sorry. Couldn't help myself. I'm a sucker for innies."

I would laugh at his playfulness, but at the moment nothing is funny. By some miracle, I am standing in just my underwear in front of the floor-to-ceiling mirror. The lighting is wildly unflattering. The man behind me may be the best-looking human being on the planet, and somehow...

I'm okay.

More than okay.

I am so turned on.

I suck in a deep breath, watching my chest expand and rise. I find my courage and say as firmly as I can, "Finn—"

"Hush, Avery." His eyes snap to mine as he raises one brow. "This is the last thing I'll say, I promise."

"Fine."

"I'm nervous, but don't let me stop. Undress me all the way. I can handle it."

As he slowly wets his lips, I'm certain my body catches on fire. "I was going to leave your underwear on. Your period and all."

I allow my cheeks to flush crimson red. *Ah, who the fuck cares?* We've made it this far. "You're just looking, not touching. Does it bother you?"

"Not at all. I just didn't want you to be too uncomfortable."

I scowl at him. *Uncomfortable?* We're so far past uncomfortable. We're at throw caution to the wind and let's see what the hell happens.

I blow out a shaky breath, feeling bolder by the second. I ride the wave of my bravery before it's too late. "Take off my underwear. Tell me what else you see that you like." *Lie if you have to.*

Finn nods and squeezes my hip bone. His fingers tease the waistline of my black cotton panties. He has a sexy Midas touch apparently. There's nothing impressive about this pair of plain bikini-style underwear. But now that he's touching it, it's the sexiest article of clothing I own.

Finn traces my panty line back and forth, teasing me as he talks directly into my ear. "Avery, listen to me. You're beautiful. You're worthy. Don't you dare let any man treat you like garbage. Don't let any man tell you you're lacking. If he doesn't see you as sexy, he's not using his eyes." He hooks his finger around my chin and guides my view so I'm looking into my own eyes. "But confidence starts with you. A man is going to treat you how you treat yourself. *So please, for the love of God, act like a fucking queen.*"

Everything is wet.

I'm turned on. I'm teary-eyed. This is the most intimate I've been with another human being in my life. *I want him.* Stupid fucking period...ruining everything. Maybe he doesn't mind—

"I have to stop here." He drops his hand, leaving my panties securely around my hips, and steps backward. Suddenly, my wall of support is gone and I'm holding my own weight.

I spin around in a huff to face him. "*What*?" My wide eyes must look accusing because he raises his hands in surrender like he's trying to calm a wild animal he provoked.

"It's been way more than five minutes, and I can't go any further without getting carried away. So...I should go."

He's not technically rejecting me. I didn't offer. But shame rears its ugly head anyway, and the confident woman from two minutes before exits the stage. We're back to the same ol' Avery. Unsure...embarrassed...scared.

"Okay, I understand," I say, crossing my arms over my bare chest, covering my nakedness as best as I can. "Good night, then."

He takes a few steps toward the closet entry. He stops, then spins around. "Hey, I have a long run planned for tomorrow morning. Eight miles at least."

"Uh, okay," I sass. This man is fucking crazy if he's inviting me to run eight miles with him. "Have a good run."

His shoulders shake as he laughs, understanding my sentiment. "What I mean is I'll probably need the hot tub after. Say around eight?" He points to me. "This is either your warning to avoid me or your invitation to join me. Whatever you choose. Good night, Avery."

With that, he's gone.

He leaves me with a clear choice.

Did I like what just happened? Or is this man who is way out of my league and much too tempting a dangerous choice in my life right now? Finn has unrequited love written all over him, and I'd be an idiot to let myself go there. But then again...

The way he was just looking at me in the mirror...

The way he made me feel about myself...

I think I'm standing at least an inch taller at the moment. I've never met a man in my life who treats a woman that way. Finn has the answers to a lot of questions on my mind. Questions I only have one summer to answer before reality punches back.

So it's easy to make my choice.

I need to buy a swimsuit.

Chapter 9

Finn

Her eyes.

The lukewarm water from the showerhead cascades over my shoulders, runs down my back, and splashes at my feet.

Those fucking eyes.

I shut my lids and see Avery's eyes engrained in my mind. They were so light in front of the mirror, underneath the bright closet lights. They were the prettiest shade of seafoam green, with a hint of fire right when she told me to take her panties off.

I should've.

What stopped me?

The dickhead she wanted to marry who cheated on her then dumped her instead. That's who. He even had the nerve to blame her sex appeal. Avery is now the most emotionally fragile woman in the world. What's gratuitous sex going to do except confuse the shit out of her? She doesn't need to spiral like I did after Nora and I broke up. Hooking up left me feeling so much worse and constantly nervous that I'd contracted an STD or accidentally gotten a one-night stand pregnant. Add anxiety to heartbreak, and what do you get?

A fucking hot mess.

Avery's better than that. It's probably why I like her. I like her company. I really like her tits. I really, *really* like that she's the only woman outside of Lennox who doesn't see me as something to use or possess. It's obvious from how comfortable she is around me that she thinks I'd never be interested in her. She's wrong, of course. But she's comfortable, which means the conversation flows. Maybe I'm an ass for doing this, but Avery is my little experiment in building trust with women again and relearning how to let my guard down.

How many conversations do I need with her to really get over Nora? Let's find out.

Still, though...

Those goddamn beautiful eyes.

The more pornographic part of my brain is envisioning her looking up at me from her knees, my tip in her mouth as she smiles between sucking. In my fantasy, Avery's taking her time sucking me off because she's already thoroughly sated. I've taken care of her three times. Once with my fingers, then with my tongue, last with my cock.

I fist my erection in the shower, hard, as if I could stop it from growing.

This keeps happening. Every single time I think about her, I need relief. It's more of an annoyance than anything because I haven't been able to stop thinking about her since last night. Glancing down at my eager cock, I grumble. *Dammit.* I'm already worked all the way up. Not even an eight-mile run was enough to exhaust me. *Stroke.* I give in to running my hand up and down my shaft, massaging myself under the water stream.

I wonder what she likes in the bedroom.

Stroke.

If she trusts me enough to see her naked with the lights on, I bet she'd let me fuck her with the lights on too.

Stroke.

I wonder what she sounds like when she's com—

Pound! Pound! Pound!

"Finn! You in there?"

The aggressive knocking on my bathroom door makes me jump out of my skin. She even attempts to jiggle the bathroom handle. I locked it. Maybe I sensed my cousin would once again barge into my home, unannounced.

"Goddammit, Lennox!" I bark. "We need boundaries."

She yells back, loud as all hell so I can hear her over the shower stream. "I have your phone. Your dad called."

Fuck. I roll my eyes and shut off the water. "Cool. I'll get back to him." The mention of my asshole of a father has deflated both my erection and mood. I grab my towel off the hook, pat myself dry, and then wrap it around my waist.

"Yeaaahhh...about that." Now that the water is off, I can hear her apologetic tone clear as day through the door. *What did she do?*

Ripping the door open, I see Lennox holding out my phone... which is connected...to a call with my dad.

What the fuck? I mouth at Lennox.

"He's on mute," she says out loud.

"Why in the hell would you answer my phone?" *Especially if it's my dad calling*? Lennox should know better. She knows how strained my relationship is with my dad. I'm his only son out of three children. He's desperate to connect. I'm desperate to keep him at arm's length.

She shrugs innocently. "Sorry. He called like three times in ten minutes. I thought it was an emergency. You know, you've been up here forever." She smirks at me. "Were you rubbing one out?"

I snatch the phone from her hand. "Can you go downstairs, make a fresh pot of coffee, and then *leave your key to my home on the counter*," I say through gritted teeth.

She snorts. "Fat chance." But she scuttles off to follow at least the first part of my demands.

I fill my lungs with as much air as possible and let out an irritated exhale before I unmute the phone and place it by my ear.

"Hey, Dad."

"*Son.* Hey! How are you, Champ?"

Jesus, he's so fake.

"Pretty good. How are you?" *Then again, so am I when it comes to him.*

"Good, good. Great, actually. I just got my schedule for next month. I'm flying a Boeing into Vegas on the eighteenth. Can I interest you in a Wagyu steak, on your old man?"

No. "Um...the eighteenth?" That's in a month. It gives me plenty of options for an excuse. "I think I have back-to-back sessions that day and I can't afford to cancel. Damn, if you were one day earlier or later, I'd be free." That's the great thing about my dad's schedule as a pilot. He has very small windows of opportunity to visit when he's in town. *Unfortunately,* I don't get to see the man often. *Bummer.*

"Well, that's the great news. I arranged for a little time off. I've got three days and two nights. If you're busy on the eighteenth, how about dinner on the nineteenth? You just said you were free."

Shit. Walked right into that trap. I clear my throat, stalling. I try to think of any emergency that could've happened in the last seven seconds to get me out of dinner with my dad, without me actually having to tell him how much I hate his guts. "I guess I did."

"Great. The nineteenth it is. I can get us a VIP table at the new Wolfgang Puck restaurant. The chef is a friend, and I know the head maître d' personally. Sweet girl."

Of course you do. The real question is if he knows her or *fucked* her. The two words are interchangeable for Dad.

"Why don't you bring Nora along? I can make a reservation for three."

Yup, keep twisting the knife. "Nora and I broke up, Dad."

"When?"

"Last year, at the end of summer."

He blows out a heavy breath into the phone. "Griffin, I'm sorry. I wish I had known, but you never talk to me."

"Please don't call me that," I mumble.

"Why? It's your name."

No, it's your name, and I hate that we share it. Griffin Harvey is a pilot. Finn Harvey is a photographer. Griffin Harvey is a womanizer. Finn Harvey builds women up. I am nothing like my dad. I will never marry a woman, cheat on her for nearly two decades, impregnate two mistresses, and then drag my ex-wife through years of litigation in an attempt to starve her of any alimony. I will not ignore the fact that she's waiting tables in twelve-hour shifts and can still barely pay the bills, while I'm sipping rum in Fiji and trying to fuck everything in a bikini.

"Hey, I hate to cut this short, but I have to prep the studio for a client who'll be here soon." *Lies, lies, lies.*

"How's the business going?" Dad asks, clearly desperate to prolong our conversation.

"It's...going," I answer honestly. "Could be better."

"You know if you need a loan—"

"I'm fine."

"It doesn't have to be a loan. If it helps, a gift—"

"Dad, I'm good. Thank you, though."

He sighs heavily. "I'm proud of you, Finn. It's not easy staying afloat as a small business owner. If you ever need anything, I'm here."

"Okay, thanks."

"I mean it, Champ. What good is my money if not to help my son?"

A knot twists in my stomach. Dad traveled a lot when I was growing up, but he made a point to keep his flight schedules strictly domestic when I was in little league. He couldn't catch every game, but he made it to more than any of the other pilot dads.

He was a great dad.

I just didn't realize what a shitty husband he was until I left for college and Mom finally felt free enough to leave his sorry ass. For ten years now, I've tried to separate the two versions of my dad. My mom tells me not to fight her battles. She's given me her blessing to have a good relationship with Dad. He's never treated me poorly.

But I just can't ignore the kind of man he chose to be. He unapologetically stole the best years of my mom's life. He tore our family apart.

"Dad, I have to go. I'll see you on the nineteenth."

"All right, son. I'm really looking forward to it."

"Mmhmm," I say right before I hang up. It's all I can manage without sounding like a dick. I didn't want to end the phone call with, *I'm not.*

I pull on some sweatpants and a clean athletic shirt before heading to the kitchen. The smell of coffee fills the halls and the entryway of my house.

"Poured you a cup," Lennox says without looking around. She's sporting quite the goth look today. Black jean shorts, fishnet stockings, black tank top, and her hair is jet-black once again.

"Hey, you got rid of the purple?" I ask, pointing to her hair.

"Meh," she says, shrugging, "I bore easily."

I glower at her. "Is that why you're here so much?" I grab my steaming cup of coffee off the counter and inhale. Lennox does make a great cup of coffee.

"You're better company than my roommate," she says, sipping from her own mug. "Do you want creamer? I bought some of the oat milk stuff you like."

"Oh yeah?" Opening the fridge, I find it stocked with a few new items. Tonic waters, yogurt, fruit, my preferred brand of orange juice, and some deli meat for sandwiches. "Well, Lennox, you've redeemed yourself. I think I'll keep you." I pull the safety seal off the creamer and douse my coffee.

"Sorry about your dad," she offers. "He called the first time, and I figured if you were around, you'd let it go to voicemail. But then he called again and again, and then something dawned on me."

"What dawned on you?" I ask, leaning against my kitchen island.

"How else would you know if something happened to your sisters?"

Fair point. I wouldn't. I don't really keep in touch with my dad's daughters.

"I know Griffin is a dick and all, but you always said your sisters were innocent in all this. You'd want to know if either of them was in trouble."

It's true. My half sisters and I have a shared disdain for my dad. From what I understand, Molly and Alaina also keep him at arm's length. We're spread out across the country. I'm in Las Vegas, Molly lives in Baltimore, and Alaina attends college in Fort Lauderdale. We keep him busy with his annual apology tours; he treated all our mothers like shit. But we have nothing against each other. We just don't have much in common. We're connected by blood, but nothing else.

"He's coming into town on the nineteenth of next month. Do you want to go to dinner with us?"

Lennox sticks her finger in her mouth and makes a gagging sound. It's worth noting that Lennox is my mother's sister's daughter. They are the lead chairmen of the *We Hate Griffin* club, so I'm not surprised she doesn't want to break bread with Dad.

"Fine. Abandon me then."

Lennox takes a tepid sip from her cup. "Why don't you just tell him to get lost? Cut ties if you don't want him around, Finn. You're justified."

"He's finally paying Mom her fair share of alimony. He even gifted her flights to Greece for her and her boyfriend. Everything is at peace. I don't want to kick up the drama again." I rotate my finger in the air. "Not to mention he cosigned the mortgage for this house. I owe the man my company for one dinner a year, at least."

"If I were you, I'd kick him in the teeth after the way he—"

"Can we change the subject?" I ask. "This is far more Griffin and family drama than I want to deal with on a late Saturday morning."

"Fine. What are you doing tonight? There's a whiskey tasting at Rue 52 that my friend is hosting. It's far tamer than the foam party. Want to come?"

"Nope, I have plans. Although if you plan on once again popping by uninvited tomorrow, please pick me up the Southwest rolls with the black beans. The eggrolls always taste better the next day for some reason."

Lennox holds her mug to her lips and blinks at me. Her glib smile grows. "You have *plans*?"

"Yes." I think. Maybe. I plan on heading over to Dex's hot tub at eight. I'm not sure if Avery will be in the tub waiting for me or hiding under the bedroom covers upstairs. I don't know what the fuck that was last night.

I've done the mirror affirmations thing for my clients a hundred times, but never like that. When a boudoir client is really insecure or nervous, I'll place them in front of a large mirror and get them comfortable with looking at themselves, with smiling naturally. I've never undressed any of my clients. I am a consummate professional. Never once has that scenario been sexual...until last night.

Watching Avery cry, or more like twist up her face and try not to cry, broke my heart. I wanted to fix it. Last night, she didn't need someone to tell her she had a sweet smile and great charisma for the camera. She needed a man she was attracted to, to tell her she was fuckable. More than fuckable. She needed me to see her naked and *want* her. Approve of her. Praise her. So I did.

But today, I'm wondering if I did more harm than good. No matter what happens, I r*efuse* to be the second man to break this girl's heart. If I'm not ready for something legitimate and real... if she's only here for a few months...we should probably just be friends.

"What plans?" Lennox asks.

"I'm hanging out with the girl next door again." *Hopefully.*

"Ah, Dex's fish babysitter?"

"Yup. Her name is Avery. Cool girl. She's easygoing, funny, and smart. Hey, speaking of which—what do you think about our website?"

"It sucks," Lennox responds without hesitation.

I roll my eyes. "*Excuse me.* I built our website."

"Yeah," Lennox says, flashing me a snarky smile. "I said what I said."

"Lennox...if I could fire you..." I take a long, drawn-out sip of my coffee, enjoying the taste of oat milk. It's probably the only good thing that came out of my relationship with Nora. She turned me on to oat milk. I like it better than regular milk now. "What do you know about search engine optimization and click traffic... all that stuff?"

"I know enough to know we should be doing it," Lennox says, hunching her shoulders. "I don't know enough to actually be useful."

"Yeah, me neither." I nod. "That's what Avery does. She's a brand strategist—whatever that means. I was thinking about asking for her help."

Lennox drains the rest of her mug. "Do we have 'help' money in the business account?"

Not really. I guess I could take Dad up on his offer. "How much could a consultant cost?"

"I don't know. Let's find out," Lennox says, placing her cup in the kitchen sink. She grabs her laptop from her large purse and sets it on the dining table. I pull up a chair right next to her.

"Her name is Avery Scott. Brand strate—"

"Got it," Lennox says, typing away. "She's the first result on the search page."

I blow out a breath. "Yeah, well, that's kind of what her job is, I guess..."

"Fuckin' shit, Finn. You can't afford this." Lennox clicks and scrolls through Avery's website. Her firm is called Arrow Brand Consulting. Everything about her site is clean. It's fresh, interesting, but extremely professional. It looks elite. This is exactly the kind of presence I need for Finn Harvey Photography.

"How much is it?"

Lennox angles the laptop screen toward me. She opened up the services page. I read the top line where Arrow Consulting explains that a lot of brand strategists will hide their consultation fees in an attempt to bait new clients. Arrow chooses to be transparent, and while they are willing to create custom packages, their minimum fee for a basic audit and review is...

"*Sixteen thousand dollars*?" I balk. "For the basic services?"

Lennox meets my wide-eyed stare. "Dude, we are in the wrong business." She cackles. "And your new girlfriend must be rolling in the dough. Look at her client list. There are Fortune 500 companies on there. I bet they are paying way more than sixteen grand."

"Fuck me," I mutter under my breath. I find Avery's headshot on her company's website. It's a flattering photo. I'm sure I could take a better one, but this is decent, except it's in black and white. While it looks professional, I'm missing those seafoam green eyes.

"You think she'd cut you a deal for some help?"

"Isn't that rude to ask?" My eyes are still fixed on her picture. It's uncomfortable when friends ask for big favors. When people find out I'm a photographer, they want hours of free labor. I'm happy to oblige, but I've got bills to pay too.

"Doesn't hurt to see if you guys could exchange services. Offer her a free boudoir shoot. I can do her hair and makeup. All together that's worth about a sixth of her fee." Lennox laughs in short huffs. "Sixteen grand for one job? *Damn,* your friend is a baller."

That she is.

I would've never expected Avery to be a boss lady. She's so down to earth and humble. It's refreshing. There's nothing that screams six figures about her raggedy T-shirts and faded pajama bottoms. I like that. I like her witty sass. I like how chill she is. I like—

Oh, hell.

I think I really *like* her.

Fuck.

Chapter 10

Avery

"Aves, I'm so sorry. I'm still stuck out here with your car," Palmer whines into the phone. "I didn't expect to actually get the part."

I roll my eyes. "Palmer," I groan.

"What?"

Popping in my right AirPod, I swap our call from audio to FaceTime. I wait until her face is on the screen. "Um, my best friend just landed her big break. I don't care about my car. I'm not doing anything out here, and I can have anything I need delivered." Including the four different swimsuits from Target I ordered for rapid delivery this morning. I realize Finn has already seen most of me naked, but I'm still determined to find the most flattering suit Target has available in store. I needed options.

"I'm not even sure if the pilot will get picked up..." she says with a defeated half smile. Geez, the entertainment industry is kicking her ass.

I prop the phone up against the pitcher of orange juice I have in the middle of the dining table. Holding up one finger, I ask, "Can we just dream big for a moment? Manifest."

She blows out a breath. "Fine."

"You're the star of this pilot—"

"*One* of the stars. It's an ensemble cast—"

"Palmer, work with me here."

"Fine. I'm the star of this pilot."

"Good. And what happens when the pilot gets picked up?"

She slumps her shoulders, and her slinky tank top falls off her shoulder. I can see her nipples clear as day through her thin top. Palmer has the kind of small, perky breasts that don't need to be contained at all times by sturdy bras with underwire. "I don't know..."

"Yes, you do. It's okay." I give her a reassuring nod.

"Okay, my career picks up."

"And?" I tuck my knee to my chest and rest my chin on top of it, giving her a lunatic smile.

"I get a steady paycheck."

I nod enthusiastically. *"And?"*

"And I can pay back my debt, get a better agent, get more jobs, maybe a movie deal, maybe walk the red carpet one day."

"There you go!" I clap my hands together. "Honey, you can *do* this. You are beautiful and talented. I want this for you as much as you do. *This will happen.* This pilot *will* get picked up. You're going to do big things, best friend."

Palmer immediately tears up. She's been crying nonstop lately. You would've thought she was the one who was dumped. Every time we've talked in the past week since she drove off to Albuquerque, she's been an emotional wreck. She's just probably in her actor mindset. She's playing a single mother, living on the streets, who is trying her best to kick a heroin habit. If that's not emotionally taxing and dramatic, I don't know what it is. She's embracing her role. Palmer is a truly phenomenal actress. If success in the industry was based on talent alone, she'd be famous. Unfortunately, the reality is that luck's been a bitch to her. Her entire career is filled with near misses and almost opportunities.

"You're a better friend than me," she says in a hushed whisper. "A much better friend."

"Palmer," I grumble, rolling my eyes. "It's just a car. It's fine— but hey, I have to go. It's Mason on the other line." As much as I'd like to ignore that asshole's call, we need to chat business today.

Palmer's face twists. "Fuck Mason," she says.

"Yep, well, someone is, that's for sure. Okay, honey, bye.

Talk soon." I reluctantly press end call and answer on my screen. "Mason," I say, my tone dropping to the icy depths.

"Hey, Avery. Can I start with—"

"No, you may not. I looked over the Legacy Resorts reports and I have a few ideas for a proposal, but I need to understand what kind of organic leads are coming to their site. Have they shared that with you yet?"

"Not quite."

"Once I have that data, I'll be able to proceed. Email me when you have it."

He sighs into the phone.

Sigh all you want, jerk. This is strictly business.

"They want a live pitch."

"I would assume so if they are willing to pay in the millions. Are you concerned about my pitch?" I've handled client meetings since the establishment of our business. I don't care how much money is in a potential client's suit pockets. I'm not intimidated. I'm confident in what I do.

"No, I'm not concerned, but..."

"But what?"

"Their head of marketing emailed me—"

"Yeah, Mason, why are they emailing you instead of me? I handle client relations. Put me on the email thread."

Mason sighs again, testing my patience.

"Whatever you need to say, spit it out," I snap.

"The guy is a total misogynist, Avery. And he's the one making the final decision on firms. You may be the talent, but he wants to talk business with me—"

"Over scotch and cigars?"

"Exactly."

What a dick. A dick that's willing to pay us millions if I can pull this off. With that kind of payout, I could afford to get out of my lease with Mason and get my own place. L.A. is getting more expensive by the minute. Then again, I wouldn't even have to stay in L.A. My business is virtual, and my best friend, with any luck, won't be residing in California much longer. I could start over wherever I want. I could probably afford a house if I moved somewhere cheaper.

"So we need to pitch together?"

"Their resort in Cancun is under renovation. It'll be done at the end of summer. They want to invite us to a complimentary weekend and have us give the proposal to the CEO, CMO, and VP. Drew from Maynard Realty said that one point five million is lowballing for what they can afford."

"Hm," I mumble into the phone as I head to Dex's fridge and pull out a Diet Coke. The loud hiss of a soda bottle fills the silence. I take a large glug, ignoring the aggressive little bubbles that attack my throat. "How much does he think we should ask for?"

"Five million and then expect them to meet us in the middle. So we'd walk away with about three point five."

It becomes apparent why Mason is so nervous.

"Are you asking me whether I can come up with a proposal that's worth a little north of three million dollars?"

"I can help you, Aves. Whatever you need..." His pleading tone turns knots in my stomach. I've been so shocked and angry that I forget that four years of my life have melted away. Four years that were good...for me.

Mason used to moan a little when he kissed my forehead. He'd inhale slowly, like the smell of my hair was intoxicating. A small breath in, and then his soft lips would touch right between my brows. It made me feel so cherished. It was perfect and peaceful until the gory end I never saw coming.

"Mason, you've underestimated and underappreciated me in all aspects of our relationship. At least when it comes to work, how about you trust me? I'll do my job. You do yours. We'll present the proposal together, and when the summer is over, we need to talk about dissolving the business. I don't think I can—"

"I didn't cheat on you," he interrupts, seizing his opportunity.

My heart begins to thump angrily. "I saw the text. It is what it is... Don't try and lie—"

"It was an app. Let me explain."

I am not a saint. I am not perfect. When the man I loved for nearly half a decade wants to explain how he didn't cheat on me, curiosity becomes king. I can't help it. "Explain then."

"There's an app called Rumble. I was talking to a woman I'd never met. It's just texting...no videos or anything like that."

"So an app just for dirty texting?"

He blows out a harsh breath. "It was just a role-playing thing. I was pretending like she was a call girl I'd hired before, and...I don't even know how that message got sent to you. We were talking earlier and, I must've accidentally...well, you get it. But I didn't cheat on you, Avery. I was just trying to have a night off from all this shit."

I choose to sit in the stiff dining chair instead of getting comfortable on the couch. It seems more fitting at the moment. "A night off from what? *You dumped me.*"

"It doesn't mean this doesn't suck for me too." His voice jumps an octave. "I know I'm not allowed to say it, but *this sucks for me too.* I miss you. It breaks my heart that we're not going to spend the rest of our lives together."

"And whose fault is that?"

There's silence for a moment, and he asks the question that's been on my mind for days. "Were you happy...with our intimacy? Or were you settling?"

Of course I was settling. But there's more to love and commitment than sex. We had everything else. "Why didn't you talk to me about it? Why did you choose to break us like this?"

Another long pause, and then he says, "I honestly don't know. We just didn't do that... We never talked about that stuff. We were always a certain type of way with each other, since the beginning."

Mason and I were lights off, missionary, once a week at best. Toward the end, once a month. That was our legacy. I almost can't blame him for wanting more. Tears begin to form. The pain I've been running from almost catches me. But what Mason doesn't understand is the pain isn't just from heartbreak; it's from fear.

My identity was so wrapped up in a man that the minute he didn't want me anymore, I lost my identity.

I used to look in the mirror and see myself. Now, I look in the mirror and see what I'm not. At least, until last night...

Until Finn.

I don't know if it was what he said in the mirror or how he said it, but I walked around topless most of the morning, feeling proud of my breasts. I grab my left tit, giving it a hardy squeeze. Mason, on the other end of the line, is silent, none the wiser that I'm fondling myself. These aren't the breasts Mason passed on. They are the ones that made Finn smile and lick his lips. I wish it were as simple as hooking up with Finn for validation purposes. I think he'd sleep with me. Maybe it'd be for pity on his end, but I bet I'd still enjoy it.

The problem is I don't want my identity wrapped up in any man. I don't want to only like myself until Finn doesn't want me either. I want my confidence back. I want to never ever again believe a man when he says I'm disappointing in the bedroom.

I want to feel safe to explore. I want to use a stupid app like Rumble and role-play. I want to experience *all* the things my so-called bland relationship deprived me of for four years.

But I need help...someone to show me how to be something I'm not. *Finn.* He's the answer. I don't want something as unattainable as his heart. I just need his body. I want Finn to teach me how to have great sex...

No. Something more extreme.

I want Finn to teach me how to fuck.

"Aves, maybe I was rash and I panicked. What if we just take the summer off to breathe and think about things? Maybe this isn't a breakup...just a break. I know you're furious with me right now, but hopefully, by the time Cancun rolls around, we can *talk* in person. About everything. Even the uncomfortable stuff."

"What's there to talk about? I don't think I can ever trust you again," I say, pressing my back against the wooden dining chair, wanting the pressure to hold me in place.

"I *didn't* cheat on you. I will show you the app. I swear on my life—"

"I don't care," I say. He already pulled at the thread and unraveled us. The truth is? I don't feel good about myself when I'm around him. And what's more, I no longer think it's all my fault.

I think of the shitty, artery-clogging takeout food we ate every night. Yes, it made me feel like garbage. But I'm not a great cook, nor did I have time to learn. I was too busy building Arrow's client list and reputation. Never once did Mason offer to go to the grocery store with me and pick up healthier options. Never once did he suggest we cook at home together.

Never once did he cook *for* me. Finn's steak was the first meal a man has prepared for me since I was in pigtails and my dad used to make me hamburger mac 'n' cheese.

I let out a deep sigh. "Just send me the reports." I clear my throat. "Let's take it one step at a time. We need to see if we can work together. That's the most important thing right now." Otherwise, we have a business to divvy up.

"Okay," he says, sounding slightly relieved. Did I just give *us* hope? *Shit.* "Good night, Avery. And hey, just so you know, I'm not sleeping around. I didn't get over our breakup that easily. I'm not planning on having sex with anyone right now."

Why was it so much easier to believe he was actually cheating on me? I trusted Mason blindly for four years. Why is it so hard to believe him right now?

"You should, Mason."

"What?"

"You should. Have sex with someone new. I certainly plan to."

I end the call before he can say another word.

Chapter 11

Finn

There's a nervous jolt in my chest as I push through the tension-filled gate separating my yard from Dex's. I hear the buzz and bubble of the hot tub.

Avery's already in the tub.

Her hair is pulled up in a sloppy bun, little strands of loose hair caressing her face. She's makeup-free, and her cheeks are pink and flushed from the heat. Her pretty eyes are sparkling under the dim deck lights.

I hold up the six-pack of beer. "I guess you chose to keep me company tonight."

She smiles and nods. "That I did. How was your run?"

"Grueling." I set the six-pack down, pull off my shirt, and lay it on the back of a patio chair. I feel her eyes on me, but she quickly diverts her gaze when I turn around. "You can look, Avery. I'm not shy."

Chuckling nervously, she covers her eyes. "Okay, you're unnaturally hot. You have to know that, right? Good grief, you're fit."

What the fuck am I supposed to say to that? "Thank you?"

"It must get annoying when women stare at you like a piece of meat. My best friend Palmer is a total knockout. Every time we go to a bar, she gets groped or fed some sleazy line just because she's good-looking and has a great body." Avery twists her lips as she teeters her head from side to side. "You'd think it'd feed her ego, but it doesn't. Men want to see her naked, but they don't care about her name or what she does for a living. It's crass, and it gets to her more than she admits. Her entire identity is wrapped up in how she looks, and it's not fair. I'm trying not to do that to you in case you feel the same."

"That's awfully considerate of you."

"Well, I respect hot people problems, you know? It's not like I have them, but I respect them." Avery chuckles at her little joke while I plunge into the water without testing the temperature. I know the heat is turned all the way up, the way Avery's skin is so pink and raw.

"Do you work out?" I ask.

Avery rolls her eyes. "Finn, you've seen me pretty much naked. You know the answer to that question."

"I *don't* know the answer. That's why I asked."

Avery flicks a little water in my direction across the tub. "I like to walk sometimes, but that's about it."

"I work out a lot."

"Shocking," she says with a wink.

"Not to look good," I admit. "For stress relief. It's the only way I can work out my anxiety and frustration. So you may see a hot body"—I gesture to my chest—"but this is all the product of a lot of shitty stuff I'm working through." I shrug. "Looks can be deceiving."

Her smirk flattens, and the corners of her lips turn down in concern. "What stuff?"

"Nope. Not going there tonight. The hot tub is for relaxation." I waggle my finger at her before I wade across the tub to stretch out my legs and quickly return to the six-pack I brought. I pop the lid on two Alaskan Ambers and hand Avery one. I stay standing, lingering by her side. "How was your day?"

"Good," she says, smiling wide.

I'm silent as I take a swig from my beer. But she doesn't continue. She clearly doesn't like being the center of attention. "What did you do?"

"I just worked a little."

"On what?"

She lets out a little huff of annoyance, understanding what I'm doing. I'm trying to get her to talk. I'm trying to give her some much-needed attention.

"I think I accidentally overfed one of Dex's fish today. I feed his saltwater fish this nutrient thing from an eye dropper every Monday, Wednesday, and Saturday. It ate and then went belly up for a minute but seems to be okay now...I think." Her eyes widen in concern. "I don't know, actually. It's not like I can reach in there and snuggle the damn thing. I didn't realize how high-maintenance fish are."

I laugh. "Just Dex's fish. They are all exotic."

"Yeah, I really didn't know what I was getting into when I said I'd help. I have to feed them and check their water temperature twice a day. The auto lights over the tanks upstairs are broken, so I have to adjust them manually until they get repaired." She shrugs, unintentionally pushing her breasts together. I don't even bother looking away. I thoroughly enjoy the view of her cleavage in a black bikini halter top. "I'm just going to say it—Dex hustled me."

We both break out in laughter. Dex is the kindest, goofiest dodo on the planet. It's from all the years of breathing in an oxygen tank underwater. He couldn't hustle someone if he tried.

"How much is he paying you?"

"Nada. Free rent for the summer." Avery licks her lips before she hangs her head. "I would've done anything to get away from home."

I suck down half my beer in one glug. "I take it you live with Mason?"

"Yep."

"What's your game plan when the summer is over, then?"

She drops her jaw before showing me a cute pout. "I thought we said the hot tub was for relaxation?"

"True."

She drains her bottle, and I move across her to get us another round, but she stops me. "Wait, I want a clear head when I talk to you tonight."

"Oh? About?"

"After I unintentionally poisoned Dex's fish this morning, I did run an audit on your website...your entire business, actually. I went through your service page and looked at the packages you offer."

I grumble. *So much for relaxing.* "All right, tell me. What am I doing wrong?"

I watch her entire demeanor change. Her shoulders straighten. She sits up a little higher. Even her chin slightly elevates. This is exactly what it looks like when a queen is about to give a command.

"You're not doing anything wrong. Your portfolio is great, but you are missing out on a lot of opportunities for revenue. First and foremost, you're not charging enough for any of your services. Second, you have headshots, family portraits, and boudoir photography on the same service pages." She purses her lips and shakes her head. "I understand the need to be versatile, but you have to separate your boudoir clients. My suggestion is to keep your current website and place a link to a private site—eighteen and up. Require an age confirmation for entry and then show a warning of explicit images. *All tasteful examples.* Tease the idea; don't become a landing page for perverts. But I think you need to demonstrate that you are capable of more risqué shoots. You said you photograph full nudity sometimes, right? I checked out your competition. They are far more forward with the services they provide. Bold sexuality and female empowerment are welcome in the current market. Women don't want to hide anymore. It's a great time to be in boudoir photography. You just have to give your potential clients a way to find you."

Avery continues on about separating the sites and driving the right kinds of click traffic to two sides of the business. She discusses rebranding and merchandise ideas for additional streams of revenue. I try to soak up every word, but she's talking so fast, my head is spinning.

"What's your annual income before operation costs?"

I finally experience the shame Avery says she feels around me all the time. This is how it feels when you think someone is so far out of your league. "It's embarrassing."

"Finn, I'm not trying to embarrass you. I'm trying to tell you there's potential here. Are you making nearly 150K a year? Because you should be."

"Barely a third of that."

"I can get you there," she says with such confidence. "Give me the summer. I can definitely get you on track."

I scoop a handful of water and wet my hair. "I happened to check out your website too. As much as I want your help, I can't afford you. Sixteen grand, minimum?"

She cringes. "Oh, that's outdated. Mason must not have updated the website. I should've caught that. We don't take clients for less than twenty-five now, but that includes investment into paid advertising—look, Finn," she says, holding up her palms and shaking them in the air, "it's neither here nor there because I'm offering to help you for free...kind of."

"I couldn't ask that of you—"

"Actually, I'm asking it of *you*." She shrivels again. Her queen-like presence, diminished. Avery looks so nervous all of a sudden as her thumb knocks against the water line, making little splashes. "A trade. I help you... You help me."

"You want a free boudoir session?"

She scoffs with such force, she chokes on her own spit. "Oh, hell no. No, no. No. Seeing me is one thing, but photographing me? Documenting all my insecurities with a camera that adds ten pounds? No...no...just *no*."

And now, just like that, I want her naked in my studio more than I've wanted anything in my life. Just to prove to her that she doesn't see herself accurately.

I touch my fingertips to my temple. "What do you want then? I have nothing I can give you that's worth twenty-five thousand dollars."

"Yesterday..." she says, as though it's an explanation.

"Say more."

Her eyes shift to the left, away from me. "I was with the same man for four years."

"I know. You told me..."

"Never once did he see me naked with the lights on."

"Really? Not in four years?"

She shakes her head. "Nope. He never acted like he wanted to. The way you"—she clears her throat and forces herself to look at me—"talked to me and...touched me. It made me feel brave. I want to be able to do that. I want to stop missing out."

"Missing out on what?" I can feel my forehead crinkling. *Where the hell is she going with this?*

"Good sex. I want to know what men like, and I want to enjoy it. I will save your photography business if you *teach* me how to have good sex. That's the deal."

Holy shit. I need another beer. Actually, I need a whole keg.

Reaching over Avery, I grab another bottle. I don't bother grabbing the opener. I angle the tip against the side of the deck and pound the bottleneck. The lid rolls away as the beer foam spills over my hand. I chug the entire thing, trying to buy a little time to think. Avery is patiently quiet. She's nervous but not pushy.

"So you want me to tell you what positions men like best or something?"

She shakes her head. "No. I could watch porn for that. I need you to *show me*. I need practice and real-time feedback, so when I do get back out there, I'll know next time..." Her bottom lip trembles, and she quickly covers her mouth.

"Next time you'll know what?"

Inhaling deeply, she composes herself. "That if things don't work out, it's not my fault because I suck at sex."

Where does her prick of an ex-boyfriend live? I really want to pay him a visit.

"I understand how crazy this sounds, but last night it seemed like you wouldn't mind sleeping with me—"

I snatch her hand out of the water immediately and put it to my lips. Her lips twitch into a little smile. "If I'm hesitating, it's not because of the reason you're thinking. But this is complicated." I drop her hand and step backward. "You're asking me to take advantage of you while you're at your lowest. And I don't know how to represent the entire male population. Every man likes something different. I mean, what if I'm into really kinky stuff?"

Her brows quirk up. "Are you?"

I shrug. "Nothing...degrading, just sometimes I like—ah! No. Avery, I'm sorry. I can't do this. I couldn't even ask you out because I'm still not over my ex."

"Oh." Her entire face falls, and I can tell it's taking every ounce of restraint for her not to flee from this hot tub. "Okay, that's okay. I know this was out of left field. Let's forget it..."

I let out a heavy sigh. "I mean, I'm not over the way my ex treated me. I don't love her anymore, but I'm still angry. I'm not ready to get involved with anyone right now."

"I get it," Avery says with a nod. "Me neither. I think I got a little in my head last night in front of the mirror and all. If I'm being honest, it was kind of exhilarating to be that brave. I think I'm chasing a high. *Sorry.* Can we forget I brought it up?"

No. I'm never going to forget how stupid I'm being right now. I should just pony up and fuck her properly. I'd make her forget her ex's name. I'd ruin her for every single man on this planet. But that's not what a good guy would do. This is a deal my dad would jump at.

"Sure."

"I'm still going to help you, though, with your business." Avery's smile is sincere. Her eyes look even lighter, almost full gray...ghost-like. I notice they lighten when she's about to cry. "And we've got a lot of work to do, buddy, so strap in."

"*What?*"

"Oh, come on, Finn. Don't be offended. It's no secret you've been neglecting your marketing. You're in a hole. We have to pull you out one step at a—"

"No, I mean, you still want to help me for free? Even though

I told you I wouldn't..."

"Yeah. Of course. I have one big project for the summer, but the rest of my contracts are on maintenance. I have the time, so why not? I'll help a friend, no strings attached."

No strings attached. Is that possible? Can we honestly do this with no strings attached?

"How would this go?"

"Well, we'd start with rebranding the boudoir website. Darker colors, clean transitions—"

"Not that part, Avery. Sex. You and me. If I were to *teach you*, how would that go?"

She reaches for her beer and tips it to her mouth to no avail. It's empty, so she sets it behind her. She could stall by opening another bottle, but instead, she decides to be brave. "It's simple. We'd have sex the way you like. You'd tell me what to do and how to do it. You'd just be patient with me and help me try new things and get better at them." She rolls her wrist in the air. "I think confidence is key. Like you said in the closet. But I have to *practice* confidence in the bedroom. It's not natural for me."

"Okay... New things such as?" *I'm going to pass out if she says anal.*

"Do I really have to say it right now?"

I lock my gaze on hers. "Explicitly."

She grumbles and rolls her eyes as she sinks lower into the hot tub so the water is coming up to her neck. "Have you heard of that app called Rumble?"

Fuck. "I could lie..."

"Okay, so then you know it's for like...dirty talk."

"I'm aware."

"I thought I'd try my hand at dirty talk. I downloaded it." She smacks her lips. "May I just say it's kind of terrifying that it took me less than ten minutes to purchase the app, download it, create a username, get into a chat room, and read a message from a man who said he wanted to watch cum drip down my chin as I choked on his mammoth rock-hard cock."

I snicker at her incredulous expression. "And what did you say to that?"

She tents her hands over her face, hiding. "I said 'Cool. Sounds good,'" she mumbles through her fingers. "He left the chat room immediately."

I burst out into laughter. "That's the best you could come up with?"

"See? It's why I need your help. I don't get it. Why do men think that's sexy? It's hot for a girl to be gagging and choking and crying? I don't understand this. Is it just crude talk, or is that really what men want?"

I sigh and set my drink aside. Advancing closer, I use my body as a wall to lock her into the corner of the hot tub. I hover over her, purposely puffing up my chest. "Hold out your hands," I command.

She does as I ask, and I lock both of her wrists in one hand. Squeezing hard, I raise her hands above her head and put my lips an inch from hers. Her chest pulses up and down, and I can almost feel the nerves.

"When you get down to it," I say in a low grumble, "we're just animals and it's about domination. It gets our testosterone flowing when we feel powerful. Our cocks are harder and bigger, and we have more endurance. When a woman gets on her knees or is pinned down and agrees to do whatever we ask, when we ask for it, we feel like the masters of our own universe. It's a fleeting moment in time when we have control in this chaotic world. It's not about seeing you suffer. It's just about us feeling powerful. It's a turn-on."

She's stunned, her eyes fixated on my lips. "Yeah," she barely whispers, "okay, that makes sense I guess—"

"But a really powerful man knows the secret," I continue, purposely making my voice low and growly, trying to test whether this brooding attitude works on her.

"What secret?" Her voice cracks.

Oh, it definitely works. Avery doesn't need lessons. She needs a man who's willing to give it to her rough and dirty. She just wants to feel wild...and wanted.

"That you come harder when your girl comes first. That's real power." I release her wrists and plant a quick kiss on her forehead, retreating back to my side of the hot tub. "So," I say, lightening my tone, "how'd you find out about Rumble?"

She blinks at me. "Does that also make you feel powerful? Teasing me?" Her narrowed eyes and low tone lead me to believe she's a little pissed.

"You asked me a question." I shrug innocently. "I answered."

She rolls her eyes with a huff. "Mason was using it. I thought he was cheating on me, but he wasn't. He was role-playing with some girl from that app."

My jaw clenches when I understand where this is headed. "That's still cheating, Avery. Phone sex is still sex."

"It's not cheating if we were broken up," she mutters.

"Technicality. Why does it even matter?"

"Because," she says coolly as her eyes narrow further, "I can't forgive a cheater. But I could forgive an idiot."

I might've crossed a line. Avery's a big girl and can make her own decision...but she cried in my lap last night over what this guy did to her. It's not right. "You want to get good at sex to win him back?"

"No, Finn. I just want to feel better about myself." She hunches her shoulders. "I don't know how else to say it. I want sex to be exciting, not so nerve-racking that it's scary. That's all."

"Okay," I say, and her eyes perk up, so I quickly clarify. "*Okay* as in I get it, but I need some time to think about it, Avery. It's not because I'm not interested. It's because..."

Because we can talk. And you're fun. You're comfortable enough with me to ask me to teach you how to have good sex? It's clear we already like each other. If we fuck, we're going to fall for each other. I'm sure of it. And neither of us can handle that right now. Neither of us can handle the fallout of yet another breakup. Not to mention Avery's clearly not over her ex. Nora still haunts me...

This is a terrible idea.

"Because what?" Avery asks, reminding me I didn't finish my sentence.

"I just need to think about it. I want to help you, but I don't want to hurt you. I have to think about what that means."

She gives me a small smile as she nods. "Okay. Think about it. In the meantime, let's get back to business." She sits a little taller again. "I seriously think you should consider a new logo."

Avery

It could've gone worse...

Definitely.

Maybe.

Shit. What is wrong with me? Finn intoxicates me with his humble sexiness. It's annoying really. He tempts me on purpose, just to prove I'm like every other woman in the world—enraptured by him. But then he adds to the pile by playing the good guy? Concerned about hurting me? Not wanting to be reckless about casual sex? Who is this guy? It'd be easier if he was just a sexy pig. But it's clear there's way more to Finn than I realize.

I shut off the hot tub and cover it back up. Finn got a call and left ten minutes ago, abandoning me with a heaping serving of regret. I can't believe I asked him to teach me sex. I grumble out loud in frustration. I've never felt more stupid in my life.

I collect the empty beer bottles from the deck and rinse them before I throw them away. It's 9:48 on a Saturday night, but it feels more like a stroke past midnight. The pumpkin has smashed. My dress is torn. My horses are rats. The spell is officially over.

Walking past the aquarium in the living room, I wish Cherry a good night. *Sweet fishy dreams, my friend.* The little red fish, whom I've dubbed *she*, is darting across the tank again, back and forth, back and forth, tirelessly. *I'll see you in the morning, you little goof.*

I'm on the fourth stair when I hear a heavy pounding at the door. *What in the world*? Palmer? No. The police? Still in my swimsuit, I tighten my towel around my body and head to the front door.

I open it a crack until I realize it's Finn. Opening the door wide, I see he's flushed and a little sweaty. He takes a step forward and leans into the doorframe wordlessly.

"Hey," I say. "Did you forget something? Or did you miss me already?" I tease. He doesn't match my humor. His brooding eyes are dark. Clouded with something heavy.

"You're really serious about this?" he asks in a strained mumble.

What is wrong with him?

"You want me to teach you how to have good sex?"

Why be ashamed? My foot is already in my mouth. I should go ahead and swallow it.

"Yes."

Finn walks through the door, grabbing my hand as he passes. "It's time for your first lesson," he grunts as he leads me past the kitchen to the staircase.

"Where are we going?" Dumb question, I know. *Bedroom, obviously.* But I'm really nervous.

"Where do you think?" he asks, sounding a smidge on the side of annoyance.

"Bedroom."

"Closet," he says over his shoulder as he pulls me up the stairs. *Oh no.*

"The big mirror." Finn tightens his grip around my hand. "I want you to see everything I'm about to do to you."

Chapter 12

Avery

I lost my virginity in the back of a Pontiac the summer before college. It was to a boy named Lucas. Thirteen years later, I don't remember much about the mechanics. I just remember it being uncomfortable, brief, and just about the biggest letdown that year, and that's even after I got my rejection letter from Berkeley. Lucas praised me afterward, telling me we were so hot together, but what we did had nothing to do with *together*. I got nothing from it.

I was simply a vessel for his release.

I really think the way I lost my virginity cursed me and set the entire tone for my future sex life. Mason was the third guy I'd ever had sex with. Let-down Lucas. Quick-to-come Cameron. And last, but not least...mundane Mason. But I loved him, so what was mundane, was tolerable. It was fine. I was *fine*.

Until tonight.

When the curse is broken.

Because the way Finn is looking at me like he's going to devour me whole makes me think this one night is going to be the redemption of my entire lackluster sexual saga.

Here. We. Go.

Finn lifts me like I'm light and places me on the counter in the middle of the master closet. I flinch when the cool granite touches the bare back of my thighs. That's how you know this is a multimillionaire's closet. Why the fuck do you need granite in a closet?

I swing my dangling legs out of nerves, my heels hitting the back of the cabinets like an antsy child.

Finn pulls off his shirt, disorienting me with his chest and abs that are so perfectly sculpted I want to touch them to make sure they're real. He stands between my legs and presses his palms against the tops of my thighs to stop my fidgeting. "I know you're nervous," he says with a sly smile. I nod in reply, expecting him to tell me not to be, but he goes in a different direction. "You should be."

"Should I?"

He scrunches his face. "Yeah, of course. I always get a little nervous when something really fucking amazing is about to happen." It's like a shot of adrenaline pools between my thighs.

My lips part in surprise. "See? How do you do that?"

Wrapping his muscular arm around my back, he runs his lips up and down my neck. I start to go hazy from his heady smell of sweat and cologne. He smells so damn good I want to taste him. "How do I do what, Avery?" he growls into my ear.

"You talk about sex like it's natural."

"It is."

"You seem so sure this is going to feel good for both of us."

He nods into the crook of my neck. "I am."

"How do—"

"Are you still on your period?" he asks, interrupting my questioning.

I shake my head. "No, it was the tail end yesterday, completely gone today." I clear my throat. "Would that have been a...should I not...you know. Is that a deal breaker for guys?"

His forehead crinkles as he raises his brows.

"Not for me. Dex has the best walk-in shower to fuck in. It has a bench."

He's not wrong. I love Dex's shower. There are two rain shower heads and massage jets in the center. His large, built-in teakwood bench is clearly custom-made. Although, my stomach churns when I think about how Finn knows Dex's shower is ideal for sex. He's done it here before. I wonder how many other women he's put in front of this mirror.

But it's not my business. That's not what we're here for. He's my teacher, and I'm a student with questions.

"Dammit," I say as I cringe. "I don't have condoms."

Finn bites his bottom lip. "Dex does. Third drawer of his nightstand."

I close my eyes so Finn doesn't see me roll them. *And why the hell is he having so much sex at his friend's house anyway?*

"But we may not need them. Are you on birth control?"

Of all things to wind me, of all moments...why now? *Don't cry. Don't you dare cry.*

"Yep," I squeak.

But my stupid eyes give me away. Finn won't move on from the subject when he sees me tearing up. "Why are you upset? We can use a condom if that makes you more comfortable. I just know you're not the fuck-around type, and I got tested a while back. I'm clean, and I haven't been with anyone since."

"Okay," I say, trying to push the intrusive thoughts away from my mind. "That's fine."

The truth is when I found Mason's engagement ring in the closet, I made an appointment with my gynecologist about family planning. They were booked out for six months, but I figured it was perfect timing. Within six months, surely Mason would've proposed.

I'm thirty. I want kids, and I already feel a little late to planning. I figured Mason and I would have a brief engagement and would want children shortly after we got married. I made an appointment to have my IUD removed. An appointment that I missed last week because I'm not in California, I'm not engaged, and I'm about to have sex with a man I've known for about a week for the sole purpose of understanding what I'm doing wrong in the bedroom. I would've never guessed this is where I'd be when I booked that damn appointment.

"Talk to me," Finn says. "What's on your mind?" He finds my eyes and cocks his head to the side.

Relaxing my eyelids, I press my fingers to my temples. "I need to think a little less, Finn. I just want to feel. Can you kiss me now?"

His lips are on mine before I can open my eyes again. All suspicions confirmed, Finn tastes like...

Man. Fresh. Breath. Air. Flesh.

I can't cohesively describe it. He kisses with intention, his tongue massaging mine. His bottom lip is tucked between both of mine until he decides it's not deep enough. He tilts his head and claims my mouth, but eventually his craving grows, my lips unable to satiate him...

He moves down my neck while toying with the knot of my bikini top. "Avery," he whispers, "you taste so sweet." He uses his teeth to tug on my earlobe gently. "I am going to make you feel so fucking good. Tell me where you want my lips."

"Wherever you want."

He stills and steps backward. I immediately shudder, missing his warmth. Finn turns to adjust the giant mirror. His biceps and forearms tense as he angles the heavy mirror and frame, accentuating the images on his tatted arm. Taking the opportunity to thoroughly inspect his sleeve, I realize how much more intricate his tattoo is than just the ghost ship. There's what I can only assume is a kraken tattooed on the back of his arm, dancing across his tricep. Below the crook of his elbow, a cluster of mermaids or sirens look out at the dark sea. I think this whole design is meant to look angry...intimidating perhaps...but right now, to me, it only looks hot.

I want to be pinned down, those pictures pressed against my skin as Finn makes a puddle out of me. Except for some reason, he's stalling.

I'm now on display, right in the middle of the mirror. I expect him to return to me so I can wrap my legs around him and continue our make-out session, but Finn grabs a rolling stool from the corner of the closet and positions himself between my legs. He sits down slowly, his eyes locked between my legs. Eye level with the apex of my thighs, he has to tilt his head upward to meet my eyes.

"Your first lesson," he says with a wicked smile on his face.

Oh, for a moment, I forgot why we're doing this. He's not just here for pleasure. He's here to teach. "Is?"

"Dirty talk."

The corners of my lips turn down, and I watch my pout in the mirror. I don't want to talk dirty at the moment. What I really want is to turn the lights off and let Finn climb on top of me. I just want to feel safe underneath his body, where I know he can't see any part of me jiggling around. Except that's exactly what I said I was bored of. I'm here to push my comfort level, and Finn is here to hold my hand through it.

"Dirty talk is not my strong suit."

"Do you know why?" His startling baby blue eyes are dancing with entertainment. I think it turns him on when I blush.

"Um, I don't watch a ton of porn...like some. Not a lot. So I don't know what they say. I'm not really vocal during sex."

His smile grows. "First of all, I'm going to make you vocal during sex. I'm going to have you screaming when you come. Trust me."

My stomach clenches, and I instantly feel the swell between my legs.

"Second of all, you don't need to watch porn to learn this. Too much, and it desensitizes you. You already know what to say, but you won't let yourself say it because it's embarrassing. Dirty talk is just asking for *exactly* what you want." Finn places both of his hands on my knees and trails his hands up my thighs. "So when I ask you where you want my lips, why don't you go ahead and tell me the truth?"

"My..." *Fuck. Why is this so hard?* "My neck," I say. "I like when you kiss me there."

Finn shakes his head. "No, baby, that's a lie. That's not where you want them. You want me to eat your pussy like I'm starving, don't you?" He pushes my thighs apart and strokes his thumb against my swimsuit bottoms, knowing exactly where my clit is without seeing it. "I bet you're so fucking wet for me right now, my tongue could go swimming, sweet girl."

My heartbeat turns into aggressive flutters; it vibrates like a hummingbird's wings. I love the way he's stroking me, teasing me. Everything Finn does lights me on fire in the right way.

This hellish heat... *Oh.*

I want to burn.

I like when he talks to me like that in the sanctity of this closet. When we're in private, just Finn and me, I want to tell him what I want.

His eyes don't leave mine as he picks up the pace and rubs rapid circles around my swelling clit. *Oh God.* I'm going to come from his thumb. This is seriously about to happen. I know it because my thighs are tensing and I have the urge to let my eyes roll into the back of my head.

"Is this how you want to come?" Finn asks. "Because if there's something else you want"—he smiles wickedly at me—"tell me. You're safe with me, and what you want me to do, believe me, baby, I *really* want to do it too." He leans forward and plants a wet kiss above my knee. "Just say it."

"I...um..."

"*Say it,*" he growls.

"I don't want to."

"Why?"

"Because Mason hated it. Every time I asked, he came up with an excuse. The rejection hurt. It made me feel gross and humiliated, and now I just can't stand the idea of bringing it up."

Finn stops rubbing me, and his smile flattens. "Did you blow him?"

"What?"

"Would you give Mason head when you guys had sex?"

I mean, we rarely had sex, but when we did... I nod.

"Lesson number two, Avery—and this is a very important one. Are you listening?"

I nod again as I try to swallow down the lump in my throat.

Finn looks right into my eyes and says, "If a man doesn't *give*, he doesn't *get*. End of story. Don't waste your time on selfish assholes."

He kisses all the way up my thigh this time. When he reaches the fabric covering my sex, he yanks it aside and blows across my crease and over my clit. It's a seductive, yet blissful stimulation. Like a sweet cool breeze on the hottest day. It feels so good I lose my head. I let myself get drunk off this man's potent sexuality, and the words just spill out of my mouth...

"I really like that," I moan.

"You look so good, baby. You're so hot and pink and swollen." He chuckles. "I haven't been this excited about pussy in a long time."

It's the first moment I notice how into this Finn is. Like sex with me is more than a friendly favor to white knuckle through. Am I desirable? Am I appealing? Does he *actually* want me? My confidence soaks through my body like liquor in my bloodstream. I let the hazy feeling flow through me, intoxicating me until it reaches my lips and my mouth falls open...

The first words I can think of just come rolling out.

"I want to come on your tongue, Finn. Please. Kiss me *hard*, right on my clit."

He stops blowing against my sensitive skin and smiles at me wider than I've ever seen before. "There you go, Avery. There's the dirty talk. *Good girl.* You're such a quick learner. That was very sexy."

I soak up his praise as he unties the bows of my bikini bottoms. I bridge my hips so he can pull the swimsuit from underneath me and then toss it aside. Tenderly, he scoots me to the edge of the counter then secures my heels against his shoulders. I'm spread, on display, and my most intimate area is an inch away from Finn's face. I should be writhing with humiliation, but I just don't care right now. I'm so turned on. All I care about, *all I can think about,* is finding my release. I'm so needy, the pressure is too much.

"And just so you know," he says before he licks my inner thigh half an inch away from my center. "This is my pleasure to do, Queen." *Oh dear God.* He teases me with soft kisses, apparently to make me erupt from the anticipation alone. I try to lie backward, but Finn protests. "No, sit up. Eyes on the mirror. I want you to see how fucking beautiful you look when I make you come."

He drags his tongue across my slit, up then down, starting on one side, then attending to the other. "Goddamn, I knew you'd taste sweet," he moans.

There's no way. I am a thirty-year-old grown adult. I thoroughly understand a woman's anatomy. It is not cotton candy and bubblegum down there. But he's certainly treating me like I'm dessert. The way he moves, moans, and tells me how soft and warm and delicious I am, I actually believe him.

I'm sweet.

I'm savory.

Following Finn's command, I watch myself in the mirror. My crazy hair, loose strands falling out of my messy bun. My cheeks are so flushed, they're red and splotchy. My lips are permanently parted. I can't get enough air through my nose, so I have to gulp and gasp to fill my lungs as Finn tries to suffocate me with pleasure. His broad, muscular back in the mirror is blocking the view of anything intimate. But I can clearly see the mermaids of his tattoo on the back of his arm. They are perfectly shaped, with hourglass figures, tiny waists, and voluptuous chests under their clamshell bras. They are beautiful. They are inviting me to be beautiful with them as they sit on their rock, smiling wickedly, egging me on.

You're beautiful. You're worthy. Go ahead, girl, get yours.

Feeling my orgasm building, I flex my hips and push harder against Finn's tongue. As subtly as I can, I grind my hips and immediately feel him smile against my womanhood.

"Sorry," I mumble, ashamed I'm being too greedy.

Finn reaches for my hips with both hands and grabs as much of my ass as he can in this position. He squeezes firmly before pulling me tighter against his face. "Don't you dare be sorry. That's so sexy. Enjoy yourself, Avery. Use me. Use my tongue."

He guides my hips, encouraging my feral behavior. I push all reason away. Don't think too hard, don't worry so much...just *feel*. I weave my fingers into Finn's dark, coarse hair. It's trimmed on the sides, but the top is plentiful enough to grip. And when I'm almost on the brink of my orgasm, I make a fist.

"Oh, ho, ho," he says between breathy chuckles. "*Good girl.* Pull my hair. Don't you dare stop."

He's saying all the filthy things because he knows, believe it or not, I like it. The Rumble chat room was cringe-worthy, but not because of the words—because of who was saying it. All the things I used to find awkward...hm, maybe it was timing, maybe it was the company. Finn could ask anything of me right now, and I'd do it. Including...

"Fuck my face, baby. I want to taste how hard you come," he growls.

I make a point to find my eyes in the mirror.

Then I explode.

And Finn's right.

It's so fucking beautiful.

He's patient through my orgasm. He even stands and lays me backward so I can relax. The cool granite touching every inch of my skin is a welcome relief.

"I'll be right back," he says and then disappears through the closet to the master bathroom. I hear water running. *Understandable.* He's probably rinsing off his face, seeing as I drenched it. Finn returns with a robe draped over his arm. It suddenly dawns on me that my bikini top is still on. That was hands down the best orgasm I've ever had in my life, and my top is on, covering Finn's favorite part of my body.

This night has barely begun.

"Why are your pants still on?" I ask, nodding toward his shorts. Never have I been more eager to see a man's erect penis before in my life.

Except Finn cringes. Apologetically.

"Hop down," he says, holding out his arms to catch me. Draping the robe over me, he kisses my cheek. "Come on." Grabbing my hand, he leads me to the bedroom. He just tasted the most intimate part of my body, but it still gives me nervous flutters when he holds my hand. Leading me to the bed, Finn pulls the corner of the cover down and guides me into a sit. He joins me, sitting right beside me, shoulder to shoulder. "Can I get you anything? Water? A beer?"

"Why do I feel like you're leaving?"

He lets out a big sigh. "Because I am."

"Did I do something wrong—"

"Don't even say it, Avery." He kisses my shoulder. "You are perfect. In fact, you really got into it."

I turn my head to face him, and he's smirking. I roll my eyes. My confidence has sobered, and I'm embarrassed at how animalistic I just acted on that closet counter.

"Sorry. It's not my usual style..."

"Don't be. It was great. But I realize that you must be really comfortable with me to let your guard down like that."

I pat his knee. "I am." *It's strange. It doesn't make sense. But I am.*

"Which means I have more responsibility in this than I realized," he says softly.

"What does that mean?"

Finn turns his knee in to face me. He tucks a loose hair behind my ear as he speaks, "When I left you in the hot tub, I got a call."

"I know." I'm worried about why he's grimacing. "Who called?"

"Someone who really pissed me off."

"Do you want to talk about it?"

He releases something between a laugh and a grunt. I'm not sure exactly. I just know it means *hell no*. "I was upset, so I came over thinking we could have some fun and comfort each other, but I want tonight to stay just for you. Can I take you out before we go any further?"

Out? Like into the world? Where people would see us together? "Finn...you told me you weren't ready for a relationship, and I heard you loud and clear. Mason and I just broke up as well. I have no expectations from you. I'm not trying to trick you into dating me. I really just needed a safe space to explore this side of myself." A secret, safe place. Because if people knew what we were up to, Finn might be the one embarrassed for a change.

"I wasn't thinking that." He cocks his head to the side. "I meant, let's go to dinner as friends. Just because I'm not your boyfriend doesn't mean I don't respect you. You told me you want me to teach you how to have good sex. No matter how you look at it, it gives me the upper hand and puts you in a vulnerable position."

"True." I'm impressed with his intuitiveness here. *Really impressed*. It's strange, almost.

"I think we're going to have fun doing this, but let me be a good guy about it. Okay? So have dinner with me tomorrow night, and then I'll fuck you senseless right after."

Why the hell are you single? How is this possible? Now I need to see his penis immediately because there must be something horrendously wrong with it. Maybe he murdered someone? Maybe he tortures puppies? What's wrong with this man?

"Okay, thank you. That is incredibly nice."

Finn smiles. "I have a client tomorrow afternoon, but I'll be done well before six. Do you have a nice dress?"

Literally one. It's the same dress I wore to my thirtieth birthday dinner. I don't even know why I packed it. It's the only dress I feel good in, and I didn't want to leave it behind with Mason.

"Yeah."

"Okay, good. The place I want to take you to has a dress code." He kisses my forehead. "Get changed and comfortable. I'll lock up on my way out then go through the back gate."

He stands, but I stop him, my hand clenching his forearm.

"Hey, Finn?"

"Yeah?" He blinks at me expectantly with his baby blue eyes.

His light eyes in contrast with his jet-black hair are so striking. Finn's an interesting combination of sexy, yet beautiful. I don't know whether I want to fuck him or paint him.

"Do you read women's magazines or something? Or, like... follow Oprah? It's weird. You told me to fuck your face, yet you also want to be a gentleman and take me to dinner before sex."

Finn chuckles. "You just haven't seen my dark side. *Yet.* I'm taking you to a really nice restaurant, and I'm going to pick up the tab. Then, when we get home, I'm going to make you earn your meal."

I press my legs together as the stirring between my thighs kicks up again. "All right then, Finn. Keep your secrets. Good night."

I stand up, intent on grabbing a clean pair of underwear, but Finn pauses in the bedroom doorway. He spins around to look at me across the room. "Avery, my dad is a womanizer."

"What?" I'm caught off guard by his odd declaration.

"My dad treats women like shit. And I swear, I'm his spitting image. My entire life is basically my apology to the world for his behavior and a desperate attempt to prove that even though I look just like him, I'm nothing like him." Finn's eyes are on the hardwood floor, one of the rare moments he's not making eye contact with me. "That's why I'm nice."

"Oh my God...I, um...*shit, Finn.* I'm not usually lost for words..."

"It's okay, don't say anything. I just wanted you to know I'm not playing you." He looks up and his smile returns. "I'm for real. I'm a good guy."

I nod because I believe him. *Finn is for real.* "Okay," I whisper.

"All right, Queen. Get some rest. You're going to need it." He winks. "Dream of me tonight."

Chapter 13

Finn

"That was fucking grueling," Lennox says as she pulls the pig puppet off her right hand. She proceeds to help me load my equipment into the back seat of my truck. I didn't need to bring much. The sky was perfect today for family photos at the town park. It's bright out but a little overcast, so we had no issues with a glare. It went much better than last year.

We learned. When you're photographing an extended family that has eighteen members, eight of which are under the age of four, bring puppets, balloons, and snacks.

"That little kid, Jaxon, has a shocking resemblance to the Chucky doll."

I shoot her a look.

"*What?*" she asks defensively. "I mean, like before the scar... but still with the evil eyes."

I don't say anything because she's right. Jaxon is terrifying-looking. The kid was mean mugging me through the entire photo shoot, and I have the pictures to prove it.

I love the Richmond family. I've been photographing them for six years now. Their extended family is huge, and it's the patriarch, Grandpa Jack, who always pays the bill. He tips me as much as my services cost. I think he pities me, but I'm currently in no position to decline. He's the main reason Finn Harvey Photography is still in business. It's always why when he calls, I bend over backward to accommodate him.

I don't normally do weddings, but I made a special exception for his favorite granddaughter, Katie. They hire me for everything—back-to-school photos, newborn pictures, engagement photos, and annual family photos. I even talked Katie into a boudoir photo shoot as a wedding present for her now husband, Bryce. She told me he loved them, but it's been three years and the dude still won't look me in the eyes. He'll just shake my hand and smile at my shoes like he's intimidated.

Believe me, Katie doesn't turn my crank. Nothing turns me off more than the idea of cheating. I hated cheaters because of my dad, and Nora's antics put the final nail in that coffin.

"Thanks for your help today," I say. "Also, what the hell are you wearing?"

Lennox has swapped her normally dark, gothic look for a beige, floral dress. Come to think of it, her hair is pulled back into a neat ponytail and I think she's wearing pink lipstick.

"I have a lot of looks," she says noncommittally.

"True. But I've never seen this one."

She shrugs. "It's summer."

"You're seeing someone new, aren't you?"

She flashes me a sarcastic smile, her nose crumpling. "I put some southwest eggrolls in your fridge, by the way. Your dinner awaits you."

"You're a good woman, Lennox. Thank you. But I'll get some more fresh tonight. I'm taking Avery to Rue 52."

Lennox smiles so wide her face might split in half.

"What?" I ask.

"You're honestly going to throw on a sports coat? You hate wearing a monkey suit and going to Rue 52."

"Yeah, I wanted to take her somewhere nice."

"Wow." Lennox's eyes are full of snarky condescension. "Is this a *thank you* dinner?"

"Uh...in a way?"

Lennox pushes against my arm playfully. "That's awesome. So she's going to help with the website?"

"She is..." I wonder if Lennox can tell I'm trying to dodge the details.

"When does she want to do the boudoir shoot?" Lennox asks as she follows behind me.

I open the door, crawl into the driver's seat, and crank the car to get the air conditioner flowing. It's disgustingly hot today and I don't need my equipment warping from the heat.

"She doesn't."

"What? Why not? The set is fucking amazing if I say so myself. I've almost finished staging."

"She's not into that sort of stuff. We have a different... *arrangement.*"

Any other person in the world would shrug and think nothing of it. But it's Lennox. She's family, my best friend, and is not too shy to call me on my shit.

"You dog." She clasps her hands together as she looks up at me. "I mean, I never thought you'd pimp yourself out to save our business, but hey, whatever keeps the doors open." She's snickering in glee, watching my unamused expression.

"It's not what you're thinking."

"I'm thinking you slept with her."

"I didn't." More like I sat with my head between her thighs for about fifteen minutes.

"Liar," Lennox snarks. "It's nothing to be ashamed of. She's really cute, and here's hoping she's an upgrade in personality from your usual type."

"She's way more than cute... She's got a lot of layers." Avery toggles between shy and insecure to intimidatingly intelligent and direct. It keeps me on my toes how I can't quite pin down her personality. All I know is that I like it. "She's also going through it with her ex."

Lennox tents her hand over her eyes as the sun pokes out from behind a cloud cluster, blinding her. "So you guys have that in common."

I blow out a breath as my jaw twitches in irritation. *Speaking of exes.* I have no one else to talk to about that phone call from last night than Lennox, so I might as well get it off my chest. "Hop in? Air's going."

Lennox walks around the truck and opens the passenger side door. She's dramatic as she grabs the interior handle and hoists herself up like she's mounting a horse. She hates my truck because of how high it sits off the ground. I don't love it either. It's like driving a monster truck around town. But I didn't exactly pick it out. It was an over-the-top present from my dad a year ago.

"What's up?" Lennox asks.

"Morgan called me last night. I'm trying to shake it off, but he got to me."

"What the fuck did your ex-girlfriend's ex-boyfriend want with you?" Lennox turns in her seat, facing me directly, her brows pulling in concern. "And how did he get your number?"

"They're back together. They've been back at it for a couple months apparently—"

"Of course...typical Nora. Always needs a stand-in—"

"He must've grabbed it from Nora's phone. He called because he wanted to ask me *man to man* if I was sleeping with her behind his back. He suspects she's cheating on him again, and since I was the culprit all those years ago, naturally, he figured I was at it again." I knock my thumbs against the steering wheel. "His words, not mine."

Lennox grumbles to herself. "It's been three years, Finn. It still bothers you?"

I bury my hands in my face, letting the memories I push away daily bubble to the surface.

Nora was a stripper. I met her at Ruby's, a gentlemen's club my grandpa owns. One of his many random properties amongst the Las Vegas Strip. It's probably the only one he isn't keen to brag about, but it happens to be his biggest cash cow.

I hosted a bachelor party for one of my buddies at Ruby's. I watched Nora dance on stage all night, and after the final call, when she was dressed and had wiped off most of the body glitter, I asked if I could take her to breakfast.

Our first date was at an IHOP right outside the Las Vegas Strip at three in the morning. The next day, I woke up to a slew of congratulations texts from my buddies for taking home the hottest stripper in the club, but I didn't actually take her home.

She ordered a double stack of plain pancakes and soaked them with boysenberry syrup. I got chocolate chip pancakes. We switched halfway through. It was that tame. We talked about how she used to be a blackjack dealer, but stripping paid much better. Ruby's treated her well. She felt safe and in control. My grandpa's club has very strict rules in place to protect their dancers, and they don't tolerate illegal activity. You'd have to find your happy ending elsewhere. Ruby's was one hundred percent law-abiding. And plus, Nora stayed out of the private rooms...unless her car needed repairs.

I've never fallen in love that fast. Within three months of us dating, she stopped stripping at Ruby's. I bought my house for her. I asked my dad to cosign the damn loan...*all for her.*

It was a few weeks after she moved in with me that I learned Nora wasn't single.

And I was the other man.

When I found out about Morgan, she had every excuse in the book. She didn't know how to break it off, he was abusive and controlling, she was reliant on him, he owed her money. She didn't love him. She just didn't want to see me end up in a fight over her.

That's the part of the story where I'm no longer the victim because I listened to all the bullshit and I still chose to stay. I loved her that much. I kept her. I believed her. When she ended it with Morgan, I forgave her.

And then somehow I became the asshole who snaked his girl right from under him.

"The narrative bothers me, that's all. I didn't know about Morgan until it was too late. I'm not that guy."

"Everyone who matters knows that." Lennox reaches over the center console and gently pats my shoulder. "But it's okay if you're upset that she's back with him again. You don't have to love her to be hurt over her."

"I know..." There are two sides to Nora. I won't deny there is good in her. But in the end, the bad far outweighed the good.

"But I'm glad to see you're moving on." Lennox pats my shoulder. "We should all hang out. Double date? You, me, Avery, and Alan. Look at that—we're both dating A names."

I chuckle. *Alan who likes sundresses, huh?* "Avery and I aren't dating. We're just friends who apparently are going to hang out for the summer."

"What's a four-letter word for *hang out* that starts with f?" She flashes me a wicked smile. "I think it's spelled f...u...c—"

"Lennox—"

"It's not a big deal, Finny," she says as she opens her passenger side door. "Whatever keeps the lights on in the studio. Bring her around. I'd love to get to know her. Plus, you're no longer authorized to enter into a relationship without my prior approval. I have a knack for sniffing out the rats. I told you Nora was bad news from day one."

"Yeah, yeah... Get out of here. Go see your new boy toy. Wait, do you want a ride to your car?"

"Nope," she says, pointing across the small playground. "I'm parked just on the other side." She hops out of the truck but holds the door open. "For the record, you were really smiley today. Way more than usual."

I raise my brow at her. "Really?"

"Definitely." Lennox points at my chest. "Must be the change in company." Proving her point, I smile to myself as she shuts the truck door and heads to the overflow parking lot.

Hm, must be.

Chapter 14

Avery

I am *exhausted.*

I don't know how women do this every single freaking day.

Lucky for me, Palmer talked me into full-body laser hair removal years ago, so shaving wasn't necessary. Still, it took me hours to pluck my eyebrows, put on a face mask, then wash, blow-dry, and curl my long hair. I spent an ungodly amount of time going down the rabbit hole of smoky-eye tutorials, which turns out I suck at, so I ended up settling on several thick coats of mascara, black eyeliner, a little pink eyeshadow, and matching blush. This is about as glam as I can get it.

It's not about impressing Finn. It's about impressing myself. *I can do this.* I can learn to appreciate more about myself than the business I created. Looks shouldn't be the most important thing...but should they still be a *thing*? Is a man wrong for wanting a woman to try a little bit? Maybe with Mason I should've put on makeup and worn clothes that didn't look like they barely survived a moth attack. There is a part of me that knows I'm partially culpable for Mason's lack of interest in our sex life.

But I can turn this around.

This is my decade. I won't wallow. I won't whine. I *will* figure this out. I will have my cake and eat it, too. I'll find a man who can do more than tolerate me. One day, I'll have children with a man who loves to be cozy with me in sweatpants but appreciates me in the bedroom too. A unicorn? Perhaps. But I'm great at research. I'll find him if it's the last thing I do.

Or die single.

Whichever comes first.

I head to the fridge to grab a bottle of water. I'm walking around in my bra and underwear because Finn did not tell me what time he was picking me up tonight and I don't have his number. I'm assuming he's picking me up. There's a small chance he thinks I'm meeting him at the restaurant, but seeing as I don't know *which* restaurant we're going to, I sincerely hope he's not that clueless.

He told me he was done with work around six o'clock, so I've been primped and polished since six on the dot. My dress is on a hanger, dangling from the staircase railing, and my strappy black heels are lined up neatly underneath. My satin dress is restricting, so I figured I'd enjoy my comfort until Finn rings the doorbell. If this is going to continue for the summer, we need to plan better. I'm not sure if I'm going to be in my underwear for minutes or hours. I'm a dinner at five thirty kind of girl, but Vegas people are a different breed.

Cold water bottle in hand, I hunch over, peering into the enormous built-in fish tank in the living room that doubles as a see-through wall. *Where is she...ah, there's my little goof.*

"Hey, Cherry, so dumdum, as in my ex-boyfriend Mason, hasn't sent the reports on Legacy Resorts yet. Therefore, instead of working on my big proposal, I did some research on you today. I'm pretty sure you're a Cherry Barb." *Wow. I'm talking to a fish...a fish that paces like it's high on cocaine.* "I'll ask Dex when he's back, but if I'm right, can we pause for a moment and appreciate how apt and intuitive my nickname is for you? I started calling you Cherry a week ago."

I raise my brows at the tank as if I expect the little fish to answer.

"Also, please don't be offended, but I've dubbed you she because you're so shiny and pretty. If you are a male and that's offensive, I sincerely apologize. Apparently, the only way I can confirm your gender is by scooping you out of the water, gutting you, and checking your intestines, and we're just not going to do that, Cherry. But it seems rude to continue to call you 'it.' You have such a big personality for a fish. I watch you all the time. You either have severe anxiety, or that fish goop the aquarium guy feeds you once a week has you on uppers. But I don't mind. You're up at all hours of the day and night, and it makes me feel less alone. Mason and I are a mess. Palmer's so wrapped up in her show. My parents are on another planet. You're the only one I can really talk to whenever—"

"You can talk to me."

I shoot up straight and immediately try to cover my bare ass that my thong does not conceal. Spinning around, my heartbeat doesn't calm when I see Finn leaning in the doorway of the sliding glass patio doors.

He's chuckling at me. The smug bastard is in stitches as I try my best to cover my nakedness. "I already saw your bare ass bent over, sweetheart. I licked your pussy clean last night. What're you trying to hide?"

I open my mouth and then close it. I can't think of anything better to say, so I blurt out, "Lurker. How long have you been standing there?"

"Not long. Just since you told Cherry you wouldn't gut her to check out her equipment."

I'm not sure what's more concerning at the moment—that Finn caught me talking to a fish, or caught me in my underwear, talking to a fish.

"Why wouldn't you ring the doorbell?"

"I did," Finn says, holding up three fingers. "Three times. You didn't answer. I came through the back to make sure you were okay. You live alone here, Avery. If we make plans and you don't answer the door...I'm going to check on you."

I take a moment to eye him up and down, and as my shock and mortification simmer, I have time to notice how handsome he looks dressed up in clean black slacks and a baby blue button-down that matches his eyes. He has a sports coat draped over his arm.

"I guess I didn't hear the doorbell from upstairs."

He shrugs as he enters and closes the sliding door behind him. "Well, I'm here now. You ready? Or do you need more time? Our Uber is outside."

"Uber?"

"Yeah, it's a pain in the ass to park my truck on the Strip. It's easier to get dropped off."

"We're going to the Strip?"

He clenches one eye closed. "Is that okay?"

I nod, still stupefied at his attire. He's dazzling. There's no other way to describe it. *Good grief.* He's so sweet and normal, I forgot he's a god among men. How the hell did I trick this man into taking me out to dinner? We're not even the same species.

I pull my gold clutch off the kitchen counter and make my way to the front door. My head is a little fuzzy. I really felt in control of this situation until now...

Finn is wonderful in every way. I thought I completely understood that he's too good to be true...*for me.* He needs a princess, a real prize. I'm just his friend. That's why this works. He's safe with me just like I'm safe with him because our hearts are not involved. I tighten my jaw as I reach the front door. *Stay out of it, feelings.* I don't want to walk down the painful path of unrequited love.

"Hey, Avery?"

"Yes?" I ask, spinning around.

"Should we put on your dress? As much as I'm enjoying the view, the restaurant has a dress code, and at the bare minimum, you need to be *dressed.*"

"Oh, fuck me," I mumble, palming my forehead, mumbling to myself. *Okay, I officially need to calm the hell down.* I was about two seconds away from walking outside in my thong and bra, not to mention barefoot.

"That's the one?" Finn asks, pointing to my dress hanging from the staircase.

"Yep."

He fetches it for me, pulling it off the hanger. "Do you step in, or does it go over your head?" he asks, examining my sleek black dress.

"Overhead," I say as I grab my shoes and slip into them. I reach for my dress, but Finn doesn't hand it over. He swivels his finger in the air.

"Turn around." There's a determination in his voice. "Arms up."

I do as I'm told, relieved that he can't see my face. This is a level of intimacy I wasn't quite prepared for. Rough and tumble sex, sure. *That* I was expecting from a man who'd make professional models feel insecure. But his tenderness? His slow, sweet touches? Checking on me instead of abandoning our plans when I didn't answer the doorbell? Taking me to dinner to show me kindness and respect?

I think I bit off way more than I can chew...

Once the fabric cloaks my body, Finn traces my curves with both hands, smoothing my dress in place. "This fits you like a glove." Spinning me around, he keeps his hands on the outward curve of my hips as he studies me. I feel my cheeks reddening. *Shit.* What can I do? I can't control it. "Your makeup is really pretty and your dress is stunning, Avery." He hooks his finger under my chin and tilts my head upward, forcing me to stare into his eyes. I notice he always does this when he's about to compliment me when he really wants me to soak up his praise. "You look like royalty—a goddamn queen."

I couldn't control my smile if I tried. I want to say thank you, but I'm speechless.

"Just remember, you're going out with me tonight," Finn continues. "I don't care who hits on you this evening. You're coming home with me." He taps the tip of my nose. "No trading me for something better."

He releases my hips and strides past me, grabbing my hand in the process and leading me toward the front door. He snags my clutch off the entry table then tucks it under his arm so all I have to hold is his warm hand interlaced with mine.

Something better, Finn? Ha. No such thing.

* * *

Finn seems slightly agitated, but I'm happy as a clam. It might have something to do with my third whiskey sour. I can't even feel my feet anymore, which is great because we've been standing for forty-five minutes at the bar. Finn made a reservation, but the restaurant clearly gives zero fucks about calling ahead.

"Sorry," he mutters, scouring the restaurant. "It shouldn't take this long."

"Finn, I'm fine." I pop a maraschino cherry into my mouth and munch happily. Just give me a few more cherries, and we can call this dinner. It's already the perfect evening. This restaurant is fantastic. I'm not used to such a swanky, club-like vibe paired with the most sophisticated menu I've ever seen. It just feels nice to be out and dolled up for once. I wish Palmer could see me now, with my makeup, in this dress, at this restaurant, *with this man.* I swear she'd tear up and slow clap—her life mission complete.

"We're packed like sardines. You must be uncomfortable," he grumbles. "*I'm* uncomfortable."

He's spot-on. About thirty of us, waiting on our tables, are huddled around a bar that would barely seat twelve. Elbow to elbow, everyone is crammed, hungry, and grumpy...except me, especially when I find a bonus maraschino cherry at the bottom of my drink. *Munch, munch, munch.*

I'm about to tell Finn to calm down because I'm thoroughly enjoying myself when I notice a small hand with red manicured nails slink over his. Finn freezes and turns his alarmed expression to the woman standing next to him.

"What're you drinking?" she says over the dull roar of the restaurant. "That looks good."

Finn flashes me a quick telling look, his eyes bulging. *Save me*, he says wordlessly. But I don't. Because the woman standing next to him is slim, blond, beautiful, and I suddenly feel very out of place standing next to Finn.

"It's their signature whiskey." Finn takes the opportunity to remove his hand from under hers and points to the top shelf of the bar. "That one right there."

He angles his shoulders to face me, but the blond woman isn't dissuaded.

"Would you recommend it on the rocks or neat?" she asks. But I'm almost certain this woman with the pouty red lips and platinum-blond hair doesn't drink whiskey. She wants to drink Finn.

"Depends on what you like, I suppose," Finn replies with a clipped smile.

"What do *you* like?" she basically purrs.

Wow.

I can tell Finn is torn. He doesn't want to be a dick. It'd be easier if I was the kind of woman who'd throw her drink in this poacher's face and tell her to back the fuck off my man. Except I'm not that kind of woman...

And Finn is not my man.

"I like what I have." Finn taps the side of his glass, making the ice clink in his whiskey on the rocks. But it's obvious his response is edgy and laced with double meaning. *I like what I have.* Does he mean me?

"You're more than welcome to order me one on your next round," she replies, shooting him a wink. I watch his strong jaw twitch. Now he's annoyed.

"I'm with a friend this evening," he says.

In the most unsubtle, mean-girl way possible, the blonde woman leans backward, looking me up and down. She scoffs to herself. "Oh well, then excuse me," she snarks. "I didn't mean to interrupt you and your *friend.*"

Yes, you did. You meant to interrupt. You just couldn't fathom he'd pick me over you.

"Hey, do you want to go somewhere else?" Finn asks. "I'm sorry about all this."

I shake my head. "No, this place seems great. I can wait." I try to sound chirpy, but it's too late. He notices my mood slightly deflated and my eyes that are probably just a shade less sparkly. It's the result of a stranger subtly insulting you.

"Miss," Finn says sternly as a hostess, dressed from head to toe in black, passes by the bar. I'm surprised when he catches her by the wrist. She looks alarmed as well, even as Finn immediately drops her arm. "Is Angelo in tonight?"

The hostess narrows her eyes. "As in the manager?"

"Yes," Finn says, trying his best to curb his annoyance.

Overworked and dealing with endless customer complaints, the hostess matches his annoyance. "He's in his office, but there's nothing complaining will do for you. We're overbooked. We'll let you know when your table is ready," she all but hisses at Finn.

Pulling his wallet out of his back pocket, Finn produces a one-hundred-dollar bill. He folds it between his fingers and holds it out to the hostess. "Will you please take a moment to tell Angelo that Griffin Harvey the Third is here, waiting at the bar, and would really like to say hello before I leave?" He wiggles the bill at her. "Can you remember all that, or do you need me to write it down?"

Snatching the bill from his fingers, she grumbles something under her breath. "I'll let him know," she says clearly before disappearing into the back of the restaurant.

Finn places his hand on my lower back and leans down to whisper into my ear. He smells intoxicating. His rich cologne is sweet and earthy, with a touch of sandalwood. "Will you do me a favor?" Finn asks.

"Sure."

"Don't order any more drinks."

I immediately shrivel in place. How insensitive of me. Actually, I'm all sorts of confused. On one hand, Finn's business is struggling, hence our deal, but on the other, he just tipped the hostess one hundred bucks to simply deliver a message. I haven't been to Finn's house yet, but I know it's much smaller than Dex's. Then again, I saw Finn's truck, and either his car payment is more than his mortgage or he stole the damn thing.

"I'm sorry. I got carried away. These *are* expensive," I say, nodding toward my whiskey sour on the bar. "Let me at least pay for my drinks. I insist."

Confusion briefly flashes over his face until he realizes what I'm insinuating. He chuckles. "Oh, no, Avery. It's not the money." He leans in closer, dropping his tone. "All I want to do right now is rip off that dress, get you soaking wet for me, and then bend you over. You have no idea what's coming for you tonight. But I can't fuck you if you're drunk."

"Oh..." My breathing kicks up. When Finn says stuff like this in private, I know it's part of the game. But in public? It feels dangerously sincere. Like he actually wants me all of his accord.

"That's another lesson, by the way." Finn winks at me.

"Huh?"

"Flirting in public. It's good for your sex life."

I nod in a hurry, hoping no one can hear us over the sea of chatter at the bar. "Got it. Public flirting. *Noted.* Um...but I'm not drunk, just so you know. Not even close." *Partial lie.*

"You sure? Spell hippopotamus backward."

I give him a deadpan stare. "I couldn't do that completely sober, Finn."

His laughter is playful as he rubs his palm from side to side across my lower back. I don't remember Mason ever touching me like this in public. He'd open doors and pull out my chair like a gentleman, but he never touched me like this, at every opportunity, just because he wanted to.

"Mr. Harvey?"

We whip our heads around to see the hostess from before, back, with a tucked-tail expression on her face. "Angelo wanted to apologize for the delay. He'll be out a little later to say hello. In the meantime, we have the VIP table ready for you."

"Thank you," Finn says *expectantly.* I'm incredibly impressed, but Finn nods like he knew exactly the card he played and what the end result would be.

"I'm sorry about before," the hostess says, obviously nervous. "I've been getting yelled at all evening...but anyway, I didn't realize who you are."

"It's *fine*. No apologies necessary. Thank you." Finn smiles at me. "You ready, Queen?" He holds out his hand.

"Yes." In perfect timing, my appetite hits me like a freight train. I'm starving. "Oh, we need to pay for our drinks, though." I spin to try to flag down the bartender, but the hostess interrupts.

"No need. They're comped. Right this way." She gestures away from the bar, and my hand is almost in Finn's until I notice the rude blond woman giving me a nasty stare with her lips pursed. I almost ignore it, taking a few steps behind Finn, but I suddenly change my mind.

"One second," I say. "I forgot something." I double back to the bar and grab my now watery whiskey sour. Making a point to brush up against the blond woman, I clear my throat. Her eyes, full of contempt, snap down at me. I take in a deep breath as I do something I've never done before...

Maybe it's the drinks, maybe it's Finn's energy, or perhaps it's the fact that I actually fixed up, went out, and am feeling damn good about myself tonight. *You have no right to take that away from me. I won't let you.* So I proceed to put this bitch in her place.

"Your jealousy is warranted," I say before I take a small sip of my drink. "His dick is huge, he fucks like a god, and he's also the kindest man I've ever met." I flash her a cocky smile. "Enjoy your evening."

Spinning on my heel, I don't bother to stick around for her reaction. But I hope her jaw is dropped and she's shocked at my audacity.

"All good?" Finn asks. He's waiting, his hand still outstretched for mine.

I lace my fingers in his. "All good."

Chapter 15

Finn

I think I've figured it out.

The reason I'm so drawn to Avery is because she can't help but be herself. She embarrasses easily but can laugh at herself. She startles like a buck during hunting season but recovers so quickly with grace. She's shy yet forward all at the same time. Shy enough to feel like a fish out of water in the bedroom but forward enough to ask me for help with her insecurities.

"Do you mind if I order for us?" I ask Avery, sitting on the other side of the booth. This table could seat at least eight. It's completely unnecessary for just Avery and me, but I'm assuming Angelo's pissed at his staff and a little worried about his job at the moment.

"Not at all," she says as she taps away on her phone.

"You sure? It drives some women crazy."

She lifts one eyebrow but doesn't look away from her phone screen. "I'm assuming you know this restaurant well?"

"I do."

"Then you know what's good." She finally looks up at me and tucks her phone away in her clutch.

"Work emergency?" I ask.

She shakes her head, causing her long hair to jostle. I'm not used to seeing her thick, dark hair down. It's hard to picture Avery without the sloppy bun. The woman in front of me is almost unrecognizable.

"No. I was Googling how to spell hippopotamus. To be

honest, I wasn't one hundred percent sure I could spell it forward, let alone backward."

"For shame, Avery. College educated and can't spell hippopotamus? What were they teaching you?"

She points both fingers at me. "You know something? College was useless for me. Everything I've learned that's helpful for my job, I taught myself. All college got me was a mountain of student loan debt."

"I can empathize," I say. "My degree is in economics."

"Oh." She cringes. "I'm sorry."

I snort. "And marketing is more interesting?"

"My degree isn't in marketing. It's in—"

Our waiter arrives in a huff, cutting Avery off. "I apologize for the wait, Mr. Harvey...Mrs. Harvey."

Avery shoots me a pointed look, almost demanding I correct him.

What is it with this girl? So she clearly likes me, but the idea of being with me repulses her? *What the hell?*

I hold out my hand, gesturing across the table. "This is my friend, Ms. Scott."

He flushes. "I am terribly sorry. Can I get you another drink, miss? Our signature cocktail for the evening has dark rum and Tahitian vanilla bitters. It's quite popular."

I raise my brow at Avery, and she smirks back.

"No, thank you. I need my head this evening."

I freeze and watch our waiter's face turn beet red.

"*Pardon me,*" Avery says with a sly smile. "I mean, I need to keep my head this evening. Just water, please."

"And you, Mr. Harvey?" The waiter pulls the oversize menus from underneath his arm, but I hold up my hand to stop him.

I'm not in the mood. We've been waiting too long. We should've been wrapping up dinner by now. Avery and I should already be back at my place...*studying.*

"Water is fine. We're ready to order. The southwest rolls, but not with the mango salsa, with the pickled cilantro slaw. Then the pot stickers with the duck sauce, the crab fritters, not too spicy, and for dessert, raspberry tiramisu. Don't split it. One plate, two forks is fine. Bring it out individually as it's ready. No need to wait."

"Of course, sir. Great order."

We both wait until the waiter is out of earshot and talk at the same time.

"You said *head* on purpose, didn't you—" I start.

"What the hell was that—" she also begins.

I rub my brow with one finger. "Ladies first."

"Why is everyone here so skittish around you, Griffin Harvey the *third*? What's up, Finn? What aren't you telling me?" There's a glint in her light eyes, eager to hear a juicy secret.

A secret I really don't want to share.

I shrug. "My grandpa owns this restaurant. Apparently, that translates to I can get anyone here fired, which is not true, nor would I want to."

"*Oh.*" Avery runs her fingertip across her lips as she contemplates my response. Even her nails are painted in a light pink. She really did go all out tonight.

Was that for me?

"I don't mean to sound spoiled here, but then why did you have to call and make a reservation and why did we wait at the bar for so long?"

I let out a deep breath and sink into the tufted booth. "My grandpa owns a lot of places on the Strip. I try not to play the Harvey card. But I invited you out, and I just wanted to treat you to a nice evening. I get the feeling you don't get taken out a lot." I don't know what I said wrong, but I sure as hell said something wrong. *Shit.* Her eyes hit her lap immediately, and I scramble. "I didn't mean that no one would ask you—"

"No, no," Avery replies, her eyes still down, "it's fine. You're right. I haven't been single in years, and Mason and I were homebodies."

"There's nothing wrong with that."

"Finn, this is the *only* nice dress I own."

I stay silent, too worried I'm going to say something wrong again.

"I mean, I make well into the six figures. I can actually afford to live in a decent part of L.A., which a lot of people can't say...and this is the only nice piece of clothing I have. It's the only dress I have that makes me feel pretty."

I run my hand through my hair and grumble, "Is this whole arrangement just so I'll call you pretty, because I already—"

"Stop." Avery locks her eyes on mine, startling me with the fire blazing in them. "Please do not misunderstand me. This is not a shallow validation thing. It's not about *you* calling me pretty. What good is it if you and every other man on this planet calls me pretty if *I* don't believe it? Even more terrifying, what good is it if my entire worth is wrapped up in a man's opinion of me? Look, Finn, my mom gave me the sex talk at age sixteen. You know what she told me?"

"What?"

"Don't do it. Don't get pregnant."

"Oh boy..." Although my dad's rendition wasn't much better. His advice? Fuck early. Fuck often. Don't settle down. Advice he gave me right in front of my mother.

"So I went from awkward sex to boring sex, eventually to no sex. I don't know if Mason was the problem or if I was, but I just know I don't want to have *that* problem ever again. I want to find someone who is a good match, who brings out the best in me. But I don't know how to match myself because I don't know what I like. I haven't tried much of anything. Sex is behind closed doors, lights off, obligatory, and awkward. Would you be okay with that kind of sex life with your wife?"

Truthfully? No. "In a good marriage, if you're unhappy, aren't you supposed to talk about it and work on it together?"

Avery points square between my eyes. "Exactly. That's what we're doing." She flits her hand in the air dismissively. "Without the marriage part, of course. This is *research*. A trade. It's the perfect way to safely test the waters. I don't know anyone else who has your confidence in the bedroom who needs my help with something too. Or at least I thought you did until I realized you're secretly rich."

My chest tightens as my jaw twitches. "Excuse me?"

"Oh, please," Avery says then vibrates her tongue against her bottom lip. "I was confused for a minute, but it's all making sense now. Your Rolex has diamonds on it," she says, nodding to my wrist. "You pulled out a hundred-dollar bill from your wallet without flinching, so I'm assuming there's more where that came from, and everyone who hears your last name is quaking in their boots. Plus, I lied to you earlier. I wasn't looking up hippopotamus. I have an uncanny knack for spelling. I was looking up Harvey Griffin Senior, who owns two hotels, a dozen restaurants, and several parking garages all on the Strip. Net worth roughly in the ballpark of a quarter billion. Is that true? Those online estimates are never accurate." She pumps her eyebrows at me. "They're usually a lowball. How am I doing here?"

I match her stare. "Are you interrogating me?"

Her smile spreads. "Your wealth is not my business, Finn. But I do wonder why you're mooching off Dex's nice steaks and borrowing his hot tub. I get the feeling you could certainly afford your own."

I could lie about this so easily. I do it all the time. It's a secret I managed to keep from Nora. To this day, she thinks my grandpa is actually broke because of tax evasion and my inheritance won't be enough to cover a Happy Meal. It couldn't be further from the truth.

But this is Avery. Without a doubt, I know my money doesn't interest her. She's not exactly a woman after the finer things in life. Yet another reason why we get along so well.

"My inheritance will come in stages. Twenty percent when I turn thirty. Another twenty percent when I turn thirty-five. So on and so forth."

"*What*?" Avery asks in a shrill voice. She clears her throat, her prior tone accidental from surprise.

"My grandpa is a level-headed man. He's established trusts for all of his children and grandchildren, but he set up the disbursements to make sure we still had to work our way through adulthood. I was raised never to count on his money. Plus, there are all sorts of stipulations to get the full disbursements. We have to be married by a certain age, have children—or prove we medically can't. We have to live in a certain radius. It's controlling of Gramps, actually."

It's the only reason my dad married my mom. She married for love. He married for a payout. My grandpa thought he was doing his son a favor by trying to rein in his dickish behavior, but all he did was make my mom an easy target.

Before I can say more, Angelo, dressed in a full suit, tie and all, arrives at our table with a plate of steamed dumplings and spicy duck sauce. He looks like a walking contradiction. His jet-black hair is slicked back, pulled into a tiny knot on the nape of his neck, yet his three-piece suit is pristine. I can see part of a tattoo wrapping around his thumb. Angelo and I use the same tattoo artist. His big-boy job as Rue 52's manager was only because of my insistent recommendation to Gramps. I stand by it. He's a hard worker and a good guy.

"I am so sorry, man," Angelo says as he slides the platter onto the table. Avery's eyes follow the heavenly smelling dish, and she's practically drooling. Poor thing was lying. She's starving. It's been nearly two hours since I picked her up, and I bet she was saving her appetite.

"What's going on? The bar is a mess."

Angelo rolls his eyes. "I had two waiters call out on me ten minutes before their shift due to legitimate medical emergencies. My best busboy burned the shit out of his hand, and my sous chef sliced his hand open on a bottle of merlot. It's the house of fucking horrors in here tonight. I was actually back there washing dishes myself. I threw on this monkey suit to come apologize to you. Why didn't you call me and tell me you were coming tonight?"

He holds out his hand and clasps mine in a brotherly

handshake.

"I didn't want to make a fuss, Lo. I'm simply taking my friend to dinner."

Angelo gives me an impish smile as he turns his gaze to Avery like a hunter eyeing his prey. I'm not sure what his intentions are with that look on his face, but I'm either about to laugh or knock that stupid smirk right off his face.

His move.

"Where are my manners? Hello..."

Avery sticks her hand out in a hurry. "Avery. Nice to meet you." She points to the dumplings. "These smell divine. You are the first person to bring me food all evening, meaning you are officially my favorite person in this restaurant."

Angelo tsks his tongue but doesn't take his eyes off Avery. "Shame on you, Finn. Starving your date like that. What's your favorite kind of wine, hermosa? I owe you a bottle for making you wait."

"Lo," I gripe, "keep your wine and your compliments and just bring out the rest of our food."

I know he's messing with me. He used to do the same thing with Nora whenever I brought her around. A friendly pissing contest. Except when it comes to Avery, I'm not feeling very playful. Just protective. Angelo's not good enough for her. He's never going to take the time to appreciate all the layers—her humor, her charm, her elegance, *and* her flat-out goofiness. He doesn't realize she has a secret weapon she likes to tuck away. That sweet pussy for starters. Bare, pink, and puffy—all my favorite adjectives for that part of a woman. But Avery plays the part of plain Jane because it's comfortable for her. She's trying to hide behind Clark Kent's glasses. When they come off and she dresses up the way she is tonight, every man can clearly see what they are to her...

Undeserving.

Me included.

But I'm a hell of a lot closer than *Angelo*.

Angelo's laughing at me, enjoying my agitation. "Fine, how

about a picture?" He pulls his phone from his pocket. "You both look so nice tonight. I'll frame it, and you can go on the celebrity wall."

"No!" Avery practically shouts. Angelo and I both jump a little. "I'm sorry, I mean no, thank you. No to the picture, and most definitely no to my face on a wall. Please...just, no, thank you..."

I can feel the hot discomfort coming off her skin, so I reach across the table and ask for her hand. Obediently, she places her hand in mine and I squeeze the tips of her fingers. "Lo, go check on my eggrolls, man."

"All right, all right. Oh, hey, while I have you, are you still looking to sell your truck? I might have scrambled up the cash. Can I take a look before you leave tonight before I make a final decision?"

I reluctantly pull my gaze away from Avery's eyes. Her eye makeup accentuates the green perfectly. Natural, yet her lashes look a little darker. Those pretty eyes don't need any help. They catch my attention all the time on their own.

"I didn't drive it tonight. We took an Uber."

"An Uber?" he squawks. He bows his head and shakes it from side to side. "Just sad. I would've brought you in a limo, hermosa." He puckers his lips at Avery, and she snickers. I truly can't tell if she's enjoying the attention. I certainly am not.

"Bye, Lo. I'd say it was nice seeing you, but honestly, I could take you or leave you right now."

He laughs heartily as he retreats from the table. "Have a good dinner, you two. Finn, I'll call you about the truck."

I give Avery's fingers one more quick squeeze before I release her hand and point to the dish between us. "These are best while they're hot."

She rubs her hands together in glee. "You don't have to tell me twice." She grabs her appetizer fork, stabs the smallest dumpling, and dunks it in the bowl of sweet and spicy sauce.

"By the way," I ask her, twirling my own fork in my hand.

"Did you not want your picture taken, or you didn't want your picture taken *with me?*"

She screws up her face, taken aback. "Nothing to do with you. I just hate pictures. My face always looks like a balloon. I have no camera charisma. I smile so big my eyes look crooked. I've never once taken a good picture."

"Your headshot on your website is nice."

She rolls her eyes. "That was my high school senior picture, and I photoshopped the shit out of it."

"*High school?*" I ask, incredulous. She simply nods in response. "You are a highly sought-after brand consultant who works with Fortune 500 companies, and you haven't had a legitimate picture taken since high school?"

"What's your point, Finn? It's clearly not inhibiting my business," she mutters.

"My point is, I can help with that. I might know a guy who takes some damn good pictures." I point to the middle of my chest. "I could take some really nice professional headshots for you. Let me help you."

For a moment, I think she considers it. But she eventually shakes it off. "You already have your work cut out in helping me. Believe me." She takes a small bite of the dumpling, chews, then swallows. She nudges the plate in my direction across the linen-covered tabletop, inviting me to join her. "These are the best things I've ever eaten in my life." Avery moans in appreciation.

"What do you mean I have my work cut out for me?"

She points her fork at me. "One of us is about to have the time of their life in the bedroom tonight." She dunks the other side of her dumpling back into the sauce. "And sorry to tell you, buddy, it's not going to be you. I may be a quick learner, but I'm basically starting from ground zero. You're going to have to take the lead and pull me across the finish line."

I chuckle to myself. Does she really think that's a problem? Little does Avery know, a woman like her letting me take the lead...?

There's no bigger turn-on than that.

Chapter 16

Avery

"Motherfucker." Finn growls with frustration when he sees the limousine waiting for us in front of the restaurant. It's in a no-parking zone, and the driver is holding a bottle of expensive-looking champagne. "That son of a bitch actually wants to fight," Finn mutters under his breath.

I have to clutch my hands around my ribs I'm laughing so hard. Our waiter informed us that Angelo called us a ride and would send us home with a nice bottle of champagne. I don't know when this cutesy pissing contest started between the two of them, but since I'm reaping the rewards, I'm rolling with it.

"He did say I deserved a limousine."

"You do," Finn grumbles and rolls his eyes. "Let's go. Might as well make the most of it."

I'm beyond titillated with the fancy ride, the champagne, and the tiramisu Finn's carrying, which we were too full to eat at the fancy restaurant. This is better than my birthday dinner by far. A make-up evening that was worth waiting for. I feel like a princess. I'm being treated like a prin—

No.

A queen.

The driver opens the door, takes my hand, and kisses the back of it before he helps me into the vehicle. It's awkwardly charming, but I'm soaking it all up. How often do I get to ride in a limo down the Vegas Strip?

I've been in a limo before, but not like this one. The plush leather seats are grouped together with a small table in between. There are built-in compartments for champagne on ice. There's even a slim, elegant throw rug in the center of the vehicle.

"Good grief, Finn."

"It's normally for VIP events," Finn responds, ducking his head into the limo. "When Rue 52 hosts celebrity receptions or dinners."

"*Oooh*, and what exactly do VIPs do in the back of a limo in Las Vegas?" I pump my eyebrows at Finn. I meant it as a joke, but his lips tighten into a flat line before he licks them.

"Want to find out?"

Honestly, I don't know. I don't respond, just play dumb and shrug, but I know exactly what the look on Finn's face means. Straightening up, he converses with the driver with the vehicle door wide open.

He fishes out his wallet and hands the driver a hundred-dollar bill. "This is to keep the partition up for the entire ride." To my surprise, he hands the driver another bill. "This is to take the long way home." Finn hands him a final bill. "This is to never, ever put your lips on my date again. Clear?"

"Yes, sir," the driver says. "Should I..." He holds out the bottle of champagne and points inside the limo with his thumb.

"No, I'll take it from here. Thank you."

Finn slides into the vehicle and climbs over me, purposely rubbing his legs against mine as the driver shuts the door behind him. He sets down our takeout and deposits the bottle of champagne into the ice bucket but makes no moves to open it or fetch the glasses nestled on the built-in rack. The minute he settles back into the seat beside me, his hand finds my upper thigh, uncovered due to the deep slit in my dress.

"Why do you keep doing that?"

"What?" he asks, his eyes on my chest. The limo rumbles to life and I hear the sound of a blinker, but we don't budge. Looking through the tinted windows, traffic is bumper to bumper. It'll be a while before we can start our trek home, unless some gracious vehicle halts and makes room for this extended limousine.

"With Angelo and then the driver...you keep acting really protective. Like we're actually dating. Why?"

Finn's answer is simple. "Because it turns you on."

I scrunch my brows. "What?"

He smirks. "Not just you. Most women." He rubs up and down my thigh, the heel of his palm pressing against my skin so hard it begins to redden. "There's something about a man who's protective of his girl that just gets women all kinds of wet. This entire dinner has been foreplay, Avery."

I clear my throat and give him an unimpressed stare. "I realize that me asking you to teach me how to have good sex makes me seem easy, but I don't consider feeding me *foreplay*."

"Really?" Finn's brow quirks in confusion. "So it doesn't turn you on when I make every excuse to touch you in public? When I turn down every other woman in the room and keep my eyes only on you? It's not sexy when I'm willing to break a man's jaw for thinking he has a chance with the beautiful woman who showed up on my arm?" His hand moves farther up my leg and then slides between my thighs. Instinctively, I press my legs together harder, but his large, strong fingers wedge between them. "Spread your legs, Avery. I've been a gentleman all night. It's time for my reward." His voice seems to drop an octave as he whispers in my ear.

Hesitantly, I do as I'm told. I'm not hesitating because I'm nervous. I'm hesitating because Finn is inebriating and I'm going to let him fuck me in this limo. The way my breath is ragged and the adrenaline is pooling between my thighs...it's a done deal. But I'm taking a moment to brace myself because Finn is bringing out my inner freak. I've never met her before. What if I meet her and I like her? What if she wants to hang around? What if she only shows up for Finn? What happens when I tell her that she can't keep him...he's not mine...this is a game...between friends...

"So, tell me, are you wet for me?"

"Soaked," I respond.

His lips turn down as he gives me an impressed head nod. "That dirty talk is coming along nicely."

I give him half a chuckle, and then he's back to business. "Show me."

"Like..." *Wait...huh*? "How do I show you that?"

Finn holds up his index finger.

I squint one eye. "You want to finger me?"

He shakes his head, wearing a smug smile. "No, I want *you* to finger yourself."

My inner freak goes dormant, and I'm suddenly on the brink of nervous chattering again. The uncomfortable pang in my chest goes from aroused to nervous in an instant. "Well...what are *you* going to do?"

"What do you think?" he snarks. "*Watch*."

The limo finally lurches forward, pulling into traffic. Finn removes his hand, rises as best as he can in a covered vehicle, and moves to sit on the adjacent bench seat. He settles in his seat, his hungry eyes trailing over my body. "Come on, Avery. We're on a time limit now. Show me how you touch yourself. Don't even think about lying by saying you don't do it. Mason didn't satisfy you a day in your life. Show me what you've been doing in private for four years."

"Is this um...another lesson?" I ask stupidly. I'm just buying time, hoping my bravado catches up. I've never masturbated for a man before, let alone in the back of a moving vehicle. Hot or wrong? Sexy or degrading? Delicious or embarrassing? *I don't know.* "Is this what men like?"

Finn shrugs as he bites down on his lower lip. "It's what I like."

I'm torn between my self-respect and burning desire to do what Finn likes.

He's been sweet all night. I talked. He listened. He's been patient and playful, protective and proud...he—*oh*.

I get it.

The foreplay.

He's been priming me all night, acting like such a gentleman. Now he's asking because he knows he deserves to get what he wants. There's no other way to see it. He earned it. *The clever bastard.*

Yanking my panties to the side with my pinky, I trail my middle finger against my crease. I look anywhere but at Finn. "Like this?" I mutter.

"You look a little uncomfortable," Finn says.

"*Because I am.*"

"Why?" he asks.

The answer is obvious. I'm on display. But why does that bother me? All Finn has done is praise and worship my body. The bulge in his pants right now is telling me his feelings aren't all lip service. *What do I want from him? No. What do I want from me?*

It's permission.

To enjoy this.

To get from this what I want. To be selfish and think about what the fuck it is that I need. I watch Finn's chest rise and fall. It's clear he's trying to control his breath. He's got both hands half tucked underneath his thighs, securing them as if he doesn't trust them. What if, for just a moment in time, I let myself believe that a man who looks like Finn is turned on by a woman like me?

I slip my longest finger into my slit. Feeling my own wet heat, I swivel my finger around until my arousal coats my entire finger. Holding my middle finger in the air, I say, "See? Wet."

"Holy shit," Finn says as he dips his head and rakes his hand through his hair. "I didn't actually think you were going to do it." He smiles. "Such a good student."

"Are you coming back over here?" I pat the seat next to me with my unoccupied hand.

"No. Please, for the love of God, Avery, do it again." His eyes are burning, pleading, desperate...the way I imagine women look at him. I consider my response as I float right out of my body and become a woman far bolder than I've ever been.

"Once I start, I don't know if I can stop."

Finn lets out a low, shaky breath. "Good. All the way. Let me see how you make yourself come."

The funny part is that the logistics are a well-rehearsed dance. How many times did I have to take care of myself when Mason finished and didn't bother to ask if I was okay? How many times did I get myself off fantasizing about my boyfriend fucking me somewhere, *anywhere* other than the bed in the pitch-dark? How many times did I wish a man wanted me so damn much that missionary wouldn't satisfy the craving? That he'd need more... deeper...wilder.

That man is right in front of me, watching me finger myself until I forget to care. I forget to be embarrassed. I forget about any and everything except finding my release as I slip my finger in deeper, over and over, trailing my slippery arousal over my clit. I hike up my knee and press my heel into the edge of my seat when I feel the pressure of pleasure building. The heat saturates my skin and goose bumps rise as my body tenses.

"Good girl, Avery. You look so fucking good. You have no idea how turned on I am..."

Finn's words are garbled like he's watching the show underwater. I stay focused on his eyes. His eyes, which are normally the lightest shade of baby blue, look like coal as they fixate between my thighs. I hike up my other heel and widen my thighs in a deep V, unashamed at how exposed I am.

I'm so close. I tickle the tip of my clit, tensing at the ticklish sensation, but I need something more to push me over the edge.

"Finn...say something..."

"Say what, baby?"

"Anything." My head hits the back of my seat as my orgasm teases me, bubbling to the surface and then dropping back below. *I need something.* His hands? His tongue? His dick? Maybe one thing even more tempting...*his heart.* "Tell me this means something. Even though we're just friends. Tell me I'm safe and you care."

"Don't fucking stop," he says as he crosses the space between us at record speed. His lips smash against mine as he embraces me the best he can in this position. I whimper into his mouth as I come, twitching and trembling in his arms as he pins me tightly in place. The blinding pleasure has barely subsided before Finn's passionate kisses turn soft and tender, just light pecks beneath my ear and down my neck. "I care about you, Avery." He kisses the tip of my nose. "This means something."

I smile and nod into his neck. "Thank you."

"That was really hot."

I chuckle, my breath hitting his skin. "It's despicable, Finn," I say teasingly. "You made me wait for dinner, didn't book a limo, and you made me do all the work back here?" I tut my tongue.

"If you think what you just did was work, then you have no idea how I fuck."

I poke my tongue out at him. It suddenly dawns on me that the vehicle is stopped. *How long have we been stopped?* "Are we home?"

Finn nods slowly.

"How long?"

"A while. You were really getting into it... You were pretty loud back here."

My skin shrinks around my face, the reality of shame washing over me. "So basically, I shouldn't make eye contact with the driver?"

Finn nods, trying to hold in his laughter. "Probably wise." Releasing me, he scoots over to the door and pushes it wide open. After stepping out first, he holds his hand out for me. I adjust my panties, smooth out my dress, and collect my clutch before grabbing our takeout bag and the fancy bottle of champagne. I have to scoot awkwardly to the edge of the limo with my hands full and my clutch tucked beneath my arm.

Finn relieves me of the bottle and takeout bag, securing my hand in his. I love when he does this. What man likes to hold hands? I thought it was just for show at the restaurant, but here we are in the privacy of our neighborhood. With butterflies in my chest, I feel like a teenager again.

"My place or yours?" Finn asks, leading me to the right, toward his home.

"Wait." I pull back. "My place. I have to turn down aquarium lights so the fish can rest."

"God forbid the fish lose a night of sleep," Finn grumbles.

"Hey, how would you feel if the sun rose and never set, hm? It'd be jarring. Plus, I made a promise to Dex to take care of what matters to him. I take my commitments seriously."

"Fine," Finn says. "I suppose location doesn't matter anyway. Are you ready?"

"For what?" We pause under the porch as the limo driver pulls away from the house. Finn leans against the doorframe as I fish for my keys.

"To find out what real work means."

My eyes snap to his face.

His sexy smile grows. "Open the door, Avery, and take your dress off. It's time for class."

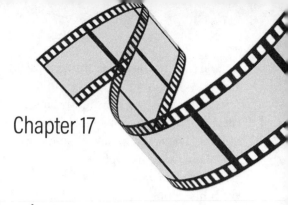

Chapter 17

Avery

Finn looks impatient as he watches me come down the stairs. I thought he'd follow me to the bedroom when I went to adjust the aquarium lights, but he stayed behind in the living room. Perhaps he wants to talk first. It's probably a good idea to establish some ground rules anyway. I lost my mind a little in the limo, all but asking him to hold me through my orgasm. The only flaw to my grand master plan is that I'm having trouble separating emotional and physical feelings when it comes to sex.

The bottom line is they go hand in hand. Affection...safety... love... I'm realizing these are all things necessary to have a completely fulfilling experience. Therefore, with Finn, I'm going to have to find a way to accept the missing pieces of our situation.

"Finn, I think we should lay down some ground rules—"

"*Hush.*"

"Excuse me?"

Finn rises from the couch and reaches for my hand. I hold it out playfully, like a queen to a loyal subject, but there's nothing proper about the way Finn yanks me into his body so hard, I crash into his chest with an audible thud. *Oof.*

"How about we play a little rough tonight and see if you like it?"

"Rough?" I mutter, still smashed against his pecs as he grabs the hem of my dress, pulling it upward.

"Nothing crazy. But I bet you'll like it if I take control."

I nod as I raise my arms so he can pull my swanky, sleek dress up and over my head. He tosses it aside, well out of reach. "Okay, I'm in. What should I do?" Glancing to my right, I see my fish friend Cherry doing her nightly laps. I don't know why it comforts me, but it does. The world is still spinning. Everything is okay. I'm still me. The crazy, lonely, old maid who talks to fish and yet...

Finn wants it rough.

"You do everything I tell you to. Don't think. Just do it." He trails his thumb over one of my cheeks. "And don't be nervous. I'm not going to hurt you. *I'd never.* But I'm going to boss you around and show you how I like it. Just tell me to stop if you're not happy."

"Okay," I say, cursing myself when my voice cracks.

"Avery?" Finn drops his head and finds my eyes. "I'm serious. If you're unhappy at any point, tell me. I'll take you upstairs to the bed, turn off the lights, and we'll do this in whatever way makes you the most comfortable, okay?"

I keep my eyes locked on his. *Deep breath.* "I don't want comfortable, Finn. I want *hot.*"

His hands expertly unclasp my bra strap, which is no easy feat. This strapless bra is reinforced with eight clasps. It's effectively a corset, but it doesn't slow Finn down one bit. My breasts have barely popped free before his mouth engulfs one nipple, while he rolls the other between his thumb and forefinger. I gasp at the sensation. One side of my chest is warm and wet. The other is teased and taunted, my right nipple becoming angry and rock-hard between his fingers.

"Oh *God,*" I moan as he switches. My tortured nipple is instantly comforted against his warm tongue, while the other is completely unprepared for the almost painful pleasure.

"Fuck, Avery," Finn growls as he suddenly rises and yanks down my underwear. "I'm sorry. I can't even do the foreplay. I'm so turned on right now. I need you." He yanks my hand over the hard bulge in his pants. "You're going to take good care of me, right?"

I nod obediently. *Desperately.* More than anything, I want to take *good* care of Finn. While I unbuckle his belt, Finn undoes his shirt, making me more and more crazed as each button pops free.

"Get on the couch," he commands. "On your hands and knees."

The flit in my chest turns into an aching pound when he talks to me like that. Domineering. Impatient. *Needy for me.* I make a mental note for future reference, I kind of like it when a man growls at me like that. It makes me want to growl back.

I position myself on the couch, grateful that at night we only have the low lights on. Finn can see everything...just under a hazy, flattering ambiance. The brightest part of the room is the blueish glow of the aquarium, but it barely touches us from the couch.

Finn situates himself behind me after ditching his pants and briefs. He slides the tip of his dick up and down, against my crease, and I have to bite down on my upper arm. *Goddamn, that feels good.* Flesh against flesh. Slick, wet, wanting... *So. Damn. Good.*

But I squeal when he nudges forward, the tip barely in. "Ah!" The invasion is overwhelming. Not like this. It won't fit like this. I know he feels it too.

"*Shit, baby,*" Finn says in a hiss as he rips away. "You're way too tight like this." Clutching my waist, Finn flips me over. His smile is haughty and amused. He pushes my knees apart, scooting forward between my spread thighs, and that's when I see his full erection for the first time.

I gawk. In horror. *What the actual fuck? He just tried to put that in me?*

"You've never been stretched properly a day in your life, have you?" Finn asks, seeming to enjoy my shocked expression.

"Maybe I just snap back." I'm surprised my wits are still about me. My brain was wiped clean when I saw the mammoth proportions he's packing. I don't see his dick as fun at the moment...only terrifying. It's not the length I'm worried about most. Although that'll be worrisome in time. For now, it's the girth. Why does that look like a penis and a half?

Finn scoffs. "You're not going to snap back from this, baby. You're going to wear my cock like a glove, and no man will compare for the rest of your life."

Yeah, that's exactly what I'm worried about.

"Hold your knees," he demands.

I plead with him first. "Finn, in all seriousness, go slow. I feel like I need an epidural to take you. I...just... Please don't get carried away and hurt me."

His brooding, bossy demeanor instantly deflates. "Oh hey now," he murmurs as his eyes soften. "Come on, I would never." He leans forward and caresses my shoulders then proceeds to massage them for a brief moment. "Relax, Avery. I got you. I've had a big cock my entire adult life. I know how to do this." He touches his lips against mine. "You're going to love it," he says, his breath warming my lips. "I'll stop if you don't."

"Okay." I grab my knees, pulling my legs out of his way. He wets the tip of his thumb and rubs little circles around my clit. Instantly, I'm at ease. The warm flood of pleasure seeps through my bones, and just as he says, I relax. He enters so slow, so smooth, that the pressure is nothing but welcome. I feel myself adjust with ease as he continues to stimulate my most sensitive area, so much in fact that when Finn is finally as deep as he can go, my eyes roll into the back of my head as my orgasm crescendos. I cry out so loud, I startle myself, throwing my hand over my mouth as I explode on his dick.

"There it is. Scream for me, baby," Finn groans as he abandons my little button and squeezes the insides of my thighs. He doesn't move, just closes his eyes and enjoys the electric waves of my release. "You're so damn tight, I can *feel* when you're coming."

I'm immediately wiped, ready to tuck under the covers and sleep this exhausting, senseless sensation off, but Finn's just getting started.

"Are you comfortable? It doesn't hurt?"

"Not at all." I'm pushed almost past my limits, but it isn't painful. I just feel full, like he's touching every part of me that's been neglected for so long.

"Good." He rips out of me and sits back on the couch. "Climb on top. I want to get deeper."

Fuck. This I don't like. I blink at him, trying to think of an excuse.

"Now," he adds sternly, returning to his prior assertive attitude.

I'm awkward as I straddle his lap, trying to widen my legs so all my weight is on my knees. There's half an inch between his thighs and mine, and I try desperately to suspend myself in midair.

"What the hell are you doing? Have you never been on top before?" Finn asks, trying to figure out why I'm tense and grimacing like I'm in the middle of a workout as I try to hover over him without letting him feel my full weight. I decide to be honest. That's what we're doing here. Finn is my safe space, and even if this is embarrassing, it's not forever...

"I'm not exactly a size two, Finn. I'm trying not to put my weight on you. I don't want to squish you."

He groans in frustration as he positions himself at my entrance and then pushes out my knees on either side, throwing me off balance. I literally fall onto his dick, wincing as he fills me to the brim. Grabbing my ass, he pulls me tighter into his lap, my thighs melded with his, our hips interlocked.

"Stop it," he whispers in my ear then lets out a low moan of satisfaction. "Put your weight on me," he growls. "I fucking love how it feels. If you want to enjoy your sex life, you have to stop apologizing for your body. It's beautiful. Exactly what I like. Your ex couldn't handle it, so he didn't deserve it."

It's like he's a pussy whisperer. Every time he talks to me like that, confidence emerges from a place deep inside me that I'm still unfamiliar with. He coaxes her out. He makes me feel brave, wild, and beautiful. So I grind on him. I kiss and nip at his neck while he praises me for riding his cock. His appreciative groans drive me to unhinge, and I forget about being self-conscious. I forget that he outmatches me in appearance. I completely forget that this whole arrangement is bizarre. I ride him like a savage, taking his dick like it was made for me. All that's going through my head is how much I want to see what he looks like when he comes.

"Oh, baby, *good girl*. What do you need lessons for, hm? You ride cock perfectly."

My eyes are closed, but I smile as he gently wraps his large hand around my throat.

"Go ahead," I mumble between raspy breaths. "I'm curious." Finn can choke me. Finn can do anything he wants to me. I'll love it. It's dangerous how much power he has over me right now.

"Not tonight, Avery. I'm too close." To my utter shock, he scoops me up, his forearms tucked under my thighs as he stands, lifting me in the air.

"What're you doing?" I squawk in alarm, but I don't wriggle down like I want to, for fear of toppling him. Sitting on top of him was a concern. Him carrying me like this is mortifying. What if he breaks his back?

But Finn doesn't even hesitate. He carries me across the living room with ease, still nestled into my sopping crease, and presses my back against the aquarium tank. The cool glass shocks every inch of my skin.

"*Ah*! Wait, Finn, we're not supposed to touch the glass."

"Ask me if I care right now," he growls in my ear as he thrusts into me, hard.

"But the fish—"

"They'll live," he mutters as he presses me firmly against the tank, pinning me with his body so his right hand is free to elevate one of my knees. He sucks in his lips as he scours my chest then leans back slightly as he dips his head so he can see where he's entered me. It dawns on me why he put me against the aquarium. It's the glow of the tank. Finn's visual. He wants to see it. Fucking me isn't enough. His eyes are hungry too.

"I think it's jarring for them. It's something about the vibra—"

"Avery," he interrupts. "Enough about the fish. Just let me fuck you, *please*." He thrusts into me like a madman while my ass and back are smashed against the aquarium. I toggle between, *I'm so sorry, Cherry,* and *oh dear God, yes, harder, Finn,* in my mind over and over. I'm shocked at his stamina. He holds me, fucks me, and kisses me all in tandem until his panting gets louder. The beads of sweat on his forehead drip down to my chest, mixing with my own. We're so slippery. Back and forth, slipping right into each other, holding on for dear life.

"Where can I come?"

I wrap my hands around his cheeks. "Wherever you want."

"Can I ruin your makeup?"

My chuckle is breathy between pants. "It's already smeared, I'm sure."

Finn stops pumping his hips and looks right into my eyes. "It's an expression. I want to come on your pretty face."

Oh. Another unknown. A new lesson. Never once did Mason ask me for this. "Um, yes. Okay. How do I—"

"On your knees, get low," Finn barks. "Open your mouth."

I debate telling him I've never tasted cum before. Precum, unintentionally sure, but I never let Mason finish in my mouth. He never asked, and I never offered. But with Finn, I welcome it. He makes me feel so damn good. I'm grateful for how powerful he makes me feel. Whatever Finn wants, I'll gleefully give.

He strokes his massive member a few times as he watches my eyes. I bat my eyelashes at him and poke out my tongue the way I've seen women do in videos. They act like they're thirsty for it, and I try my best to mirror the sentiment. It works. He growls in pleasure as the warm, thick spray coats my cheek and dribbles over the corner of my lips. He misses my open mouth, maybe on purpose as a courtesy, but curiosity gets the best of me, so I run my tongue over my bottom lip and taste the salty tang. I'm not ridiculous. It isn't gourmet, but it is deliciously satisfying to see how impressed with me he looks at the moment.

"You're full of surprises." Using his thumb, Finn carefully wipes away a droplet of his release that is dangerously close to my eye. "And you are so beautiful, Queen."

I love when he calls me that. I'm naked, on my knees, Finn's cum coating my face, and yet—*I do.* I feel like a goddamn queen.

He makes his way to the kitchen and wets a handful of paper towels. I hold out my hand when he returns to me, but he insists on cleaning me up himself. "Was that weird?" he asks as he wipes underneath my eye, then my cheek, and then finally my lips. He drags the warm paper towel underneath my chin one more time, ensuring he's thoroughly cleaned me up.

"Which part? When we traumatized the fish or when you finished on my face?"

Finn laughs. "I'm not worried about the fish. The latter... I won't do it again if it bothers you." He taps my nose.

"It doesn't bother me." *At all.* I like thinking that Finn wants to be kinky with me. Maybe he can get something worthwhile out of this part of the deal too.

Finished cleaning me up, Finn balls the paper towel in his fist, but he doesn't rise. His eyes turn down, a touch of sadness coating them as he scours my face. "It's such a shame."

"What is?"

"How he treated you."

"Mason?" I ask, and Finn nods in response. "He honestly wasn't bad to me until he broke up with—"

"Yes," Finn interrupts, an angry edge in his voice. "Yes, he was an idiot. Lesson numbe...whatever number we're on. Don't ever forgive him for being in the presence of royalty and refusing to bow. You're sexy, smart, kind, and loyal. You should be *earned* every day of your life. Don't ever let any man make you question that."

I inhale, my chest rising. I hold my breath for a moment before I release it. "You're supposed to be giving me sex advice. Not advice on matters of the heart."

Finn stands, then cups his hands underneath my elbows, helping me to my feet. "They're *one and the same*. For a girl like you, Avery, sex and matters of the heart are one and the same."

I'm honestly not sure if his words are a compliment or a warning, but either way, I'm two skips past uncomfortable. All I want to do is curl into bed, Finn by my side. I can visualize waking up together to coffee and leftover tiramisu for breakfast. I am picturing all sorts of scenarios that are not just gratuitous sex, and

I need to stop before I cross a line I can't come back from.

Finn is pulling on his briefs when he says, "I need to lock up my house and set the security alarm, and then I'll come back. Why don't you take a hot shower, and I'll meet you in bed in a bit?"

That sounds amazing. *Too amazing.* "I think you should sleep at your place."

He raises his brows at me. "I don't mind staying. I wasn't going to fuck you and leave."

"I know, I know." I cross my arms around my bare chest, feeling a little self-conscious again. "You're a good guy, Finn. Believe me, I get it." I wink at him to try to lighten the mood. There's no way I can tell him that if he sleeps over, if he keeps taking me to dinner, if he keeps telling me all the ways he thinks I'm wonderful, and how it's not my fault Mason fell short...I'm going to fall in love with this man. It's going to hurt like hell when he doesn't fall in love with me back. "But this is the first time I've been single in almost half a decade. I am enjoying sleeping alone again. I need space."

"Oh, okay." He crosses the space between us and kisses my forehead, easily believing my lie. "Yeah, I understand. I liked sleeping alone when Nora and I broke up too. For a while, anyway. Just let me know if that ever changes." He pulls on his pants but doesn't fasten his belt. He drapes his shirt over his back and pushes his arms through the sleeves, but he doesn't button it up. Finn looks like the quintessential male version of a walk of shame.

I wish him a good night, promising him I'll let him know if I change my mind and want him to come back. It's the first time I've had sex with a new man in a very long time. Finn's doubting my ability to process this in the moment. He leaves me his number, convinced I might change my mind in the middle of the night.

And I think I have. But I won't say it.

I should be crying over Mason, not swooning over Finn. I should be in California dealing with my problems, not living in this fantasy I somehow looped Finn into. I should be more worried about my business and Legacy Resorts and probably shouldn't be having amazing sex on my favorite client's couch.

But Finn's right.

My mind is changing. *I'm changing.* After getting a taste of how I should be treated, I'm no longer going to settle for seeing myself as undeserving. It's time to ask for what I want and demand what I need.

I'm turning it around. *Starting right now.*

Thirty will indeed be my golden fucking year after all.

Chapter 18

Finn

I reach across my nightstand and flip over my phone to check the time and my nonexistent missed calls. *One fifteen in the morning. Well, shit.* I wildly misjudged that. I really thought she'd call. I left Avery my number but didn't grab hers.

Best sex of my life.

And I didn't grab her number.

And plus, I'm her...*what*? Sex coach? Friend? Client? All of the above. I'm also the guy who's more into this arrangement than I should be.

It's simple really. Avery is open about her insecurities and asks questions because yes, maybe she trusts my so-called expertise in the bedroom, but she's also very clearly written me off. She can't fathom that I'd want her when it comes to a real relationship. *She's dead wrong.* Would I spook her if I told her that I'd never been that hard during sex before and I *really* wanted to stay the night? I left like it was nothing, but it fucking bothered me. Would she snap closed like a bear trap if I told her I really like her and she's sort of restoring my faith in genuine connections?

Here's the problem—I like Avery because we can talk. I would bet the last dollar in my pocket that if I told her I was legitimately into her, she'd turn into the rest of them. Overcompensating, paranoid, defensive, and possessive. It happens every single time. What I have with Avery is perfect because it's riskless. All reward... Okay, *mostly reward*. We should be in the same bed right now. That's the next lesson I'm going to teach her. After great sex, you fall asleep next to each other then wake up at one fifteen in the morning and do it again—

Buzz. Buzz.

Well, speak of the damn devil. My phone subtly vibrates, and my prayers are answered. A little later than I expected, but hell, I'll take whatever Avery's willing to give at this point.

Looking at my screen, I see it's an unsaved number, an area code I don't recognize.

"Hey, you," I answer with a wide smile on my face. "Change your mind?"

"Finn?"

I nearly choke when I hear the voice on the other end of the line. Shooting up in bed, I pull the sheet over my lap, trying to cover up like I got caught naked. This seems to be my default around Nora. I've done nothing wrong, but I'm always jumpy. "Nora?"

"Change my mind about what?"

I suck in a slow breath. *I could hang up. I should just fucking hang up.* But I loved this woman for years. Never once in all that time did I treat her poorly. When I ended things, I asked her for civility. Maybe I shouldn't provoke her. "Nothing, I thought you were someone else. Did you get a new number?"

"Yeah. I'm on Morgan's plan. Who's calling you in the middle of the night, Finn?" Her tone grows cool, and my jaw twitches with agitation.

It's not your business who's calling me at any time of the day or night.

"Apparently you. Why are you calling me this late? Is it an emergency?"

"I had to wait until..." She trails off.

"Until Morgan fell asleep?" Who am I kidding? Of course they're living together. Nora can't stand the idea of living alone. "If he doesn't want you calling me, then you shouldn't be calling me. I have to go—"

"*Wait.* Finn, please. I'm just calling to apologize. I know he called you. If he was an ass, I'm sorry. He's so...so...controlling. He shouldn't have called."

I press the speaker button and toss my phone on the bed. It sinks into the down comforter about a quarter inch. This duvet is overly fluffy and not my taste. Nora picked it out. I need to get rid of this thing.

"*You* shouldn't be apologizing for him. And it's not a big deal. I cleared it up, but just so you know, he thinks you're cheating on him—"

"I'm not."

"I didn't ask if you were. I simply said he thinks you are. Whatever you two are going through, leave me out of it this time."

I hear a door creak open and click closed on her end. I imagine her tiptoeing out of her apartment, well out of earshot. She's silent except for the sound of her shoes clicking against iron stairs. When she's finally reached her destination, she says in a huff, "I'm trying, but I...I just don't love him, Finn. I've been trying really hard to move on, but I miss you."

"Nora, stop—"

"*No, please,*" she pleads. "Finn, I swear I can do better. I've been working on myself. All the things you said, all the *awful* things you called me out for...you were right. *You are right.* I've been reading some books about anxiety and how sometimes people who come from bad childhoods can kind of project their insecurities—"

"Nora." One word silences her. It's my tone. Flat. Unconvinced.

"Please? Can we just meet? For coffee? It's been a long time. People can change and grow up... I want to show you that I can be a different person for you."

Nora's easier to deal with when she's being unreasonable and cruel. It makes sense to walk away. But every time she's about to cry, my natural instincts kick in. My primal urge to *fix it* and *make it better* gets the best of me. So instead of hanging up, like I should, I do what I've been trying and failing at for years—I try to explain.

"It never bothered me that you had anxiety or insecurities.

What bothered me is how you treated me. What bothered me is how I was paying for mistakes I never made. I treated you with respect, love, and patience from the very beginning, and for some reason you punished me for it. Maybe if I'd been an outright dick to you, you would've respected me back."

"I know," she whispers. "I wasn't in control of—"

"Nora."

"*Finn*," she says through a sniffle. "I'm not happy. You're the only one who makes me happy, and I will do better. I will treat you better. I promise. We don't have to rush. Can we *just* meet up and talk?"

For once when it comes to Nora, my head and my heart are in the same place. "No. Listen to me. If you don't love Morgan, leave him. But if the reason you're unhappy is because you're holding on to the idea of us...*don't*. We're not going back to our awful relationship. I'm sorry. It's time to move forward, and us together is not the future."

I exhale and rub my hands over my face. *Thank you, Avery.* I needed to know that talking to a woman doesn't have to be painful, full of miscommunications and misunderstandings. I should look forward to a call, not dread it. I should be laughing more often than trying to hold back my anger.

The line is silent for a while before she speaks again. I can feel the atmosphere shift. I can picture her eyes narrow and her hand on her hip as her tone turns frigid. "You're seeing someone." She says it like an accusation.

I'm silent. *Just hang up, Finn. This is a textbook trap.*

"Did you hear me?" she asks, her tone still icy.

"I did."

"Well, are you?"

I carefully compose my words. "Whether I am or not doesn't change anything I just said."

"*Who*?" Nora asks in what can only be described as a hiss.

"Why? So you can put a target on her back?"

"No. I just want to know who is so *damn great* that they'd

make you close the door on us. How could you just move on like—"

I howl in irritation. "Are you fucking kidding me with this hypocrisy? You're living with Morgan. You're on his cell phone plan. Of all the dudes you could pull—*Morgan*? After what we went through?"

"It's not like—"

"Stop. We've been broken up for almost a year now. Yes, I'm seeing someone. Yes, I'm really into her. No, I won't tell you who. There's nothing left to accuse me of."

"I've been trying to call you for months, Finn. It takes a new number for you to even answer your phone? You left me and *broke* me. You didn't keep any of the fucking promises you made. I actually thought you loved me."

I ignore the tug in my chest. "The gaslighting is old, Nora. You say you've changed, but this is exactly the shit I left behind. We're not together. I *care* about you. I want good things for you. But I don't love you anymore." I blow out another breath, trying to calm my rising blood pressure. When the heat of my frustration subsides a little, I add, "Look, we're better apart. End of story. I'm happier now."

"You're a goddamn liar. You're never going to stop thinking about me. Just like I'm never going to stop thinking about you. You can act like you don't care, but you are never going to love someone the way you loved me."

"Yeah, I hope not. That love almost destroyed me."

"Fuck you, Finn. I hate you," she says through sobs before she abruptly hangs up.

They aren't crocodile tears. They're legitimate. Nora's furious enough to cry when she doesn't get her way and she loses control of a situation. It used to work on me. I'd see her wet eyes and the tear-stained cheeks on her pretty face, and I'd completely forget I wasn't the one in the wrong. That kind of love is dangerous. Blinding. Manipulative. It will steal a man's soul. I barely escaped with mine. I'm not risking it again.

One thirty-two a.m. Dammit. I'm up now.

I pull off the covers and swing my legs around, my feet hitting the wood floor with a soft thud. This house always sounds so hollow at night. Every step I take toward the kitchen echoes loudly off the walls.

Opening the fridge, I decide on an Alaskan Amber. I grab the magnetic bottle opener from the fridge door, and I've barely popped the top on my beer when I hear the faintest knock at the front door. It's past one in the morning. Either this is Avery or the politest burglar in the world.

Pausing by the security alarm, I disarm the front door and open it to see Avery, her hair in its usual disarray. She's wearing pajama shorts and a tight tank top that's so long it hugs the outward curve of her womanly hips. I never thought I had a type before, but fuck, do I like her full hourglass figure. I love how she feels in my hands, like her body was made as my personal playground. Why is she so confused about how enticing she is?

Avery holds out my sports coat and speaks before I can. "You're up."

I can't help my smug smile. "I tried to sleep. A call woke me up. Not *your* call, which was a little disappointing." I lean against the doorframe, and she takes a tiny step backward, still holding my jacket out. "This might be better, though."

"I'm crazy for bothering you this late, but you forgot your suit jacket. I wasn't sure if you'd need it tomorrow."

I cock an eyebrow. "For what?"

She sucks in her lips, her cheeks flushing. "You know...for like meetings or...meetings." She snorts in laughter at her lame excuse as I take the jacket from her and toss it behind me. It hits the floor with a clank, the metal buttons meeting the hard floor.

"What's up, Avery? Do you want to come in?" I hold out my hand, but she doesn't take it. She only shakes her head and shrugs.

"The last time I had sex outside of a relationship is when I was seventeen. It was so awkward, I was happy to leave for college and never see him again."

I nod along, unsure of where this is going. "Okay."

"I'm not a hookup kind of girl, so this is new. Everything is new. I thought I was okay, but I couldn't sleep. Tonight was..."

I raise my brows fully, feeling my forehead crinkle. "How was it?"

"Physically? Spectacular. By far the best I've ever had... But my heart feels a little empty right now. I guess I wanted to come by and ask you for more advice."

"Being?" I scour her eyes, looking for a clue. *Is she okay? Is this too much, too soon?*

"Does it go away? How many hookups until sex doesn't feel so...hollow?"

If you'd just take my hand and come upstairs, get under the covers with me, let me hold you, you'd know... It wasn't just a hookup. "Honestly?" I let out a breathy, humorless chuckle. "I'll let you know. According to my research so far, it's a lot."

She rolls her eyes. "Ah, dammit."

I want her to come inside, but I know if I close the space between us, she'll just back farther away. I have to play this carefully. I don't even know what I'm playing for. Let's say Avery and I give it a go...we'd be on a timeline. One summer to decide if we're the real deal. That's a lot of pressure for two people with broken hearts. Avery's wounds are fresh. Mine are older, but they never really healed.

"Is that what you're looking for?"

"Hm?" she asks, lifting her eyes to match my intense stare.

"Hookups? I thought you were a relationship kind of girl. Are you wanting to explore your options when you go back to California?"

Her laugh is bitter, mixed with a scoff like I said something ridiculous. "I just want to have options, Finn." She points to my chest, then to hers. "We are different. You walk into a bar and you see options. I walk into a bar and just hope I'm even seen. It's why..." She takes another little step backward as her eyes drop once more.

"Why what?" *Don't stop. Talk to me... Just come inside.*

"Why I fell in love with Mason. He was the first guy to ever really see me. He was the only man to ever pick me over Palmer. It's hard to look past her. She's stunning, obviously—"

"She's attractive, I'll admit," I interrupt.

Avery bobs her head, pretending like my statement doesn't offend her. How many times has she been passed over while her best friend gobbled up the attention?

"But I think you put more stock in that than you should..."

"Huh?" Her face screws up in confusion.

Ah, fuck it. I take a large step forward through my doorway. My bare toes nudge against the edge of her flip-flops.

"Real beauty isn't loud and demanding. It's subtle." I tuck a loose strand of her rich, dark hair behind her ear. "Men look past you because you represent what they're scared of. Palmer's the kind of attractive you enjoy for the night. You have the kind of beauty you worship for a lifetime."

She rolls her eyes and tries to step away, but I grab her by her shoulders.

"Stop that," I command.

Her eyes bulge. Clearly, my tone startles her. "Stop what?"

"New lesson. You want your love life to be satisfying, right?"

She simply nods in response.

"Then learn to take a compliment. Stop flinching every time I tell you you're beautiful." Hooking my finger under her chin, I slide my arm around her waist.

"What're you doing?" she asks in a whisper.

"Listen to me, okay?" Using my finger, I move her chin up and down, forcing her to nod. "Avery, look at me."

Her eyes lift, but she's trying to look over my shoulder. I'm not satisfied.

"*Hey*, I mean *really* look at me." I try to control my breathing, but my chest tightens when her misty green eyes lock on to mine. "I noticed *you* in the car that day. Not Palmer. You're *exactly* my kind of beautiful. I'm looking... I see you."

At first, I think my finger is shaking, but turns out Avery's chin is wobbling. "Okay," she mumbles.

Shaking my head, I lean in a little closer. My lips are almost touching hers. "If I were to tell you you're *great* at your job as a brand consultant, what would you say?"

"Thank you," she says without hesitation.

"Why?" I stroke my thumb across her soft, warm cheek, still holding her head up with my finger tucked under her chin.

"Because I know. I'm great at my job because I work really hard. It doesn't mean I can't get better, but I know I'm good."

"Exactly. So when I tell you you're beautiful..." I press my lips against hers. It's hardly a kiss. Just a curious, reassuring touch. "Just *know* it... Say thank you."

She finally smiles, understanding my message. But much to my dismay, she cradles my hand in both of hers before pulling it from her face. "Thank you, Finn. That was sweet." She drops my hand but doesn't pull away.

"What is it?" I study her clouded expression, her eyebrows angled, her thoughts clearly racing. It's a familiar look, and I can't quite put my finger on it.

"Maybe that's what went wrong with Mason. How could he want me if I didn't want myself? Maybe he would've complimented me more if I had just said *thank you*. I always used to brush him off and tell him he was only saying things to placate me."

I suddenly realize I recognize the look on her face. I used to wear it whenever Nora and I broke up. When we weren't together but I was still in love with her. Avery's not ready. They *just* broke up. *What was I thinking?* You don't forget four years in a couple of weeks.

"Maybe if I had talked to him more," Avery continues, "it wouldn't have ended like it did. Maybe I can learn to talk to men the way I can talk to you."

I touch my knuckle to my lips and ask the question that's been burning in my mind since the moment I met her. "Why do you talk to me like this? Why are you so at ease?"

She gives me a guarded smile as she lifts her shoulders.

"Because you're *Vegas*." She retreats. Taking one large step backward, she nearly falls off the concrete step. "Thanks for talking to me. I'm going to get some sleep. This week, I'm going to work on some design ideas for your website. I haven't forgotten my end of the deal. I'm going to do a really good job for you. We're going to make your business soar."

"Okay." I blow out a breath, hoping she hears my reluctance. *Don't go. You're already here. You wanted to see me...so stay.* "So I'll see you soon?"

She nods overenthusiastically. "Yes. I'll text you." She turns and scuttles down the concrete steps. I call out to her when she reaches the sidewalk.

"Avery, wait!"

She halts in place and pivots to face me in the doorway.

"You said I'm '*Vegas*.' What the hell does that mean?"

She holds her palms up and shrugs like it's obvious. "What happens in Vegas, Finn..."

Oh. I hide my annoyance as she waves and heads down the sidewalk. I wait on the stoop, watching her until I'm sure she's made it safely into Dex's house before I groan in annoyance.

Stays in Vegas. What happens in Vegas stays here. *Fuck.* That's why she's so willing to be vulnerable and open with me.

One summer. That's all she wants. *One fucking summer* to build up her confidence so she can go running right back to the man who doesn't see her.

Chapter 19

Avery

"Sorry I didn't call you back sooner, Aves. I've been so busy," Palmer exaggerates on the phone, drawing out all the syllables in her response. "The network is really interested but hasn't made a final decision, so the studio is just taking a chance and filming the first four episodes. It's literally been go-go-go. I haven't had a minute to myself."

I exhale into the phone, hoping she can hear my agitation. I'm silent for a moment as I snuggle into Dex's throw blanket, a steaming mug of coffee in one hand. Stalling, I watch Cherry swim her morning laps, back and forth. *I'm pissed.* That's the truth. I called Palmer after Finn and I had sex a couple of nights ago. I wanted to talk to my best friend. I wanted her to help me process all the mixed emotions I was having. She didn't answer. I texted Palmer that I needed her, and she left me on read for almost three days.

I'd understand if she was truly that busy, but she hasn't been too go-go-go to keep her entire social media following updated on her whereabouts and budding career. I already knew Palmer was filming more episodes...because of Instagram. Her thumbs must be too tired from name-dropping minor celebrities to push the call button and get back to her best friend of twenty years.

"How's filming?"

"I mean...this show is...*fine*. It's a good stepping-stone. But I'm ready for bigger things, you know?"

"After a week?"

"This industry moves fast," she chides. "People find fame overnight."

"I wasn't..." I release the air in my lungs, forcing my attitude out with it. "I want the best things in the world for you, friend. But I miss you. I've been calling..."

"Shit, I'm sorry. I know. I'm such a piece of shit. I'm just never alone. It's hard to find time to talk. I really miss you too, and I'm sorry I missed your call. I've been putting everything into this job, trying to network and get in good with the directors and some castmates, you know? Connections. I don't know what to do if it doesn't work out. Did I tell you my lease is up and the complex is raising rent again? I can't afford it anymore. If this show doesn't work out...I'm homeless."

I tut my tongue. "Homeless? Isn't that dramatic?"

"No, it's accurate."

"*I'm your home, goof.* You think I'd let you sleep on the street?"

She laughs into the phone. "You're about to be homeless too. We all know you're going to let Mason keep the apartment when summer's over."

I take a sip from my mug, annoyed at how well she knows me. It's not a crime to be noncombative. Plus, why would I want to live in an apartment haunted with memories of my failed relationship? "We can get a place again. It's been years since we've lived together."

Palmer breathes out into the phone. "What a way to ring in our thirties, right?" The last time Palmer and I lived together was before I moved in with Mason. We said parting ways was bittersweet. Our official entry into real adulthood. For me, my first live-in boyfriend. For Palmer, it was the first time she lived alone, period. She had to have three jobs and loans from her parents to get by, but still, she managed. We thought it was the end of an era. Turns out it was just a break.

"Are we regressing?" I chuckle softly. *Fuck. Are we...regressing?*

"Well, if I'm going to regress, it's going to be with you. I love you, Aves. And I'm so sorry I didn't call sooner. You said you needed to talk. What's up?"

My annoyance dissipates. Just like that, I'm hurtled back to high school when I used to confess my secret crushes to Palmer. The conversation would always be the same. I'd tell her who I liked. She'd insist she set me up because of course Palmer had all the boys at school wrapped around her pinky. I'd cry and plead that she leave it alone and let me *crush* in private...in peace. She'd never listen. Bold, brave Palmer, convinced I was the best thing since sliced bread, would chat me up to a guy, best intentions at heart...but it always ended up the same way. Me, rejected and humiliated, and Palmer getting asked out instead.

Eventually, I quit telling her who I liked.

But I suppose it's safe now. Finn has probably clued into the fact that I like him. I'm doing my best to keep the degree to which I like him under control so my heart and ovaries don't get carried away, but overall, our friendship is budding even faster than this fictitious romance I've created in my mind.

Finn texts me daily. *Always first.* Sometimes it's dirty stuff. My sexting is still awkward, but we're working on it. And sometimes Finn just texts me to send a funny GIF or to recommend something. I'm quickly learning all the things he likes—oat milk creamer, alkaline water only, and blending strawberries into *vanilla yogurt.* Not strawberry yogurt...vanilla yogurt mixed with ripe strawberry chunks. Apparently, there's a major difference. Finn might be more of a foodie than I can handle because my idea of fancy is plating a Hot Pocket instead of eating it from the microwaveable pouch.

"Remember my new neighbor?"

"Hot guy with tats?" Palmer asks in a chirp.

"Sure. 'Hot guy with tats' is Finn Harvey. He's a bit of a unicorn, Palmer. I've never met a guy so...*everything.*" I don't know how else to describe it. Finn is manly, sexy, and commanding at the perfect moments. Yet, his personality is that of a golden retriever. He's so sweet and approachable. He's a character written for a fairy tale. I'm waiting for the twist in the story, his giant flaw that negates his absolute perfection in my mind...like finding out he's a serial killer. That would literally be the only thing that could offset his charm."

"Are you..." Palmer trails off, lost for words. "So you like him?"

I sip my coffee, smiling to myself as I enjoy the last few seconds where my secret is still in the bag. "I had sex with him."

"*What*?!" Palmer squalls. "Stop it! Why didn't you call me?"

I have to remove the phone from my ear she's shrieking so loud.

"I did..." I unsubtly clear my throat into the phone.

"Well, if you had led with that, I might've called you back sooner."

Wow. Her lack of filter from her brain to her mouth...I swear.
"Good to know you only want to talk when I'm entertaining."

"Aves," she groans, "come on. I mean, I would've called to make sure you are okay. I know you don't take sex lightly. I can't believe you rebounded with a guy like that. I mean, hell, he's so fine. If I was there. I sure as hell would've taken my shot."

My annoyance immediately bubbles back up. *Back off. Back the fuck off.* Uh-oh. Jealousy is not good. Jealousy is the enemy of casual sex. Finn is my teacher. My coach. My friend. He's a whole lot of things that I shouldn't be acting jealous over.

I overcompensate my casual reply, trying to calm my jittery heart. "Funny. I don't think we've ever shared a guy. First time for everything, I suppose."

"Oh, stop. I wouldn't... Um, so how are you? How do you feel? Does Mason know?"

"Why would Mason know?" I set my coffee mug down on a coaster and tuck my knees to my chest before pulling the throw up to my chin. *Why is it so cold in here?* I remind myself to check the thermometers in the tanks. Dex's air conditioning is always running now that the Vegas summer heat is picking up. I wonder if Cherry feels like she's swimming in the artic. She seems a little slower lately.

"I don't know... If I were you, I'd call him and shove your new boy toy right down his throat. It sends a clear message."

"What message?"

"That you guys are over. Done. No going back. You've moved on."

Palmer missed the whole Rumble chat fiasco, so there's no need to defend how Mason didn't cheat on me after all. But again, the more Palmer tells me what I have to do with my love life, the more I want to do the opposite—just to prove a point. *Talk about regressing.* There's obviously still a rebellious teenager that lives inside me.

"Finn and I are friends. That's it. There's nothing to shove down Mason's throat. I'm spending the summer trying to figure out how to love myself. Once I figure that out, I can decide how I feel about this breakup. I've seen couples come through worse, you know? I've also seen couples walk away for less. I don't know what to think. The bottom line is Mason said he was unhappy and we broke up. He didn't hit me, cheat on me, or lie to me... He was just *unhappy.* Should I hate him for telling the truth? Plus, he told me he may have just needed space. Maybe I needed space too. What if this is what we needed to wake ourselves up?"

"He said that? He actually said he wants to get back together?" She literally sounds disgusted. What the hell is this hypocrisy? Palmer's had endless boyfriends who have cheated on her. Her relationships are usually short-lived, but she's run back to them before. She only saves *this fuck him, he doesn't deserve you* energy for me, apparently. Or maybe she wants Mason out of the way. I'm not sure.

"He said maybe this is a break. You know, my parents took a break for a while and got back together."

"Right...shortly before their divorce. Remember how hard you took it? Do you honestly want to do that to your kids too?"

Jesus, Palmer. Her sharp mouth. "Regardless of how things pan out, Mason and I still have a business to run. We have a huge contract at stake. A career-making contract that we have to secure, *together.* Right now, I need support. Not demands."

"I agree. When it comes to business, he should be

supportive—"

"*No.* Palmer, from you. I need support from you. Don't tell me what to do. *Just listen.*"

How long am I going to have to coach her on how to be a good friend? *It's been two decades. Don't you know me by now? Can't you understand what I need?*

She mumbles something under her breath before she says, "Okay, fine. I support you. I'm listening."

"Thank you." The heavy silence settles between us, and as much as I want to dish about Finn and how he's turning my world upside down, instead, I decide to keep my treasured secrets to myself this time. "I'm going to get my day started, but good luck on set. Break a leg."

"Thanks. Oh, and, Aves?"

"Yeah?"

"I know I say the wrong thing sometimes, but you know that I, um...you're my best friend...the only person who ever believed in me and stood by me, and uh...I'm just sorry that I'm the weak link in this friendship. I really do love you in my way. I wish I were better...more like you."

"Palmer," I say amidst a heavy sigh.

"No, no, just let me own it. I know how I can be. Sometimes I don't think I deserve you."

"Doesn't matter, best friend. You have me. I love you too."

"Good." She breathes out in relief. "Go have fun with your boy toy. I hope you went to the store and bought yourself something other than granny panties."

She can't see my glower, but she can sure as hell hear my sass. "How can I? You still have my car."

"*Shit.*"

I chuckle as I hang up the phone. Hot mess Palmer. Yeah, she's rough around the edges, but she's my oldest friend. I know where each of those edges comes from.

I know her heart. *And it's a good heart.*

* * *

A soft pounding coming from Dex's front door pulls me from my nap. Who could that be? I check my phone lying on the coffee table in front of me in case Finn texted to tell me he was stopping by. There are no notifications. Just the time on the screen telling me I've been napping for one hour and it's past three in the afternoon.

It's been a few days since Finn and I have *hung out,* and I'll admit...I've been avoiding seeing him in person.

Because I'm sore.

It's a good sore. Simply evidence of his massive proportions, but I don't think I could've slept with him again without cringing, and the last thing I want to do is make him feel guilty and scare him off, so for the past few days, I've been pretending I'm buried in work. I'm not. Mason still hasn't gotten back to me with the reports. I texted him yesterday, and all he said was he was traveling and would check in when he gets back. *This is why I handle the clients.* Too bad the marketing director at Legacy Resorts who holds the key to the next level in my career apparently can't handle a woman who's smarter than he is. *Ridiculous.*

I make my way to the door, wishing I'd downloaded the security system app like Dex instructed me to. Had I done so, I could see who was at the door, tap a button, and politely tell them to please go away without leaving my spot on Dex's comfy living room couch.

Opening the door, I see a stranger I certainly wasn't expecting. She has striking features. Her angled features and high cheekbones are entrancing. Her straight-cut bangs, jet-black hair, and dark and heavy eye makeup are a stark contrast to the light jean shorts and flowy, floral top she's wearing. It's such a unique look, composed of contradictions. Is everyone in Las Vegas interesting and beautiful?

"Hello," I say, nodding to the pink, polka-dot bakery box in her hands. "I'm sorry, wrong house. I didn't order any deliveries." I glance past her shoulder, but there's no car. Finn accidentally got my groceries. Maybe I got his...baked goods?

"Hey, Avery," she says, wiping one hand on the back of her shorts and then holding it out to me. "I'm Lennox, Finn's cousin. Sorry if my hands are sticky."

I shake her hand anyway, my urge to be polite winning out over my concern as to why her hands are sticky. She must sense my hesitance because she elaborates as she holds up the pink box. "I brought you the best cinnamon rolls in Las Vegas as a welcome neighbor gift. But I had to sample one to make sure they were up to their usual par."

I throw my head back and laugh. "How are they?"

She smiles, her ruby-red lips spreading across her entire face. "So good that you're down to three." She holds out the box. "Finn drove out to Scottsdale to see his mom today, so I thought I'd take the opportunity to be a creeper and come introduce myself. He's been talking about you nonstop."

I try to contain my smile and fail miserably. Whatever. He's my friend. I'm allowed to like my friend and enjoy the fact that he's talking about me.

"All good things, I hope?"

"Phenomenal things," she says. "I had to come by and make sure you were real."

I chortle under my breath. *Flattery gets you everywhere, Finn. Like right back in front of the closet mirror doing whatever you want to me.*

"Do you want to come in? I can make some coffee." I point to the box in her hand. "You must be a mind reader because I haven't had lunch yet and those smell divine."

"I'd love to."

I step aside, making room for her at the doorway. She gives my shoulder a little squeeze as she passes me, and instantaneously, I feel at ease around this stranger. It's the same way I felt immediately at ease around Finn. Maybe it's a family trait. They share a certain charisma.

Lennox makes herself right at home in Dex's house. She's

obviously been here a time or two as well, because she knows where the little appetizer plates are in Dex's massive kitchen. She pulls the dishware from the cabinet and plates two enormous cinnamon rolls that cover the entirety of each six-inch plate. My empty stomach howls with excitement.

After pressing the brew button, I join Lennox at the kitchen breakfast table—the only table I use in this house. Dex's fancy dining table in his grand dining room is still staged and untouched. I have zero plans of eating at a table that could comfortably seat twelve. The round kitchen table is plenty of space to eat and work at.

"You're really pretty," Lennox says.

As a knee-jerk reaction, I look over my shoulder and then flush at my evasiveness. *Confidence, Avery. That's what we're working on.*

"Yes, I'm talking to you," she adds with a chuckle.

"Sorry," I say, burying my face in my hands. "I just...I was in a relationship for so long. No one says that to me anymore."

She purses her lips. "Your boyfriend didn't tell you you're pretty?"

Come to think of it... "He always told me it was implied. He wouldn't be with me if he didn't think I was beautiful. Then again, we're no longer together, so..." I laugh awkwardly. *Good grief.* When was the last time I had normal social interactions with other women? Just Palmer. And that's usually ducking and dodging her snarky commentary on my life.

Lennox pretends to gag. "That's lazy."

"You know what?" I say, raising my brows. "It is lazy. How hard is that? It's barely a sentence. 'You look pretty.' Not that hard, right?" Mason should've said it more. I deserved more than *implied.*

"Not that hard at all," Lennox parrots back. "Do you guys still talk?"

My shoulders tense, and I immediately feel my defensiveness rising. "We own a business together. We still have to communicate."

"That's cool. In a perfect world, we're all still amicable with our exes. It makes moving on so much easier. If you guys can own a business together, that's really mature." She peers at me, her big brown eyes narrowing just slightly. "Personally, I want to chop off my ex's balls and feed them to him one by one." She tugs the neckline of her shirt, exposing a name tattooed underneath her collarbone. "In hindsight, getting his name permanently marked on my body was a bad omen. Jinxed it."

I cut a generous piece from my cinnamon roll. The side of my fork cuts through the fluffy dessert with ease. Covering my mouth as I chew, I say, "Are you getting it removed? And *holy shit* this is delicious."

"Right? And no, no need. My artist has a whole plan to cover it by working it into a new design." Lennox pats her shoulder. "As soon as I have a little cash, I'm copying Finn's ship."

"*Oh*, yeah...his tattoo is..." *The sexiest thing I've ever seen in my life.* "Pretty cool. Is there a story behind it?"

"Not really. Finn's always been into ships. Which is funny because he has his pilot's license. I always figured he'd want to become a ship captain, but—"

"Finn has a pilot's license?"

"Just a private pilot's certificate," Lennox says with a shrug. "It's not like he could apply to fly for Delta or anything. I'm not even sure if it's still active. He hasn't flown in years."

"Wow. I would've never guessed. He wanted to be a pilot?"

Lennox twists her lips. "In another life. Has Finn told you about his dad?"

I cut another piece of my cinnamon roll, stalling. Finn mentioned Lennox to me. They are more than cousins. This is his best friend, and they work together. I can speak freely, right? "He might've tossed around the word *womanizer*."

Lennox guffaws. "Finn's so polite when he likes a girl. What he meant to say is Griffin Harvey Junior is the shit stain of society and an affront to womankind. Sexually active eighteen-year-olds with daddy issues are his favorite type. It's a miracle he's only fathered three children. I truly suspect there are more. Dirty fucker apparently doesn't know what a condom is."

I blink at her with my jaw dropped. Okay, so she's candid. Actually, I like it. There are no smoke and mirrors with Lennox. What you see is what you get.

"That must be embarrassing for Finn."

She nods in agreement. "Finn and his mom are really close. Which makes it hard for him to love his dad."

I wet my lips, tasting the remnants of the sweet icing on my tongue. "Should we be talking about this? You know...behind Finn's back?"

She reaches over and pats my hand. "My loyalty is to Finn. I know what I can say and which secrets to keep. My job is to protect him. Speaking of which"—she points to my chest—"what's your deal?"

"Ah," I say with a forced laugh. "So these aren't friendly, neighborly cinnamon rolls after all."

"Indeed. Baked goods come at a cost."

I smile. *Calm down. I couldn't hurt Finn if I tried.* "How do you take your coffee?" I ask as I rise.

"More cream and sugar than coffee, please."

I grab two cups, pouring a generous amount of half and half into Lennox's cup. I pour her cream but bring the silver container of sugar to the table with a spoon. "I'm not good at guessing people's sugar tolerances. And as for '*my deal*,' I'm happy to tell you whatever you'd like, but you know Finn and I aren't dating, right?"

Lennox grabs the spoon before unlatching the lid of the sugar container. She spoons three heaping teaspoons of sugar crystals into her cup.

Yup, my kind of girl.

"He said you guys were hanging out."

I suck the air in between my teeth, exaggerating the squeaking sound. "We *hung* out. Once."

"Did you guys sleep together?" she asks with a mischievous

smile. Her smile is contagious, and I catch her playful mood.

I clear my throat. "I mean, we didn't do much sleeping."

She squeals with laughter and taps her feet against the floor rapidly, making the table shake. "I *knew* it. I should've known just by the way he was talking about you. Finn finally likes a good one. Thank the heavens."

"Oh, oh," I say, holding up my palm and waving my hand in the air. "No. Not like that. I just...we're..." Okay, I'm going to need to figure out how to answer this question because someone else is bound to ask. "I just got dumped from a very long-term relationship about three weeks ago, and I'm not quite sure how to do the whole dating game. Finn's showing me the, uh...ropes so to speak. And in exchange, I'm going to use my expertise to help you guys build more business."

I picture the cogs spinning in Lennox's head. She keeps her quizzical expression on me as she takes a sip from her mug. "This was Finn's idea?"

I can't help but laugh. "Oh, no. I asked him. More like... convinced him. *Completely my idea.* He's innocent in all of this. And I know I must sound crazy, but I'm a hands-on learner. Sex isn't something you can just learn from a textbook. Actually, scratch that—*you can*. I did. Which is probably why I'm so awkward at it. Finn is confident in the things I'm not, so I figured he could teach me what men want and how to have a decent sex life."

Lennox tries to control her smile. "So you asked a man you barely knew to have sex with you for tips?"

"Pretty much." I cover my eyes. "It's not my usual style, but I've never been able to just talk to a guy so easily. And plus, sorry, I know he's your cousin, but Finn is beyond hot." I drop my hands and shrug innocently. "I saw an opportunity. I seized it. But I promise, I have nothing devious planned. We're just friends helping each other out."

Lennox turns her lips down and nods slowly. "Okay, let's pretend this won't end in a total disaster. What happens at the end of summer? This is the last question of my interrogation. I promise."

I give her a small smile. I like that she's protective of Finn. It makes me immediately like her. "I go home, move out of my apartment with my ex, and feel good about dating again. Hopefully, by then I have enough confidence to eventually attract a guy who doesn't see a life with me as *settling*. Meanwhile, you and Finn are so busy with bookings, you'll be quietly cursing me for making you guys so busy and rich." I raise my brows. "Sound fair?"

She tips her mug in my direction. "I could work with rich. I think I like you, Avery. I officially approve of this whole situation." She nudges my plate toward me. "You may eat your snack in peace."

Lennox joins me in laughter. When we catch our breath, I add, "Just so you know, I do consider Finn a friend. I have no expectations, and there are no hearts at risk. We're helping each other get...unstuck, I suppose."

"I think we should be friends," Lennox says, raising her brows. "I mean, you and Finn can't just fuck all the time."

I beg to differ. I'm no longer sore. I will live underneath that man...or on top of him...or on my knees...

"You're living here all by yourself while Dex is away?"

I nod. "Well, my best friend was supposed to visit now and then, but she's an actress and she booked a role last minute and hightailed it to New Mexico with my Jeep."

Lennox widens her eyes in surprise. "You're here alone with no car?"

I nod in reply.

"Damn, babe, that's lame."

"I'm okay," I say. "Walmart and Target will deliver most anything, and I go on quick walks in the morning before the heat becomes unbearable, so I get out of the house on occasion. And Finn took me to dinner the other night."

Lennox rolls her eyes. "I'm liberating your imprisoned ass." She chugs her coffee, and at first, I'm impressed, but then I remember how much cream I put in there. I'm sure her drink is barely warm. "I'm headed to Town Square. Not that I can afford anything there, but my credit card is a little dusty. I'm going to go make some bad decisions in Sephora. Want to come?"

I gesture around my eyelids. "If you teach me how to do a smoky eye like yours, I'll *buy* some makeup for you. I can't figure out how to blend it properly. It comes out looking like I failed miserably when trying to cover up a black eye."

Lennox chuckles. "Ah, it's all about the blending brush. And I have a trick that involves Scotch Tape. Come on. I'll show you what brushes to get. Let's go." She rises, her chair screeching against the wood floor.

"Um..." My shirt is stain-free at least, but it's still frumpy and two sizes too big. It's from a 5k charity event that I most definitely did not run. I volunteered to hand out little water bottles at the end of the race. "Do you want me to change?"

She squints one eye at me. "Um," she mimics, "that's a weird question. Do you want to change? I can wait."

"Oh, I... I don't know. Is Town Square fancy? I don't want to embarrass you." I glance down at my frayed blue jean shorts. I hate wearing shorts. My legs are not tan or toned. They belong in the security of compression yoga pants. But it's so damn hot here. What choice do I have?

"Are you planning on participating in a flash mob while we're out?"

"Definitely not."

She pops her shoulders. "Then how the hell would you embarrass me?" Lennox throws her head back as she lets out a breathy laugh. "I'm going to pull my car around. Want to meet me out front in five? Oh, and that needs to go in the fridge," she says, pointing to the pink box on the counter. "The icing has cream cheese in it."

The front door closes with a click, and I find myself, for the first time in a long time, looking forward to a girls' day out. I put my cinnamon rolls into the fridge as instructed and collect my purse and keys before passing by Cherry's tank.

Sorry, girl. Have a good day. I won't be watching you all day

like a sad, old spinster fish lady.
I apparently have plans.

Chapter 20

Finn

"What's up, Lenny?" I ask through my truck's speaker. I turn the blasting air conditioning down so I can hear my cousin.

"*Lenny?*" she asks. "Someone's in a good mood. Also, please don't call me that."

I laugh. "No? Why not? Brings me back to the good old days when you had braces and headgear."

"Exactly. *Ass.* Anyways, why are you so cheery?"

"I'm just in a good mood. Mom's doing well. Her new boyfriend is a good guy. We got a few more booking requests through the website—"

"And you got laid," Lennox adds, interrupting.

Perhaps... "Why do you say that?"

"Because I hung out with your new girlfriend all day today. I might've implied you already told me what was going on, so she literally spilled everything."

I wish Lennox could see my expression right now, a direct mix between irritated and rageful. "So you accosted Avery? I'm a big boy. I don't need you to protect me."

"Yes, you do, Finn. You may look like a grown man, but you're fragile like a teacup puppy when it comes to the women you fall for." She snorts in laughter.

"If she told you everything, then you know we're not actually dating." I pump my brakes when the red sedan in front of me slows down for no apparent reason. I hate traffic driving back from Scottsdale. Everyone on the road drives like they're lost.

"Do you like her?" Lennox asks.

"I slept with her. Of course I like her." I instantly regret my statement because I know what's going to come out of Lennox's mouth next.

"Um, you've slept with plenty of women you don't like. Cass, Anette, Rayna, Molly, Heather, that one stripper from Ruby's whose first name was legally Sprinkle. As a reminder, she was the one who squealed like a little piglet when she came."

Oh God. "When the fuck did I tell you that?"

Lennox roars in laughter. "You were so hammered. Tequila is like truth serum for you, dude."

My cheeks fill with air as I roll my eyes. "I *liked* all of those women. I just didn't want a *relationship* with them. And they didn't want a relationship with me either."

"Wrong. Molly was in love with you for years, and Rayna cried for three days straight when you got back together with Nora."

"Do you keep tabs on all my hookups?"

"God, no. The volume alone would be way too much work. Who the hell would have that kind of time? I saw Cass last week, though."

I've only had one friends-with-benefits situation that didn't end in total disaster. Cass is a legitimate friend, but I've had her in every position you could imagine. The only reason I haven't called her in a while is because I was taking a break from fucking around. Cass is extremely apathetic about sex and relationships. She's not remotely close to being interested in a relationship with me, which is probably why Cass was the only woman in the world Nora wasn't jealous of. It's why Nora invited her into our bed so many times. "How is she?"

"Good. She's still working at Ruby's."

"I figured as much." *Obviously.* I'm convinced Cass is the best-paid bar manager in Las Vegas.

"She asked about you. She told me to tell you to call her."

"What'd you say?" I ask distractedly, flicking on my blinker and hauling ass to pass the little red sedan on the two-lane highway.

"That you were involved with someone."

I let out a deep breath. "Am I?"

"Aren't you?" Lennox is quick to reply. "I mean, this sex coach thing is real cute and all, but it's obvious you guys like each other. What's the problem?"

"The problem is that the last time I got involved with a woman who wasn't over her ex... Need I elaborate?"

"I just spent all day with her, and I can confirm—Avery is Nora's antithesis."

I shrug even though she can't see me. "She's only here for the summer."

"She lives like five hours away, Finn, and she's a consultant, which she can do from anywhere. By the way, your girl is a total baller. You won't believe how much she spent on me in Sephora today. She didn't even flinch when they read the total at checkout. I nearly had a heart attack."

"*Lennox*," I scold.

"What?"

"Don't take advantage of Avery like that."

"She insisted!"

"It doesn't matter."

"How about this. In a year and a half when you get the first chunk of your trust fund, you can afford to pay her back with interest for me. Deal?"

"You need my inheritance for that?" The first chunk of my inheritance is a little less than four million dollars. *What the fuck did they buy at Sephora?*

"I mean... You'd need a hell of a lot more money than you're making now."

"Thanks for that," I grumble. *Not emasculating at all.*

"But worry not, I talked you up all afternoon."

"Do I need talking up?" I ask absentmindedly. My exit is coming up, and it's easy to miss in the dark. It's the last stop before the final two-hour stretch home. With a quarter tank left, I'm not risking it.

"I think she really likes you. But you need to be careful, Finn."

"I told you we're not actually dating." I flick on my blinker. "But out of curiosity, why?"

"Because it's weird. She dated her ex for four years. He dumped her *on her birthday* seconds after he gave her an engagement ring. That happened a few weeks ago. She should be a hot mess, but she's *fine*. When Charlie and I broke up, I couldn't eat, sleep, or get out of my pajamas for ages. I was devastated. It's bizarre. Avery shouldn't be okay."

"Maybe she knows she dodged a bullet," I say, turning at my exit and pulling into the truck stop right off the highway.

"Or maybe she's not dealing with it yet. And *maybe* sleeping with you is a way for her to postpone the inevitable meltdown that's coming."

I pull into the only free pump with a green diesel handle. "What's your point, Lennox?"

"Talk to her. Don't be the rebound guy this time, Finn."

Her words rub me the wrong way. I know my cousin means no harm, but it was always my weak spot with Nora. No matter how much I loved her, no matter how hot our chemistry was, we were doomed. Maybe because I started as her rebound guy.

"Avery needs a friend right now. That's all. I need a friend."

"You know what your problem is?"

"My meddlesome cousin?"

"You think that loving a woman means letting her get away with whatever she wants. You're not a dick if you set some boundaries and stand up for what you need from a relationship."

I shut off the truck and pick up my phone, bringing my conversation with Lennox with me. "Except Avery and I aren't in a relationship. She's preparing herself for when she wants to get back into the dating game again. I'm basically her practice field." I insert my debit card and want to gag at the cost of diesel fuel per gallon. When the fuck did this jump a whole *dollar*? Gas prices keep creeping up, and it's half the reason I only see my mom about once every two months now. I used to make the drive every weekend just to check on her. I normally spend the night, but this time it felt like three was a crowd. Mom's happy and her new man seems obsessed with keeping her that way. There was no need to linger.

"Well, if Avery is practicing how to date again, maybe you should too. Ask her how she feels about her ex and you. Ask her what she wants. Tell her what you want."

I ignore the sign that clearly says don't leave the pump unattended. Heading into the gas station, I respond, "I've known her for a couple of weeks. It's a little early to talk about feelings, Lennox."

"How long did it take before you knew you loved Nora?"

Less than a week. "Doesn't that mean I should do things differently moving forward?"

"Yes. So, tell her what you want."

Maybe it's sound advice, but that would require me to know what the hell I want. Finding out about Morgan and Nora stung. I won't admit it to a soul in the world, but it drives me crazy that she ran back to him after she spent years telling me I showed her what real love felt like. There was no way she could go back to a man who didn't make her feel the way I did. It was all lip service. It's not that I'm jealous. It's just tough to face all the bullshit. The reality is, Nora didn't just treat me like garbage... *I let her.*

Avery's been nothing but honest and vulnerable with me. Maybe we should talk. Maybe this could be more than casual. I enjoy spending time with her. She's so easy to talk to. This game of good sex doesn't really feel like a game. If it is, I think I'm winning every time.

Apparently, if you want to find a nice girl to connect with, just swear off dating, and then she'll come barreling into your life...naked in a hot tub. *Shit... Okay, so I like her. But are we both ready for me to do something about it?*

"Fine. I'll talk to her," I mumble, holding the phone between my shoulder and my ear as I fill my arms with gas station snacks.

"Good," Lennox says as I head to the cash register. "Then my work here is done. All right, get home safe. By the way, I used the last clean towel when I showered, so I threw a load in the washer, but I didn't run it yet. Oh, and you're out of beer, cheddar cheese, and Chex Mix. I put them on the grocery list, but could you buy the Bold Mix flavor next time? The blue bag is so bland. I mean, I ate it...but it was bland."

The gas station attendant widens his eyes and looks startled at the very unamused expression I'm wearing. I point to my phone and whisper to him, "Not you."

He nods and begins ringing up my snacks, one by one.

"Lennox, I'm changing my locks."

"Bye, *Finny.*"

* * *

> **Finn: I'm in the hot tub. I have junk food.**

> **Avery: You are NOT in the hot tub. I know this because I, in fact, am.**

I smile as I read Avery's response and head through my backyard to the adjoining back gate to Dex's home. It's quiet. She must not have the jets on. I figured by the time she saw my message, I'd be relaxed and soaking.

"I hope you're *not* decent. Are you topless or bottomless? Or my favorite—completely naked," I say over the fence. Pausing, I wait for a flirty response.

"I'm wearing a swimsuit, Finn. I can't just give the goods away. My new teacher keeps telling me I have to make a man earn it."

I tuck the snacks and energy drink under one arm as I

unlatch the lock and use my shoulder to push the tension-ridden gate open. Avery's in the tub, in a black, one-piece swimsuit. "Ah, damn. Your new teacher is an idiot."

She laughs. "I wouldn't say that. He's all kinds of sweet, *and*"—she points to my hands—"he brought blueberry-flavored Red Bull?"

I set the blue can next to her arm resting on the deck, along with the bag of snacks, and proceed to pull off my shirt. There's no need for space tonight. I dip into the tub and find my place right next to Avery, even going as far as wrapping my arm around her shoulders.

She holds up the can. "How did you know I have a weakness for these? They are always sold out when I go to the store." She snuggles into me, and I feel a sense of relief. She feels it too. No way I'm alone in thinking this is more than just gratuitous sex.

"I didn't. I happen to like them too. But I don't drink them during long drives. They do nothing to keep you awake because the sugar crash cancels out the caffeine."

"*Exactly*," she says, "but they taste like candy." She peeks into the white plastic bag I brought and then hands the can to me.

"No, you go for it," I say, refusing to take it.

"You only have one. I don't want to take it from you."

I squeeze her shoulder suggestively and wink. "Take it. I'll make you earn it later... As in I'd really like to give you another private lesson tonight if you're up for it."

"Aren't you exhausted? Lennox said you were in Scottsdale today. I didn't expect to see you tonight."

"A little. I left at about six this morning. Scottsdale is about five hours away if traffic is decent. But lunch didn't take long."

Avery crinkles her forehead and looks at me head-on. "You drove five hours each way in one day and now you want to have sex?"

I study her pinched expression. "Why is that weird?"

She opens the can, and the hiss of carbonated beverage fills the silence between us. After taking a little sip, she says, "Because

'I'm too tired' was Mason's favorite excuse, I guess."

It's a rare moment when I can see how Avery is feeling. She's not as impervious as everyone thinks.

"Can I ask you a question?"

"Sure." Her eyes are forward and steady; she's lost in an unpleasant memory.

"Was it just your sex life, or was your entire relationship with Mason disappointing? And before you make some ridiculous self-deprecating comment, I've had sex with you, Avery. I can say with full confidence the problem wasn't you."

"I'm not convinced," she says with a scoff. "Look, honestly? I guess I didn't put my best foot forward. I never wanted to be a girl who found validation in how she looked. I don't think that makeup, sexy clothes, or my weight should be the most direct path to a man's heart. I wanted to be loved for me—my mind, my generosity, my work ethic, my loyalty... But I wonder if sometimes I brought out the worst in Mason by neglecting something that is fundamentally important in a relationship."

"Which is?"

"Attraction...on every level. Maybe when you love someone, you're supposed to be your best for them, not just be comfortable around them. I don't know. We never talked about it. I'll never know how Mason was feeling. I'm not even sure if I know how I was feeling. I was too busy to stop and think about it." She takes another swig and sets the can aside.

"How do you feel now?" I clear my throat. "About your breakup?"

She playfully rolls her eyes at me. "Well, Dr. Phil, obviously I feel *sad*."

"Do you? Because I've never seen someone so analytical about a relationship ending. Especially when it was so abrupt. You said everything was fine, and then he pulled the rug out from under you. You should be hurting, crying—"

"I did cry," she interrupts. "I was on your lap, remember?"

"You were upset when you thought he cheated," I explain.

"But how do you feel about the actual breakup? You ran away for the summer, and you're living here alone, yet you're acting so nonchalant. It's a little bizarre."

She turns and then digs through the bag of snacks. Pulling out a bag of salt and vinegar chips, she asks, "May I? These are my favorite."

"You may... And you can also answer my question if you'd like." I raise my brows at her.

"Fine," she says, dropping the bag of chips and covering her face with both hands. I immediately regret my pushiness when I see her frustrated reaction. "I'm so fucking freaked out, Finn."

"Well, that's norm—"

"No!" She flicks the water in my direction, and it hits my neck. "Not because we're not together, but because of how relieved I am. *I didn't know.* I literally didn't know I was unhappy until Mason said it. And yes, my pride is hurt. Yes, my ego is wounded, and of course, I'm embarrassed he blamed it on sex. But all that will fade in time. What freaks me out is, what if he never said it? What if he didn't dump me? I absolutely would've married him. I would've been on my death bed never *knowing* I was unhappy. So, yes, I'm a little stunned right now because I'm running every single scenario in my mind and realizing how fucked-up it was. I thought I was being a good woman. Everything I did was to make him feel comfortable. He's a slow-moving guy, so I learned to be patient. He's impressed with a woman who works, so I built us a business from the ground up. He said he didn't like materialistic, shallow women, so I didn't spend my time and energy on that stuff. But here we are, four years later, and I don't know who I am. I just know who Mason wanted me to be. And spoiler alert—being exactly who he said he wanted *still* wasn't enough to keep him."

I blink at her, shocked at her candidness. How is she talking to me like this? Is this real? Women are just vulnerable and honest without being manipulative and playing mind games? Is this a thing? *Where the fuck have you been, Avery?*

"I don't know whether to say I'm sorry or I'm happy for you."

She chuckles. "Right? That's exactly how I feel. Look, Finn, I know how I'm coming off, like I'm on the verge of a psychotic break—but that's not what this is. I'm thirty years old. I'm not a child, and I know it isn't Mason's responsibility to patch up my insecurities. But it is my job to figure out what I want and what I like. That's hard for me. I've been a people pleaser since the day I was born. Ask my mom. She said even as an infant, I wouldn't cry if I was hungry or wet. I came out of the womb trying not to bother anybody."

I laugh, making the water jostle. "I had colic. I came into this world guns blazing and ready to torture my poor mom with my constant screaming. Or so she says."

Avery reaches up to tap my nose. "I don't doubt it. You are unapologetic about being you. I love that. I like your confidence. I'm just hoping you rub off on me before summer is over so I don't end up changing for the next guy I end up with, you know?"

Next guy? How come I hate when she says that? *Aren't I the next guy?* "You wouldn't have liked me much if you saw me with my ex. I was a different guy. Much like you, I didn't realize how unhappy I was until I ended it for good." I run my wet hand through my hair.

"Well," Avery says, picking up the can of Red Bull, "cheers to fresh new chapters and to new friends." She takes a sip and then taps the corner of my mouth with her finger. When I part my lips, she pours a little of the sweet liquid into my mouth.

"Friends, huh?" I ask after I swallow.

She shrugs. "Yeah. Friends."

Except the way she touches me, smiles at me, and shares all her most precious thoughts and feelings doesn't feel so friendly. Or maybe this is how it's supposed to be. It certainly wasn't this way with any of my exes. Did I have it backward all this time? Are you supposed to be friends first and then fall in love? Maybe you should get to know the person before you've fallen for them. Maybe knowing the good and bad up front would prevent all the jarring realizations. And if friends first is the right path, where does fucking fall into place? Are Avery and I behind the curve or ahead of it?

Before I can overthink this anymore, Avery sets the can down and unties the bow behind her neck.

"So you said you're feeling up for lessons tonight?"

I force myself to be patient instead of yanking her suit down and exposing her full tits. "I am."

"What should we study?" Her smile is so cute and mischievous, I just want to suck on her lips. She makes me feel so light and full at the same time. Flirty and serious. Avery is every single piece of the pie.

"How's your blow job?" I ask.

"On a scale of one to ten?" she asks, grimacing.

"Sure."

She inhales, her chest rising high. "Solid four." She blows out her breath. "And a half. Four and a half."

I can't help but chuckle at her. "Why do you say that?"

"I don't know. I only have one move, and I feel like it's boring. And sorry to overshare, but it'd take Mason forever. I think we both ended up hating head."

I hate this guy. So fucking much. "Well, sweetheart, I can guarantee you, I'm a melt-in-your-mouth kind of guy. I won't be bored." I tuck a wet piece of her hair behind her ear.

She clamps her eyes shut. "Would you be willing to talk me through it?" Avery laughs at herself a little. "Most awkward question I've ever asked in my life," she mumbles under her breath.

"It's not awkward. I'm more than happy to tell you what I like." Using my teeth, I tug on her earlobe before whispering in her ear. "But do you remember what I already taught you about giving head?" The way I feel her shudder with anticipation sends me straight into the zone. My cock presses uncomfortably against my swim trunks.

She nods. "Yes."

"Say it."

"If a man doesn't give..." She trails off, and I raise my brows at her, so she continues, "He doesn't get."

"Good girl. Such a good student." I pat the deck, indicating she should hop up. She sits on the edge of the deck, her feet still dipping into the tub. Moving between her legs, I place my face right in the center of her chest so that when I peel her swimsuit down, her round tits drop right onto my face. I allow myself to get lost for a moment, nipping and teasing her plump nipples, encouraging her to lean back onto her hands and arch her back.

I'll never get my fill of her tits. I could breathe them in for hours, so I have to force myself to keep moving south. She bridges her hips so I can pull her swimsuit past her full hips and fleshy thighs. God, I love her legs. I love how they look and how they feel, and I know for damn sure what she sees in the mirror and what I see in front of me must be two different women. Avery has nothing to be ashamed of and *everything* to flaunt. All my favorite parts of a woman are plentiful on her. There's more to touch and squeeze, and I wish she knew how her body drives me wild.

"Here?" Avery asks as I pull her swimsuit all the way off and toss it over my shoulder. She glances around the privacy fence.

"Yes, here. And now," I command. "Lie back. Spread your legs. I'm going to show you how to do this. The equipment is different, but the strategy is the same." Pushing on her shoulder, I guide her into a lying position before I run my tongue over her clit a few times. I'm so gentle, I know it has to be frustrating. By the third time, she bucks her hips so hard that she slams back onto the deck with a loud thud.

"*Fuck*," she wails.

"It's the teasing that works you up. I like that too," I say before I blow on her wet slit. "The anticipation is almost as good as the release."

She throws her forearm over her eyes and moans in agony as I continue to tease her. "Oh my God, please just..."

"Please what?" I flatten my tongue and drag it against her crease. For a moment, I give her the pressure she's aching for. Then I pull away. "Ask me for what you want."

"I just... You already know," she says, her breath growing ragged.

I run my hands against her thighs and suck on her clit, hard. Her quad muscles instantly flex and tighten as she tries to create enough tension for her orgasm to build. I immediately rip away again.

"Not yet, baby. I said, *ask me*," I growl. "I want to hear it."

"Does me begging get you off? *Fine*," she says in exasperation. "Um, please make me come."

I could...so easily. I want to. But all the growing feelings aside, Avery asked me for help. There's a purpose for what we're doing. I'm supposed to teach her.

"Hey, sit up for me."

She sits up and lets her legs dangle into the tub, the water going up to her knees. Using the back of my fingernails, I rub up and down the sides of her thighs, trying to comfort her. "What do you want?"

"Finn, you know dirty talk isn't natural for me. I'm trying, but it's going to take some time before it—"

"No, no, sweetheart. Look at me." We're almost eye level with me standing in the tub and her sitting on the edge of the deck that surrounds the in-ground hot tub. She barely has to shift her gaze down. "I'm trying to get you to be more assertive in the bedroom because I get the feeling that you're one of those women who fake their orgasms. What do you want from sex?"

"I just want you to like—"

"No, I said what do *you* want from sex?"

She pulls her eyes from mine and looks over my shoulder. "I honestly don't know."

I snake my arms around her hips and squeeze the top of her ass. "That comes from years of sleeping with a guy who doesn't care if you finish."

I watch her eyes freeze. She's quiet, trying not to blink, and I know with my whole heart she's trying hard not to cry. I don't rush her. I wait for her to collect herself as I rub soothing circles with the heel of my palm against her lower back.

"It also comes from the humiliation of asking to try things and being told no one too many times," she finally says, her voice cracking. "Rejection is one of those things that sticks with you."

"Avery, right now you have a man between your legs who will try whatever you want. More than that, I would be delighted to give you whatever you ask for. So be a queen, baby. Tell me what to do. I'm at your command. Look at me."

She finds me with her misty green eyes.

"This is the most important lesson I'll ever teach you. Are you listening?"

She nods. "Yeah."

"Good sex means being generous, but it means being selfish too. You have a right to enjoy this. Sex should be satisfying for you too." Her face is stoic, but I find the single tear trickling down her cheek and wipe it away. "Promise me, right now, you'll walk away from any man who doesn't make your happiness a priority."

"I promise," she whispers, her voice breaking. She clears her throat and then says clearly once more, "*I promise.*"

"Good. Now, do you want to try again, or am I making you uncomfortable?"

"You're making me very uncomfortable." She places her hands around my cheeks. "But change is uncomfortable. And I'd like to try again."

"Okay." I smile at her, my gaze fixed on the glowing embers in her eyes. *There it is.* I found the fuse. All this girl needs is a little reassurance. For someone to actually give a shit about what they can give to her versus what they can take. That's all it'll take for her to ignite. "So what do you want?"

She presses her lips together for a moment then forces herself to speak. "I want to flip over, get on my hands and knees, and feel you fuck me from behind."

"You got it," I say, grabbing her hand and pressing it against my stiffening cock underneath the water. "My pleasure, baby."

She shakes her head. "Not yet. I want this later." She tightens her hand around my cock. "But when I said *fuck me*, I meant with your tongue."

Chapter 21

Avery

Oh, sweet hell.

I've never been this greedy in my life. I'm comfortable on my hands and knees on the hard deck because Finn fetched me a towel. That's the kind of man I'm sleeping with. He folded up a beach towel for my knees so I was more comfortable when he buried his tongue into me from behind.

I'm not rushing. I don't try to find my release in a hurry. I simply enjoy myself and all the appreciative moans he's making from between my legs. This is how the pretty girls must feel. Deserving. Do I deserve this? *Yeah... Maybe I do.* When did what I want start to become less imp—

"*Whoa!* Finn," I squall when I feel his finger tap gently against the wrong hole.

"Sorry. You don't like that?" he asks in a mumble, immediately removing his finger. Using both hands to spread me, he slips his tongue inside my crease. He tilts his head so he can get even deeper.

Every time he enters me like that, the heady fog of pleasure takes over my entire body. It feels so good, I might do something insanely irresponsible like allow this Goliath of a man to take my ass, shortly before meeting my end. *Death by giant dick.*

"No, it feels kind of exhilarating actually, but—*ah! Oh God...*" It's too damn hard to focus when his tongue is darting around like that. "Just not tonight. Baby steps."

"Mmm," he moans. "Okay, we'll just do this tonight." He cocks his head to the side and flicks away at my clit, sending me down the river of indulgent pleasure again. I whimper and moan shamelessly. It feels natural. It feels right. I want him to know what he's doing to me and how accepted I feel, just as I am. I couldn't even fuck Mason with the lights on. I now have the sexiest-looking man I've ever laid eyes on with his tongue gliding all over my pussy like a rehearsed dance. Is this all it takes? Asking for what I want?

"Finn?"

"Yeah, baby?"

"Can I have your fingers too?"

He sinks his finger into me in reply. "Good girl for asking. Of course you can. You're so wet. You love this, don't you?"

I moan as he coaxes me along with his sexy talk.

"You want another?"

"Yes, please."

"So polite," he mumbles as a second finger joins the first. And then to my great surprise, he curls them inside me.

Wait. I'm not new to this. I've been fingered before, but Finn is going off-road. Instead of a pumping motion, he seems more focused on stroking something. I mean to ask, but he's moving too fast for me to understand what's happening. The pressure builds, but from a place I don't recognize. It's far more intense, far more overwhelming. I can't even speak. I just bite down on my forearm as my knees go weak.

I open my mouth, but only a raspy groan comes out as he starts to move his fingers furiously. The deck begins to shake... *Or is it just my body?* Something doesn't feel right. I'm on a brand-new cusp, and I have no fucking clue what's on the other side. But the intensity is so punishingly delicious. The overwhelming waves of pleasure make me want to slip under the water and drown in this sensation.

I bite my lip when my orgasm explodes in a blinding rage, more intense than I've ever felt before. I'm about to scream out Finn's name when—

Holy shit. Something slips...no...sprays. *No, please no.* I freeze in place. Absolutely mortified, I refuse to let myself enjoy the post-orgasmic relief. Because I feel it dripping down the back of my thighs. I swear I thought it was a pornographic myth. Surely I didn't just...squirt?

Oh, sweet humiliation. Welcome back. It's been a little while. Thank you for rearing your ugly head and ruining this for me.

I turn over, like a dog with its tail tucked between its legs. Finn's still standing in the hot tub, the water rising to his hips. I pray the beads of liquid on his chest are sweat, condensation, or splashes from the tub. I have to believe that, or I'll die of embarrassment at this moment.

"Don't," he says sternly when he sees my expression.

I study his furrowed brows, assuming he's horrified too, but the smile on his face is nothing but wicked. "I'm so sor—"

"*Don't,*" he repeats, cutting me off.

"Don't what?"

"Apologize for the sexiest thing I've ever fucking seen. Lie back," he grumbles. "Right now, Avery, I'm serious. I'm so hard, I'm going to fuck you better than you've ever had it in your life. *Lie back.*" He grabs me by my hips and scoots me to the very edge of the deck. He must be standing on the raised bench seat in the hot tub, because suddenly he's a few inches higher and his erection, which he just freed, is positioned right at my entrance.

"You're not grossed out?"

"*Grossed out?* You know that was intentional, right?"

"Was it?"

"Hell yes, it's my special skill." He smirks as he hovers over me and presses his lips to mine. I taste a hint of chlorine and myself. A little sweet, a little musky, but completely hedonic. "I take it you've never done that before?"

"I didn't even know I could."

"I'm going to teach you a lot about what you can do. You're mine to play with. *All summer.*" His tip nudges my entrance, and I push against his chest.

"Wait. I thought we were going to practice my blow job skills."

Finn narrows his eyes, his lips turning down in contemplation.

He seems suspended between lustful need and sweet amusement. He chooses the former. "You got yours. Now it's my turn." He presses his lips against my ear. "And I want that wet pussy, right now."

Straightening up, he strokes along his cock, staring at me with my legs spread, like he's debating how he wants to play this. "Hold your knees, Queen. I need your legs out of my way so you can take my entire cock. Every inch."

Goddamn, his dirty mouth stirs something up inside me. I immediately obey, pulling my legs up and outward by my knees.

He spits on my clit, and I writhe in place as he uses his thumb to rub his saliva all over my crease. He's moving so slowly, and I know what he's doing. *The anticipation.* It's killing me. I feel like I could come again from the look he's giving me.

"This is going to go fast. Not my usual style, but that's what you do to me. Do you know that? I'm putty in your hands, Avery."

His loud, grumbly moan is all I hear when he slams into me. I lose track of time and space. We're fucking amongst the stars for all I know. Maybe I come again, maybe I don't. I'm not really able to tell the difference anymore. It all feels so good. The build-up, the anticipation, the release—*it's all so good.* I need it all. I'm going to ask for it all. It's clear I don't know what my body is really capable of. But I'll find out. Finn's willing. And I want him to take me there.

"Such a fucking queen," he whispers into my ear right before he roars, spilling inside me.

* * *

My sensitivity is still so heightened, the beads of water from the hot shower tickle my skin. It seems like I feel them one by one, cresting and breaking against my body. I can't wipe the stupid, goofy smile off my face. *This is satisfaction.* I wiggle my toes against the tile floor of Dex's oversize walk-in shower. *How have I gone this long without satisfaction?*

Finn's waiting for me with a towel outstretched in his hands when I turn off the water. He rinsed and wrung out his swim trunks before putting them back on, but I know he must be uncomfortable. And here's the awkward part. He needs to go home and change...

But should he come back?

I step out of the shower and let Finn wrap me up in the fluffy towel. Being naked around him finally feels comfortable. I feel like my body is his to explore now as much as it is mine. He kisses the top of my head, breathing in my damp hair.

"I like your shampoo. There's a scent I can't quite place."

"The ginger, probably. It's this ridiculously expensive designer brand. I don't usually spend a lot of money on beauty products, but I buy good shampoo. I think it's citrus, ginger, and a little mint. Those scents shouldn't work together, but somehow—"

"They do," Finn finishes for me. "It reminds me of this soap my dad used to bring back from the Caribbean for my mom. She loved it." Finn rubs my shoulders with his large hands. It feels like home when he touches me. Like I'm where I should be.

"Did you guys get to travel a lot with your dad as a commercial pilot?"

"No. He didn't want us to."

"Ah, makes sense. I'm sure he didn't want you missing school and such."

"No. Nothing like that." Finn grunts, his agitation apparent. "It's just harder to cheat on your wife when she's around, you know?"

"*Shit.*" My open palm finds my forehead, making a loud, echoing smack in the large master bathroom. "I didn't mean to bring up—"

"Oh, hey," Finn says, "it's fine. It's old news. I told you, the stuff with my dad...it's complicated."

I pat my body underneath the towel, soaking up the water droplets. "How so?"

"Because he's such a dick to my mom, but if you take all

that bullshit out, he's a pretty great dad. It's confusing. I hate him strictly for how he treated my mom, but I feel guilty about it because he's always been good to me. I normally can dodge his calls just fine, but I have to see him when he's in town. It keeps the peace, I suppose."

Reaching up, I smooth the worry lines on Finn's forehead. His brows are cinched in dismay. "Do you have to see him often?"

"Nah, not really. A few times a year. He's actually in town next month. We're having dinner. Want to come with me and be my decoy?" He lets out what sounds like a nervous chuckle. I half expect him to add, *just kidding.* This is a layer of Finn I haven't seen before. He looks a little vulnerable.

I smile at him like the world's biggest smart-ass. "Ask me."

"What?"

"If you want me to go, I will. Just ask me for what you want. Don't be shy." I wink at him.

"And the student becomes the teacher," Finn says. He taps his fingers together in a sarcastic golf clap. "Fine. Avery, will you please go to dinner with me when I have to meet my dad? I could use a friend to get me through it."

I rise to my tiptoes, but I'm still not tall enough to kiss his cheek. I reach around the back of his neck and pull him a little closer. "I'd be happy to," I say into his ear before I press my lips against his smooth cheek.

"Thank you."

I snuggle into my towel and smile at Finn, right before I shoo him away. "It's a date. But now, I need to sleep off all our shenanigans from this evening." Perfectly timed, a large yawn overcomes me. "And I *know* you must be wrecked as well."

I can almost see the words on his lips. I swear if he asked, I'd say yes tonight. I'm so happy. I could pretend for just one evening that I could keep this man to myself forever. *Say it, Finn. Ask me if you can stay over.*

He settles for a lingering kiss on my forehead then follows up with a quick peck on my lips. "Get in bed. Get cozy, Queen. I'll lock up behind me. See you soon."

Finn waves over his shoulder as he exits the bathroom. I dry myself off and make my way into the bedroom, where I've finally taken advantage of some of the drawers Dex cleared out for me. After weeks of staying here, I no longer live out of a suitcase.

I pull on a pair of my most comfortable black cotton panties. Omitting a bra, I yank on a thin tank top in a hurry as it hits me. *This evening shouldn't end like this. Stay with me... Hold me... We're already in way over our heads. Let's just dive in.* I fly down the stairs, thudding loudly as I sprint like I'm headed to an emergency. But it took too long for me to come to my damn good senses.

It's too late. He's already gone. I debate calling, but my descent down the stairs was enough time to remind myself that Finn deserves a friend who stays true to her word. I asked him for a favor. My intention was not to trap him. If I asked him to stay, he would, out of guilt...maybe pity. Either way, for some reason, I have a hold over him, and I don't think it has anything to do with infatuation. I think he feels bad for me. A lesser woman would exploit that.

I am not a lesser woman.

I stand alone in the living room, feeling deflated, watching Cherry glide across the dimly lit tank. I'm sure she thinks it's moonlight. *It's all synthetic, sweetheart. Just a ruse created by your daddy, who is off swimming with fish in the real ocean. She's moving so slowly, it's strange. How quickly do fish age?* Taking a step closer, I peer into the tank, following her slow, languid movements. It startles me when she pauses in place, seemingly motionless, except for her fins barely waving to keep her afloat. *Odd.* I swear if my fish friend is belly up tomorrow, I'm going to lose my shit.

"Hang in there, girl. I'll call the aquarium guy tomorrow." Maybe their pH is off. That would be my luck. I offer to take care of Dex's fish, and I end up murdering them all by neglect as I'm living out my dirtiest fantasies all over Dex's home. He told me to make myself comfortable, but by comfortable he probably did not mean naked on his couch with my legs hooked over Finn's shoulders.

Damn. I cringe to myself. That does not come off well. I wonder how he'd take it if he knew what Finn and I were up to. It might be the first time a client has ever fired me. And hell, Dex would be justified in doing so.

Chapter 22

Avery

All my instincts are telling me Mason's dodgy, lazy behavior is going to cost us the Legacy Resorts contract. I'm not sure why he's so distracted. It's a simple request. I need the numbers so I can get to work. We're pitching in less than two months, and this is the most significant contract we've ever chased. So, after weeks of no reports, I take matters into my own hands.

After hours of scouring our common LinkedIn connections, I determine that Hunter Mahan is the marketing director at Legacy Resorts. Due to our numerous contacts in common, I'm able to snag his email address.

Misogynist or not, surely he's capable of responding to an email.

* * *

From: Avery Scott, Arrow Consulting
To: Hunter Mahan, Legacy Resorts

Dear Mr. Mahan,

My name is Avery Scott. I'm one of the principal owners of Arrow Consulting. It's very nice to meet you. It's my understanding that Legacy Resorts has requested a proposal presentation from Arrow Consulting at the end of the summer.

First and foremost, thank you for the opportunity. I know you've been in touch with my business partner, Mason Richards, but in an effort to make sure I'm thoroughly prepared with a strategy suggestion, would you kindly send over your current marketing reports? Mainly, I'm interested in the click traffic so I can assess your current customer demographics and how many leads are resulting in sales.

If necessary, please feel free to send over an NDA. I'll be more than happy to sign. I've included my number if you have any immediate questions or concerns. I will make myself available.

Thank you.

Regards,

Avery Scott

* * *

A soft knock at the front door sounds, and I click send in a hurry before I can talk myself out of going over Mason's head. I shut my laptop and head to the front door, the butterflies in my stomach kicking up.

It's been a few days since I've seen Finn. I decided after our last encounter, he's more than holding up his end of the bargain. It's time for me to do my part. I've spent the last few days immersed in boudoir photography and all things freelance photography-income related, and I have some initial ideas on how Finn can get his business on track.

I open the door to see Finn's broad back. He's wearing a thin T-shirt that hugs the bumps and ripples of his well-defined muscles. I know what these muscles feel like. I've caressed them, licked them...scratched them. He whips around, two blueberry Red Bulls in his hands.

"Surprise," he says with a charming smile.

"My hero." I reach for the drink in his right hand. "These will go great with dinner." After spinning around, I make my way down the hall, hearing Finn's heavy footsteps behind me.

"There's dinner?" he asks. "I thought this was just a business meeting." I did in fact specifically tell him there would be no sex tonight. I wanted to make sure I wasn't taking advantage of him, so tonight all we're doing is talking shop.

"Dinner might be a stretch." I stop in place and rotate, facing Finn head-on. "I can only really make three things."

He looks amused. "Being?"

"Baked potatoes, cereal—"

"Does cereal count as making something?" he asks with a teasing smile.

I proceed to roll my eyes. "And dip," I finish, pointing to Dex's kitchen table that is currently displaying five different bowls of various dips.

"Holy crap." Finn follows my finger and assesses the table. "That's a lot of dip."

I nod so enthusiastically, my hair falls over my face. "I'm pretty passionate about dip."

Finn chuckles. He smacks my ass casually, ignoring my girlish yelp as he passes by me. Finn sets his drink down and proceeds to pull the Saran Wrap off each of the glass bowls. "You made these just for me?" he asks, cocking one brow.

"Yep." *Slaved away all day.*

He immediately shoves his finger into the first bowl then shamelessly sucks it clean. "What the hell is this masterpiece?" He dunks his finger in again.

I proceed to fetch the new bag of pretzel rods off the kitchen island and hand it to Finn. He opens it with ease, gleefully dunking the thick pretzel stick into the dip once more. "Honey mustard but with a twist—I use spicy brown mustard and Dijon. I know—it shouldn't work, but it's tasty, right?"

Mouth full, he nods and gives me a cheesy thumbs-up.

"Don't fill up," I say. "We still have buffalo chicken dip—yes, with actual chicken so I can try to pass this off as a real meal, French onion dip for the potato chips, I have French baguette for the bacon cheddar chive dip, and for dessert, banana cream pie dip with vanilla wafers."

Finn looks at me the way you'd look at a puppy tripping over its big ears. Adorably...with a little pity. He's silent, but his shoulders are shaking, so I know he's laughing at me.

"What?" I ask. "Look, it's the best I can do. I struggle in the kitchen..."

He shakes his head, a goofy expression on his face. "You are so cute. Never have I been treated to a feast of dips. This is a new standard for date night, by the way." Grabbing the bowl of banana cream pie dip, he places a quick kiss on the top of my head as he passes me. "Can we start with dessert?"

Wait, date night?

"Of course." I collect both of our drinks and a box of crunchy vanilla cookies and join him in the living room. He scowls at me when I join him on the couch, leaving at least a foot of space between us.

Raising up his arm, he invites me to cuddle into his chest and is less than pleased when he sees me grimace. "Okay, what's with you tonight? Did I do something?"

I don't think anyone else in the world would notice, but I see it—Finn seems to shrivel in his seat. Just a hair. Almost unnoticeable...except I notice.

"Are you upset with me?"

"Why would you think that?"

"No kiss hello. You only want to talk business tonight. You're sitting over there like I'm contagious. I'm counting down the minutes until you start giving me the silent treatment."

I roll my eyes so hard they strain. "I hate the silent treatment. Such a waste of time. I'd rather be in a screaming match than play the ice-out game."

Finn points to his chest emphatically. "*Me too.*" He shakes his head like he's trying to shake off a bad memory. "It was my ex's favorite game to play. After a while, I started picking up on the little tells that I'm in trouble. Starting with"—he gestures to the space between us—"she wouldn't let me touch her."

"Oh, hey—no." I reach over to squeeze his knee. "Okay, I just... Look, I feel guilty."

He raises his dark brow. "Why?"

"Because all we do is talk about my needs. I promised to help you with your business, and I haven't been doing that. Every time we're around each other, we seem to—"

"Get naked?"

"Exactly. Is this too much sex? It was just supposed to be a favor." Leaning forward, I collect the energy drink from the coffee table and pop the lid. These are even more delicious when Finn brings them to me. It's a telltale sign he's thinking of me, even when we're apart.

"It won't last forever," he says. My chest immediately tightens as the pang of rejection shocks me.

As a knee-jerk response, I nod enthusiastically, pretending like I'm not caught off guard. "I know. I wasn't thinking this was serious or anything."

"No, I mean, it's fun right now because it's new. It's exciting. It always starts this way when you're with someone new. There's nothing wrong with enjoying it while it lasts. So yeah—it's a lot of sex. *Great.* Let's have a lot of sex while we can."

Funny. Mason and I never had a honeymoon period. Did it fade? Absolutely. But I can't remember it starting off passionate like this. Everything from my past relationship was so careful and calculated and...boring.

"Did you and Nora have a lot of sex?"

"Yes," Finn responds without hesitation. "Pretty much daily when we were together."

"Oh."

"But it wasn't like this."

The light flutter in my chest comes alive. My mouth begins to water in anticipation like he's about to say something really important. All I have to do is ask. "Like what?"

"Nora used sex for control, I think. If I was having sex with her constantly, I couldn't possibly have the time or energy to be having sex with anyone else. It wasn't for enjoyment; it was more of a way to prove myself. To prove how much I loved her and wanted her, but even daily wasn't enough. Nothing I did made her feel less insecure. I was always in trouble. I'd get side glares, silent treatment—hell, sometimes she'd all out scream at me in public. She never trusted that I loved her and only her. No matter what I did, there was always something wrong. I literally was afraid to be around the woman I loved because I knew our next big blowout was just around the corner."

How strange. Here I never thought people who looked like Finn would have intimacy issues. We were both starving in our prior relationships—just starved of different things.

"That sounds a little like..." I bite down on my lip, debating whether it's my place to say. But we're friends. This is something I'd say to any friend. "Emotional abuse."

Finn closes his eyes and nods. "It took me a really long time to admit that. It didn't sound manly to admit I was being treated poorly in my relationship."

I wrap my hand around his fingers and squeeze. "I'm sorry. I'm glad you're doing better now."

Returning my warm smile, he brings my fingers to his lips. "If you're thinking I'm only doing this so you can save my business, you're wrong. I like being around you. You make it easy to smile."

Oh geez. That jolt in my chest. The pulsing shocks and vibrating tremors taking over my body from the inside out are most definitely feelings. *Real fucking feelings.*

"But I'm starting to feel like I'm using you." That's a half-truth. More accurately, I'm starting to worry that I'm blurring lines. It started with *no feelings*. Now we're at *okay, just feelings for the summer*. And I'm getting dangerously close to, *heart freaking ripped to shreds when I have to leave this man and get back to reality*. "I don't want you to feel like my sex toy."

Finn rubs the back of his neck, a sheepish smile creeping across his face. "I'm good with it. Consider me your toy." He opens his legs into a wide V, as unsubtly as possible. "Play with me."

I try to hold a straight face, but we both burst into laughter. "Wow, that was bad...just *bad*."

"I know," he says between breathy chuckles. "Sorry. If I'm being honest, I am so fucking horny right now. It's been three days since I've had you, and I'm getting a little dizzy, nauseated, hot flashes, and my vision is blurry." He puckers his bottom lip.

Is he...begging...for me?

"Are you horny or pregnant?"

He howls in laughter as he pats his lap. "Get over here. You're my cure, Avery. How about we play first, and then business after?"

"Three days isn't that long. Also, you have a hand for that."

He shakes his head. "Nuh-uh. You know how once you've tasted real New York–style pizza, you can't go back to cheap delivery?"

"Eh, I'm more of a Chicago deep-dish kind of girl."

For a moment, he's distracted as he shakes his head in disbelief. "*Deep dish*? What the fu—okay, we'll come back to that. The bottom line is *you*, sweet girl, are gourmet, and now there's no way my hand is going to cut it." He carefully wrestles the can I'm holding out of my grip and sets it aside. Before I can protest, he wraps his hand behind my neck and pulls me to his lips. I briefly allow myself to get swept up, and I kiss him back furiously, enjoying the feel of his tongue on mine. I melt into the powerful way he holds me, so steady, so sure. I start picturing a life with Finn where I'm *this* happy all the time, and it scares me because the minute you like someone...*love someone*...they have the power to completely destroy you.

"Finn," I mumble into his mouth when I feel the bulge in his pants starting to grow against my belly. He's reluctant to break our kiss, and when I keep talking, he moves down to my neck as his hand scrambles for the clasp of my bra. "I've spent the past few days buried in research. I worked so hard on some ideas for you. I really want to share them with you."

"After," he mutters between kisses.

"No. *Now*. Please." I fight my body, my heart, and my mind. *Stop. Stop before I lose control.*

I said the magic word. The two-letter little word that Finn and every man with some goddamn sense should respect: *no*. He immediately leans back on the couch, letting out a shaky breath and trying to calm his arousal.

"Okay. Sorry. You can't blame me, though. You just look so pretty tonight, all dolled up like that. It's like you're purposely trying to tempt me." Finn eyes me up and down, and I am embarrassed he noticed.

Shit. Okay, so yes, I curled my hair and left it down tonight. I also put on a little makeup. Just the color-correcting moisturizer Lennox showed me at Sephora and a little of the sun-kissed bronzer I bought for both of us. She also introduced me to a line of tinted lip balm that may be my new favorite product. But I'm not trying to look desperate, so I wish Finn would stop drawing attention to my efforts of being a little more...visually appealing.

Finn tugs at the waist of my shorts. "Are these new?"

Lennox also took me to a couple of clothing stores during our shopping trip. The outfit I'm wearing—high-waisted black Bohemian-style shorts with a thick bow around the waist, paired with a form-fitting cream tank top—is the outfit she insisted I buy. Lennox was pulling items off the rack left and right for me to try on at the boutique as if I were her little Barbie doll. She complimented me nonstop, but I felt so out of place. The store was too fashion-forward, all the material was too fancy, and every look was far more chic than I could ever pull off. What I'm presently wearing is the only outfit she could talk me into bringing to the register. When I had second thoughts and tried to put it back on the rack last minute, she ended up buying it for me. I immediately felt guilty she had to whip out her credit card due to my stubbornness.

"Lennox took me shopping. She has a good eye for fashion. She helped me pick a couple of things that would be more flattering for my body type."

Finn blinks at me so slowly that his eyelids look heavy. It's almost like he's trying to force himself to hold something back. "What's your body type?"

I roll my eyes childishly. This is awkward. I hate talking about it. I've never been a confident girl when it comes to looks, but I've also never let looks rule my life. I thought I was being mature. Perhaps I was just being avoidant. "What do you think my body type is?" I ask, meaning to make him uncomfortable. Maybe he'll clam up like I am and we can move on to a different subject.

Except it's Finn...

I should've known he has all the right answers when it comes to this.

"Your body type is *damn lucky.* Blessed in all the right places." He traces an hourglass figure in the air with his hands. "Natural and tender and soft. Your body makes me want to curl up next to it, day in and day out. I don't know what type I'd call it—just know that it's my favorite type."

I want to roll my eyes again, scoff, and say he's just saying all of that to pacify me. But the whole point of our arrangement is teaching me to be more self-assured. What good are his lessons if I refuse to learn?

"Thank you," I say. "That makes me feel really good about myself. And thank you for noticing I got dressed up." I bite my bottom lip in contemplation. *Go there? Don't go there?* "For you," I add. "I got dressed up *for you.*"

He wears the sweetest smile I've ever seen on him. "Well, if that's true, it makes me feel really good about myself. It's hard to know what you're thinking sometimes. You keep a lot to yourself."

I squint at him. "Are you kidding? I asked you to be my sex sensei because I'm wildly inept in the bedroom. It really doesn't get much more in your face than that."

"Your feelings," Finn says like it's a clear explanation. But I don't understand, so I just shrug. "You'll openly admit to your insecurities, but you won't actually say how they make you feel. It's like you try to judge yourself before anyone else can. It's strategic. In fact, everything you do is poised and careful. And sure, you cried around me once, but I think those tears were more out of frustration than anything. If you think you're being vulnerable... eh, well, I can tell you try really hard to be more realistic than emotional. It seems lonely."

I lean back against the couch cushions and tuck my knees to my chest. "Since when are my emotions someone else's responsibility? My issues are *my* burden to bear."

Finn waits until I meet his eyes. He's so demanding when it comes to eye contact. Maybe because he knows his icy blue eyes seem to tear down my walls. "Burden me, Avery. I want you to."

I let the stupid tears well in my eyes, and I feel smaller than I ever have before. I wish Finn could understand that we don't see the world the same way. He will never understand what it is to be the ugly duckling. He will also never understand that I'm okay with being the ugly duckling. I'm okay with pajama bottoms, messy buns, and a couple of stains on my T-shirt. I'm fine with pizza pockets for dinner. I don't want to lose myself. I just want to like myself. I want to figure out what I need from my sex life, and then I want to find another ugly duckling so we can live happily together, in the same world where we can swim and waddle at exactly the same pace.

I don't want to fall for a man I would be terrified of losing because I'm not good enough for him. I'm a nice person, I'm easy to talk to, and I'm right in front of Finn's face. Of course he's intrigued...for now. But it won't last. The moment we step out of this bubble, he'll understand how mismatched we really are. But I know if I say all this to Finn, he'll just come up with some poetic excuse to tell me how wonderful I am, and honestly, I'm sick of hearing it.

"Do you still want to have sex?"

He cocks one eyebrow. "That's one hell of a response."

"I'm serious."

"Of course I do."

"And you'll listen to my ideas for your business later? And pay attention?"

He tries to hide his gleeful smile. "Absolutely."

"Okay, then for our next lesson," I say as I drop to the floor and kneel between Finn's legs, "teach me how to give good head."

Finn

She actually looks studious with her head cocked to the side, waiting for instructions. Avery's kneeling in front of me, her pretty eyes blinking at me expectantly. Her low-cut tank top is a siren's song, and the top bumps of her perfect round tits have my head muddled with all kinds of disgraceful thoughts. I'm pining for her, but in a way, she's already mine. Right? But then why doesn't she feel *mine*?

I like Avery exactly the way I met her. Every time I call her beautiful, it's genuine. But the way she brought her A-game tonight is stirring up something territorial in me. I'm jealous for some reason, and I don't know why. It's just the two of us here.

"You're not sleeping with anyone else, right?"

"*What?*" she asks, incredulous, her face twisting up in surprise. "Why would you ask that?"

"We never established we'd be exclusive throughout the deal." I run my thumb from the base of her earlobe to the bottom of her chin, and she leans away from my touch, her surprised expression turning into an accusatory one as her eyes narrow.

"Um, I thought that was implied when I let you fuck me without a condom. *Wait*. Are *you* sleeping with other women?"

Her eyes widen to cartoon proportions, and she begins to rise off her knees. I immediately plant my hands on her shoulders and press her back down as I scoot to the edge of the couch.

"Avery Scott, calm the fuck down. *No. Of course not.* I just wanted to make sure we were on the same page."

"Same page, same page," she mutters, but I can see her chest still rising and falling rapidly.

Good. It's not just me. I hope the idea of me with another woman makes her sick, because I'd be willing to rip another man to shreds right now.

Reaching over Avery's shoulder to the coffee table, I dip my finger into the bowl of banana cream pie dip and scoop out a large dollop. I taste it first. "Mmm, that's *really good.* I love banana cream pie. Second only to coconut cream pie. Although this dip has me reconsidering." I hold my finger, still half-coated in dessert, to her lips. "Open your mouth."

Avery drops her jaw, and I insert my finger a little farther back than she was expecting. She gags on the tip of my forefinger when it touches the back of her throat. "Sorry," she says, sputtering. "Wasn't ready. I'm okay now. Try again."

"Don't overthink this, baby. Suck."

She takes my finger into her mouth again and this time swirls her tongue around the tip before pulling her mouth away. My finger falls off her lips with a pop.

"*Good girl.*" My cock twitches in anticipation. Goddamn, I love our sexy games. Especially because I know she only plays them with me. "It's simple. Lots of pressure, keep it really wet, and make sure you let me know how much you like it."

"That's it?" she asks, licking her lips and making the last remnants of the sweet dip on her lips disappear.

"That's it."

She reaches for my waistband, and I bridge my hips, letting her pull down my athletic pants and briefs. After she tosses them aside, her gaze toggles from my growing erection to my eyes. "This would be a little easier if you were smaller."

I chuckle at her roundabout compliment. She's cute, but my mind is elsewhere. I want her warm, wet mouth. Right now. "I'm sure you'll manage. Also, give me those perfect tits." Leaning forward, I scoop her breasts out of her tank top and bra, one by one. I palm, squeeze, and knead firmly, possessively. *Mine. She's mine. These are mine to enjoy. I want to wake up next to these...to her. Every day.*

My wandering thoughts are wiped clean when I feel her tongue flicking at the tip of my cock. Avery's wearing a mischievous smile, a little glint of angst in her eyes. "You like to be teased, right?"

"At the moment? No." I inch forward, trying to guide myself into her mouth, but she presses her lips together—no entry.

"You make me beg for it almost every time," she mumbles. She flicks her tongue once more, swirling it around my now glistening tip. The sensation is just enough to ignite me but not to satisfy anything. "Payback is a bitch."

"Avery," I grumble. "You're so sexy." I fix my eyes on her heavy tits and pert nipples, jostling around as she scoots forward on her knees. "We can play any other night, but right now I need you. Please, just—"

"Ah, there's the magic word," she mutters right before she engulfs me.

I groan in relief. *Fuck, it feels good.* If her pussy is my home, her mouth is my vacation. Covering her teeth with her lips, she clamps down and runs her mouth up and down half of my shaft. I'm losing my fucking mind from her moans and whimpers. She even sings my praises in between sucking—*you taste so good, you're so big, I want your dick forever, Finn.*

She executes flawlessly. I'm more than pleased, but Avery pulls back, unsatisfied. Wrapping her hand around the base of my shaft, she tries to take in more of me but can barely swallow down half of my cock.

"Dammit," she says, frustrated at her failed attempt to deep-throat.

"You don't have to do that," I say. "This is perfect. You'll make me come just like this."

"No...I..." She leans away and leaves my needy dick unattended for a moment as she examines the length. "It's possible, right? Or are you too big? Could Nora do it?"

"*Whoa, hey.*" I wipe the dot of spit from the corner of her mouth with my thumb. "Don't do that. I don't want to hear her name when I'm with you. Don't compare yourself." *There's no comparison.* "You really want to try?"

She nods, a look of determination mixed with stubbornness flickering in her soft green eyes. "Just out of curiosity."

"Spit on it, get it really wet." She does as I ask and strokes my throbbing cock, ensuring the entire thing is slick with her saliva. I weave my hand through her hair, cupping the back of her head. "Good girl. Relax. Breathe through your nose and don't panic. Just take as much as you can. Believe me, that's plenty. When it's too much, just pull back. We'll stop."

"Okay."

"Hold out your tongue."

I play there for a minute, rubbing my tip against her flattened tongue, and then before she can close her lips around me, I pull her head forward, sliding half of my length into her mouth, nudging the back of her throat. She immediately sputters and gags. *Shit.* But when I try to pull away, she grips my hips. Determined, she takes in more and more until there are tears running down her cheek and her eyes grow red. She draws me in again. Over and over. Determined as all hell. I eventually watch her breathing start to steady—in and out, through her nose. The panic subsides. After several more tries, I watch in surprise as most of my cock disappears down her throat. She can only hold it for a second, and she rips away, gasping for air. She's breathing hard, her face flushed, her eyes still watering, but she looks thoroughly pleased with herself.

"There we go. That's closer. Seventh time's the charm." There's a silly smile on her face. But I'm in no mood for jokes.

Goddamn, that was sexy. So fucking sexy. My balls clench, and

I grab my pulsing cock in my hand.

"Avery, baby, can you swallow for me?" I ask between my ragged breaths.

"Yes."

"Good girl. Just take the tip and hold my balls."

Stroking myself, I talk her through my release until I spill down her throat. I go rigid as I groan in delight, emptying every last drop into her mouth. I wait for her audible gulp until I slump back into the couch, the fabric soft against my bare ass. *Sorry, Dex.*

"Good job, baby." I praise her wholeheartedly, and she's glowing under the attention. "You did so—"

I'm interrupted when Avery's phone rings loud from the kitchen, cutting the tension between us. She immediately jumps up, but her legs must have fallen asleep from being on her knees for so long. She winces and stumbles, and I reach out to help steady her, but she recovers too quickly, darting over to her phone. I watch her puzzled expression as she scours the caller ID.

She points to the phone. "I think it's work. I have to—"

"Go ahead."

"Hello, this is Avery Scott," she says into the phone as I proceed to pull on my briefs and pants. "Mr. Mahan, I wasn't expecting a call. Thank you."

The angry beast in my chest rumbles. It's the "Mr." that irks me. *It's work. Calm down, Finn.* This could be a crusty old dude in his sixties for all I know, but I can't shake this greedy urge that reared its ugly head tonight with Avery. It's official. I want her for myself. No one is going to treat her like I will. No other man will be as dedicated as I am to making this woman see how beautiful she is, inside and out. If I can do it best, then she should just be with me. It's that simple. Yes, it's too soon. Sure, we're on a timeline. *I know* it's just a damn deal for the summer—but I don't care.

I'm happy. *I'm fucking happy.* I bet I can make her happy too.

Avery, completely unaware of my sudden revelation, continues to talk in a foreign tone. I'm learning her business voice sounds just like a flight attendant.

"Well, that was my primary concern as well. From the preliminary research I've done, it looks like commercials are a good idea, but I don't think local cable is your best option. Streaming services are ideal, but timing is everything. Especially for your click traffic, summer is not the time to heavily invest—trips are already planned. You needed to make the placements around the end of February. That's the sweet spot. Consumers have mostly recovered from the holidays and are debating between investing in spring break or summer travel plans... Right, exactly..."

I don't know what the hell she's talking about, but she adjusts her tits back into her tank top and straightens her back before she begins pacing. Even barefoot, she looks like a boss at the moment. She's suddenly wearing her sexy, take-over-the-world, confident, I-got-this attitude. It's such a turn-on, and if she's up for it, I'm going to rest for ten minutes and then bend her over this couch.

"Mr. Mahan, I'd love to talk numbers, but would you mind holding for just a moment... Okay, thank you."

Turning her attention to me, Avery asks, "Finn?"

"Yeah?" I ask.

"I just put the Chief of Marketing for Legacy Resorts on hold. That's the multimillion-dollar contract I told you I'm trying to land. He's about to conference in the Chief Financial Officer and VP because apparently, they've been eager to chat with me. I have to—"

I hold up my palms as I rise. "Say no more." I cross the space between us.

"You don't have to go," she says. "But...this might take a while."

Leaning down to plant a kiss on her forehead, I breathe in her hair, enjoying the smell of tropical, ginger, and mint. "You focus. I'll see myself out." I grab the bowl behind her on the kitchen table. "But I'm taking the buffalo chicken dip."

She giggles. "All yours. Oh, but heat it up first." She catches my hand and squeezes it tenderly. "Thank you for understanding."

"Of course. Oh, and, Queen?"

She melts under that nickname. I love it when the color fills her cheeks when she swoons for me.

"That head? Ten out of ten, baby."

With that, I leave her to her call, feeling a medley of new emotions at once: satisfied...hopeful...happy...ready.

I'm ready for this.

Chapter 23

Avery

I thought a virtual morning coffee date with my best friend would be a good idea. Sassiness aside, I miss her. She's more family than friend, and this is the longest we've gone without talking in at least a decade. But the problem with very long-term friendships is that sometimes you've excused the bad behavior for so long, you almost don't recognize it.

"Palmer," I say, staring at the side of her face, her eyes clearly on her phone off screen as she's texting. "Do you need to go?"

"One sec," she mumbles, and I hear her pecking away at her phone. Whomever she's messaging must be getting an earful.

"Because I can call you back." She's been ignoring me for at least five minutes now. I thought a face-to-face conversation might help us connect.

"Just one sec."

Over the past month, I've been spending all my free time with Finn—*okay, under Finn*—and with Lennox. It's never this complicated with them. I never have to beg for eye contact or their attention. Why does Palmer treat me this way when it'd be so easy to be decent to me? *Why do we trample on the ones we love?* I'm almost bothered that my new friends are unintentionally pointing out the glaring issues in my oldest friendship.

I wait another two minutes before I inform her, "Okay then. I'll try and catch you another time when you're—"

"There," she grumbles. She puts her phone down and faces me head-on. She adjusts her iPad, realizing she was only in half of the frame this entire time. "So sensitive. It was a work thing. Sorry, there's drama going on, and it's stressing me the fuck out. Some girl is trying to get me fired."

And here is the quintessential problem with my relationship with Palmer. Instinctively, I'm too protective and overly concerned. *I* can complain about her obnoxious nuances, but I'm the *only* one who can. Because I love her. Because I always have her best intentions at heart. And while I have to gently remind her, *almost daily*, how not to be a shit friend, nobody threatens Palmer. I become a bulldog with a big bark when it comes to my best friend.

"Who? And why?"

"The director's assistant. It's fucking ridiculous. Jealous bitch. I think she wanted to be considered for my role, but instead, she's basically a glorified stagehand." Palmer twists open a bottle of water and takes a hurried sip. "She even asked me for acting advice once. Can you believe that? Then she wants to stab me in the back by whining to the director when I'm late—I mean once. I was late once. Well, twice, but the other time I was sick, so that's not my fault."

I wrap my hands tightly around my jumbo novelty mug, which was a gag gift from Finn. It must be for soup because I'm certain it holds at least twenty-four ounces. He proudly showed up at my door one morning with this giant black mug with hot pink writing that reads: *I had great sex in Las Vegas.* He told me it made him think of me while he was at the store and he left with a snicker.

Needless to say, it's now my favorite mug in the world. I smile into my cup as I ask Palmer, "Why would she be so devious after you helped her?"

"Helped her what?" Palmer snaps.

I swallow my sip of over-the-top sweet coffee. "You said you gave her advice..."

Palmer snorts. "No, I said she asked for advice. What I told her was to lose twenty pounds, save up ten grand, and buy herself a set of tits."

I inhale and exhale slowly, debating whether this is even my battle to fight. "Should you say that kind of thing to people? You probably pissed her off, and now she's out to get you. Not everyone understands your humor."

She raises one brow at me. "I wasn't trying to be funny."

Oh for the love of God. "I seriously doubt one grudge can get you fired from a role. How many episodes have you filmed now?"

"Five. And rumor has it, we're about to be picked up by a big streaming network. I'm not technically allowed to say who, but if you can read between the lines, it's Net—" She silently flicks the air in front of the screen.

Clever. "Really? That's amazing." I drop my jaw and force my eyes into wide, enthusiastic circles. "Why aren't you more excited?" I click my manicured nails against the side of my mug, and it apparently captures Palmer's attention. She leans closer to the screen, peering at my nails.

"Are you wearing acrylic? You hate acrylics."

"No, it's actually this hybrid dip thing. My friend Lennox recommended it." That's quite literally my best description. Lennox and I went to the salon, and all I know is this is somewhere between gel polish and acrylic, except it's vegan, cruelty-free, and smells like pears. I examine my mint green nails, which are the color Finn suggested when he saw me off to my day date with Lennox a couple of days ago. And by *suggested* I mean he pulled me into his chest and whispered in my ear that my hand decorated in green would look beautiful wrapped around his cock.

"Who the hell is Lennox?"

"Finn's cousin...and employee...and best friend...and sort of roommate, I'm not sure. She's just always around."

Palmer's eyes narrow at the smile on my face. "Who's Finn?"

Setting my mug aside, I then press my fingers against my eyelids. "The guy I'm sleeping with, Palmer. The guy I've told you about countless times now."

"Hot tattoo guy? Your sex coach thing is still going on?" She tsks her tongue in a way that screams condescending. "*That's adorable.*"

My smile instantly dissipates. The familiar feeling washes over me, and I shrivel. What is it? It's hard to put my finger on it... It is the special, passive-aggressive way Palmer keeps me in my place and reminds me that no matter what I have, no matter how shiny it is, it's small...cute...*adorable.* And now that I've had a taste of support, it's clear as day—she needs to do better. *She's capable of doing better.*

"Does it make you feel good about yourself when you make me feel like that?"

"What?" Her light eyes widen as she tucks a strand of her platinum-blond hair behind her ears.

"That word, '*adorable.*' It cheapens what I'm doing. Finn doesn't pity me. I think he's actually really into me. We're good together. Better than good. We're over-the-top, hot together. And even if it's just for the summer, I feel alive. I feel bold and brave, and for the first time in...ever, I'm learning to appreciate my body exactly the way it is. If you love me, please don't poke at that or make a mockery of it. If you don't have something kind to say, just don't say anything."

I steady my breath, slow inhale, slow exhale, amidst my pounding heart. I hate having to stand up to Palmer, but not because of an impending screaming match. It's because she's sensitive. And by drawing boundaries...I just made her cry.

"Oh, Palmer," I say, "please don't cry—"

"No, no," she says, sniffling. Her face instantly turns red and blotchy. "You're right. I'm sorry. I think I'm just jealous. Lennox and Finn—they're a big part of your life now, and I'm not there to experience it with you. Adorable is just a word, Aves. I didn't mean anything by it. And I'm so proud of you. You could've been a hot fucking mess after your breakup with Mason, but instead, you've come out on top. *You always come out on top.* I'm so sorry if I was mean—"

"It's okay," I say. "Thank you for listening and apologizing." I know what she's about to say next. It's always the way we end these uncomfortable exchanges.

"I don't deserve you," she mumbles.

I follow up with my part, like a rehearsed scene. "Doesn't matter, best friend. You've got me."

* * *

The stone path that leads to Finn's photography studio is beautiful... but uneven. I've nearly rolled my ankles three times in my heels by the time I make it to the clients' entrance. Across the yard, I see the gate that leads to Dex's hot tub. Finn's backyard is beautiful and well-kept, but small—it's about half the size of Dex's.

Strangely enough, in the entire time we've been hanging out, I haven't been inside his studio once. Finn always picks me up or meets me at Dex's. Plus, he claims Lennox is always lurking at his home, and we wouldn't have privacy. What a wonderful freaking change of pace. A man who puts in the effort. The next man I date most definitely needs this quality. There's nothing better than opening the front door and seeing your hunky knight in armor smoldering at you.

As a break from our normal tradition, Finn asked me to meet him in his studio before we head to dinner with his dad. I'm barely in front of the glass doors before he greets me with a smile as he slides the door open. He clutches his heart.

"God, I love this dress on you. You look gorgeous." He cocks an eyebrow and stares at me warningly.

"Thank you," I say.

"There it is." He winks at me. "Good girl."

"I wish I had something new to wear for tonight, but it's my only fancy dress." I shrug. "Sorry you've seen me in this before."

"Why be sorry?" His dimples deepen as he looks me up and down. "You should live in this dress, Queen. Day in and day out." He plants a quick peck on the top of my head and brushes my hair behind my back, following up with a kiss on my neck then my bare shoulder.

"You clean up nice yourself." To no one's surprise, Finn is dressed impeccably. His clean tan slacks are wrinkle-free and pair nicely with his long-sleeved black dress shirt with subtle gray pinstripes. Does he have this much style on his own, or does Lennox dress him too? I poke him in the chest playfully but let my fingers linger when I feel the electricity pulsing through them. When am I going to get tired of this? When will enough be enough? Because lately, I have to cross my legs when I'm around Finn to control the instant urge. I've never felt like this. I've never *needed sex* like this before. It's never been this fun.

My fingers trail down his chest, over the bumps of his tight six-pack covered by the thin fabric of his shirt. He lets me tap teasingly against his belt a few times before he grabs my hand. "No time, Avery. And anyway, I want to show you something."

He laces his fingers with mine and leads me past the small seating area. We pause in front of a closed door, and Finn turns to face me. Sometimes, he takes me off guard. At times when I'm least expecting it, he stuns me with his gaze. I gawk at him like a deer in blinding headlights because it's so easy to talk to him that sometimes I forget how fucking incredibly good-looking he is.

"You okay?" he asks, his brows furrowing in puzzlement.

I clear my throat and force myself to blink, feeling how heavy my fake eyelashes are. "Yes. Fine. What's up?"

"Remember how you said I should use a model for the new website?"

"Yes..."

I ran Finn through a lot of suggestions. None of which he seemed particularly thrilled about. I suggested that he set up partnerships with lingerie stores within a twenty-mile radius and offer a discount on his services for customers of boutiques willing to hand out his card. He shrugged. He said it felt like heckling.

I also suggested he film a few photography lessons for educational purposes to give tips and tricks to amateur photographers just starting out in the business. Educational content is fantastic for SEO. Again, he thanked me for the suggestion but brushed it off.

I ran him through click traffic, promotion packaging, raising his pricing, adjusting the studio hours, and paying for ads in newsletters and bulletins. All fell on deaf ears, except the rebranding. I came up with a new logo and new business name. *Finn Photography*. No Harvey. We ditched the lousy tri-circle design he had, and instead, I mocked up an iridescent shark fin on a clean black surface. *That* he loved. He was really enthusiastic about the designs I drafted for the new business cards and flyers I emailed him. They are just mockups. I'll send them to a professional designer to really take them to the next level. In the meantime, we've been stuck on the website.

I always tell my clients that a website needs to tell a story... without telling a story. It has to be subtle. It has to be an *energy*. There is a way to evoke emotion with colors and fonts, and good branding is what hooks and keeps a client.

Finn needs a model to show off his boudoir photography skills. We need images that are tasteful, yet edgy. We need women to see an image and want to picture themselves in the scene. I was under the impression Finn would reach out to a former client to get their permission to use certain pictures, but judging by the look on his face, he wildly misjudged what I meant.

"You," he says simply. "I want you. You're perfect." He opens the door, and I suck in a sharp breath at the sight.

The floor is covered in black flower heads. It's a sea of wrong-colored roses. It feels like walking right into a black-and-white photograph. The entire room is decorated in black, white, and cream. There's a coolness...and edge...a certain moodiness. The four-poster bed is made up with white sheets and sprinkled with pearl-white rose petals. What looks like ink is spilled across the edge, dripping to the floor. I run my finger over the dark spill. It's glue...or wax. Whatever it is, it's solid. Every detail, down to the string of pearls draped over the vanity mirror, is intricately placed.

"This is *incredible*, Finn. It's tragic and haunting but beautiful. It's so...sexy."

"All Lennox," he says from behind me as I step farther into the room, trying not to squish the fake roses surrounding my feet.

"It reminds me of..." I roll my wrist in the air as I trail off and search my brain. "What are those black-and-white movies called?"

"Film noir."

"Exactly. Film noir. I love this. This is going to do *so well* with clients. When are you going to start shooting in here?" I spin around to face him, a wide smile on my face. He returns a half smile, his expression sly and teasing.

"I have to adjust the lighting, but I'm ready to do a test session. How about after dinner, you be my guinea pig?"

"No."

"Tomorrow?" he offers.

"Not good either."

He scrunches his face. "Well, when's good for you?"

I return his quizzical stare. "When guinea pigs fly." I shake off his ridiculous expression and hold my hand out. "Come on. Aren't we going to be late to meet your dad?"

"Avery," Finn scolds.

"Finn," I say just as sternly. "Let it go. It's not happening. You're not photographing me in here or anywhere. *Especially* not with my clothes off. End of discussion. Let's go."

He grabs my hand but doesn't take my lead. Instead, he yanks me against his body. He wraps his strong arms around my waist and holds me in a bear's grip. When he feels my body relax, he reaches up with one hand and traces the slope of my forehead, down the bridge of my nose, finally tracing my lips with his finger. "I know you're a little camera-shy. I can help you with that."

"No," I mumble.

"I'm so good at my job, Avery. I take beautiful photos. I promise."

"I've seen your work and I don't doubt that for a second, Finn."

"Then what's the problem? You watched yourself in the mirror when you rode my tongue until you came. You're not as shy as you're pretending to be. You don't even have to be fully nude if you don't want to."

"That's different. *No*."

"I just want you to see yourself the way I do."

"Well, I don't." I am on the borderline of a tantrum. I feel so ridiculous, but Finn doesn't understand. Whatever spell I have him under is emotional. A picture can't convey the feelings Finn gets around me. A picture can't describe the bonds of friendship we've built. All he'll see in front of him is a woman who is probably twice the size of the rail-thin models he's likely used to fucking. I'm a phase for him. An over-correction. A safeguard around his heart. I've never seen Nora, but how much do you want to bet she looks otherworldly gorgeous?

I just want to stay right where we are. I want to keep pretending for as long as we can. One summer. I was promised *one freaking summer.*

"What's wrong?" Finn murmurs. "Haven't I spent the past month teaching you how to love yourself? Remember what I told you? It's confidence, Avery."

I raise my shoulders and drop them. "I appreciate it. And I feel great being with you. But you don't erase a lifetime of insecurities and doubt in a few weeks. This isn't part of the deal. You're supposed to show me how to fuck, not how to love."

I wish I could take it back. I want to swallow the words back down and shove them into the depths of my stomach. I don't mean a damn word, but I'm scared to tell him how I feel. There is no good answer. Even if he returns my feelings, the clock will immediately start ticking. We make sense in the bubble. But what happens when we step out? Finn isn't going to feel this way about me forever.

His eyelids droop as he presses his lips into a firm line. "Okay, I hear you."

"I'm sorry."

"It's fine. But it's clear what we're doing isn't working. I wanted to help you, not make you feel even more insecure. So..."

The flicker of a playful smile teases the corner of his lip. "Until you're ready to do this"—he juts his thumb over his shoulder—"we should probably stop our lessons."

"*What?*" Oh no, buddy. No, no. *One whole summer.* I've got six more weeks at least of enjoying your body.

"You heard me." Now he's wearing a full-blown, shit-eating grin. "Come on, Queen. We're going to be late."

He leaves me behind as he moves toward the door. Like a child robbed of her candy, I can't help but pout. My hands find my hips, and my toes nervously twitch in my high heels. "You're seriously trying to cut me off from sex? You really think that'll get you your way?"

"Excuse me," he mumbles with his eyes locked on mine. My gaze immediately falls to his crotch as he makes a meal out of adjusting himself through his pants, his thin slacks easily outlining the shape of his dick. Even unaroused, the man is Hulk-sized. "There we go. Much better."

"Was that necessary?" I ask. I blink at him, unimpressed. "That's playing dirty."

"Don't worry, sweetheart, it won't take you long. You'll be posing for me soon, and after, we're going to christen this studio. I'm going to fuck you ten different ways in this room. I promise you that," he says, following up with a light chuckle.

"I'm not getting in front of the camera, Finn." Of all the stupid things I just said, that part remains to be true. I take his outstretched hand and weave my fingers in his.

"Oh, Avery," Finn singsongs. "I know how I affect you, and I have *every intention* of playing dirty."

Chapter 24

Finn

I give the upscale restaurant a once-over, but there's still no sign of Dad. We reconfirmed. Last week, I even texted him and asked him to update the reservation to accommodate three. So why he's late, I don't understand. I'm not particularly upset. I'm enjoying this pretentious restaurant, with my date. I'm not sure if Avery would call this an official date—but she's wearing her sexy black dress, her makeup is done, and she's even wearing golden hoops in her ears. I didn't even realize Avery's ears were pierced until tonight.

That has to be something. If she's putting in this much effort to fix up like this to meet my dad, she must want to make a good impression. Because...*she cares, right*? She has to be feeling the way I'm feeling.

Our waitress, who politely introduced herself as Penny, returns to our table and smiles, and she silently refreshes our water glasses.

"Excuse me, Penny, could we start with an appetizer, please?" I ask, and the waitress grimaces.

"I'm so sorry. Restaurant policy is we can't put in food orders until the entire party has arrived. I can get you another round of drinks and more wasabi nuts, though."

I glance at the tiny dish of almonds that Avery hasn't touched. Avery isn't a picky eater, and I've learned in the past month that both in the kitchen and in the bedroom, she's open to trying pretty much anything at least once, but wasabi is off the table. She nearly gagged when the waitress set them on the table.

"Would you like a drink, Queen?" I set my eyes on Avery, and after a quick smile, I let my gaze wander down to her ample cleavage. *Ah, damn.* Holding out might be a little harder for me than I realized. But I don't know how else to get her in my studio. I know she doesn't want me to document her body, but it's not for me. It's for her. She needs this. I've seen it so many times before. It's why I got into boudoir photography. The pride I get when a woman finds her confidence and finally sees herself as all the things she never thought she was... It's unrivaled. I like giving that gift.

Penny turns her head and stares right at Avery. Her shoulders relax, and she changes her tone to a casual one. "Excuse me, girl. He calls you Queen?" she asks.

Avery covers her eyes as her smile spreads and her cheeks turn pink. "Every time he sees me. He treats me like one too."

Penny whips her head around and glances at me. She clutches her chest. "How long have you two been together?"

"A little over a month," I respond.

Avery raises her brows at me, and I shoot her a little wink. She keeps her eyes on me as she grips her water glass and brings it to her lips. "It's been a really good month," she says before taking a small sip.

There. There it is. Validation. I knew she wanted more too. I felt it. But how? Should she stay in Vegas? Should I go to California? Long distance isn't an option. I watched that travesty unfold with my parents. Maybe we're not ready for this conversation yet. Maybe we're just ready to own up to what this really is, no matter how it got started.

"You two," Penny says, pointing back and forth between us on opposite sides of the booth, "are perfect together." Her eyes land on Avery again. "Hold on to him tight, honey. When a man calls you a queen every day, hold on *damn tight*." She clenches one of her fists in the air, showing off her red-manicured nails. "What can I get you to drink?"

Avery taps the long, skinny drink menu to her left. "I can't decide between the Show Me Love or the Start Me Up. What's your recommendation?"

"Um, let's see. Show Me Love has a delicious lychee puree. It's unique and fresh. You'll never taste anything like it, but it's light and a touch sour. Start Me Up is much sweeter and bolder. The passion fruit puree mixes perfectly with the pineapple rum. Both are fantastic choices."

All right, time to flex a little. I know Avery isn't after the finer things in life, but if she's with me, she can have them.

I pull out my wallet and fish out a few hundred-dollar bills. "Bring her both. Johnnie Walker Blue for me." I fold the bills between my ring and middle finger and hold them out to the waitress. "And please put in an order for the calamari and the brie-stuffed mushrooms." I try to make sure my smile is kind but assertive. I don't love acting like a Harvey, but fuck if I'll let my girl go hungry because my dad can't get his ass to a restaurant on time.

Penny doesn't even hesitate. She snatches up the bills. "Our little secret," she says with a wink and hurries off to the back of the restaurant to put in our drinks and appetizer order.

The minute she's out of earshot, Avery leans into the cloth-covered table between us. "Okay, Finn Harvey—fess up. Are you already loaded? Is that why you don't care about making money from your photography business?"

"Who says I don't care?"

"You didn't take any of my suggestions. I'm *great* at what I do. I've helped companies near bankruptcy make it into the Fortune 500. Strategic partnerships, brand positioning, SEO, and local newsletter ads would make your business soar, but you ignored all of it. You only care about the stinking shark fin logo."

"Because it's pretty damn cool. I'm Finn. It's a shark fin..." I tap my temple with two fingers. "That should've come to me sooner."

Avery doesn't return my smile. She blinks at me with a blank expression.

"Okay, okay, you want the truth?"

She nods. "I think I know the truth. You doubt me."

Reaching across the table, I grab the tips of her fingers, decorated in light green polish, and squeeze tenderly. "Not for a damn second. I'm, uh...overwhelmed...and pretty intimidated. You kept talking about metrics and measuring campaign success..." Releasing her fingers, I bury my face in my hands before blowing out a sharp breath. "I take pictures, I have a studio, I edit, but the business part? I was never cut out to be entrepreneurial. If I start all that stuff you told me to do, I wouldn't know how to handle it after the summer, when you go back to California."

She tilts her head to the side, a look of pity washing over her face. "Finn, you could call me whenever, for whatever, and I'd be there for you. I get this kind of thing can be a lot at first." She lets out a frustrated sigh. "Dammit."

"What?"

"When I asked you to help me in exchange for my services, I guess I made the thickheaded assumption that your business was your main source of income. But I make pretty good money, Finn, and never once in my life have I tipped a limo driver or waitress hundreds of dollars to get my way. So be honest... You don't actually need my help, do you? Your photography business is more of a hobby. You're already filthy rich."

The temperature of my blood begins to rise. This is the side of my life I prefer not to highlight. It attracts the wrong characters. But this is Avery...

"Not yet," I mutter. "Yes, I'll get part of my inheritance when I'm thirty, but until then, the next year and a half will be a little tight financially—"

"Then why are you wasting your money on showing off?"

My jaw drops open. "I'm not showing off. It's not really my money."

I have almost one hundred thousand dollars that I've tucked into a separate account. It's a culmination of money from my dad, which he gifted for birthdays and holidays. The account also contains the huge chunk of change he gave me when I built an in-home photography studio. I try my best not to touch the money. My dad is convinced he can buy relationships. It's dirty money. *Forgive me. Love me. Love the monster.* But yeah, sue me, I made a few withdrawals to take Avery out and show her a nice time.

"Look, I'm trying to be—" *How do I say this? I don't like dipping into that account...but I do it for you. To prove a point. You're worth the white glove, five-star, royalty treatment. The way no one's ever treated you in your life.* "I don't want you to see me as a guy who is all looks, has a failing business, and can't treat you to nice things." I gesture around to the extravagant restaurant.

"That's funny," she mutters almost under her breath. Her face falls as her eyes land on her lap.

"What's funny?"

She flashes me a brief, clipped smile. "I just liked it better when I thought you needed me."

"Oh, I do—"

A loud bellow of laughter sounds at the entrance of the restaurant, causing me to stop midsentence. Even Avery whips her head around at the commotion. The hairs on the back of my neck rise as I watch him charm the young, brunette hostess. Fine, my dad has game. But she's thirty years his junior, at least.

Twenty seconds. No, less than. *Less than fucking twenty seconds* and we haven't even spoken and I'm already irritated. I raise my hand to beckon him over to our booth at the back of the restaurant, but he doesn't see me. His eyes are fixed on the young hostess's chest as he makes an excuse to touch her arm. I don't know what they're talking about, but *"your table is this way"* really shouldn't involve so much flirting.

Avery straightens in her seat, her bugged-out stare landing on me. "That's your dad?"

"Mmhmm, that's Junior."

"Junior?"

"Yes, Gramps is Senior, Dad is Junior, and I'm Griffin Harvey the Third." I cock my head at the glazed look in her eyes. She seems both alarmed and amused at the same time. "What?" I ask.

"Nothing," she says, shaking her head. "You guys just look a *lot* alike..." But the way she says it...

Ugh. I roll my eyes. "Don't say it."

"I didn't say anything," she insists, trying to cover her giggle.

"You're thinking it."

"I'm not."

I glare at her. "You are... Fine. Just say it."

"I have nothing to say."

"Just get it out, Avery," I grumble.

"You'll forgive me?" she asks, giving me an adorable, innocent smile.

"Of course."

She makes a big ordeal of coughing into her fist. "Your dad"—*cough, cough*—"is hot." She bursts out laughing. "Okay, I'm kidding. Kind of. It's just, he doesn't look his age. Actually, how old is he?"

I narrow my eyes at her again. "Why? You want his number?"

"Oh, stop, Finn."

I'm not proud to say it, but it would not be the first time one of my dates ditched me for my dad.

"He's fifty-six, a pilot, disgustingly rich, and has the sex drive of a man in his early twenties."

Avery shakes her head, her long, brunette waves falling over his shoulders. "Oh, geez. Your poor mom."

That. That right there is why Avery's the one. She gets it.

I glance over Avery's shoulder, watching the hostess heading to our table with my dad in tow. He purposely trails a foot behind so he can watch her ass. It's like watching a lion stalk its prey. Maybe I should warn her, but judging by that stupid giddy smile on her face, she's happy to walk right into his trap. *Use a condom. Getting child support out of him will be a bitch.*

"Look," I say in a hurry, "my dad is a nice enough guy, but if you're uncomfortable at any point, we can leave—"

"Finn." Avery reaches across the table and squeezes my hand. "You asked me to come here for support. So I'm here. Unless your dad slaps a hockey mask on and starts chasing us around with a machete, I'm not going anywhere. Don't worry about me." She raises her brows. "Worry about you," she says in a hushed tone as my dad approaches.

"You have my number, honey. Call me after your shift, and maybe I'll let you buy me a drink," Dad says with a wink to the hostess, who scuttles away, blushing. "Champ!" he bellows. He holds out his arms, and I scoot out of the booth to embrace my father. "You look good, son. I'm so happy to see you." He clasps his forearm around my shoulders and pats my back with gusto. "So happy."

"Hey, Dad," I mumble into his shoulder. My dad still has a solid two inches of height on me. I have a bit more muscle, but not by much. Admittedly, he's in great shape for fifty-six. "Why are you so late?"

"Ah, I'm sorry, bud. I didn't mean to be rude. Truthfully, I fell asleep in my hotel room. If I wasn't staying right upstairs, this dinner might've turned into a nightcap. By the time I threw on a sports coat and ran out the door, I was already twenty minutes late."

I nod, but I'm skeptical. I believe he was sleeping. I just doubt he was alone. "Dad, this is Avery Scott." *Ah, fuck it. I'm just going to say it. Let's see what she does.* "My date."

She wiggles to the edge of the long booth and rises, her dainty hand extended. "Mr. Harvey, it's a pleasure to meet you. May I just say Finn is your spitting image."

Dad takes her hand with a huge smile on his tan face. His salt-and-pepper brows lift animatedly. "Hey, honey. Call me Junior, please. It's so nice to meet you, too. And no, no way. My boy got all the good looks. Such a handsome fellow."

"Well, with that, I agree."

Still shaking her hand, Dad pulls her into an uncomfortably tight hug. Avery's breasts flatten against his abdomen. "We're huggers in this family, little lady."

Penny returns to the table as if she was summoned, and I'm

suddenly aware our fanfare of a greeting is blocking the thruway for the servers. She's holding a platter of drinks and appetizers, and she needs us to take our seats.

"Sit with me, baby." I hold out my hand, pulling Avery to my side and ushering her into my side of the booth. I sit down, closing her in protectively. Dad replaces Avery on the opposite side of the booth after unbuttoning his suit jacket and neatly hooking it on the dedicated golden hanger on the outside of our booth. *Man, this place is pretentious.*

"Show Me Love, Start Me Up," Penny mumbles as she slides Avery's colorful cocktails her way, "and a Johnnie Walker Blue, neat, for you, sir." She places the platter of fried calamari with four different dipping sauces and the piping hot plate of stuffed mushrooms between us. "Careful, the mushrooms are scorching hot."

After Dad requests a scotch, we assure her we're all set and need a minute with the menu before she hurries off again.

Dad raises his brows. "Show Me Love and Start Me Up? Are those drink names?"

Avery lets out a light laugh. "They are, indeed. I ordered two. Would you like one while you wait for your drink?"

"Hmmm," Dad says. "Which are you willing to share?"

"Either. I liked the sound of them both and couldn't choose."

My jaw clenches as Dad waggles his brows at Avery. "How about we try them both? We can switch halfway."

I slide my whiskey over to Dad in a huff. "Take mine, Dad. You're not a cocktail guy."

"A man can change," he says through a chuckle.

Or stay exactly the same.

He takes a sip of my drink and sighs with pleasure. "I do like my Johnnie, neat."

Wedging my arm between the small of Avery's back and the cushioned back of the booth, I squeeze her hip. "Can I try the light green one?" I ask before planting a kiss on her temple. I like playing house. I like touching her like this. It's how it should be.

She's mine.

She takes a little sip of her drink in the martini glass first and puckers her lips like it's sour. "*Oof.* Tangy, but *really good.* I think you'll like it." She slides the glass across the table toward me, careful not to spill a drop on the clean white linen tablecloth.

"Aren't you two cute? How'd you meet?"

"I'm Finn's neighbor for the summer. I'm house-sitting. We ran into each other, and I offered to help him with his photography business."

"How so?" Dad asks.

"I'm a brand strategist. I'm helping to develop some growth plans for Finn's studio."

"Growth? So, like marketing?"

Avery teeters her head. "There's a little crossover in services when I work with smaller businesses. With any company with annual revenue in the six figures, I'll do it all. I'll help establish a brand image, provide insight into growth tactics, and even help implement marketing strategies. But mainly, when I work with larger companies, I create a vision for the company, and usually the established marketing team of said company executes that vision. For example, Finn said you're a commercial pilot?"

"I am."

"Who do you fly for?"

"Royalty Airlines."

"Ah, see, I'm familiar with that brand, and it's an interesting story—" Avery stops abruptly and looks up to meet my eyes as if to ask if she's talking too much. I squeeze her hip under the table tenderly.

"What's interesting, baby?" I'm not sure if I particularly care about the story behind Royalty Airlines. I'm just liking how she's letting me call her baby all over the place, especially in front of my dad.

"So Royalty Airlines' logo is purple, as are their seats and uniforms."

My dad nods along. "Everything is purple. Thank God I look

good in it."

Her light laugh is forced. The way you'd laugh in obligation at your boss's joke. "Well, a lot of people assume purple means royalty and the color choice is obvious, but that wasn't the company's intention—a happy accident maybe. About forty years ago, Royalty Airlines had a blue logo, but what they discovered at the turn of the century was that it was the matriarch of the household that was the one researching options and making the final decision on flights and travel. So, if the flight price points were competitive and a woman had to choose between very similar airline companies with masculine logos and colors, there was a slight advantage to appealing toward a more feminine style."

"Interesting..." Dad says. The way his brows are furrowed and Avery has his full attention, I know he means it.

"So Royalty did a complete branding overhaul. And the more feedback they got from their new consumer base, the more they changed about the airline policies. Families boarding with children age five and under would be seated first versus the other airlines at the time that was only offering early boarding for families with children two and under. They made their snacks more kid-friendly and offered organic juice boxes and were one of the first companies to offer free in-flight Disney movies. The lavatories are a little bigger to accommodate changing tables. The planes are stocked with sanitary cover-ups for breastfeeding. Royalty went a step even further than appealing to women. They became the airline for—"

"Mothers," Dad finishes for her.

"Exactly. After the rebrand, they went from the fifteenth most lucrative carrier in the United States to the second...because no one can compete with the American Airlines loyalty program." Avery shrugs. "Glass ceilings, you know?"

"All that because of a little color switch?"

Avery shrugs with a sweet smile on her face. "It's a little more complex than that, but yes. Pretty much. That's the power of brand identity."

I fight the urge to kiss her right now, in front of this entire restaurant. I like every shade of Avery, but this might be my favorite. She's so intelligent and confident when she talks business, and it's so refreshing to see a woman so powerful in what I lack.

"So how did you become a brand strategist?" Dad asks, looking as impressed as I am. "Is that a degree?"

Avery takes a small sip through a cocktail straw from the reddish-purple-colored drink in front of her. "Ooh, try that one," she says, sliding it my way. "Delicious." She clears her throat and continues. "I actually started my degree in nursing, but I had trouble with science. My grades were lackluster, and one day, late in my junior year when I was forcing myself to study in the library, I stumbled upon a seminar. One of the tenured professors from the business school was talking about jobs that would be exploding in the next decade. Her name was Dr. Ruth Donovon. I just loved the way she spoke, with such confidence. She became my mentor and convinced me to switch my degree to business. She taught me everything I know."

"You switched your major *late* in your junior year?" I ask.

"Oh yeah." Avery bobs her head. "I had to do two extra semesters of school, but Dr. Donovon was very convincing. It's worth noting, the Royalty Airlines story I just told you? She was the brand strategist they hired, who told them to switch their logo to purple. They personally thanked her at their annual executive meeting and credited her vision with their leap of one hundred billion dollars in revenue in their first year after the rebrand."

"Goddamn," my dad says with a grunt. "She must've been richly rewarded."

Avery laughs as she picks up her drink once more. "She's retired in a very nice house in Key Largo. We still talk about once a year."

"You're a smart man, Finn," Dad says, pointing his appetizer fork at me before he stabs one of the cheese-stuffed mushrooms. "You got yourself a working lady. There's nothing more appealing than a woman who can hold her own in the business world."

My chest tightens as I take his words in the worst way possible. I wish this defensiveness would go away, but there's a wall between Dad and me. That wall is called Mom. "There's also nothing wrong with a woman who stays home to take care of your house, raise your child, and ensure you never have to lift a finger when you're home."

"That kind of woman comes with a hefty price tag," Dad scoffs obnoxiously. "And a lot of lip." He pops a mushroom into his mouth and chews vigorously. "Oh, these are fantastic. You have to try one, honey." Dad scoots the plate of appetizers toward Avery. "They're plump and juicy," he says before I watch him shoot her a disgustingly flirty wink.

Chapter 25

Avery

By the time dessert is served, I'm so stuffed I feel like my dress could spontaneously burst. I only sampled everything, but Mr. Griffin ordered so much food that merely tasting all the dishes became equivalent to taking down an entire Thanksgiving dinner. The food was so rich. Delicious, but heavy. Once a year is plenty for this restaurant.

I want to offer to pay for dinner to be polite, but I'm a little worried I can't afford it. Thanks to my dad's constant nagging, I tuck most of my money away in high-risk, high-reward mutual bonds. Apparently, I can be daring right now with my money.

But not *this* daring.

The average cost of an entrée at this restaurant is ninety dollars. Mr. Griffin ordered about eight different dishes, four rounds of drinks, dessert, and a bottle of French champagne—a brand I've never heard of before, but apparently, it makes Dom Pérignon look like a case of Pabst. This is Finn's other side. The side he works very hard to keep quiet.

I squeeze Finn's thigh under the table, and he looks my way. The hazy fog in his eyes tells me he's a touch past tipsy. I tap my clutch. "Should I offer to—"

"What? Pay?" Mr. Harvey interrupts. "Don't be ridiculous, honey."

I really thought I was whispering, but apparently not. Our waitress, Penny, approaches the table with perfect timing, and Mr. Harvey pulls out a matte black card. "Honey, would you have the kitchen box this up? Son, you guys should take it. It's rude to the chef to waste it, and I wouldn't dare offend my friend."

Penny nods and says, "Speaking of which, Chef Roren says your meal is on the house—"

"Nonsense," Mr. Harvey interrupts and holds up his hands. "No chance. This meal was superb, and I am more than happy to support my friend." He wiggles the card between his fingertips. "Ring this up, tell the chef the meal was superb, and can you messenger the leftovers to my son's hotel? Champ, you said you got a room on the Strip somewhere, right?"

Finn blows out an exasperated breath. "It was a surprise, Dad..." He pivots his attention to me. "It was a surprise. I booked a penthouse suite at the Bellagio with a nice view of the fountains. You said you'd never actually stayed on the Strip before, right?"

Finn tells Penny our room number, and she retreats from the table with Mr. Harvey's credit card in hand.

"You didn't have to do that," I say, feeling my cheeks ache from my enormous smile.

"I wanted to. I figured it was a good opportunity. The Bellagio is only a block to our right."

"Thank you." I trill my fingers against his hand sweetly as the rest of the restaurant melts away. It's just me, Finn, and the heavy-eyed, sultry look he's giving me that says we should just probably fall asleep in each other's arms tonight.

It'd be the first time.

Of all the things Finn and I have done together, we haven't crossed that line. I've never felt his muscular arms around me when I woke up in the morning. And I'm ready to.

"Adorable," Mr. Harvey says.

I flinch right before my fist tightens. *That stupid word.*

"Avery, honey, I am terribly sorry to be rude, but may I have a private word with my son? Just some family affairs I don't want to bore you with."

"Dad," Finn intones, "I'll just join you at the bar."

Except it's crowded with patrons waiting for their seats and most certainly not private. "Don't be silly," I say, squeezing his hand reassuringly. "I have to run to the ladies' room anyway."

Finn lets me out of the booth, and I scour the restaurant for the bathroom. *Far back right.* I strut gracefully in my sensible heels right into the luxurious bathroom. I don't understand the bathrooms in these elegant restaurants. They are cleaner and better kept than the dining room itself.

I'm in a stall with my thong around my ankles when I hear a voice I recognize and one I don't. Our waitress and another woman.

I'm convinced there's a sixth sense women have when they *know* someone's talking shit behind their backs. It's a feeling. Your muscles go wobbly. Your skin constricts. Your face flushes, the blood filling it at least a few degrees hotter. Every instinct in my body tells me not to pull up my underwear, flush, and present myself.

So I stay quiet.

And I listen.

"...if I get the shit Monday brunch shift again, I swear I'm quitting," says the unfamiliar woman's voice.

"You've been saying that for months. Who would pay better?" Penny asks.

"Emeril's new restaurant has openings."

"Then apply," Penny snaps, her tone full of irritation.

"What's wrong with *you*?"

"Sorry, I've worked six nights in a row. I'm exhausted. I'm about to cash out, clock out, and head home. I just rang out the VIP booth."

"Speaking of which..." The other woman's voice drops to a seductive purr. "Can you deliver a note for me?"

"What?"

"Your VIP table. You know who that is, right?"

"According to the credit card, his name is Griffin Harvey."

She lets out a shrill chuckle. "You have no idea who the Harveys are, do you?"

Penny sighs, clearly trying to express her disinterest. "Outside of being the roadblock between my pillow and me—no. No, I do not."

"Old money. The Harveys own like half the Strip. Worth billions."

Penny grunts. For the first time in this conversation, she seems amused. "Well, that explains the fifty percent tip—"

"*Fifty percent?*"

"And the old guy slipped me his room number. Can you believe that? My wedding is in six weeks, for Christ's sake."

"Ha. He's worth the trade. You take the old man. I want his son."

"Emma, you're somethin' else. And anyway, sorry to bust your bubble, but the woman he's with is his girlfriend."

The woman, whose name is apparently Emma, scoffs heavily. An obnoxious, condescending cackle that makes my skin crawl. "Who? Ms. Piggy? Yeah, I'm not so worried."

My intestines twist. I draw in a deep, silent breath through my nose to hold back my tears. My bank account could swallow up this waitress whole. I am vying for a multimillion-dollar contract with one of the biggest luxury resort companies in the world. I am one of the most sought-after brand strategists on the West Coast. I know I'm better than this. But I allow myself a single tear because nothing stings worse when a snarky bitch calls you fat.

"*Wow, mean girl,*" Penny says. I can't see her face, but her tone is incredulous.

Thank you, Penny.

"Not cool. I bet his girlfriend and I could share a closet. If she's fat, what am I?"

"You," Emma coos, "are curvy and voluptuous and a total showstopper. *She...*is in my way."

"You're ruthless. And I can promise you, he's not interested. His eyes were locked on his date all night."

Emma's laugh is villainous, causing my hurt to morph into red-hot, putrid anger. "Look, just slip him my number and tell him it's from the waitress with the great ass, and I'm willing to let him play in it."

"You mean *with* it," Penny replies.

"Nope," she says, popping the P.

And with that, I've heard enough. I yank up my thong and smooth my dress before I flush. I all but kick open my door, enjoying the look of the shocked faces in the bathroom mirror as they see me emerge. Penny flushes scarlet red, and I finally get a good look at Emma.

Maybe she's pretty. I'm not sure. I think her light-blond hair and dark eyes would be considered striking to some. Yes, she's probably at least three dress sizes smaller than I am. But it's hard to process beauty when it's sheathed in such an ugly personality.

They are completely still, frozen in place as I wash my hands with my head held high. I glance at myself in the mirror, ensuring there's no evidence of the single tear I set free and my makeup is still perfectly set.

After I've dried my hands with the cloth towel and dropped it into the laundry bin, I turn to face the two women. I nod at Penny reassuringly. *My fight is not with you.*

I look at Emma, but she avoids my gaze. If Palmer were here, she'd take a swing. She's defended me my entire life from mean girl energy. But Palmer's not here, and it's time to stand my own ground.

"Emma," I say, my voice unwavering and smooth as silk, "I'll make sure to let Finn know you're interested, but if he contacts you, I sincerely hope you have more to offer him than your asshole." I flash her a smart smile. "Good evening, ladies."

Twice. Twice now, I've had to make a green-eyed bitch look silly in a restaurant. It seems every time I'm out in public with Finn, there's a fight brewing. A fight for my pride. A fight to prove I'm worthy. If I don't have the looks, I sure as hell have the wits. But how long can I do this? I never asked for this battle.

I ride the high of adrenaline as I float back to my table. I was hoping by now, Finn and Mr. Harvey have had plenty of time to discuss their family affairs. But as I near the booth, I see Mr. Harvey huddled into the table, the look in his eyes aggravated. He's so invested in their conversation, he doesn't see me approach and his words ring loudly over the sea of murmurs and clanking silverware hitting porcelain plates.

"Champ, what are you doing? You can pull a much hotter woman than Avery."

My knees go weak, and I immediately slump into the empty booth behind Finn and his dad. I bury my head in my hand. This part I wasn't ready for.

Emma was a small battle won.

I have a feeling I'm about to lose the war.

Finn

"What did you just say?" I snarl at my dad across the table, feeling my blood pressure rise.

"Avery," Dad repeats. "I mean, she's sweet and very smart. That's kind of sexy. And she's got a great set of tits. But come on... compared to your last girlfriend? Nora was a fucking ten. Avery's a steep fall from grace, Champ."

"Well, have at it. Nora's available now." *Sort of. Maybe she's cheating on Morgan, maybe she's not.* "Go ahead and give her a call. You have my blessing," I practically spit at him.

"And take your sloppy seconds? I don't think so." He bellows in laughter, misreading my tone. There's nothing funny about this conversation or about disrespecting Avery. We don't see the world the same way. All I see with Nora is pain. All I see in Avery is hope. Hope is beautiful and sexy and seductive. Dad hasn't had hope for a day in his life.

My eyes narrow before I throw back the last sip of my whiskey. Dad finally notices my scowl.

"Oh, come on, kid, I'm just saying. If you're with this woman to appease Senior, I can tell you right now, there's a way to sidestep that mess."

"What mess?"

"Senior's bullshit about the inheritance."

Gramps's rules make sense to me. Twenty percent of my inheritance is in the ballpark of eight million dollars. If I don't have a family to support, I'll only get half. Gramps also has the stipulation of vetting our significant others first. It's his way of protecting us from gold diggers. We'd have to pry his money from his cold, lifeless hands before he handed over half of his empire to a shallow, money-hungry woman with no morals. *His words, not mine.* It's why I never told Nora what I stood to gain. I wanted to know she loved me, not my worth. At least that part was true. I don't think Nora loved me for my wallet. In fact, I don't know if she really knew how to love me at all.

"I don't see the point in complaining about *gifted* money."

"It's your birthright, son."

I roll my eyes at his melodramatic statement. "You know what? I'm not worried about it. And I'm not with Avery to prove a point to Senior. I'm *with* Avery. *Period.*" Okay, a little preemptive, but I know where this night is headed. The penthouse suite I booked is covered with rose petals. The room has a jetted tub where we can play naked footsie under the bubbles all night. The champagne is already in an ice bath on the balcony table that overlooks the Bellagio fountains. There's no better way to say I'm whipped for Avery than the most cheesy, over-the-top declaration of my feelings.

"I'll make up the difference," Dad breathes out.

"What?"

"Don't let Senior dictate your life. Getting married was the worst decision I ever made. The only good thing that came out of that relationship was you. But you don't have to settle for a woman like Avery just for the extra money. What Senior won't give you, I will. Have fun. Enjoy your life. Travel. Visit Ibiza, Brazil, and Croatia. Take pictures abroad and fuck all the beautiful women there." He pinches his fingers together and kisses them. "Nagging and bitching from a frumpy, killjoy of a woman is *not* what I want for you and your life. Especially when she leaves you and tries to take you for all you're worth."

I had one too many drinks. That must be why I can feel my temples pounding. "Frumpy killjoy, huh? Ladies and gentlemen, there you have it, my father's words to describe the woman who gave me life." *Fuck you, Junior.* Fuck whatever got twisted up inside your brain as a baby and turned your heart wretched and your dick insatiable.

Dad smiles at me like this conversation is chummy. "*Oh, Champ. Still such a mama's boy.*"

I raise my brows warningly. "Should I be ashamed of that?" I love my mother. I'm protective of her. Where's the crime in that? "I thought you two were finally at peace. I just saw Mom last week. She said you guys are done in court. You're giving her alimony and back pay, right?"

Dad's eyes turn down and his lip curls, like a perturbed villain. "Senior," he mumbles. "I didn't give that bitch a dime. Senior paid her out."

Something snaps in me. Maybe it's my patience finally breaking in half. "What did you just say?"

"She went to Senior with some sob story about how she barely broke even after selling the Vegas house. She needed a cosigner for her place in Scottsdale, so she aired out all our dirty laundry like the rat she is, and he just caved for the little bitch. *Fuck* did I get an earful from him. The man is in his seventies and still yells like—"

"Take it back," I seethe. "Do *not* call her that, especially not to my face."

Mom told me none of this. All she said was that she was finally at peace. It dawns on me that Mom was doing what she did my entire life—she protected me from seeing Dad's true colors so I could enjoy the good parts and be blind to the worst of him. She didn't want me to know...

What a fucking monster I came from.

"Champ, relax. It's just the fallout of a lover's—"

"*Stop*," I bark. "You did a lot of things to my mother. Loving her is not one of them. I'm so sick of this. You know something, Dad? I wake up every day, and I don't try to be a good person. That's not the standard I live by. Every day I wake up, and I just try to be less like you. That's how I know my life is moving in the right direction. I can't...do this anymore. I can't excuse all the disgusting parts of you anymore. I'm done." I release the breath I've been holding for ten years. "I'm fucking done."

Dad's startled by my outburst. Never once in the past decade have I been honest with him about how I feel. Maybe I should've said all this sooner, because he finally looks ashamed of himself.

"Champ, I don't—"

"I don't want to see you anymore. I want you off my mortgage. I'm selling the truck. I don't want a damn thing tying you to me anymore. Not until you grow the fuck up, Dad." I slam back into the back of the booth in frustration. The entire seat shifts an inch, and I rise to peek over the back of the booth and apologize to the diner behind me.

My heart drops when I see the top of Avery's head. *Goddamn it. How long has she been sitting there? She must've heard everything.* I scramble out of the booth and around to her side. She does her best to turn her head, but it's too late. I see her wet eyes.

And it's the straw that falls on the already broken camel's back. It should've been enough that Dad took the best parts of my mother and made her into a depressed, anxiety-ridden shell of herself. But now he just made Avery cry, and that's a line no one gets to cross.

Never again. Not while she's with me.

I hook my finger under her chin and turn her gaze toward me. She rolls her eyes and shrugs her shoulders in defeat as I survey her glistening cheeks.

"I'm caught," she mutters under her breath. I wipe away her tears with my thumbs.

"Ready to go?" I ask softly.

She nods. "Yes."

"I'm sorry, Queen. I hate seeing you cry." I kiss the top of her forehead. I take her hand in mine. "Let me make it up to you."

Chapter 26

Avery

We're in the jetted two-person tub in the enchanting penthouse suite when Finn finally asks me the obvious question on his mind...

He was mostly silent on the walk over here. He was distracted in his thoughts as he retrieved our keys from the concierge and took the elevator to the top floor. He only smiled at my shocked expression when I walked into the room and saw it decorated as if it were our honeymoon suite.

With rose petals everywhere, it looked picturesque. The scent of sweet amber and vanilla filled the air. And the view...

From the balcony, it's a bird's eye view of the lit-up, dancing fountains. We're on top of the world tonight. But Finn's mood is deflated.

When we first arrived, after unbuttoning his dress shirt, he immediately filled the tub, even going as far as throwing a handful of loose petals on top of the water. He stripped me down, careful not to rip my dress. He took his time peeling off my lace thong and matching strapless bra before he ushered me into the tub, assuring me this was only part one of his apology. After taking off his clothes, he joined me but made sure to take his seat across from me, keeping the distance between us.

"How much of that conversation did you hear?" he asks, his eyes fixed on the water line.

"What conversation?" I play dumb. I'm already uncomfortable. Finn's guilt for something he didn't do or say makes it ten times worse. I want to comfort him, but I'm still licking my own wounds.

"Avery," he grunts out.

"From the moment your dad informed you that you can pull a much hotter girl than me." My laugh is harsh and bitter. "He's not wrong." I try to wink playfully, but Finn is not remotely amused.

"He's an ass—"

"Finn, it's fine. If I was upset, it was because of something that happened in the bathroom." It's a half truth. Emma's antics hurt my feelings. Mr. Harvey's words obliterated them. It's one thing for a jealous woman to be cruel when she desperately wants what you have, but Finn's dad's disapproval...especially over the way I look? I don't know how to process that...

"What happened in the bathroom?" He cocks one eyebrow.

I lean back, letting my head rest on the ledge of the deep tub. "One of the waitresses wanted your number. I overheard. Apparently, she does butt stuff."

Finn tries to control his smile but fails. A cackle breaks free from his lips. "I'm sorry. I think I momentarily blacked out when you said butt stuff. Where did we land on that subject, by the way?"

"Oh yeah, let's go for it."

His eyes perk up, not understanding my sarcasm. "Really?"

"*No.* Are you crazy? That'd be like shoving an ear of ripe summer corn into a cocktail straw. You'd have two fake girlfriends to bury when you literally split me in half, Finn."

"Fake?" He pokes my shin with his toe under the water.

"Wasn't all that for show?" I ask but can't hide my hopeful tone. "I'm not sure if our situation would make sense to anyone else. I suppose it's easier to say 'girlfriend.'"

He licks his lips and stares at me with a gaze so seductive, I swear the water surrounding us grows hotter. "Maybe I was testing the waters. Maybe I called you my girlfriend all night because I wanted to see how the words tasted." He blows out a long breath, leaving my nerves on the very edge of their seat. "It's been on my mind... Has it been on yours?"

"Well, yeah. Of course," I say honestly. "It's natural. We spend a lot of time together. We're sleeping together, but..."

"But what?"

"There's just the small matter that I don't actually live here."

"But your job is remote, right?"

I nod slowly as I run my hand across the top of the water. "True. But it'd be sort of crazy to move your entire life based on the feelings you have for a few weeks." I squint one eye. "Right?"

Finn shrugs. "It'd be sort of crazy to move back to a life you hate if you have other options."

I pinch my fingers together under the water, trying to control the nerves. It's not the worst thing in the world to know that Finn might have real feelings for me. Would it be so crazy to tell him that I have real feelings for him too?

I mean...is it too soon?

My relationship with Mason was over long before I realized it was. I'm single. This is no crime. Life happens when it happens, and I'd be stupid to refuse a gift from the universe like Finn. But there's just one thing that has me worried, and it's not the geographic distance between us.

"Do women always hit on you so openly and aggressively?"

Finn blinks at me, his lips flattening into a firm line. Clearly, he wasn't expecting that question. "Uh, honestly...I'm used to getting attention. But I wasn't looking at anyone tonight besides you—"

"No, no, of course not. Finn, we're fine. I wasn't accusing you of anything." *There's nothing to accuse him of. We're not together.* "I'm just curious. Do you like the attention, or does it get exhausting?"

He juts his chin toward me. "You tell me."

I snort in response. "If and when I get endless waves of beautiful men throwing themselves at my feet, I'll let you know if the attention becomes tiresome."

Finn chuckles, but it falls flat, and I'm slightly worried I hurt his feelings. Was I supposed to offer to move to be with him? I just... How? We're not ready. *I'm* not ready. Plus, I feel like I'd need a full suit of body armor to survive the attacks I'd get for dating

Finn. There's nothing more vicious than a confident woman with her eyes fixed on a prize.

Finn finally breaks the lull by saying, "I like the attention from *you*. Sexy is great, but I also need genuine. You're the first woman I've met who seems to be both." He licks his lips and bends his fingers, beckoning me closer. "Come here."

I show him my slyest smile as I slowly lean forward, eventually crawling onto his lap. I'm relieved to be on top of him. I was worried his sex strike was legitimate. "I knew you'd cave." Both of our bodies jostle as he chuckles. "I like the attention from you too, Finn. I've been ignored for a really long time, and it feels so good to be seen. Thank you."

My lips find him urgently. I suck in his bottom lip and run my fingers through his hair as I try to inch forward on his lap, just the idea of his erection kicking up the tingling sensation between my thighs. But Finn, his lips still intertwined with mine, grabs my hips and holds me in place.

"Slow down," he murmurs into my mouth.

I try to wiggle forward again, but he holds me firmly in place at least two inches away from his dick. "What's wrong?" I ask. "Are you still upset about your dad?"

"Yes," he says, "but that's not why we're not going to have sex. I thought I told you earlier."

I flatten an irritated stare at him, but he isn't dissuaded. He brushes my hair away from my shoulders and presses his lips against my collarbone. "I'll compromise. Kisses are fine." His breath feels cool against my damp skin.

"Seriously? You're going to reject me when I'm wet, naked, and on top of you? Is that a smart move?" The edge in my voice isn't from anger, it's from agitation, because all I can think about is sliding on top of him and riding until I'm thoroughly sated.

His stupid huffs of laughter at my nonintimidating threat only irritate me further. "I'm not rejecting you. I'm showing you I'm a man of my word. But you're in control of this, baby. Promise me you'll get in the studio..." He wraps his hand around my neck and guides my ear to his lips. His voice becomes low and grumbly. "Promise me, and I'll fuck you so hard right now, you won't know what you're swimming in—this tub or your cum. You know I can hit that spot that makes you explode."

Damn, I love his dirty mouth. I'm weak when he talks to me like that. He warned me he'd play dirty. And it almost works as the aching urge between my thighs almost answers for me. *Yes. Whatever you want.* I'm tempted until the shrill cackle of a woman's laughter pops the fantasy bubble in my mind.

Who? Ms. Piggy?

That's adorable.

I didn't mean to interrupt you and your "friend."

The mean girl chatter is all I hear before I wiggle off of Finn's lap and back to my side of the tub. "Fine. We won't have sex."

"All right," he says. "No worries." He stands in place, the water plunging off his body as he rises from the tub. Finn's gargantuan dick is fully erect and right in line with my eyes. He makes a meal out of raising his arms above his head to stretch as if flexing his taut six-pack is simply natural. He reaches for a towel as he steps out of the tub. Leaning down, he plants a kiss on my cheek. "Just let me get dressed. We can"—he smirks—"talk...or whatever else you want to do tonight."

Just take some damn pictures, Avery. It's not that fucking hard.

But it's always been my kryptonite. I've been camera-shy since the day I hit puberty and I started hating what I saw in pictures. Junior high is when I really noticed the stark difference between Palmer and me. My mom took a picture of us on the bus with our matching puffy paint T-shirts we made for the first day of school that read "Grown Girls," because everyone knows at twelve years old, you're totally equipped and ready to take on the world.

I was so excited for Mom to get that picture developed. But the day she brought it home, my whole world changed. I ignored our big smiles and the bright-pink T-shirts we spent hours making for the first day of school. All I could see was how much thicker my arms and thighs were than Palmer's. My chin was soft, and my cheeks were far fuller. I spent every waking minute with Palmer. She ate way more than I did. I actually *enjoyed* carrot sticks and cucumbers with ranch dip. Palmer's version of healthy was baked Lays, fruit-flavored gummy bears, and Diet Coke. Yet we were growing so differently, and I seemingly had no control over it.

I noticed we were different. And I haven't been able to stop noticing since that day.

Getting dressed became my main sense of contention through junior high and then high school. *Curvy wasn't always cool.* Rail thin was all the rage when I was at my most vulnerable in adolescence. Clothing stores like Abercrombie & Fitch and American Eagle made all their cutest clothes in size double-zero. So I learned to shop elsewhere. I learned to enjoy the beauty of comfort. I wasn't about to play a game I knew I couldn't win. *I played to my strengths.* I was smart and a hard worker and kept my head down in the arena of dating outside of a few awkward dalliances, until one day...

I met Mason.

He had a clear choice in the bar that day. The wild child beauty, Palmer. *Or me.*

And for the first time in my life, a man chose to pursue *me.* And not by default. Palmer was flirting pretty heavily that night. Mason didn't seem to notice. He kept his eyes on me.

I thought I'd made it through my awkward, uncomfortable, camera-shy phase unscathed until, at age thirty, I was catapulted right back into the shaky, fragile waters of insecurity and singlehood.

And here's what Finn can't get through his sexy, beautiful, thick skull: what if he sees me in a picture and notices too? The bus picture was almost twenty years ago, but that pudgy pre-teen is still ingrained in my brain. What if Finn notices how mismatched we are? Everyone else seems to. Once he sees it...

He'll never be able to unsee it.

The spell will be broken, and I'll lose him before the summer is over.

Finn stands in front of me, the waistband of his briefs hugging his hips tightly. He holds out a fluffy white hotel towel, and I reluctantly drag myself out of the tub. It's so cozy I could sleep in here. But Finn pats my body dry and drapes an oversize satin robe over me that feels cool and silky against my skin.

The only flaw to Finn's grand romantic gesture with this room is that I have no change of clothes. There are complimentary toiletries—makeup wipes and a disposable toothbrush—but I'm forced to put back on my thong and uncomfortable strapless bra from earlier this evening. Finn probably wasn't worried about it, assuming we'd be naked all night. When I'm situated, I join him on the private balcony, the gust of warm Vegas air filling my lungs.

"Do you like champagne?" he asks, right before a loud *pop* makes my heart jump. "*Whoops.*" We watch the heavy cork fly over the balcony rail and fall endless stories down. Both of us look concerned until a solid minute passes by and there's no slew of cuss words from the pedestrians below.

"Not really," I finally answer. "I drink it for toasts, mostly. I prefer beer or fun cocktails. Anything with flavor."

"I get that." But he pours two glasses anyway.

I settle into a cushioned patio chair next to him before he hands me the skinny glass flute. For a moment, we're silent as the Las Vegas Strip beneath us sends me straight into sensory overload. The faint smell of smoke and a variety of different restaurants is still potent, even up this high. The bustle of foot traffic and punctuated shrieks and giggles are loud from below. The neon lights cast a hue on the dark sky above us, making me think there's a different measurement of time out here. There's day and night, dawn and dusk...and then there's Vegas. The sinful, sleepless city full of dreams I've never dreamed before.

"I've been here about three times before this summer but have never really *seen* Las Vegas. Not like this."

"Really? Why not?" Finn asks, touching his glass to his lips.

"I was always just passing by. Once for work, another time for a conference, another time after that to rescue Palmer."

Finn rolls his eyes. "Oh, Palmer."

I get the impression Finn doesn't like my best friend much. I've told him a few stories here and there, and I'm not sure if I gave him the best impression. I don't mean to make Palmer sound selfish, flighty, or catty in conversation, but somehow, it's how she comes across.

"Why did Palmer need rescuing?"

"There's a fancy strip club off the Strip that way, I think." I point to my left. "It's called Ruby's. Palmer went with some random guy and the bachelor party he was attending. Well, he ditched her and took home the stripper who was giving them lap dances all night. He stuck her with a bar tab for the entire party that was well over a thousand dollars, and she couldn't pay it. She got mouthy and was swinging punches, so they locked her in a stripper cage—like a little jail. When Palmer called me, I talked to someone from security and begged him not to call the police. I hightailed it out to Las Vegas to collect Palmer and pay the stupid tab. They probably could've arrested her that night, so I owe Ruby's one."

Finn presses his lips together in a flat line like he's debating his response.

Okay, once again... Palmer is not coming off great.

"Ruby's is that way," he says, pointing to the right. "And it's not a strip club; it's a gentleman's club."

"What's the difference?"

"Dress code and budget," he answers dryly.

I smirk at him. "Oh, and you're very familiar with Ruby's, huh?"

"Yeah," he says. "I'll own it one day."

"*What*?" That was certainly not the answer I was expecting.

"Just on paper," Finn says defensively. "I won't be managing it. It's part of my inheritance. Ruby's makes a lot of revenue for the Harvey family."

I vaguely remember walking into Ruby's and thinking it looked more like a luxury Four Seasons than a strip club. It makes sense.

"Hm, Finn Harvey, a gentleman's club owner. Who knew?"

He turns his head, watching my eyes intently. "I could sell it one day. Gramps would be pissed, but once it's mine, it's my decision."

I show him a pinched look. "Why would you sell it if it's making you good money?"

Finn turns his gaze back to the scenic overlook. He lifts and then drops his shoulders. "Let's say, *hypothetically*, I ended up with a girl who wasn't really into the Vegas thing and didn't love the idea of me owning a club where women dance fully nude for money. I wouldn't object to getting rid of it if it made her unhappy."

"*Fully nude?*" I can't help but squawk in surprise.

"Well, technically, no. We wouldn't be able to serve liquor in that case. But what's a tiny flesh-colored G-string really covering, you know?"

"Wow. In Vegas, it's cocktails or full frontal. Okay, well, now I know. You can't have both."

Finn chuckles, but his laugh falls flat. "I'm not trying to play games, Avery. If I'm in love, I just want the person I'm in love with to be happy. My ex was wildly jealous of every woman with eyes and a pulse. It's what broke us. I stopped seeing my friends. I stopped going out. There were even certain clients she wouldn't let me photograph. If it was past eight o'clock, my ass was in the house, on the couch, with her. I thought I did everything to make her feel secure, yet it was never enough.

"But the point I'm trying to make is I was willing to do anything to make her feel secure. That's the kind of man I am and will always be. For whomever I'm with."

My heart aches. It physically aches. What screw would a woman have to have loose to drive this man away with petty jealousy?

"Well, what if you ended up with a girl who was admittedly a little insecure but didn't think it was your responsibility to fix? What if you had a girl who wanted you to have friends, have fun, and be passionate and happy and whose trust you had blindly until you broke it?" I bring my fingertips to my lips and blow him a sweet kiss. "*Hypothetically*, of course."

Okay, bold. Bold move. But Finn started it. He said a relationship was on his mind back when we were in the tub. I want him to know he's not alone. Even if I don't know how to make sense of it, I certainly *feel* the same way.

Finn's gaze snaps to mine, and his face relaxes into an awestruck expression. "Can you please, *please* just agree to a boudoir session so I can take you inside and bury you into the mattress right now? It's what we both want."

I grumble in agitation. "No. To the photo shoot. But I'll get naked and grab the headboard right now if you want to end your strike."

He lets out a low whistle. "Not a chance."

"Why is it so important to you, Finn? Come on. Is this a kinky thing? Like a voyeur thing? Because you can watch me without the camera..."

"No, it's not a—" The corner of his lip twitches as a mischievous smile claims his face. "Wait, I can watch you do what?"

I shrug and bat my eyelashes suggestively. "End the strike. I'll show you just how wet I am right now, and when I'm done playing solo, you can join in."

His jaw slackens and his bottom lip drops slightly. "Listen to that dirty mouth. I created a monster."

"Are you proud?"

"Very. And I'm going to take you up on that...as soon as you get in my studio."

"Finn—"

"It's because of my mom."

I suck in a breath and hold it. I'm not sure if I should be extremely curious or completely put off. "For the love of God, please elaborate."

He holds his chest through his rich and melodic laugh. "It's not what you're thinking. I have never, nor will I ever photograph my mother like that." He shakes his head like he's shaking off the shudder-worthy thought.

"Thank goodness. So what does any of this have to do with your mom?"

He pulls the bottle of champagne from the ice bucket and fills his glass before topping off mine. "What did you think of my dad tonight? Before the drama and the dickhead things he said about you."

I try to remember before my heart bottomed out of my ass. It was such a pleasant dinner that ended so cruelly. "He was honestly so charming and charismatic, it blinded me to how deeply shallow he is."

"*Exactly*." Finn lets out a sharp breath. "I've never been able to explain it so eloquently. That's exactly it. And my mom found out when it was far too late. My dad cheated on her unapologetically. She was reaping the benefits of his income and inheritance so he felt he had the right to disrespect her left and right. He was gone so much that I think she tolerated it. But also, I think she really loved him and hoped he would just grow up. But he never did, and my mom didn't want me to know that side of him, so she kept everything hush-hush from me. It wasn't until I left for college that she finally filed for divorce. Soon after, I found out I had two half sisters, both in their twenties, only a couple of years younger than me."

"Oh, Jesus."

"Yeah, and to top it off, after over twenty years of marriage and supporting him and his career, my mom asked for the bare minimum. She just wanted enough to live by and to finish paying off the mortgage. We're talking she wanted pennies on the dollar from my dad's fortune, but he was ready to fight. He didn't want to give her anything. He hired some hot-shot lawyer to drag her through the mud, making her out to be money-hungry and coldhearted. He said it cut him when she asked for a divorce. Can you believe that shit? After everything he did to her, and yet *he* was brokenhearted."

"I get it," I mumble.

"What?" Finn actually looks offended. His face is twisted up with indignation.

I sigh, unbothered. He's misunderstanding my message, so I clarify. "Sometimes you don't see that you're a monster until the people you love most won't tolerate you anymore."

Finn sits on my words for a moment, letting them saturate. "Oh. Okay, yeah. I guess." He nods slowly. "Anyway, Mom had a tough time for a while. I lived in the dorms but went to UNLV, so I was close enough to home to visit every weekend. I watched her crumble into depression. Then, one day, she just perked up. I remember it was after finals in my sophomore year. I brought home my girlfriend at the time for the first time, and I warned her not to be offended if Mom didn't say much because she was in a bad place. But Mom had the entire house decorated for Christmas, which she hadn't done the year before. She was baking and holiday music was playing." Finn smiles at the sweet memory that's clearly playing in his mind. "She was just alive again. I asked her what changed, and she said her friend talked her into a boudoir photography shoot. She said she forgot how beautiful and powerful she was, but it helped her remember.

"From there, she started fighting back with my dad. She went to every court hearing. She sat through all the bullshit. She worked three different jobs to make ends meet. Eventually, she let the big house go and moved to Scottsdale. She even started dating again. All from seeing herself through the right lens. And that's when I decided to start looking into what the hell boudoir was." Finn laughs. "The descent into madness was swift from there."

Oh damn. Of course he had to hit me with the sweetest, most sentimental bullshit he could conjure up. "Did you make all of that up just to convince me to do this?"

He smirks. "Why? Did it work?"

I roll my eyes. "Finn."

He chuckles. "I didn't make it up. It's the truth. Every word."

Taking a small sip from my glass, I let the bubbles of champagne pop on my tongue. "Lennox mentioned you got your pilot's license."

"Just my private. I wanted to work toward a commercial license and then one day go further and get the certs to fly for commercial airlines like my dad, but after everything came out..." He trails off before finishing off his glass. He doesn't refill it. Instead, he turns to look at me hungrily. I know what's going through his mind.

Just cave. Just say yes. I want you.

"You wanted to do less of what brought your dad joy and be closer to what made your mom come back alive?"

"Right. Something like that." Finn reaches over the small patio table between us. He holds out his hand. "I just want you to have that experience, Avery. Every woman should. It's not that I want to get off to sexy pictures of you. I only want you to see how incredible you are and be brave enough to do this, because it makes me sick when I think of you being ashamed of your body. I want to give you the gift of loving yourself. And as selfish as that sounds, I want it to be from me. You asked for my help with intimacy, and this will help."

"Finn, you're already doing more for me than I could've asked anyone." I place my hand in his and squeeze tenderly. "I'm really tired. I think I'm going to tuck in for the night." I rise with his hand still in mine and then proceed to kiss the tips of his fingers. "Thank you for everything. If I'm sleeping when you come in, make sure to kiss me good night." I let go of his hand and tap my cheek where he should kiss, subtly telling him he did not get his way. The door to sex will remain locked because...

There's no way I'm going to lose this man.

My fairy-tale man for the summer.

I'm not going to risk him seeing a few unflattering pictures of me half-naked that will surely break the spell.

Chapter 27

Avery

If this weren't a dream, I'd be nauseated. I don't do well with ships. But as the water sways, I'm unaffected because, in dreamland, I'm impervious to seasickness.

My mind is alert enough to realize that my long dress, which is seemingly made of glittery mermaid scales, is clearly nonsensical, but I'm incoherent enough not to question it.

The scenery is odd. We're on a ship, but the mist is a creepy thick fog covering the stripped wood. I look up and see the tattered sails marked with skulls and bones.

Oh. It's because I fell asleep staring at Finn's tattoo. I'm probably drooling on his bare chest right now. Why am I so aware at the moment? What a weird dream. I know I'm sleeping. I know it's a dream, but I'm watching the movie unfold right in front of my eyes.

I see him approach from the hazy shadows.

His face is marred with a jagged scar underneath his eye, and he's wearing an eye patch because my brain isn't creative enough to visualize anything else for a ghost pirate. No matter, the concept is clear. And plus, I'm not worried about his costume. My eyes are on Finn's body—a perfect replica of real-life Finn. He's shirtless. Every groove of his abdomen is perfectly sculpted into six symmetrical rectangles. The broad wall of his pecs, dotted by his little brown nipples, is so enticing I immediately feel the heat between my legs.

"How are you out of the water?" he asks in a grisly whisper

that sends a chill up my spine. "Can you breathe?"

Okay, I get it. I'm a mermaid. I can breathe on land, but can I speak?

"You know what I came for," I say in a raspy voice that sounds like I'm starring in a porno. I want to laugh at the cheesy dialogue. *Come on, dream Avery! You can do better than that.*

The action sequences are distorted, and we skip the proper continuity. Somehow, now I'm on my back, my ass boring into the wooden ship deck that should be giving me splinters but in dreamland is comfy as a mattress. Finn's on top of me, cupping my sex. Somewhere in the nonsensical sequence, I've lost my mermaid dress. Finn and I are completely naked, and I can almost feel the weight of his palm against my clit.

It seems so real. The urge between my thighs grows as he rubs aggressive circles with the heel of his palm all the while taunting me, telling me not to come yet.

"I want to," I protest in my porno voice, and suddenly I feel something foreign against my neck. My brain scrambles to make sense of the scene so I can compute the sensory experience my dirty mind is trying to treat me to. *It's a hook.* Finn has a hook hand, and he's pressing the back of the cool metal against my throat.

"You're going to love it like this," he growls.

I nod eagerly, already feeling the dribble down my thigh. "Do it."

"You won't be able to scream." He smiles, almost cruelly. "But try anyway."

His hard dick replaces his hand, and I groan as he enters me. I try to spread my legs to accommodate his colossal size. Pirate Finn is even larger than real-life Finn. Comically so. I should be dead by now, but apparently, I'm a mermaid and we ethereal creatures can adapt to penises the size of anacondas. There's no pain, just pleasure...then shock.

He presses the smooth curve of his hook against my throat and gyrates his hips. A simple thrust is too tame for my mythical pirate sex god. He swivels his hips, ensuring no part of me is untouched, and as I near my orgasm, the strain on my neck grows.

The panic begins to rise, and now my shallow breaths are becoming impossible to collect. I try to whimper, but I can't make a sound. I'm not sure if it's the hook or the dream, but I can't speak. I can't breathe. All the panicked pressure in my body is collecting between my thighs, and I don't know if I can handle the explosive climax I'm headed toward.

I shake my head, and Pirate Finn must see the fear in my eyes. "Just another moment, baby." Now he thrusts—hard. I grunt in reply. "You're almost there." He pumps his hips again, nudging against that sacred spot that makes me burn for him.

On cue, the fog turns to angry dancing flames as he ruts into me like a madman. "Say my name," he snarls.

I try again to speak, but I can't. A headache begins to form, and I want to tell him to release me because I'm damn near passing out. But he only presses his hook harder against my windpipe.

"Try, baby. Just say it. Tell me who is making you come."

Summoning my strength, I fight the tension around my neck and scream as loud as I can. He rips his hook away and lets my cry ring through the night air. *"Finn, oh God, Finn. Finn. Finn."* My voice breaks through at the precise moment my orgasm unleashes.

I gasp. The air fills my lungs as my climax radiates through my entire body. The sensation is so potent, I think I come twice. Once because of the pleasure, and once because of the liberation.

It feels so real.

The pulsing sensation is so familiar. The euphoria makes my head go hazy and sink back into the ship deck, waiting for the flames around us to burn us to cinders.

Finn smiles. "Time to go home, Queen. The ship is burning."

He grazes the crown on my head that somehow magically appeared amidst our rough sex. Ripping it off my head, he then throws it overboard into the pitch-black sea. He scoops me up and, before I can ask him if he'll be okay, tosses me over the ship rail, and I begin to plummet.

I'm falling for ages. Much too long to make sense. I should've hit the water by now.

It's the feeling of falling, the swoop in my stomach that yanks me fully from my dream.

And when I open my eyes, I see Finn.

Not Pirate Finn.

Real Finn. No scar. The dim light of the lampshade across the room reveals the perfect, handsome angles of his flawless skin. And he's wearing the most amused smirk I've ever seen.

"Did you just have a dirty dream about me?"

"No." I don't know why I bother lying, but I'm a little embarrassed. I subtly rub my thighs together and feel the moisture. Dream or not, I most definitely came. That had to be the most passive-aggressive orgasm of my life. *If you won't fuck me in real life, I'll find you in dreamland, Finn.*

"You sure? Because you woke me up when you said my name a few times. And you're breathing kind of hard."

"I don't remember what I was dreaming about. Wait...I think I vaguely remember I was falling." *Lies.* I remember it perfectly. *Your pirate doppelganger threw me overboard right after you choked me with your hook and gave me the most intense orgasm I've ever had.* But I'm not saying that shit out loud.

"Okay, whatever you say." His smug smile says he doesn't believe a damn thing I'm saying. "Come here."

He yanks me back into his chest, and I snuggle against him, back to belly. This is how we fell asleep, and I must've wriggled away in the middle of the night. I've been sleeping alone for over a month, so my instincts need time to adjust.

Finn puts me back in my rightful place, cuddled into his embrace, his thick bicep sprawled out as a pillow for my head. I rest my ear on the dramatic curve of his muscle, and the mermaids on his tattoo fall into my direct sightline. They sing what they always sing to me.

Praise and encouragement. *Go ahead, girl, get yours.*

I did. Oh, I did.

I giggle silently at my own silliness, feeling playful and full. I don't think I've ever had a wet dream before. I thought those were only for the other sex. But lo and behold, I taught myself this lesson all on my own.

I shut my eyes, desperately trying to go back to the ship, hoping that Pirate Finn survived the fire and is ready for round two.

Chapter 28

Finn

I wake up to the unmistakable sound of hushed arguing. I'm in bed alone, and the sheets on Avery's side of the bed are cool to the touch. She's been up for a while, apparently.

I slept like the dead last night. No doubt it was the comfort of a woman lying next to me. I'm not sure where to go from here. When we leave the hotel and go back home, do we sleep in separate beds? Should we just keep pretending like we don't know where this is headed?

I know she feels it too. She's already mine. My woman. My queen. I just need some time to break down whatever walls she's built up, because it's clear we should be together. Every sign points to the inevitable.

Lennox really likes Avery. She isn't interested in my impending wealth. This woman knows how to be comfortable but turns on the charm whenever she chooses. She's intelligent and carries herself gracefully and isn't remotely intimidated by my dad or the Harvey name. We're hot together. The sex is glorious because it's different than what I've had. Lessons or not, when I'm with her, it feels like the deepest kind of connection. Like she needs me...

Like I need her too.

Dex was always meant to leave this summer...

And Avery was always meant to fall right into my lap.

Pulling myself out of bed, I head to the walk-in bathroom of this stupidly expensive suite. Why one night in this hotel suit costs nearly two grand is a mystery to me. Although, I suppose if I was planning on living like a real Harvey, I probably wouldn't blink at the money. But my heart is more Thatcher, my mother's maiden name, than Harvey. Two grand to me is my mortgage payment, a month's worth of groceries, and my cell phone payment. Even when she shared my dad's last name and wealth, Mom raised me to be reasonable. We bought new things only when our old things broke. She always treated our money like a fleeting privilege. Mom once told me that my dad's wealth was more of a burden than anything. She honestly believed that if Dad was born without a penny to his name, he might've had a chance at decency.

But I know better. I've seen poor men who are pussy-hungry cheaters that treat their wives and girlfriends no better than Dad treated Mom. He was always doomed. Let's leave it at that...

Because he's no longer my problem.

I splash a little water on my face and head out to the living room in just my briefs to see if Avery is really going to keep that stone wall up another day. I know she had a sexy dream about me last night. The way she was mumbling my name between moans and flexing her hips in her sleep, I don't know what I did to her in her dreams, but I wish I were there so I could've taken some notes.

"...because it was fucking stupid, Aves. You almost ruined everything."

Avery, dressed in the hotel's robe, is standing at the kitchen island, staring into her phone with her eyes narrowed. She looks ready for war. But before she can say another word, I step into the front lines because I don't know who the fucker is on the video chat who's yelling at her, but I'll be damned if anyone speaks to her that way.

I slide right next to her, forcing myself in front of the camera, not giving a fuck that I'm half naked. The man on the other line is brunette, his face fixed into a scowl.

"Lower your voice when you talk to her," I snarl at him as I snake my arm around Avery's waist. "Or you're going to hear me raise mine."

"Who the hell are you?" He holds his hand up, offended, like

I'm being unreasonable.

"Finn, this is Mason. Mason, this is my...neighbor, Finn," Avery mumbles, her eyes still narrowed at the screen.

I take my time pressing my lips against Avery's temple. "You smell nice. I didn't even hear you shower." I don't bother to whisper, and I'm enjoying watching Mason's lips flatten into a hard line. *Good. I hope it hurts.*

Avery ignores my compliment. She's clearly too agitated at something else to play the *make your ex jealous* game. "We're just talking business."

"I know," I assure her. I wouldn't have interrupted out of petty jealousy. I just didn't like the way he was speaking to her. "I'll give you your privacy."

"No need. We're done." Avery nudges me aside playfully with her hip before leaning into the phone that's propped up against the coffee maker. "Mason, are we good? Like it or not, you know I'm right."

"Fine," he huffs. "Just please don't cut me out of any more decisions."

Avery gapes as she balls her fists up by her side, out of Mason's view. "We'll talk soon," she says curtly before ending the call abruptly. Her cheeks puff before she blows out a long, frustrated breath. "Something not so nice almost came out of my mouth."

"Rough morning?" I ask.

Her pursed lips relax into a sweet smile. "Better now. So are sex coaches supposed to get their feathers ruffled when someone raises their voice at their student?"

"Fuck yes," I deadpan. *Mine or not, you're still mine to protect.* "He doesn't have to like you, but he sure as hell will respect you. And if Mason speaks to you like that again, he better not let me hear about it."

"Good God," she mumbles as she runs her hand over my shoulder and down my tatted arm. Her smile turns sly and seductive.

Ah, fuck being a man of my word. I can't believe we didn't have sex last night. If she really doesn't want to do the photo shoot, I'll let it go.

"Look, about the boudoir shoot—"

"I'm not trying to be difficult," she interrupts. Swiveling around, she fetches a clean coffee mug from the wire rack. After pouring me a warm cup of coffee and sliding the sugar and cream already on the counter toward me, she continues, "It's not that I don't want to do it. Truthfully, I'm intrigued, and if you were just some random guy, I would've done it by now."

"We've had sex at least ten times, but you'd be more comfortable getting undressed for a random guy?"

"It's the pictures. I don't want you to see them." Avery pinches her eyes closed like she's trying to separate herself from her body as she admits whatever is next. "It's just my thing. I look in the mirror, and I'm okay. But I see pictures of myself, and I hate them. And I'm worried if you see what I see...you're going to be disappointed."

I sigh sharply. "Avery—"

"Ah, stop." She holds up her palm. "I know what you're going to say, and I don't expect you to understand it. Just *respect* it." She draws out the word respect, knowing I'm powerless to combat it. If she's feeling insecure, that's one thing. If she's telling me to leave it alone, that's another.

"So it's just about *me* seeing the photos, not about you seeing them?" I ask.

She ducks her head and then lifts her eyes to meet mine, the mug in her hand grazing her lips. "Pretty much."

"I have an idea."

Avery cocks her head to the side. "What idea?"

"How about we do the shoot old-school? I have a really good film camera, and I'm still great friends with one of the TAs at UNLV. She has access to the dark room and can develop everything without me seeing it. She's a random person you'll never have to meet if you don't want to. When the pictures are ready, I'll make sure she seals them up in a box and marks them for your eyes only."

Avery blinks at me slowly, and I know she's trying to think of any holes in my master plan. "Old-school, huh?"

"Yeah, I usually shoot with a DSLR, which makes editing easier, but for your peace of mind, I'm happy to whip out my old AE-1."

"Any more acronyms that I don't understand you want to throw my way?" she sasses.

I laugh. "You should know what a teacher's assistant is. I went to school at the University of Nevada, Las Vegas. A DSLR describes a lens, but in layman's terms, it's just a digital camera, and my AE-1 is the first Canon film camera I ever bought for myself. It still works like a charm."

"Oh," she mutters, "well, there you go."

"Mmhmm. Now, I fixed the problem," I say, stepping forward and closing the space between us. Taking her mug from her hands, I let out a little moan then tuck her hair behind her ear, trying to be as seductive as possible. "Now say you're mine."

"What?" she croaks then clears throat. "Sorry, what?"

"In the studio, Avery. Say you're all mine. I promise you're going to like the photo shoot, and you're going to love what I do to you after." I wet my lips as I throw my final Hail Mary. If this doesn't work, I'm done pushing the issue. I won't make her do the photo shoot, but the way I'm feeling at the moment, I sure as hell am going to cave and fuck her mercilessly on this kitchen counter.

I wrap my hands around the smallest part of her waist and trace the outward curve of her full hips. I resist clamping down and digging my fingers into her body. How many days has it been now? I went three months without sex, and now my eyes go fuzzy when I haven't had Avery for a few days? Here begins my descent into feelings for a woman, yet again, and dear God, I hope it's for the last time.

"Okay," Avery finally answers, pulling me out of my wicked thoughts. "I'm yours... In the studio. The film camera," she says with a small shrug, "is clever. Good work-around. How's Friday?"

"That's three days from now."

"Indeed." She smirks. "That's fast calendar math."

"Smart-ass," I snark back. "What's wrong with tonight?"

She presses her hands against my pecs, but she doesn't push me away. Her hands linger. "Because I have to work—it's what Mason and I were just arguing about. It's an emergency."

"Is everything okay?" My eyes fix on hers. They look a little gray today, like a cloudy green sky.

"Yeah," she says, exaggerating her nonchalance. "*Totally.*" She lets out a deep breath before she's honest with me. "It's the first time in my career I'm worried that it's too late. When Mason told me about Legacy Resorts, I thought their rebrand was just focused on bringing in their company more revenue. They aren't performing at the top of their market, but they certainly aren't at the bottom. I thought... Well, anyway, it turns out there's so much more at stake."

I watch her brows furrow as her forehead wrinkles with concern. I fight the urge to smooth away the worry lines. "Are they fudging their numbers?"

"Oh, no. The board of directors voted, and they want to dissolve the company and sell the resorts off in pieces. They have so much potential and are already very competitive. They just want to take the simple, safe path out of this. They'd rather take their cut and sell the properties to the big names. And sometimes it makes sense for a business to do that, but Legacy could be wildly successful. And if they give up now, thousands of people will lose their jobs."

"Why wouldn't they just go work for the new resort?"

Avery removes her hands from my body and reaches for her coffee mug. "That's not how big acquisitions tend to go. In my experience, usually only twenty percent get to keep their jobs, and usually that twenty percent take a major pay cut."

I watch her eyes dart back and forth. She's not being evasive. Her mind is just elsewhere. She said she had to work. Clearly, she's already working. I'm slowly learning that Avery's biggest asset as a brand strategist is that big, beautiful brain. "You seem nervous."

"I'm not *nervous*. I'm just... I'm used to telling business owners and CEOs how to connect with their consumer base. I've never had to convince a board of directors that their company is worthy. It's hard to get people to see something that's so obvious when they are dead set on a misguided narrative."

I raise my brows at her. "The irony."

She gestures up and down her body with her free hand. "Don't even. It's not the same thing."

"It is. You are obviously beautiful and sexy and amazing in every way, but you refuse to acknowledge it. So what would work for you? What would get you to see yourself correctly?"

She grins at me as her cheeks fill with the lightest shade of pink. "Apparently, a very persistent boudoir photographer who bribes me with sex."

My laugh comes out like a roar. "Keep thinking, sweetheart. I don't think you can use that tactic on Legacy Resorts."

"Well, it won't be what I resort to first, that's for sure. Especially if I want to take the job they offered." She pumps her eyebrows back at me.

"What?" Tired of standing, I grab Avery's hand and guide us to the couch. She sits right next to me and tucks in her knees carefully, still holding her mug full of coffee.

"That feels *so* good to say out loud. Technically, I'm not supposed to say anything, but it's been eating away at me. That's what Mason and I were arguing about."

"They don't want to offer Mason a job?"

She scrunches her lips. "SEO specialists aren't exactly hard to come by. Their offer is for me and me alone—only if I can convince the board of directors to keep the company intact. Mason made up some story about how the CMO was a misogynist pig, but I think he suspected they were interested in bringing me on board, which is why he tried to keep a buffer between us. I might've gone behind his back and reached out anyway, which is why he's so furious at me."

"Fuck him," I mumble. "How's the offer?"

"Phenomenal. A seven-figure salary, perks, great benefits."

"So, is that a *promotion*?"

She must hear the skepticism in my tone. "Yes. Why?

"Well, aren't you your own boss right now?"

"Ah," she exhales. "Indeed, I am. But most of my job is laying out a plan, providing instruction, and then moving on, letting the company execute my vision. Mason does more of the website and traffic maintenance, so he gets to create longer-term relationships with clients. I've always been a little jealous of that. For once, I think it'd be pretty great to have one dedicated project and see it through. To stick around to help the company shift and pivot when things get tricky again."

I smile as I tuck my hands behind my head. When I can postpone no longer, I ask her the main question on my mind. "Where is the job?"

"There'd be some travel, but it's wherever I want. They'll even pay for relocation if I request it."

Legacy Resorts and I seem to have the same agenda. Step one, offer Avery everything she deserves. Step two, take her away from her piece of shit ex. I squeeze her knee, unable to play it cool. This is just too perfect for it not to be meant to be.

"So it's a done deal. Work your charm, save the company, secure the job, and hey, if you're looking for a fresh start, I think Las Vegas looks *really* good on you."

Her smile is half-baked at best, and for a while, she doesn't say a word. Her eyes turn down as a heaviness falls over the room. Our bodies are touching, but I can feel the distance she just put between us.

"It's not that simple."

"Mason?" I ask.

She nods solemnly. "If the roles were reversed and he abandoned me and the business, it'd be unforgivable. I don't want to be in a relationship with him, but that doesn't mean I don't still..." She trails off, raising her shoulders and then dropping them.

"Still what?"

"Respect what we built together. There was a point in time when we only had each other. When one of us doubted, the other believed. We both logged twelve-hour days, no weekends for years, trying to build something out of nothing. The funny thing is it's harder to let go of our business relationship than our actual relationship." Avery exhales sharply, and I watch her entire body tense. "Look, I already know what you're going to say."

"What am I going to say?"

Her tone grows mocking. "He's an ass. Here's your chance for revenge. He doesn't deserve you. If he were in your shoes, he'd—"

I hold up my hand to stop her. "I was going to say, I think it's very impressive how loyal and considerate you are." I tap the tip of her nose affectionately. "Whatever decision you make is the right one. And if you hate it, it's never too late to make a change." She seems startled by my response, so I ask, "What?"

"Nothing," she mutters, yet her lips barely move and her words come out as more of a whisper as her eyes widen. "Nothing at all."

"What?" I ask again. "Tell me."

"I'm just really used to my friends—well, *friend*—telling me what decision to make. It's refreshing to hear you say you think I'll make the right choice."

"Well, I do. Truly." Her eyes lock on mine and her lips part slightly. The urge to slide my tongue between them almost overcomes me. I stand up, leaving her.

"Where are you going?" She holds out her hand, but I'm a few inches out of reach.

"If I sit here with you a moment longer, I'm going to fuck you silly, and I need to keep it together until Friday."

She pats the couch with both hands and pouts like a child. "I already agreed to the photo shoot."

I smirk at her. "I realize, but I don't know if you're actually going to follow through."

She narrows her eyes, her seafoam green pupils turning to slits. "So you don't trust me."

"Oh, I trust that you're a lot smarter than me, and I only have *one* bargaining chip. I'm holding on to it." I wink at her before running my finger over my chin. "And another lesson for you, Queen. Say no every now and then. Just because you can. Make him wait. Make him work for it. It'll make a man fucking feral for you."

Her clipped smile turns into a grin. I turn toward the bedroom but whip back around when I see Avery biting her lower lip in my peripherals.

"Something on your mind, Avery?" I ask in a teasing tone.

"What's the kinkiest thing you've ever done?"

Three women at once. "Nothing crazy."

"I'm serious."

"I'm not as experienced as you're probably thinking," I say with a grimace. *I'm probably far more experienced.*

"You've still had way more sex than me." She blinks at me, the look on her face not exactly cautious, definitely not innocent... It's...

What is that? Curiosity? "Go ahead and ask me for whatever it is you want to try. I'm pretty confident I'm going to say yes."

"I had this dream last night, and you were..." She trails off and gently holds her hands to her throat. I let out a controlled breath, begging my cock to stay under control because I can't hide an erection in my thin briefs. "Did you use to do that with your ex?"

"Yes. But what did I tell you about compar—"

"Did she like it? Did you?" Avery interrupts, her curiosity at its peak.

Deep inhale. Long exhale. "Yes, and yes."

"In my dream, it was really intense...in a good way." She clears her throat, trying to fake a bravado. "I want to know how it actually feels. Do you know how to do that without hurting me?"

I nod slowly. "Definitely."

"Okay, then, if you're okay with it, I'd like to try that...among some other stuff." Now her eyes hit the floor, like her brave request exhausted her and she wants to crawl back into her cave of shame.

Nuh-uh. I won't let her. I take two strides and plant myself back on the couch. I can't seem to control my hands. Laying her backward first, I hover over with my knees planted, one between her thighs, one braced against the back of the couch. She's pinned underneath me, completely at my mercy.

I fight the urge to squeeze her full breasts and roll her nipple between my thumb and forefinger. I can clearly see she's not wearing her bra, and I just want to open her robe and lay my dick between her perfect tits. But I'm trying to prove a point at the moment.

I settle for brushing her hair away from her chest and watching her ragged breathing as her chest moves up and down rapidly.

"What other stuff?" I watch her eyes dart back and forth between mine. "Ask."

She shakes her head back and forth. "I don't know anything else specifically," she admits. She looks overwhelmed, so I take the lead.

"I take it you want me to choke you and pull your hair? You want me to boss you around, pin you down, spank your ass, and make you scream when you come?"

Avery blinks at me slowly, like she's absorbing and debating. Eventually, she nods.

"When you tell me you can't take any more"—I lean in close to her ear—"you want me to get deeper."

She nods again.

"You want me to show no mercy and take that pussy down while I praise you for how wet and tight you are, don't you?"

She closes her eyes. "I never thought I'd like it when a man talks to me like this. But I like it. *I really like it.* You've turned me into someone I don't recognize, Finn."

I trace her lips with my fingertips. "It's because *it's me*, Avery.

You trust me."

"Yes, I do," she agrees.

"Because you know I'm going to fuck you hard then hold you all night after. I promise. I just want to make you feel good. None of the bullshit. You deserve better than you've had."

Her cheeks turn pink as her smile spreads. I love watching her melt under my affection. This is a sexy game at the moment, so it seems a little out of place to tell her that I know she wants my heart and I'm ready to hand it over. All she has to do is ask.

"Friday, then," she murmurs.

"Friday, then," I parrot as I climb off her and grab her by the hands to pull her upright. Once she's seated, I turn back to the bedroom, *needing* the shower now. My cock is as hard as steel. Even still, I pause at the door and catch her gaze from across the room. "Avery?"

"Yeah?" She's a little breathless.

"I can't wait to teach you what I like in the bedroom."

She quirks her eyebrow, fierce determination painting her face. "I can't wait to learn."

Chapter 29

Avery

"Hey, so question—do you always twitch and fidget like a mouse on crack when you get your makeup done, or are you a little nervous about tonight?"

Lennox stops dabbing me with a large, round makeup brush that's so soft it tickles. I'm being a terrible client right now and making her job difficult. She's here to help me get ready for my photo shoot as a courtesy, and I'm distracted as hell. Guilty-faced, I look up from my phone and hold it out to her.

"I've been knee-deep in research for three days, and I just have a weird hunch about something. My obsessiveness is taking over, which is why I'm antsy. But it could possibly be the makeup...I've never gotten it done before—*professionally*. There were some sleepover mishaps in my younger years."

"Let's take a break before we put on your lashes and do your hair," Lennox says. "How about a drink? Do you have anything good in the fridge?"

"Actually, *yes*. I picked up some strawberry margarita mix with you in mind, my friend. Come on," I say, hopping up from the chair we pulled into the master bathroom. "Dex's fridge makes the best crushed ice. Perfect for margs."

Lennox and I have been spending more time together. More accurately, we've been attached at the hip ever since our girls' day out shopping. She usually moseys over whenever she's at Finn's place, which is constantly. When I'm not alone with Finn or working, I'm letting Lennox teach me how to be a girl. She shows me makeup styles and is always texting me cute outfit ideas. I'm officially her life-sized Barbie doll.

The new thing I've learned this summer is that skinny girls have insecurities about their bodies too. Lennox has clothes she wishes she could wear, but she doesn't have the chest or hips to fill them out. Instead, when she's out thrifting or discount clothes shopping, she'll pick out items she loves and bring them to me, all the while telling me how envious she is of my body.

I've known people to be considerate or polite about my plentiful curves, but never have I had people who celebrated my body...*envied it, even.* It's bizarre, and if I'm telling the truth, it feels really nice to be appreciated for who I am, and not the beauty I could potentially be if I just *lost twenty or so pounds*—words I heard from my mother and Palmer my entire life. Words I'm sure Mason would've liked to say but sure as hell wasn't daring enough.

Lennox passes me at the bottom of the stairs when something catches my eye and I bank right instead of heading toward the kitchen. I stare into Cherry's tank and notice a thick black stripe across her side. She even looks a little more translucent. *What the fuck?*

"Lennox," I call out, "you scuba dive, right? Is fish cancer...a thing?"

"I think so," she replies absentmindedly, rummaging through Dex's fridge for the loot. "I know sharks and whales can get cancerous tumors."

"The door," I instruct her. "I put the marg mix in the door compartment. But if a fish had cancer, what would you do? Surely, you can't *operate* on a fish? Can you? Or would you just try treatment? Are there fish oncologists?" I watch Cherry swim back and forth, not even close to her usual pace. It's a leisurely stroll and far from her normally manic behavior. I don't understand. The fish guy was just here yesterday. I told him I was concerned, and he double-checked the pH levels and the temperature of the water. He even ran a test for minerals and nutrients. The tank is flawless. In his own words, it's the fish version of a luxury resort with an open bar.

"Did you seriously just say fish oncologist?" Lennox asks. When I look toward the kitchen, she's staring at me with a befuddled expression.

"I'm a little attached to this Cherry Barb. She's my little buddy. Cherry has been keeping me company all summer." I stroke the glass, careful not to tap, still worried from the inside of the tank it sounds like an earthquake. "I'm going to ask Dex if he'd let me keep her. But I don't know how to take care of her if she's really sick."

Lennox's jaw drops. "You know those probably cost about eight dollars, right? About the cost of a venti Starbucks drink... Just saying..."

I drop my jaw and feign horror but make another mental note to ask the aquarium guy next week what to make of all this. A thick black stripe down the side of her body has to be an indication of something awry. If Cherry is getting sick, the other fish could be getting sick too. There has to be something I'm missing. *When did that stripe even develop?* I didn't notice it until now.

Albeit for the past few days, I've been working manically, reviewing investor relations reports for Legacy's major competitors for the past decade. I've been studying what has been working for their competitors and what hasn't to get as close as possible to a brand strategy guaranteed to put them at the top of their market. No easy feat.

By the time I trudge into the kitchen, now doubly distracted, Lennox has filled two glasses with the bright-pink cocktail. "Cheers." We clink our glasses together and take a small sip before she asks me, "What's your hunch?"

"Huh?" I crunch on a small piece of ice that slipped through my lips, completely forgetting about my sensitive tooth. I smack my palm against my cheek. "*Ow, shit*. Sorry, what?"

"Earlier in the bathroom, you said you had a weird hunch. Is everything okay with your project?"

I squint one eye at her. "You sure you want to know? I've been told I can drone on about work."

I'm actually dying to talk to Mason about what I found, but right now I don't feel like I can trust him. Four years in business together...and it's the first time I feel like we're working for different end goals. It's unnerving, and I hate it.

"Drone away. I'm really interested in your job. The way Finn's studio has been going, I may need an extra job. Can I work for you?"

"Seriously?" I scrunch my face at her in surprise.

"Yeah, I mean, I'm decent with graphic design, and there isn't anything I can't learn. Everything I know about photography, Finn taught me...so..." She shrugs. "I'm just really impressed by you. I've always known I wanted to go the entrepreneur path. I just wasn't sure what to do or how to do it."

Hm, interesting. "If you're serious, Lennox, I'll help you. I'm in between things right now, but as soon as I figure out what's going to happen with Legacy Resorts...one way or the other, *I will help you.*"

She shoots me a small smile. "Thank you. Anyway, sorry to digress. Please continue..."

"I dug into Legacy Resorts' financials, and they are doing fine. Are they disgustingly profitable? No. But the business is far from failing, so why oh why would the board of directors be pushing to sell? What exactly is the problem that needs to be addressed?"

"And your hunch?" Lennox asks, raising her brows to the point they disappear behind her straight-cut, long bangs. She's died her hair freshly purple again. It's such a good look on her. I love the vibrancy. Maybe I should consider a little color in my mousy brown locks.

"That there's something unsavory going on. It seems like a decision in the best interest of a specific person versus the company as a whole. Call me Magnum PI, but I've been looking up the entire board, individually. I need to get to the bottom of why these very well-off, business-savvy board members would want to let go of thousands of employees, screw over their shareholders, and basically bend over backward to their direct competition. It makes no sense unless the company is secretly near bankrupt. But I already turned over that stone and found nothing."

"If you need help," Lennox says with a sly smile, "social media stalking is kind of my specialty."

I chuckle. "I wish it were that easy. But the stuffy middle-aged board members don't seem to be active on socials. I've been digging through public earning reports. It's quite...riveting," I say, emphasizing the sarcasm in my tone. "I'm actually grateful it's Friday. I need a break and am due for some fun."

My reward for tireless, sleepless, thankless days of work for a contract or job offer I haven't even earned yet? *Finn.* Motherfucking Finn Harvey and his dirty words and rock-hard body...*all night.* All I have to do is get through this stupid photo shoot.

"Ah, speaking of fun..." Lennox takes another sip from her drink, enjoying the attention as I stare at her like a fish on a bait line.

"What? What's fun?"

"You know Ruby's?"

"The strip—I mean *gentleman's* club?"

Lennox nods. "The bar manager, Cass, is a friend of mine. She hosts her birthday there every year. They shut down the entire club for a night and throw a costume party. It's huge. All the dancers, bouncers, close friends, and even a few celebrities usually make an appearance. It's not just fun...it's *Vegas* fun. It's the Friday after next. You should come."

She's wearing that pleading look Palmer wears when she wants me to change out of my sweatpants and go clubbing with her. But a birthday bash at a Vegas gentleman's club seems a little out of my league. "If by *costumes* you mean pasties and G-strings, I'm going to have to throw you a 'no' on that one."

"*Oh, come on.*"

I quirk one brow. "So I'm right about the costumes?"

"Mainly," she mutters. "But you don't have to get that intense. And plus, Finn's going. I'm sure he'd love to show you off."

Oh. Finn's going? "He didn't mention it." I'll admit that kind of hurts. It's yet another reminder that Finn and I only make sense in closed quarters. I wouldn't fit in with his normal friends. "I'm sure he would've invited me if he wanted me there. I don't want to rain on your guys' parade."

"First of all, *I* want you there, so you're invited. Second of all, Cass just sent out the invites two days ago. He hasn't had a chance to ask you to go. You've been pretty much unreachable holed up in here." She swivels her finger in the air, gesturing to my prison— aka Dex's four-thousand-square-foot luxury home. "Finn even told *me* not to bother you while you were working."

"Doesn't your boyfriend want to go?"

She shakes her head. "Not his thing."

"I don't have a costume."

"I'll find you one or make you one."

I cringe at her response.

"We'll keep it classy. Sexy, so you fit in, but we'll cover all your bits."

I roll my eyes. "By bits, I hope you mean all my wiggly parts." I pat my stomach, which admittedly is a little flatter than normal. I don't think I'd eaten much over the past few days as I frantically dove down the Legacy Resorts wormhole.

Lennox lets out a frustrated grumble. "I see what Finn is talking about now," she mumbles under her breath but doesn't elaborate. "Okay, story for you—there's a dancer at Ruby's named Brielle. She's the most athletic, flexible, sexy piece of ass you've ever seen. She's by far the most requested and highest-paid dancer there. Nobody works a pole or a lap like Brielle."

"That's lovely," I deadpan.

"My point is that she's nearly twice your size. And she's fucking beautiful. I think you see the world as very black and white. I don't know what you think you know about Las Vegas and beauty standards, but I'm willing to bet you're making wrong assumptions." She presses her lips together like she's nervous to continue. "And it's the same with Finn. He's not patronizing you when he says he likes you, Avery. He genuinely thinks you are one of the most intriguing and stunning women he's ever met. The more you say that's not true, the more you're calling his opinion worthless."

I knew Lennox was sassy, but I had no clue she was so deep. "Wow, just call me out, why don't you?"

"I'm trying to help you get out of your own way."

"Is all this flattery just because you want a job?"

She croaks in laughter. "No. You and Finn are good together. He's relaxed and smiley all the time. He finally stood up to his dad. You don't understand the effect you have on him. He's been my best friend since we were in diapers. We were raised together, and I have never seen him this *happy*. And you seem..." She holds her palm to the ceiling and points at my chest.

"Happy too," I finish for her.

"Good. So be happy. It's right in front of you. Stop thinking you don't deserve it." Lennox winks at me.

"Thank you, Lennox. You are a really good friend."

"Okay, come on, let's go finish your makeup and start your hair. And I can't wait to show you the wardrobe Finn picked out for you." She laughs to herself as she points to the black shopping bag on the living room coffee table that she brought over with her. It's tiny. I have a sneaking suspicion that the lingerie he picked out for me is wireless. *Dammit.* Men just don't understand. Wire support under the girls is far more flattering.

"Hey, so...this costume party. We can pick anything we want to be? There are no specifications?"

"Yeah, anything."

"And if I have an idea, you can help me?"

She beams at me. "Hell yeah. What do you have in mind?"

I cover my eyes, embarrassed. I don't know why. It's not like Lennox was on that burning ship in my dreams. She has no clue what Pirate Finn did to me on the deck before he saved my life and threw me back into the sea.

"I want to be a mermaid."

Chapter 30

Finn

The rapid knocking at the clients' entry of my studio tells me one thing clearly...

Avery is not amused with my outfit choice.

I watch her through the sliding glass doors with one of her hands clutching her hip tightly, her lips pursed, and her foot tapping. I've barely slid the door open to let her in when she holds out the thigh-high black stockings I sent over with Lennox.

"I think you forgot the rest of my wardrobe."

"Well, hey, gorgeous. Can we pause for a moment?" I pull a long tendril of her hair over her shoulder. It's been brushed out into soft, sleek waves. Avery's makeup is flawless. A little overly dramatic, which is ideal for pictures. Photographs always wash out makeup, so Lennox knows to go a little heavier. "You look—"

I exhale as I clutch my chest, feeling my excited heart pump against my palm.

She tilts her head to the side adorably, and her frustration has simmered for the moment. "You think?" Avery holds her chin with the back of her fingers.

"I *know*. You look incredible." Grabbing her hand, I pull her into the studio and close and lock the doors behind me. Just to be safe, I lock the entry to the studio by the stairs as well. In case Lennox decided not to go home. I don't need any interruptions tonight. I've been salivating thinking of this moment all week. I took my own advice. Holding out made me go from needy to full-on desperate, and I'm going to wreck this beautiful woman tonight in the best way.

But first things first...

"Why don't you head into the set and get changed." I point to the door leading to the boudoir room. "I'll be in shortly. Do you need anything?"

"Yes." She blinks at me. "The rest of my outfit." She shakes the thigh-high stockings at me again. "I never agreed to do this fully nude."

"You're not fully nude." I point to her hand with a smug smile. "You have stockings. They are cozy and flattering. Give them a chance."

"Finn." She scowls at me.

"Avery." I scowl right back. "I have seen, licked, and kissed every inch of your body and have enjoyed it all thoroughly. You have nothing to hide. Remember, I'm not going to see these pictures. They are for you. But I want you to experience the full effect."

She's unable to argue with my logic. "Is the room at least warm?"

"Sweltering," I say. "I want you sweating."

"Fine." She heads toward the back room but then plants her feet and spins around. "You're not going to watch me change? You're going to see me naked anyway."

I fold my arms over my chest. *Goddamn, I'd like to. But then I'd be way too tempted to fuck you senseless before we got started.* Photographing Avery with cum dripping down her thigh is crossing the line from boudoir to pornographic. "For the next half hour or so, I'm going to be very professional. Your gynecologist doesn't ask you to strip down in front of her, does she?"

Avery flattens a stare at me like she's surprised by my absolute responses. "No, *he* does not."

"Exactly, so—" *Wait.* "He?"

"Mmhmm."

She's not my girlfriend... Am I allowed to ask her to get a new doctor? Fuck, I hate this gray area. We really need to cross this line before summer is over.

Hell, maybe we should cross it tonight.

"Anyway, I am going to treat this shoot like you're my actual client. I want you to know what I do for a living and how I do it. So—" I clear my throat with importance. "Ms. Scott, please go get changed. I think there's a clean robe on the hook right next to the door. Would you like me to grab you a cold water?"

She exhales. "Okay, yes, please." I can see the nerves in her eyes, right behind the fire dancing. I'm so fucking proud of her. I know she's nervous, and she's blowing right past it. I know she's insecure, but she's not letting it ruin her life. I am obsessed with the way she carries herself. This woman sure as hell doesn't need me... I just need her to *want me.*

"I'll knock before I enter. If you're not ready and need more time to get dressed, just say so."

"They are stockings, Finn. It's not rocket science. I'll be ready in two minutes. Let's just get this over with."

Her long hair fans out as she whips around and heads through the door to the boudoir set, shutting it behind her.

I twiddle my thumbs, giving her longer than two minutes. I want her to have a moment alone to soak it all in. This photo shoot will move fast. Not just because I'm trying to blow past dinner to get to dessert, but I was meticulous about setting up the shoot. My light kit is fixed perfectly, and I have the props staged exactly as I need them. I really wish I were doing this with a DSLR. The set Lennox designed is perfection, and it's a shame I'm going to bumble this with a film camera, but hopefully Avery falls in love with the powerful feeling of being the star of the show. Maybe she'll let me repeat this properly one day.

My fist is raised at the door, but it opens a sliver before I can knock. I hear her step away, her soft footsteps on the hardwood floor, so I push it open and enter. Avery omitted the robe but is doing everything she can to cover as much of her naked body as possible. Her forearm is wrapped tight around her breasts, nearly smashing them into flat disks. She also has her thighs pressed together so tight her legs look flushed. Her other hand is sprawled out in front of her pussy like I haven't seen it before.

Perhaps I should be aroused. I thought I'd be fighting a hard-on this entire shoot, but Avery looks so nervous at the moment, all I feel is protective.

"Deep breath," I instruct, but she doesn't obey. In fact, it looks like she's holding her breath. "Avery," I say again. "Take a deep breath. It's okay. It's just me, and this shouldn't be news to you by now, but you look incredible. So sexy and powerful."

"How long will this take? Ten minutes or so?"

I exhale. "I'm going to do something I normally would never offer a client, so you'll have to pardon the lack of professionalism."

Her eyes light up, no doubt thinking I'm going to omit the photos and throw her onto the bed. *Incorrect.* "Come here," I say, pulling her against my chest. She's so much shorter than me without heels, so I can easily rest my chin on her head. "Hey, shrimp, can you see over my shoulder?" I wrap my arms tighter around her, trailing the divot of her spine with my fingertips.

"I can," she mumbles against my pec.

"What's that sign say?"

She mutters something incomprehensible.

"One more time?" I ask.

"You're beautiful," she grumbles, fully agitated.

"And?"

"You're worthy," she says in a huff.

"And?"

She leans backward and tilts her chin up to find my eyes. "That's all it says. You're beautiful and you're worthy."

"And you're mine," I add. Hooking my finger under her chin the way I've done a dozen times by now, I rub my thumb across her cheek soothingly. "I take really good care of what's mine, Avery. I promise you."

It takes her a while to speak, and then finally she drops her arms and buries into me. Her head knocks against my chest. Her freed breasts press against the top of my abs. She wraps her arms around my neck and speaks into my shirt quietly, maybe hoping I can't hear. But her words ring through clearly. "You...are...overwhelming, Finn. I never stood a chance."

"I know," I say. It's how I intended it. From the moment I learned her name, I wanted to make Avery Scott fall for me. "Now, if you really are uncomfortable, I do actually have some brand-new lingerie you could wear."

"You do?" She looks at me, her brows furrowing.

"I took your advice and called some of those boutiques to see if they would carry my business cards in exchange for showing off their collections for my clients. They donated a few sets, and I asked for everything in your size."

She narrows her eyes. "Being?"

"Hey, now. We don't talk numbers in the studio. I just asked for everything in a size *beautiful*. Do you want to try it on?"

Peeling herself away from me and taking a giant step backward, Avery's entire body is in plain view. Every soft bow and fleshy curve of her body has me mentally salivating, especially because now she looks more determined than I've ever seen her.

"No, I'm okay. Let's do this."

"*Good girl*," I say and pump my brows.

Her jaw drops as she scoffs. "So much for keeping this professional."

I chuckle as I spin her around and pat her bare ass. "Last one. I promise." Grabbing my loaded camera from the table behind me, I continue in my most business-like tone. "Now, Ms. Scott, could you take a seat on the floor with your back against the footboard of the bed?"

She does as I ask, and I resist the urge to call her my good girl once again.

"Bend your knees and arch your back a bit—*there*. Good, that's perfect."

I cross the space between us and adjust her long hair. Avery has the perfect hair and style for a boudoir shoot. I can strategically hide her nipples underneath her long locks. When I'm satisfied with her pose, I step back and allow myself to admire the view.

"All right," I say. "You ready?"

She nods somewhat stoically, trying not to jostle her hair out of place.

"Okay, Queen, we're going to dive right in. I'm only going to put you through one roll of film—I've only got thirty-six shots I can take, so we're not going to waste any time on shyness."

"Okay," she answers.

I lower my voice. "Now spread your legs but completely cover your perfect little clit with your palm. Because if I see it, I'm going to have to stop what I'm doing and suck on it."

Avery looks like she's torn between scolding my audacity or succumbing to the sexy thought. Her lips slacken and her bottom lip parts from the top, just slightly, and even under the soft glow of the mood lighting, I can see her cheeks flush.

There it is. Perfect shot. That's exactly the expression I wanted. Thirsty, nervous desire. And now it's time to go to work.

Click. Click.

"Spread your legs a little wider. Hold that pose." I boss her around absentmindedly as I take two steps to my right for a different angle.

Click. Click.

"That's beautiful, Avery. Exactly what I want to see."

Good girl.

Avery

We did not stop at one roll of film. He's had to replace the camera film at least twice now. I was nervous for the first five minutes, and then something powerful took over me.

It was Finn's eyes and the way he was trying to control his smile as he looked through the lens. He's been scolding me for the past half hour because I have a bad habit of looking right at the camera.

Stop that. Look over there, Avery.

Over my shoulder.

Don't stare right at the lens, Queen.

I needed a lot of direction, but little did Finn know, I wasn't staring at the camera. I was staring at his eyes. He looked so pleased. *So damn pleased with me.* He's looking at me the way I imagine I look at him.

It isn't selfish or unbecoming to be the star every now and then. It feels damn good to get dressed up and feel so sexy and so... *womanly.* I never understood that definition until today.

Woman. That word. It's power, but it's tenderness. It's control, but compromise. A woman can be all things, to all people, which is why she has to be so careful about what she chooses.

I chose to step back.

I chose to be told how I should feel about myself.

I chose to love everyone else more than I loved myself.

And that's why Finn wanted to do this because there's magic in this studio. At first, I listened to his commands, adjusting myself as he saw fit. Then the tables turned and I started bossing him around. I wanted to try new poses and different angles. He photographed me with the stockings on and then off. I let the sexy black high heels he used as a prop dangle on my foot as I pretended to touch myself. I rolled around in a bed of black roses like my very essence was sin and lust. I've never known this energy. But now that I've found it, I am determined to keep it.

My ass and my breasts are bare all over that camera, and I can't wait to see what these pictures look like. I can't wait to see the expression on my face because I imagine it's complete. Satisfied. Finally...

Confident.

It's true. I thought confidence would make me feel taller or more poised. I thought my voice would get a bit deeper and my chin would be permanently fixed in an upward tilt.

But no.

Confidence feels like relief. *Goddamn relief.* That finally the way I feel about myself is more important than Mason's dissatisfaction, Palmer's condescension, or my parents' blatant lack of interest in me.

I'm beautiful to the core. I'm worthy of my own approval. I'm Finn's...

Or at least I want to be.

"Queen, we're out of film," Finn says softly, pulling me from the haze of my hedonic power trip. "We've been at it for over an hour."

"Really?"

"Time flies when you're—"

"Naked in front of a man you desperately want to have sex with?"

Finn's lips twitch into a cocky smile. Crossing the room, he sets down his camera carefully and returns to me on the bed. I'm sprawled out, with the white sheet strategically draped across my hips. I watch his light-blue eyes darken as he crawls onto the bed. I half expect him to rip the sheet away and throw my legs over his shoulder, but instead, he rolls me onto my side and spoons me from behind. I'm slightly perturbed because I can't see his handsome face. When I try to roll over, he grips my hip, hard. I wince more out of surprise.

"Don't look, just listen," he grumbles into my ear. "You did a fantastic job. The camera loves you."

"Thank you." I say it genuinely because for some reason, I actually believe him. I felt like the camera loved me for the first time in my life.

He pulls my earlobe between his lips and tugs. "Can I photograph you again?"

"Yes," I respond without hesitation.

"I'm serious. With clothes, without. You're so beautiful, Avery. My heart is sore from pounding so hard for you."

I giggle, but it seems inappropriate because Finn doesn't chuckle back. Is he not being playful? "Are you trying to sweet talk me into sex? Because I'm already there, buddy." I try to turn around to face him, but again he puts pressure on my hip, keeping me locked in place.

"No, I'm trying to tell you how I feel. If you were to move here, to Vegas, we could call this what it actually is."

"What is it?" My reply is knee-jerk. I know what he's getting at, but I want to hear the sound of his voice when he says it.

Finn brushes my hair away from my neck and plants a tender kiss behind my ear. He releases the death grip on my hip and runs his strong hand over the dip of my waist and pulls me against him even closer. His voice is low and deep in my ear. "We make each other happy. We make each other feel secure. It's easy. Just be with me."

I know he can feel my heart thudding out of control, and I don't care. He deserves to know how I feel. He calls me Queen, but he's the one who acts like royalty. Finn is the textbook definition of a fantasy man, and it's a little hard to believe this is my fairy tale.

"You'd want me to move here to be with you or move in with you?"

He must take my question as validation because I feel him smile into my neck as he grips my bare breast. "I don't care," he murmurs between kisses. "I'm open to anything except long-distance. A couple should be together when they decide to be together."

Personally, I don't mind long-distance, but maybe that's because I never felt as desperate for Mason as I do for Finn. But his aversion is understandable. His father's entire career was on the road and worked as a cover-up for leading several other lives. It makes sense that he'd want the opposite of what his parents had. I have a feeling Finn wouldn't be too keen if I were to tell him I was thinking of pursuing a life as a commercial pilot, either.

"That's a big step." I blow out a sharp breath and invite my deepest insecurity into the bed with us.

What if you end up staying with me out of guilt? What if you feel trapped because you don't want to look like the villain who asked a girl to start a life with you and then felt jilted when the spell was finally broken?

"What if you regret it?" I ask.

Now he rolls me over to face him. He shakes his head at me, his eyes narrowed. "Not a chance. Don't even go there."

"Finn, there are a lot of loose ends—"

"I know," he says. "We're not on a time limit. Why don't you figure out what's going on with Legacy Resorts first? You make that decision based on what's best for you. And then when you know where you're going to be, we can figure out us."

"You'll wait for me to get things settled first?"

He flashes me his charming, million-dollar smile. "Of course. Where would I go, Queen? I'm completely hooked on you."

Confidence is a daring vixen, and when she's feeling particularly full of self-love, acceptance, and the deepest kind of connection, she just can't wait.

"Thank you. Now, I've been naked in front of you for over an hour. Are you planning on doing something about it? Because it's been a while since we've been together, and I'd really like to have sex now."

His smile disappears. "Wait a minute. I'm confused. Last time we talked about this, you didn't ask for sex."

"*What?*" I squall. *Incorrect.* I'm pretty sure I've been explicitly clear that Finn's body is my preferred drug and my favorite kind of high.

His eyes narrow, and I clue into what he's doing right before he says it. "You don't want to have sex, Avery. You want to get fucked, don't you?"

Good grief, please, no one save me. Let it end like this.

"Yes."

"Atta girl." Finn yanks off his thin white T-shirt with one hand and discards it like a rag. The thing looked fatigued trying to hold in his muscles anyway. The shirt is probably relieved to be a crumpled mess on the floor. Sitting up, Finn presses his back against the headboard as he unbuttons his pants and frees his length. I swear it grows every time I see it. Because every time I see his smooth, hard cock I'm almost certain I can't handle the size.

He proves me wrong every single time.

"Get on your stomach," Finn commands as he throws his pants and briefs to join his shirt on the floor.

"Don't you mean my knees?"

He releases a harsh laugh. "No. I meant what I said. You're going to need to listen carefully because I don't like to repeat myself when I'm in this kind of mood." His low, grumbly tenor turns into a growl. "Knees fatigue. Get comfortable on your belly because you're going to be down there a while." When I'm lying flat between his legs, he reaches down and grabs me by the hair, firmly guiding my mouth over his cock. I open my mouth as wide as I can but gag when he puts in more than I was expecting.

Finn pulls away and gives me a moment to breathe.

"I can take it," I pant out of breath. I open my mouth again, but he stills.

"You sure?"

"Yeah... Go crazy. I want it." I dab at the involuntary tears underneath my eyes. "I'll let you know if I can't handle it. Should we have a safe word?"

Finn rolls his eyes. "The safe word is 'stop,' Avery. Just tell me, and I'll listen. This is for you, so the moment you don't like it, I'll stop."

I nod eagerly. "Don't let me give up. I want to swallow you whole." I open my mouth, flattening my tongue as best as I can, which I've learned Finn really enjoys.

"That dirty mouth of yours," Finn says with a smirk. "Open wider, Queen. Tonight, you're going to take it all."

Chapter 31

Finn

I've never fucked her like this before.

We're wild. Animals. The way she's wrapped around me, I'm damn near close to losing control, so I stop myself before I get too carried away.

"Does it hurt from behind?" I pull out and ask her for the thousandth time. Waiting for her to speak, I run my hands over Avery's smooth, round, fleshy ass. I have to constantly remind myself not to slip my finger into her other tight little hole. It spooks her. She's not ready...yet.

Her ass is poked up into the air and her face is buried into the pillow, so when she reluctantly mumbles something, I don't hear her. I've been reminding her for the past twenty minutes to speak up, but apparently she still hasn't learned her lesson. So I spank her ass, hard. By now I know not only can she take it, she also loves it.

"Speak up," I growl, rubbing where I swatted, feeling her hot skin under my palm. She purposely mumbles into the pillow again, baiting me. I smack her other ass cheek, and she whimpers before she groans.

"Oh my God. Yes."

"Yes, it hurts?"

She mumbles something into the pillow again.

"Are you trying to piss me off, Queen?"

Avery lifts her head slightly and looks back at me, flashing me those beautiful misty eyes. Her heavy makeup is smeared. She's sweating, and her hair is crazed. She hasn't looked put together since she was sucking on my cock so professionally, I ended up spilling my first load right down her throat. But the way we've been so rowdy tonight in my studio has kept me hard as steel. Not to mention I love the way she looks. Right now, make no mistake, she still looks like a fucking ten and a half. "Am I pissing you off, Finn?"

"A little."

"Good," she sasses. "Then spank me harder."

"Oh, I will, but you need to answer me first. Does it hurt?" Every time I'm in so deep that my sack knocks against her clit, she flinches like she's in pain. I'm all for playing rough, but every woman has her limit, and I care about this girl. I'm not trying to break her.

"No. I like it."

"I didn't ask if you like it. My cock is completely coated with your cum, baby. *I know you like it.* But I asked you if it hurts. Am I too deep?" I grab a fistful of her ass. "Don't lie to me."

"I can take it."

"You sure? I can stop."

She growls in frustration into the pillow and bangs her fist against the mattress, sending a few black rose petals flying. "You're killing the vibe."

"What vibe? I thought I was doing a pretty good job," I say, glancing at my soaked cock, evidence of Avery's pleasure. I wipe the sweat from my forehead with the back of my hand. There's nothing I can do about the sweat dripping down my abs. We're wet. We're supposed to be.

Avery rolls over to her back and bends her knees, coaxing me between them. The look on her face is of pure intoxication. She's fucking like she's greedy, and I love it. "Pirate Finn would never ask if it hurts. He'd tell me to throw my hips back and take him even deeper."

Pulling my eyes away from her lush tits, I raise my brows at her. "Did you just say Pirate Finn?"

"No," she deadpans.

Grabbing my chest as I chuckle, I brush her sweaty hair away from her forehead. "Is that what your dirty girl dream was about? Me as a pirate?"

She blinks at me. "I have no clue what you're talking about."

"Mmhmm, sure." I roll her nipple between my thumb and forefinger with enough pressure that we're a touch past pleasure and on the cusp of pain. She bites her bottom lip but doesn't protest. "What else did Pirate Finn do to you?" I slip two fingers into her wet crease, and she gasps. "Because you seem to have really liked it." I hook my fingers and stroke the textured spot inside her walls, and she cringes, knowing exactly what I'm trying to do.

"Wait, Finn—*oh*. This is...your...studio," she says between moans. I pick up the pace with my fingers.

"Exactly. *My studio*," I snarl. "I'll do whatever the fuck I want. Is that pirate enough for you?"

"Please don't," she begs, but her body and her words are saying two different things. "I don't want to make a mess in here."

She's unnecessarily concerned. I change the sheets after every boudoir session just for my clients' peace of mind. There's a mattress protector, and fuck it—I'd buy a brand-new bed just to watch her squirt again. I like that she can do it. I love that I'm the first one who showed her she could. But her eyes are filled with worry, and I don't want to see the stress. I just want to see my sexy queen begging to come.

"Fine." I remove my fingers and place them near her lips. "If you don't want a mess, then clean it up." I smile at her wickedly but soften my tone. "*Now, baby*. Open your mouth. You're delicious. I promise you."

She parts her lips timidly, and I shove both fingers in, forcing her mouth open wide. "Good girl. Suck on them like it's my cock. You do that so well. You never needed me. All these lessons this summer, but you're the one teaching me. You taught me how to feel good again, do you know that? Do you know how excited I am to be around you? I'm so into you, Avery. You have no idea."

Her tongue is occupied, licking my fingers clean, so she can't speak. But I can tell she's burning under the praise.

"Do you like how you taste, baby?" I ask as I pull my fingers out of her mouth.

She squints at me. "Do you?"

I slide down her body and drag my tongue slowly across her crease just to prove my point. "Fuck yes, I do." I take my time teasing her, getting a little more carried away than I intended to. Her thighs tense, and I feel her toes curl as she wraps her feet around my neck. Her whole body begins to tremble when I nip at her clit with my teeth.

"Oh fuck, *Finn*. Do that again," she begs.

"No."

Her eyes pool with disappointment as I rise and position my tip at her entrance.

"Greedy girl. I've already made you come like that twice tonight. This time, I want to feel it." I wrap my hand against her neck, softly rubbing the hollow of her throat with my thumb. "Eyes on me. If you close your eyes, I stop." I don't fuck around when it comes to this. When her eyes are open, I can tell if she's breathing. When they clamp shut, it can go from dangerously sexy to torture. That's not a game I want to play. "You ready?"

I wait for her small nod, and I plunge into her sopping heat at the same time my hand closes powerfully around her throat. It's sensory overload, and she begins to panic through her coughing and sputtering. I loosen my grip. "Calm down. Shh. I got you." Her breathing eventually goes rhythmic. "Do you think I'd let anything bad happen to you?"

She begins to bridge her hips to match my thrusts, and her shallow, panicked breaths turn into moans. I retighten my grip and feel her getting wetter. I'd enjoy the romance just as much, but I made a promise. She held up her end of the bargain and commanded my boudoir studio like a professional model, and now she wants a rough fucking.

"Look at me, Avery," I growl. She whimpers again as she locks her eyes on mine. "I didn't spend this summer preparing you for any man except me." I'm trying to play a part, but my words are true. "You're mine. This pussy is molded to me. It's mine now too. No man is ever going to satisfy you like I do." I lean over her and kiss her roughly. Her lips are swollen, and her face is flushed. "Next time you have a dirty dream about me, roll over and wake me up. And I'll show you how much better I can do it in real life. You hear me?"

She's near her orgasm. Avery has an obvious tell; her eyes start to roll back in her head.

"Eyes open and on me, or I stop."

She tries to beg me not to stop. Her words are garbled. She's able to breathe, but it's strained, and I've had enough. Watching her fleshy tits jiggle around is enough to end me. My cock is so hard it damn near feels close to exploding. She's clenching around me, making holding back my release intolerable. I bury into her like a maniac. I let go of her throat and she gasps in relief, but she only has a minute. I rotate her hips so our legs are scissored and she's feeling every single inch of me.

For fuck's sake. I'm so deep. My entire length is on fire, burrowed inside.

"*Finn*," she cries as she clenches her fists. "Don't stop. It's so good. I can take it."

Goddamn. Fucking. Queen.

"*Good girl.* I knew you could take it. Now you have to race me and win. Come for me." My nondominant hand finds her throat this time as I lick my other thumb and swivel small circles around her clit. It takes her barely a minute to shatter around my cock, the pulsing and tightening sending me right over the edge with her. I weave both of my hands through her hair, our lips interlock, and I swallow her sweet cries as I spill every ounce into her.

It takes her what seems like forever to stop trembling underneath me. I pin her down protectively, holding her, warming her until her breathing calms. Her chest rising and falling underneath me must cause me to doze off, because I lose a moment of time and wake up to Avery pushing on my chest.

"Finn, get off me. Please."

"Sorry," I mumble, peeling our sticky bodies apart. Rolling to the side, I ask, "Squishing you?"

"No, I'm just dripping on you. It's gross."

"Gross?" Reaching down, I pat between her thighs, causing her to clamp her legs shut. She's correct. She is dripping. "Why is that gross? It's mine."

"It's just a lot," she mutters, and I smirk at her in response. "Proud of that, are you?" She giggles.

"I like to think I have a healthy, potent seed."

"Ha! And here I thought men only bragged about size." It's just the sound of our hearts pounding for a moment, and then her voice goes small. "Do you want kids?"

"Oh yeah. Definitely."

"How many?"

I reach down to find her hand and weave my fingers between hers before closing my fist and bringing her hand to my lips. "As many as my wife will give me. Preferably three boys and then a baby girl that I will spoil so hard, she'll be the brattiest little diva in the world."

"That's a lot of babies, Finn. You probably need to get started soon."

"Hm, how much do you trust your birth control? Maybe I just did," I tease.

"Okay, funny man." She takes her hand back. "I need to get cleaned up."

I point to the door to my right. "There's a full bathroom in there. Clean shower, fresh towels, everything you need. When you're done, come upstairs to the kitchen, okay? I'll make us a snack."

She sits up and looks over her shoulder, her long hair spilling over her back and her minty green eyes in a soft haze. *Damn, that's the perfect shot.* I wish I had my camera in hand. "I know we said we would talk about things at the end of the summer...but in the meantime…"

"Yeah?"

"What is this, then? I mean, should I stay over tonight?"

I clear my throat, trying to hide my agitation. The games are over. I showed my hand. She doesn't get to hold me at arm's length or run out on me anymore. "It's not like we haven't slept next to each other before."

"That was a hotel," she insists. "It's a little different. This is your home. Your space. Am I supposed to sleep over?"

I sit up and plant a few kisses across her naked back before hoisting myself out of bed. "Yes, from now on, you sleep over." I pull on my briefs and raise my brows at her warningly. "We're going to have big problems if you don't."

Chapter 32

Avery

Finn has the exact same coffeemaker Dex does. It's far fancier than a coffeemaker should be. There are more buttons here than inside of a high-rise elevator. But after more than half a summer navigating Dex's pretentious caffeine machine, I'm able to make a good pot of coffee with my eyes closed. Four scoops. Thirty-six ounces. Extra bold.

I'm grabbing a coffee mug from the cabinet when I hear the front door open and then slam shut. Instinctively, I pull at the hem of Finn's undershirt that I'm wearing. I'm a full-figured girl, and in no way is Finn's thin, white muscle shirt *draped* over me. It'd probably be much looser and longer on the model type, but between my chest, my hips, and my ass, this shirt is a baby tee on me and whoever is walking through that front door is about to get a show. I have no time to dart back to the bedroom.

"Finn!"

I'm relieved to hear Lennox's voice.

"It's me," I call out. "And fair warning, I'm in my underwear."

Lennox turns the corner and sees my flushed, sheepish smile. I cross my right leg over the left in a show of modesty. She smirks at me, looking thoroughly pleased. "You guys really hump like bunnies, don't you?"

I blink at her. "We had...an *adult* sleepover after the photo shoot," I say wryly as I cross my arms.

She begins to laugh, and then her face flattens in concern. "Wait, you mean you guys did the photo shoot and then came back to the main house, right—"

I give her a guilty, closed-lip smile as Finn turns the corner and answers for me. "We definitely did not. We christened the shit out of my studio. We're going to need to clean up in there a little."

Finn's shirtless, showing off his taut, firm abs. They look extra swollen today, like he put them through a hellish workout. Hmm, how much does thrusting work the ab muscles? I feel a twinge of guilt as I appreciate Finn's perfectly defined body knowing what's firm on him is soft on me. I am never going to measure up to his level when it comes to looks. I have no idea what this man sees in me. Maybe kindness? Respect? Smarts? But is that enough to carry a relationship? It certainly wasn't enough for Mason and me.

"You horny assholes. Do you know how long I worked on staging?"

Finn ruffles Lennox's hair as he passes, the way an annoying big brother would. "You did a great job. The set worked beautifully. We'll have pictures back in a couple weeks or so...not that I get to see them." When he gets to me, he wraps his arms around me, letting his hand rest on my half-covered ass. He kisses me unapologetically as if Lennox is nowhere in sight. When I'm good and breathless, he pulls his cool lips from mine and tugs on the T-shirt I'm wearing. "This looks so sexy on you. Keep it. I want to see you in it again tomorrow when I wake up."

God, I love the attention.

Is that so wrong to admit? Can I be a sensible, hard-working, un-shallow woman and still melt into a puddle when this Adonis of a man looks at me like this?

Finn glances at my empty mug and takes it from me, seeming to understand I haven't had a chance to pour a cup yet.

"Your phone is over there charging. You must've forgotten it out here last night, so I plugged it in." I point to the outlet on the kitchen island. "It rang like four times this morning."

"Who's been calling?" Finn asks absentmindedly. He fetches another cup from the cabinet to match mine and proceeds to fill both cups.

"I don't know."

"*You don't know?*" he parrots in a mumble. "You said you plugged in my phone."

"Yeah."

"So you didn't see who was calling?"

"I didn't look. Wouldn't that be an invasion of privacy?"

Finn spins around, and his puzzled eyes meet mine. "You can. I have nothing to hide."

I return his befuddled expression. "I believe you. But I respect your privacy."

Maybe I should've gone through Mason's phone from time to time. I could've gotten a tip-off as to what was going on. It's more than possible that his adventures on the Rumble app didn't start *after* we were broken up. I just have never been a snoop. Getting dumped isn't going to change that.

Finn crosses the room with intention and wraps his forearm around my shoulders, yanking me against his chest. He smells earthy and musky, mixed with the last remnants of his cologne and my shampoo. He smells like we fucked all night. Because we did. Finn plants a firm kiss on the top of my head before releasing me. His unspoken outburst of emotion is obvious. I may be the first woman who's respected Finn's privacy.

It's in this moment that I realize I'm not the only one who was in an unhappy relationship. Where mine was bland and monotonous, Finn's was boldly volatile. Still...we're both survivors.

"Well, I'm going to go assess the damage, you jerks," Lennox says, reminding me we have company. Finn's embrace was so desperately emotional, the whole world fell away for a moment. "But here, Avery," she says, setting a paper shopping bag on the kitchen counter next to me. "I stopped by a friend's boutique store this morning to pick up some stuff for the set that you guys defiled, and I mentioned your mermaid costume. She had the *perfect* one. I bet it'll be smokin' sexy on you. And it covers all the important bits."

"Mermaid costume?" Finn asks.

"For Cass's party."

I think Lennox has assumed we talked about it, but we were a little occupied last night. I meant to ask Finn how he felt about me going this morning. I was going to ask if he wanted me to go as Lennox's friend or his date. Judging by the deer-in-headlights look on his face, I'm assuming he doesn't want me within a ten-mile radius of Ruby's.

"You spoke to Cass?" Finn asks me.

"No, I got a plus-one," Lennox answers on my behalf.

Finn narrows his eyes at his cousin. "And you invited Avery?

"I don't have to go—"

"The fuck you don't!" Lennox shrieks. "This costume is superior, and I already have a bunch of glittery mermaid shit. *You're going.*" She narrows her eyes back at Finn and points directly at his forehead. "And you fix your face. You're coming off like an ass. I'll be back," she mutters, heading to the door that leads to the basement, grumbling the entire way about us sullying her art.

The minute we hear the door shut, Finn raises his palms in the air as surrender. But I speak before he can.

"Finn, I wasn't trying to insert myself—"

"No, it's not that. You're welcome wherever I am—"

"It's just that Lennox was trying to be nice, and I mentioned my idea for a costume, and she's excited." I interrupt him right back and continue in a panic because the look on his face seems a whole lot like rejection. Of course. Finn and I make perfect sense in private, but I should know better than to think he'd want to show up with me at his future gentleman's club surrounded by a sea of beautiful, slim women—

"Cass and I have sex," he blurts out. "*Had* sex. For years. We just stopped a few months ago."

The timeline doesn't make sense. He had sex with Cass for years? But I thought he was with Nora for years. "You cheated on Nora?"

"No. Never."

"So you'd sleep with Cass when you guys broke up?"

Finn hands me a filled mug then steps back. "Well, technically that too."

"Can you stop being so evasive?" I take a small sip from the hot coffee. I don't flinch when it scalds my tongue. I'm too invested in whatever is making Finn look like someone is shoving nails through his fingertips. "Just tell me."

He blows out a deep breath. "Nora and I *and* Cass would sleep together."

"Huh?"

"Good grief," Finn grunts, rolling his eyes, obviously agitated that he has to further clarify. "A threesome, Avery. Most of the time, Nora and I would have threesomes—just with Cass. We trusted her. But she's only ever been just a friend. Cass likes gratuitous sex, no strings attached. After Nora and I broke up, it was easy to be with Cass when I was hurting because it was just physical."

"You stopped sleeping with her when you met me?"

Finn shakes his head. "A few months before that. I don't know if I told you, but I was abstinent for a while before we met."

I try to hide my surprise. And fail. I can literally feel how wide my eyes are. "Why?"

"I got to the point where I stopped liking sex. It got boring and tedious. I'd be with a woman and wouldn't feel anything. Eventually, I realized it wasn't what I wanted, so I stopped sleeping around to get a little clarity."

I point to my chest and mouth, *Me?*

He chuckles as he nods. "There was something about you that made me feel safe. Is that lame for a man to say?"

"Not at all," I say soothingly. "You deserve to feel safe."

But then again, so do I.

I've been waiting for Finn's kink. He seemed to really enjoy the rough sex last night. I am totally fine with fuzzy handcuffs and I would be open to more naked photo shoots, but this...

"So do you still like threesomes?"

He runs his hands through his hair and purses his lips. "How am I supposed to answer that?"

"Honestly," I reply.

"Obviously, I did. It's a lot of, um"—he scratches his head awkwardly—"parts and stimulation when you're with more than one woman." He runs his hand over his face and groans like the words taste bad in his mouth. "But I would never expect you to do that. And I was only concerned about Cass's birthday because I wouldn't introduce you to Nora, so I'm not sure what to do about Cass. She really is just a friend, but still, I don't want to make you uncomfortable."

I know he's trying to be considerate, but all I just heard was that *Finn likes threesomes and yet he'd never expect me to do that.*

"What else do you like that I don't know about?" I'm almost scared to ask. "I don't want you to feel like I can't keep up."

He tilts his head to the side and looks at me with pity in his eyes. "Keep up? You're miles ahead, Queen. I'm happy. I am perfectly content with the way we have sex."

"Perfectly *content*?"

"Yeah." Finn gives me a kind smile and taps his nose. "You're perfect."

We're quite clearly fixating on different words because he thinks perfect is a compliment, but I know exactly what content leads to. It's boredom, dissatisfaction, and after four years getting proposed to and then immediately dumped while you cry into a messy, crumbled pile of chocolate cake. I'll be damned if I fall in love again just to start over at thirty-four.

Finn grabs the shopping bag Lennox sets down and takes a peek. "Okay, to be clear, you're not going anywhere dressed like this unless I'm with you."

I scowl at him. "So I let you push me around the bedroom once, and suddenly you think you're my keeper?"

"You *need* a keeper wearing this." He pulls out what can barely be considered a bra. It's essentially two clamshells attached to each other with a thin wire. It wouldn't support a cotton ball, let alone my large breasts.

My jaw drops at Lennox's wildly misguided judgment. Finn

peeks back into the bag and smiles at me wickedly.

"Do I even want to see the bottoms?"

His smile is devilish. "There's not much to see, Queen."

"Good grief."

He drops the mermaid bra back into the bag and pulls my coffee mug from my hand before setting it aside. He takes each of my hands and wraps them around his waist. "My friend who used to be my friend with benefits is having a birthday party. I know we're in the gray area, but if you're okay with it, I'd really love for you to be my official date and show you off in your sexy mermaid costume. What do you say?"

"Okay," I say. "Thank you for inviting me. I'd love to."

"Good," he breathes out. "Now come on." He grabs my wrist in one hand and tugs me behind him, snagging the shopping bag off the counter as he passes by. "I need to do a thorough inspection to make sure this fits."

Oh boy. The urge that immediately bubbles up between my thighs is a little stronger than the tender ache. It would probably be wise to take a break after fucking for hours last night, but it's Finn. What crazy woman would say no? I just have to hope and pray his dick falls off so I can take a break from this man.

This is chemistry. Lust. Desire. Obsession. It's nothing in the realm of content. Now how the hell do I keep it that way? How do I avoid the same fate as my last relationship?

"I suppose if it doesn't fit, we can leave it off."

"That's the spirit, Queen."

Finn squeezes my hand, causing the mermaids on his forearm to dance. There are three of them clustered together on that rock. I stare at them inquiringly. Their smiles are so wicked, like they have a dirty secret. It certainly looks like they're enjoying themselves.

So be honest, ladies. Do you guys all get busy together, too? Am I missing out?

"Avery?" Finn asks outside of his bedroom door. "Are you okay? You look worried."

"No, no," I assure him as I squeeze his hand. "I'm fine."

Totally fine.

Perfectly content.

Chapter 33

Avery

"Holy shit, that's a lot of skin showing."

It's not just Palmer's words through our FaceTime call. It's the way her face is screwed up like she's in pain. It's unmistakably a look of shock and horror at me in my mermaid costume. "Do you have a shawl or something?"

"I really only asked about my makeup, Palmer," I say, stepping closer to the mirror and taking a seat on the bathroom chair positioned in front of several different eyeshadows and mini tubs of glitter.

Lennox was supposed to help me get ready, but she got horrendously ill with what she calls the super flu. It's been over three days, and just this morning we confirmed there was no way in hell she was attending the birthday party tonight. I offered to skip the party and help take care of her instead, but she insisted she felt guilty enough for infecting Alan. They have plans of commiserating in their misery tonight together, in Snuggies, in front of a Marvel movie marathon.

I'm jealous. Outside of the fever and chills, that's exactly my perfect version of date night. Dolling up for hours, like I'm about to walk the red carpet or walk down the aisle, is not a routine I want to fall into. But Finn seems so excited about tonight. I don't want to be a killjoy. For the past couple of weeks, we've been enjoying the gray area. The place where we get to flirt, cuddle, have constant sex, but don't have to make any life-altering decisions. But the gray area has an expiration date—and it's in three days when I head to

Cancun to present to the board.

I blink at Palmer, who has fallen into an awkward silence.

"Okay, fine, just say it—do I look fat? Because Lennox and Finn have already seen me in the costume, and they said I look—"

"*No.* No, Aves. I didn't say *fat*. It's just..." She pinches her brow. "What did Finn and Lennox say?" she asks in a mocking tone.

Lennox said I looked jaw-dropping bold and hot. She also made some less-than-tasteful comments about my breasts—all complimentary. And Finn didn't say much because the moment the costume was on, he peeled it right off. He did mention mermaids may be his new fetish.

"They said it looked good." The bottom of the mermaid costume is a long, flowy, pink skirt that's see-through and sheer. The delicate fabric is held together with silver chains that attach to a clamshell—that conveniently matches my bra—covering my bottom *bit*. This is the most revealing thing I've ever worn in my life, but I'm headed to a strip club costume party. And aren't I an adult by now? Who has the right to tell me what I should and shouldn't be wearing?

"Maybe just throw a crop top on over it. Like take a T-shirt and just put it over your bra and tie the ends." She demonstrates a knot with her hands like it's a foreign concept to me. "You'll feel even more comfortable."

"Thanks, Palmer. Real supportive," I mutter bitterly and pick up a makeup brush and passive-aggressively stab the bristles into the glitter pot too hard. Pink and silver shimmer goes flying all over the bathroom countertop and the bottom of my phone that's propped against the container of cotton swabs.

"Come on. I'm not saying you look bad. It's just..."

I exhale and meet her eyes on the screen. "It's what?"

"You're changing, a lot."

"And?" I'm not doing a good job hiding the irritation in my voice.

Palmer rolls her eyes at my tone. "I mean, I know you, Aves. You've been my best friend for twenty years, so I can say with full confidence that you, the real you, is pretty incredible. I don't want you to change your entire identity because Mason wasn't the one. You are perfect for someone. And I just don't think that someone is going to want you to dress up like a mermaid slut and party at a strip club."

I deadpan. "Slut?"

She holds up her hands in surrender. "Sorry! Poor word choice. You get what I'm trying to say. You're just not Vegas. You're not *going out*. You're Avery. You're cuddles on the couch, and ranch and chips for dinner, and the most intelligent, kind human being I know. You deserve everything, Aves."

As per usual, Palmer's loving and supportive message is wrapped in her candy coating of sass and judgment, but the core is sweet at least.

I gesture to my cleavage on display. "This isn't the norm. I'm the one who wanted to go to this party. Finn... I don't know, Palmer, there's something between us, and I think it's real."

She turns up her lip like she smells something rancid. "Real? You and the strip club owner? *Come on.*"

"He's a photographer—a really good photographer," I say, grabbing the aerosol hairspray and spraying it into my palm. I dab the liquid by the sides of my eyes before using the makeup brush to deposit a healthy coat of glitter where my eyeliner ends. I'll be damned. It actually works; the glitter is glued in place. All courtesy of Lennox's genius. "He wants me to move here to be with him and give our relationship a real chance."

"Stop. What the fuck?" Palmer asks, her eyes popping into wide circles. "You're not—"

"I am. If I get the Legacy Resorts job, I'm moving to Vegas."

The job is almost guaranteed.

My hunch was more than spot-on. Once I dug into the board members' financials, it was very clear what Legacy's main issue is... They have a rat.

The member most adamant about selling the company and getting everyone to rally behind him happens to be a major investor in Legacy's direct competition. My big presentation transformed from a pitch to a witch hunt. Once I tell the executive team and other board members what Mr. Wallace Frank has been up to, he'll be voted off the board and Legacy can start fresh with a supportive team and a solid new branding vision.

My vision.

I bite the inside of my cheek and brace myself, preparing for the snarky remark that's about to come out of Palmer's mouth, but instead, there are only tears.

"Palmer?" I ask.

She shakes her head and sniffles.

"Palmer...what's wrong?" My tone softens as I watch her eyes fill and her cheeks turn blotchy red.

"It's just *great* to know that I'm losing my job, my home, and my best friend all at the same time."

"*What?* That assistant actually got you fired? Because that's not—"

Palmer shakes her head again. "No. The show didn't end up getting picked up. The network changed its mind last minute. They'll have my final check tomorrow, and then we're done. I was going to tell you this weekend."

The way her head is hung makes my stomach twist. I hate seeing Palmer like this. Her sass and snark are a wall she's built up after years of rejection in an industry based on luck and endless ladders. An industry that's been rejecting her for a decade now.

"Palmer... I'm so sorry, friend. What do you need from me?"

"Anything? Even if it's much too much to ask?"

I nod assuredly. "Absolutely."

"Will you come get me? I don't want to make the drive back alone. I know you have connections in the airline industry. Could you get a last-minute flight—"

"Yes. I'll get on a flight tomorrow night. You can come to Cancun with me, okay? They booked me a couple's suite, but there's no way in hell I'm sharing that with Mason. Do you want to be my date?"

Hunter with Legacy Resorts made the incorrect assumption that Mason and I are still a couple, so he had his assistant arrange a honeymoon suite at Legacy's Cancun resort. I politely told Mason I was keeping the luxury suite and he needed to find elsewhere to bunk for the presentation. I actually was going to surprise Finn with a last-minute invitation, but Palmer clearly needs the distraction. She can get tan and drunk in Mexico while I secure Arrow Consulting's future.

"But you have to play nice with Mason," I continue. "He's going to be there, too."

She makes a disgusted face.

"Free vacation, honey. Beggars can't be choosers."

"What did you decide about all that anyway? You're really going to ditch Mason after all you guys have gone through with Arrow?"

"Wow, look who is singing a different tune," I say teasingly. "Has the war finally ceased?" I wink before I shake my head. "No. I came up with the perfect solution. I am going to keep Arrow Consulting intact and offer an exclusive noncompete offer to Legacy Resorts. So we'll get their fat paycheck, I'll give Mason his fair share, and Arrow Consulting will be an exclusive resource to Legacy." I pinch my fingers together and kiss them. "I don't want to say I'm a genius, but..." I pop my shoulders with a big grin on my face. I'm just trying to cheer her up. "Everything is going to be okay. You could move to Vegas with me. We can still get a place together."

"I have to be in L.A. for—"

"I know." I wish she'd just give up her acting career and find something that makes her feel good about herself. But I also know Palmer's talented. Everyone finds their path in their own way. "If this is what you want, then see this show as a big stepping-stone. You landed an amazing job, Palmer. It's not in your control who invests in the project. So take the experience, go home, and *go hard.* Another opportunity will come your way. I promise you, friend. I love you."

"I know." She presses her fingertips against her closed eyes. "But...I don't know...I'm scared that you have this new life, new friends, and a new man so quickly. I'm your oldest friend. I've been with you forever. You're really going to ditch me for some random hot guy? I though..."

I hang my head when I remember the promise I made to her weeks ago. Before Finn. Before I found this new version of myself. I told Palmer we were in it together and she could count on me. She needs me. Mason needs me. He's not my boyfriend, but he is still my business partner.

I don't want to be the girl who ditches her oldest friends for a shiny new life that truthfully I probably don't fit into. Maybe this is moving too fast. This summer was just a break from reality, but now real life seems to be catching up.

"We'll figure it out together, Palmer. Don't worry. I'll be there tomorrow, okay? I'll text you as soon as I have my flight details."

"Okay," she says through sniffly tears. She dabs again at her red, puffy eyes. "I love you, Aves. I don't deserve you."

"Well, you've got me."

* * *

"Finn Harvey, I have a face, you know."

Finn reluctantly peels his eyes away from my chest to meet my gaze from the opposite side of the limo. "I'm sorry, did you say something?" he asks. "It's hard to hear you over your sexy tits."

I try to scowl at him, but a reluctant smile breaks through, and he responds by unbuttoning the top of his crisp, gray polo suggestively. To my surprise, Finn showed up at my place to pick me up for the party in nice dark jeans and a gray polo. He's dressed the same way he does when he takes me out to a fancy dinner. When I asked him where the hell his costume was, he informed me that only the women dress up at Cass's costume parties, which to me seems very much like a hunter-and-prey type of situation, but hey...*when in Vegas.*

Finn reaches behind him to roll down the partition halfway. "How's traffic?" he asks the driver.

I hate to admit it, but I could get used to the limo treatment. It's not the luxury aspect. I don't give a rat's ass about the extended limo, champagne on ice, or plush leather seats. It's the fact that every time we take a limo, I get to spend the ride playing footsie with Finn and staring into his bright baby blue eyes instead of watching the side of his face light up under red-and-green lights.

"A little congested," the driver responds. "But don't worry, we'll get you there on time."

"Don't rush," Finn replies to the driver, even though his eyes are forward, locked on my clamshell mermaid bra. "We need about twenty more minutes. If we arrive sooner than that, circle the block, and under no circumstances are you to roll down this partition. Clear?"

"Yes, sir," the driver responds apathetically like he has no idea, or no interest, in what Finn is insinuating.

I've worked with a lot of top-dog CEOs in the past few years. There's a certain air of authority a man gets when he knows his commands will be followed with enthusiasm. Finn has traces of a CEO's attitude. It comes in little flashes. Most of the time he's soft, sweet, and charming, but there's a top-dog boss living inside him. A side that seems to only come out when he's turned on or pissed off.

Once the partition is up again, Finn grabs his dick through his slacks and bites his lower lip. "All right, Queen. You know what we do in limos. Spread 'em."

This time I full-on scowl. "No."

He cocks one eyebrow. "Excuse me? Sweetheart, I reminded you about fifty times that you're the most beautiful woman on the planet, brought you a limo, and rubbed your sexy little feet for the past ten minutes because you said your heels hurt."

"Yes," I admit, "you've been perfect tonight." *Every night, in fact.*

He nods emphatically. "Yep. Foreplay. Now, pay up. Touch

yourself. The clock is running."

"No."

"Why?"

"Because I..." I'm embarrassed to fess up, but I don't want Finn to think I'm rejecting him. "I spent a really long time on my hair and makeup because I want to look as good as I possibly can. I don't want all your friends to see me sweaty, splotchy, and with frizzy hair. I don't want you to be...embarrassed to show up with me, okay? You deserve a pretty girl, Finn. I'm really trying."

I'm putting in the effort for Finn where I fell flat with Mason. Maybe because I'm trying to rectify past mistakes. Maybe because Finn already matters to me more. Or maybe because I know when it comes to Finn, the competition is fierce. I've just never been interested in competing until now. But it's undeniable...

Now that I have his attention, I don't want to lose it.

"Why are you trying so hard to be something you already are? Avery, we can turn this limo around and go home right now." Finn's expression flattens as his eyes sink with concern. "We're going out tonight because *you* wanted to. I would've skipped it. These are my wild party friends. If you don't like it, they don't have to be a part of my life."

"You'd give up your friends for me?"

He nods. "I'm asking you to change your whole life and move here just to take a chance on us. So whatever you need to feel secure, I'll give it to you. I haven't seen these clowns in months, and I'm not missing anything."

I rub my lips together, forgetting how slippery they are from all the thick gloss. "Finn, may I teach *you* a love lesson for once?"

"Sure."

"Don't be with a woman who wants you to give up your friends for her. Be with a woman who wants to be a part of the things you like and love."

I wanted to tell Finn about my plan to move tonight. My big grand gesture. I know it's a risk and we haven't known each other long, but our chemistry is undeniable. Setting my insecurities aside, I wanted to see where this goes...

But then I got that call from Palmer a couple of hours ago. My old life is calling me home, and I don't want to be the woman who turns her back on her best friend of twenty years because she's currently lust-filled and sex-crazed over a man who has been treating her nicely for two months.

What kind of woman am I? What kind of friend am I? I need time to decide, and now I can't offer Finn any real answers tonight like I planned to, so instead, I kick off my shoes, bend my legs, and press my heels into the edge of my seat then spread my legs.

"Nothing crazy," I mumble as I part the strips of my skirt on either side of my thigh so he has a clear visual of my nude-colored panties. "I'm not going to mess up my hair and makeup."

He looks like a man starved as he sinks to his knees in front of me. "Fine. Then how about you lean back and relax? You can keep your pretty self perfectly intact, and I'll do all the work."

Before I can respond, he yanks my panties to the side and drags his tongue across my slit. I was already melting. Now I'm on fire.

"Oh my God," I groan.

He's not teasing me tonight. We're on a timer, so immediately he's lapping at me like a thirsty dog, and suddenly I don't care so much about how I look. I weave my fingers in his hair and grind against his wet tongue, trying to work as hard as he is.

"I said relax," he mumbles and blows against my clit, the cool air making me shudder. "I've got this. Lean back and enjoy."

He lets his saliva pool on the tip of his tongue before he flicks at my clit rapidly, following his own advice about head he gave me a few weeks ago. It went something like—keep it wet, lots of pressure, and my favorite part...lots of praise.

"Goddamn, you taste so good and feel so soft," he moans against me. "How's that feel, Queen?"

"Good," I force myself to breathe out.

"Hm, just good?" He latches onto my clit and hollows his cheeks, sucking as hard as he can as he sinks one finger into me.

"Oh fuck," I cry out, ignoring the fact the driver can probably hear everything. Is there music playing? We should turn on some music...*loud*...because I really want to scream. "Yes, like that."

He stops sucking just long enough to respond. "Good girl. That's more like it. Tell me how good it feels."

"You are a fucking king, Finn. You're so good at this. Please don't stop."

"That's what I like to hear," he grumbles as he works in a second finger. "You know something?" he asks, removing his lips from my body.

I lift my head from the back of the seat. "Keep going," I plead. "I'm close."

He looks up and shoots me a wicked smile. "You still have my fingers. Goodness, you needy girl. Let me talk to you for a minute."

I blink at him as my lips press together in a hard line. "I am zero percent amused."

He thrusts his fingers into me hard, making me grunt. "This is too easy."

"*What*?" I cry out as he picks up the pace.

"Yeah, I know your pussy backward and forward by now."

He's careful to keep his fingers long and straight, knowing if he curls them, I'll make a fuss about making a mess in this limo. I let him do that to me at home, preferably in the shower. Not here. Not in my mermaid costume, right before we're about to go into public.

"I know exactly how to make you feel good, baby. I've got this pussy on lockdown."

"Your point?" I ask through gasps.

"Now, how do I get your heart, hm? What do I need to do to keep you? To convince you that you are exactly what I want?" He latches on to my clit again with his lips and drives me to the brink, making sure my toes are curling and my thighs are tensing before he pulls away again. "I need you to start falling in love with me now, Avery."

In love?

Normally, I'd feel like this is a wildly inappropriate time to be having this conversation, but it feels right with Finn. It doesn't matter whether we're talking or fucking, the connection is the same. It's deep, and real, and so all-encompassing. Maybe my emotions will explode at the same time my body does...

"I'm halfway there, and I don't want to be alone at the finish line," Finn continues.

He nips at my clit now, knowing how it sets me off. It's the thrill of the idea of danger. He could hurt me, but he doesn't. He's so controlled, his nip almost on the cusp of pain but not quite. The perfect balance makes me explode. It's the trust I have knowing Finn is always going to dare me to jump off the cliff then be waiting at the bottom to catch me.

I come so hard it almost hurts. The way my back arches so intensely my spine aches, my thighs fatigue, and my head knocks back against the headrest so hard it bounces right back up. I have to rip Finn away from my body with both hands because he's dead set on pushing me past my limit and he continues to drag his tongue all over my sensitive entrance. The sensation is so intense that it's torture.

"*Stop,*" I beg. "I came, Finn. I already came."

"I know," he says with a chuckle as he yields and rises from his knees to slide back into his seat. "We need to work on your endurance."

"Endurance?" I ask as I adjust my panties over my swollen and throbbing center and realign my skirt.

"If you could bear through it, I could send you straight into another orgasm. Even more intense."

"I think one at a time is plenty," I huff, still catching my breath. The tingles in my toes still linger. I'm so satiated, I just want to fall asleep with Finn holding me from behind.

"For now. You'll see. There's a lot for us to explore together. That's what keeps your sex life alive, Avery. It's not different positions, dirty talk, or getting choked and your ass swatted. It's trusting each other enough to be honest and ask for what you want and need—"

"And the other person being willing to try," I add.

"That's where I think both of our prior relationships fell flat. Nora didn't trust"—he points to his chest—"and Mason didn't try." He points to me. "That's why we're good together. I don't want to pressure you, Avery, but if you were here, I know I could make you happy."

I look out the window and see that we're parked right in front of Ruby's. I remember the giant red neon sign from all those years ago when I rescued Palmer. *My best friend...*

"Finn, you know L.A. is only about four hours away."

He nods shortly. "I'm aware."

I keep my eyes on the window so he doesn't see my guilty expression. "That's almost the same distance to Scottsdale, right? You visit your mom once a month, and the drive isn't too bad." I finally force myself to look at him, and the way his lips are pressed together and his eyes are narrowed, he knows what I'm saying.

"Do you think seeing each other once a month would be enough for us?"

"Finn, I..." I trail off, and he waits patiently for me to finish my thought, but I can't. I don't want to tell him Palmer is what stands between us because he truly will hate her forever, and if Finn is going to be in my life, I need my boyfriend and my best friend to get along. It's bad enough that there's a war between Palmer and Mason. But there's only a war because she loves me and hates the man who broke my heart.

"Can I be honest?" Finn asks.

I nod in reply.

"I think we're good together, and I think you're standing in your own way. And when you figure out why, let me know. Maybe I can help you through it."

But I know why.

It's because even after all summer, it's still easier to sink back into what I know I am versus what I could be. I'm Mason's business partner. I'm Palmer's best friend. I don't know if I can trust the idea of Finn and this reinvented version of myself. It's just a fantasy. It's just a dream. Guys like Finn don't really fall in love with girls like me. I know he likes that I make him feel safe...

But do I make him feel alive the way he makes me feel alive? There's no way. And it's so much easier to think with my head than my heart.

"Finn, listen, I—"

Knock, knock, knock. The abrupt sound against the partition conveniently interrupts me.

"Sir, we're being told to move. I can't park here much longer. Should I circle the block again?"

"No, we're all set," Finn calls back, and we hear the driver's door open then slam shut. No doubt he's making his way over to let us out. Finn keeps his eyes on me. "Finish your sentence, sweetheart. What is it?"

What is it?...

I'm scared.

I grab my clutch and fish through it before I pull out a pack of gum. "Nothing. But here, you should take a piece." I hand over a single stick. "I promise I'll return the favor later."

He chuckles as he pops the gum into his mouth. He winks at me playfully, clearly trying to mask his disappointment in our conversation.

"Damn straight you will."

Chapter 34

Avery

I thought my costume was a little risqué, but in comparison to the women here, I look dressed for the presidential inauguration. There was one woman who was basically just wearing a tiny G-string and stickers over her nipples. I would've asked what her costume was, but she was a little busy with the security guard's tongue shoved halfway down her throat.

Suspicions confirmed—Cass's birthday party at this gentleman's club is a giant orgy waiting to happen. The decorations are superior. Everything is dark with colorful strobe lighting. There's confetti and glitter with giant balloons the size of my body. This party must've cost tens of thousands to decorate alone. I'm in shock—at the luxury...and the nakedness. But Finn looks unbothered like this is all business as usual.

I find it hard to believe one person has *this many* friends to invite to a birthday party. It's quite apparent this event is more of a publicity stunt than anything. I'm assuming this room is filled with minor celebrities, big-name influencers, pro athletes, and trust-fund babies. But it's not like I'd recognize anybody. I bet if Palmer were here, she'd be pointing out people left and right.

Although, nobody seems as infamous as Finn. From the moment he walked through the doors, he's been getting attention like he's walking the red carpet.

We entered together, my hand weaved firmly in his. He ushered me away from all the staring and leering and quickly led me to a VIP section, which is roped away from the mass mob of partygoers on the dance floor. Where clusters of people are packed at the bar, waiting half an hour for one beer, here in the VIP section it's Finn, myself, a few of his friends, and Cass, the birthday girl, who only stayed at the table long enough to give Finn a quick hug, me a kiss on the cheek, and tell me she loved my costume. I didn't even get to wish her a happy birthday, she was moving so fast.

It's clear as crystal that Finn has an entire other life that I'm not familiar with. Everyone knows him. Everyone knows his name. Everyone has been asking where the hell he's been and where *Nora* is tonight. He ignores the question each time, just politely responds and introduces me instead. But after the bullshit I pulled in the limo, the pretend girlfriend game is over. Finn has been introducing me as his date, but now there's a wall between us for sure. I hurt him with my hesitance about moving.

I hurt *myself* with my hesitance. *Fuck.*

But can you blame me? I look around and see everything I'm not. I wanted to be outgoing and fun for Finn, but I am so damn uncomfortable right now. All I want to do is leave, go home, take off this ridiculous costume, and wipe off all this makeup. I want to get into sweatpants and cuddle with Finn on the couch. But the way Finn's smiling and enjoying himself—does he want that? I just told him to be himself and not the version of himself he thinks he has to be for me, and now here I am, wondering if we're compatible after all.

When I really think about it, Finn and I have nothing in common. He's incredibly fit and works out daily. I consider making my bed exercise. Finn can cook everything. I make cereal and dip. Finn dresses like a supermodel, and the only thing I'll ever buy designer is sweatpants. How long can you keep up a façade to be with someone before you can't take it anymore? For Mason, it was four years...

I don't think I'll last half that long with Finn.

I don't like it here. This club. The music is too loud. There are too many women openly flirting with the man who is clearly here with me. The strobe lights are giving me a headache, and all these drinks are too fucking strong.

I am just not cool enough for Vegas.

I rise from my seat and lean down to whisper in Finn's ear, "Hey, I'm going to run to the bathroom."

"Okay," he says, rising as well. "Let's go. I'll show you where it is."

"No," I insist. "Stay. I can find it."

He grabs my wrist and holds me in place. "Avery," Finn says warningly. "Not by yourself—"

"Finn," I warn right back. "Don't treat me like a child. I can go to the bathroom by myself." *Plus, I don't need to pee. I need some space. I need to think. I need to be away from you and all this chaos for a moment.*

His eyes are locked on mine, and I know he's having a mental debate between respecting me and protecting me. I run my fingers tenderly across his cheek to help ease his clenched jaw. "I'll be *right back*, baby."

It's the *baby* part that makes him relax. He releases my wrist and kisses the back of my hand. "Please come right back."

I assure him I will as I duck under the VIP rope, grateful for my flowy skirt that allows me to maneuver with ease. Heading to the bathroom first just for something to do, I retreat when I see the line to the ladies' room wraps around the hallway. *Geez.* I settle for the packed bar instead, making sure I'm on the end, tucked away from Finn's view.

And for a while, I'm okay. I nod along to the club beats and try to ignore my view of the VIP section, where I can see woman after woman making their move on Finn. He smiles but turns them all away. I even see him firmly shake his head and hold up his palm when one of the strippers, dressed in confetti-themed lingerie, offers him a dance. It's like watching vultures flock, and even though he is a textbook gentleman, I still don't like the jealousy that's bubbling up in my chest. I compare myself to every single one of the women who are smaller and fitter than me, throwing themselves shamelessly at his feet.

This is what life as Finn's girlfriend would be like. Watching from the shadows as everyone tries to take what's mine.

"Water for the mermaid?"

The low voice next to me startles me from my thoughts. I whip my head to the right as the tingle of shock in my chest subsides. A blond man with a purposefully shaggy haircut that matches his scruff slides a blue cocktail toward me. His eyes are green, like mine—but so much darker. Where mine are light, his are a deep emerald. *Hm, pretty.* He chuckles as he studies my perplexed expression.

Tapping his temple, he says, "I planned that better in my head."

"What?"

He points to the drink. "I thought it'd be a cute way to break the ice. The drink—it's called Mermaid Water. You're dressed as a mermaid." He laughs again as he covers his eyes. "I did not play that off well."

I can't help but return his smile. He looks as uncomfortable here as I am, so I immediately feel a friendly bond. "Hey now, it wasn't bad after a little context."

"Don't lie."

The song switches, and it's low enough that I can actually carry a conversation. "I'm just impressed you were able to get a drink."

"Me too," he says, widening his eyes at the bartender, who has his back turned. "Cass's birthday is always ridiculous, but tonight I have to admit...it's a shit show. Of course, that has nothing to do with the party."

"Something wrong?" I ask.

"I just got into a big fight with my girlfriend," he mutters. "I wish I were enough of an asshole to leave her here, but I wouldn't forgive myself if something happened to her."

He's saying all the magic words for me to continue this conversation. He has a girlfriend. He's not an asshole.

I point to the cocktail. "Can I pay you for this if I drink it?

I don't think my date will like it if I let another man buy me a drink."

He smirks. "Yeah, Finn's got a temper on him sometimes. But don't worry, I didn't technically buy this for you." He holds up his arm and shows me a wristband. "It's an open bar for those who paid the cover."

"You're friends with Finn?" I feel a little safer looking at the tempting blue cocktail, but at the same time, this is still a stranger in a bar.

"Uh, *friends* might be a stretch. He hates me. He snaked my girl, yet I'm the one to blame." The blond man lets out a huff of frustration before he extends his hand. When I offer him mine, he shakes it delicately. "I'm Morgan."

"Avery." I can't help my curiosity. "What do you mean Finn snaked your girl?"

Morgan shrugs. "A few years ago, I fucked up. Bad. I got piss drunk with some buddies and woke up in some other girl's bed. I know how that makes me sound." He buries his head in his hands. "But I don't even remember it. I just partied too hard that night."

"Yikes."

"Yeah, I came clean to my girlfriend right away, and she said she forgave me, but"—he throws his thumb down and vibrates his tongue off his bottom lip—"it was all downhill from there. We were never the same."

"What does that have to do with Finn?"

"She started needing space. She stopped returning my calls right away. The text messages were few and far between. I'd only see her every other weekend. As far as I knew, we were a couple going through a tough time, and I accepted the fact I'd be in the doghouse for a while, but then it came out that she was living with Finn. She was dating both of us for a while, and neither of us knew."

Oh my God. And this story suddenly makes sense. "*Nora* was your girlfriend?"

He nods. "*Is* my girlfriend."

"Oh... So you guys eventually got back together and worked it out?"

Morgan laughs sarcastically. "Depends on what you consider working it out." He points to the drink. "I promise you that's not poisoned."

I take a small sip as a friendly gesture. It's delicious, so I take a bigger sip. "Thank you. I'm a sucker for anything with blue curacao in it."

"I have *never* known how to pronounce that. *Thank you.* Mystery solved."

I laugh. "Who knows if I'm pronouncing it correctly? I could be leading you astray."

"It sounds good your way. I'll roll with it." There's a lull as the song changes again.

"Are you and Nora going to be okay?" I balance the martini glass in my hand and swivel the blue liquid, trying not to spill it. There's a sinking feeling in my stomach.

Morgan beats the top of his fist against his forehead. "I don't think so."

"What were you fighting about?"

He exhales. "What we always fight about. Your date." He turns to face me head-on. "Can I give you some advice?"

Uh-oh.

"From one person caught up in their messy love life to another?"

"Okay."

"They are never going to be over. They are still in love with each other—"

"Finn's not—"

"Av-er-y," Morgan says, emphasizing every syllable of my name. "Trust me. This has been going on for years. And it's my fault. If I hadn't cheated, maybe they would've never met. Maybe they would've. I don't know. I'm just saying, do what you want for now. Just have your expectations in line. At the end of this story, those two will end up together. I think I'm finally starting to realize that."

"I don't think that—"

I don't get to finish my thought because suddenly Morgan's yanked backward from the bar. He looks as shocked as I am. The next thing I see is fire in Finn's eyes as he steps between us.

I'll admit, this doesn't look good. I must've been gone for too long, and I'm willing to bet if there was one man in this entire club he wouldn't want me talking to, it's Morgan. I have no idea how much of our conversation he heard, but I can literally feel his anger.

"Leave, Morgan," Finn says. I can barely hear him over the banging music. But there's a malice in his eyes that gives me chills. "Grab your girl, and get the fuck out of my family's club."

Morgan ignores him and turns his attention to me. "See?" His smile grows cool and cocky, and for the first time, I notice his eyes are bloodshot.

Is he drunk or high? Goddamn, he has a good poker face. I didn't even notice he was inebriated. Our conversation was perfectly normal.

"No man gets that angry about a woman he doesn't love. My mere presence pisses him off because they are still fucking. I *promise* you that."

"I'm not going to warn you again. You're drunk, and you're trying to stir up shit." Finn glances at me, and he half smiles before turning a glare back to Morgan. "Leave her out of it. Leave *me* out of it. If Nora's here, take her home. *Now.*"

"Fuck you, man. I'm a guest. And why are you so angry?" Morgan asks, his voice taunting.

I can't figure out why he's poking the bear. Even I can tell Finn's one short step away from exploding. But now I'm wondering if he's agitated at the idea of Morgan with me...or Morgan with Nora.

Morgan foolishly continues, "Whether I'm with Nora or not, it's not going to stop you from fucking her behind my back like you've been doing for years."

Thud.

It happens so quickly that I can hardly make sense of it. Finn's fist meets Morgan's face with such force that I can almost feel the impact standing two feet away. I let out an involuntary gasp before I cover my mouth. Morgan is on the ground, holding his cheekbone where Finn struck it. I fight the urge to squat down and help him up. It's clear who my loyalty is to, but right now I'm staring at a Finn I don't recognize. He looks like he's standing over a man's grave, getting ready to spit on it.

Within a moment, Morgan sits up.

"I dare you to get up," Finn says with the most disdain I've ever heard from a human being before. Finn turns to me and cocks his head to the side. "Whatever story he's spinning—"

I hold up my hands. "You don't owe me explanations."

"Let me," Finn pleads. "Please."

I shrug. "He didn't say anything. Just that he accidentally cheated and then Nora drifted and fell in love with you."

"Accidentally?" Finn lets out a cruel laugh. "Avery, this man cheated on Nora more times than he can count. He verbally abused her for years. He's the reason she's so fucking insecure and miserable that she's going to sabotage every relationship she's in for the rest of her life. He treated her like—"

"What?" Morgan croaks. "A stripper? It's what she is."

There's a chill. Finn's obviously triggered, and I know the world has fallen away for him. All he sees is red hot rage. I take a small step backward, nervous about what I'm about to see. "You know what? I changed my mind. Get the fuck up." Finn cracks his knuckles. "I've been waiting years for this."

"Finn, please walk away," I say, but he doesn't hear me. Instead, I feel a small, soft hand on my elbow, pulling me away from the crowd that's forming around Finn and Morgan.

Cass's bouncy brunette curls are dancing behind her as she quickly leads me away from the bar. She's dressed tonight as what I can only assume is a Victoria's Secret model, because all she's wearing is lingerie and a see-through robe. I keep my eyes focused on the hem of her long robe, fighting the urge to just find the exit sign and flee.

This is not my arena.

I am not the girlfriend of a guy who gets into bar fights after being offered lap dances all night. The wildest thing Mason and I used to do was catch a Thursday night football game at a sports bar when they had two-for-one wings. I am not lingerie, strippers, and this much alcohol...

I'm not Vegas.

We bank left, and Cass leads me into a room with a neon champagne flute sign hanging over it. *Champagne room. Of course. How cliché.*

"Take a seat, hon. You look like you're about to be sick." She shuts the door behind us, and once the glaring music and shouts are muted, I feel so much more relaxed. "You didn't want to see all that," she says with a pitiful smile.

Cass grabs a seat in a bean bag chair in the corner of the room. She pulls a packet of candy from the cup of her bra. She opens it and offers me what looks like a gummy worm. "Something to take the edge off?"

I shake my head. "No, thank you."

I have no clue if Legacy Resorts has a drug-testing policy for their employees and contractors. It's probably a nonissue, but a quick buzz just isn't worth the stress and worry of the aftermath.

"That fight was a long time coming. I told Nora not to bring Morgan tonight. But he can't bear the idea of Nora being within a ten-mile radius of Finn without him present." She rolls her eyes dramatically as she pops the tip of the gummy worm into her mouth. "He's such a little weasel. I don't know what he said to you, but I guarantee you he saw you come in with Finn and was just trying to provoke you."

"It's fine."

"What'd he say?" she asks, tilting her head to the side. She finishes off the candy and rubs her hands together. "Nora and I are close, so I can tell you the truth. It's all bullshit, if that puts your mind at ease. Finn and Nora are not sleeping together. He's been singing your praises all night. He's so into you. I love seeing Finn like this."

"Like what?"

She puckers her bottom lip. "In love. You guys look so good together." She taps her temples with her fingertips and extends her arms. "I'm already visualizing your wedding here."

"I'm not getting married in a strip club," I deadpan.

She snorts. "Oh, stop. This place is nice. It's the most expensive gentleman's club in Las Vegas. We could turn it into a celebrity bride's dream wedding."

"Happy birthday, Cass," I say as a diversion. "I'm sorry if I've caused any unnecessary drama tonight."

She scoffs as she hoists herself from the beanbag chair and sits right next to me on the love seat. I squirm in place, wondering how many men have gotten erections in this very seat as a dancer worked them over. I'm not sure exactly what happens in a champagne room, but I'm going to pretend a hard-on is as far as it goes.

"*You*, hon, are the *solution,* not the problem." She leans in a little closer and tucks my hair behind my ear...kind of similar to the way Finn does. I don't want to be rude, so I don't allow myself to flinch. She must take this as an invitation, so she scoots in a little closer, our knees bumping together. The smell of cherry and cotton candy kicks up between us, the mixture of her perfume and mine. *Hm...not a terrible smell.*

Cass has been nothing but nice to me all night, and despite the fact that she's beautiful and has slept with Finn, there's nothing threatening about this girl at all, so I let my guard down.

"Morgan said Finn and Nora aren't done. He told me to watch my back."

Cass's chest rises dramatically, and then she exhales. "That's what narcissists do. They blame the world for their shortcomings. Look, I've been watching the Morgan, Nora, Finn love triangle unfold for a while now, and here's the vicious cycle—Morgan treats Nora like shit, she runs to hero Finn, who makes her feel safe. But she's not dealing with her hurt and trauma, so she takes out all her anger and wrath on the person who treats her best. Finn eventually gets fed up and leaves her. She runs back to Morgan. Morgan treats her like shit, and then the cycle continues."

"So Finn is really the good guy?"

Cass's smile is warm and tender. She pats my knee. "Finn's the best guy. But love will blind you. He couldn't save Nora from Morgan, and I think that bothers him. But this is the longest they've ever been broken up. And I know it's for good because as soon as he really let her go, he was able to fall in love again." She points to my forehead. "Lennox already told me you're a good one."

"Ah, yeah. She *vetted* me under the guise of free cinnamon rolls."

Cass snorts in laughter. "Oh, I love Lenny. We both tried so hard to get Finn to see the light for so long with Nora. We were both relieved when he was finally done. Hey—I love this, by the way." Cass cups her hand near my breasts, about an inch away, and makes a squeezing motion. She doesn't actually touch me, but her message is clear.

Okay, I'm not imagining it. She's absolutely hitting on me.

Wait...is she? Maybe I'm just being dramatic because I know she's been with Nora and Finn at the same time.

"Your outfit, I mean. This clamshell bra is so cute. Can I borrow it?"

Cass is pretty well-endowed up top. Her waist is far slimmer and her hips are much narrower than mine, but I bet we could share a bra. "Sure. This is definitely a one-time outfit for me anyway."

"So cute. I have one in blue, but this pink one is so much better. I can tell the sequins are hand-sewn too. Such a good find."

"Lennox," I clarify. "All the credit goes to Lennox."

"I'm not surprised." Cass smiles. "Lennox is a genius for all things fashion and design. She helped decorate my entire home."

Okay, see? This is just girl talk, totally normal. You're freaking out for nothing—

I freeze.

The sweet smell of cotton candy is overwhelming when Cass presses her lips against mine.

I'm immobilized, and it takes her a millisecond to notice. She clasps her hand over her mouth.

"Oh my God. Are you not into me?"

"Uh..."

"I thought you were flirting back." Her eyes grow wide. "I'm a little high right now. I'm sorry, I should've asked. I didn't mean to freak you out."

"No, no, um, you were sending clear signals. I could've spoken up."

She presses her hands against her cheeks. "No, it's my fault. I just assumed we were connecting—"

"Oh, I'm not—" *A lesbian?* "You're pretty. I just—" *Have never dreamed of being with a woman.* "I'm here with Finn. I don't know what he'd think." I settle for a half-truth so I don't seem too rude.

"Oh," Cass replies, seemingly relieved by my explanation. She places her hand on my knee. "Don't worry. Believe me, he prefers if we start without him."

My heart sinks to my toes. *He's done this so much that he has a preference?*

Cass tries to kiss me again, and this time I lean back. "Cass, I'm sorry. I've never done this before. I'm...I don't..."

"Wait." Her jaw drops. "You and Finn don't share? I thought you guys were..."

"We're dating, sort of. I'm not...we don't do that..."

"*Oh fuck.* Avery, I thought that's why he brought you to my birthday party. We do this every year."

If my eyes get any wider, they are going to pop out of the sockets. She covers her mouth when she sees my expression.

"Shit. You didn't know?"

There's a lot I didn't know until tonight. "So let me get this straight. Every year at your birthday party, you, Finn, and another woman have sex in the champagne room?"

She chuckles nervously as she shrugs her shoulders and cringes. "It's a tradition?" Now she outright laughs. "Oh, I misjudged this so hard. Finn usually has a type, so I just assumed—"

"*A type?*"

"*Oh*, not looks-wise or anything like that. It's just the girls he's with are usually adventurous. But look, it makes total sense. Of course, after Nora, he'd want a simple, nice girl. I'm sure he's more than content with the two of you. I did not mean to offend you."

Content. *There's that fucking word again.*

I'm on information overload, and it's not a good time for me to be making decisions. But I've already had one man leave me because I'm boring in the sack...

I grab Cass by her shoulders and pull her back to my lips a little too aggressively so our mouths collide, but so do our noses. It's a clumsy mess, and I pull away before I hang my head in shame.

"Sorry, I don't know what I'm doing."

"Hey," she says softly. "You shouldn't feel pressured. You don't have to do anything. Do you actually want to try this?"

I nod sheepishly, feeling out of my body. *What the fuck are you doing, Avery?*

Shut up, brain. I'm trying. I said this summer was about taking risks and exploring myself and my body. So that's what I'm doing.

Cass rubs my back sweetly. "Well, first thing to remember is that the way you and Finn have sex is *very* different from this, okay? You save all the emotional connection for just you guys. This is just physical. So just do what feels good, okay? Safe space."

She tucks my hair behind my ear again. "In my experience, this is a little easier the first time if you close your eyes."

My heart is knocking hard, and I know it's from excitement, but it's not the right kind of excitement. The first time Finn stripped me down in front of the mirror, I was terrified, nervous, but so excited because what was on the other side was something

I desperately wanted. I wanted to rip the Band-Aid off. I wanted to know what it'd be like for him to see me. I wanted to see me too and like what I saw in the mirror.

But this? This feels like getting a tattoo of something I'm not sure of. I'm going to endure the pain of the needle, and then the end result will mark me forever. What's my motivation? I can't give Finn what he wants. I can't move here right now. Maybe in a year or so, when Palmer's on her feet? But maybe *this*...

Maybe if I do *this*, it can hold him over.

To want to keep me.

I clamp my eyes shut and take a deep breath. "Go ahead, I'm ready."

Her lips interweave with mine. *Okay, it's not terrible.* Actually, it's nice. Her lips are soft. Her hand on my back is small and smooth. It's exhilarating, at least, because the sensation is different. I kiss back and am alarmed at how natural this feels. I've never kissed another woman, but Cass seems to know what she's doing. She waits until she feels me relax then slides her tongue into my mouth.

Again, soft...smooth...smaller than Finn's. The kissing is okay, but I clam up when I think about where else she's going to want to put her tongue.

Oh, shit. I don't know if I can do this.

"Avery," Cass says lowly but firmly as she grabs my left breast and gently squeezes. "No offense to Nora, but you are honestly the most delicious woman Finn has ever been with."

Uh-oh. This woman is smart. She's playing right into my praise kink. The flutter in my chest begins to change. Apprehension dips slightly toward excitement.

"You are *such* a fucking woman. I'm obsessed. And I'm really excited to be your first." Cass switches to my right breast and slips her hand under the cup, finding my hard nipple. "Lie back, hon."

It's right as my head hits the sofa cushion that I hear the door creak open.

"What the *fuck* is going on?"

Oh no.

Finn's tone can only be described as shock and anger.

Chapter 35

Finn

I should've broken that fucker's jaw. I wanted to so bad. But what stopped me was the look on Avery's face as Cass pulled her away. She wasn't squeamish or scared. Instead, she was inquisitive. She was studying me, waiting to see what kind of man I was.

Even when she was out of sight and Morgan was on his feet again, trying to provoke me, all I could think about was Avery watching me succumb to past hurts. Hurts I'm healing from because of her. I'm tired of fighting the past. I just want to focus on the future.

So I walked away.

I searched for her everywhere. I even had someone go into the women's restroom and call out Avery's name, but nothing. It finally dawned on me where Cass might take her—she's high and horny and has a one-track mind. I thought I made it clear that Avery and I weren't into that.

Or are we?

When I opened the door to the champagne room, all I saw was Cass, on top of my girl, her tongue down her throat and her hand on Avery's tit. Maybe I should be aroused, but at the moment, I'm just kind of pissed.

"What the *fuck* is going on?" I ask.

"What the fuck do you think is going on?" Cass snarks back at me. "Watch your tone, Finn, or you won't be invited," she says as she climbs off Avery and proceeds to tinker with the fog machine in the corner of the room. This is how Cass likes to fuck. In a hallucinogenic hippie's dream. I hate that damn machine. It makes it impossible to see anything.

"Are you okay?" I ask Avery, and she nods. Outside of looking startled by my entrance, she seems fine. *I think.*

"Is Morgan on a stretcher in the back of an ambulance?" Cass asks over her shoulder. I notice Avery's eyes dart to my knuckles. They're still red from one good lick on that piece of shit.

"Security showed him out. I didn't hit him again."

"That's a shame," Cass mutters.

I take a seat next to Avery, and she scooches to her right to make room for me. I yank her right back into my chest territorially. Kissing the side of her head, I ask her, "What're you doing in here? Are you seriously trying to hook up with Cass?"

Avery chuckles nervously. "She said it's her birthday tradition, so I figured...why not?"

I grunt in irritation. "It's not a tradition. Her libido just goes into hyperdrive on her birthday."

"Are you mad at me?" Avery asks.

Immediately, I cradle her cheek, pulling her soft green eyes to mine. "Baby, no. Not at all. I just figured we'd talk about something like this first."

"It was a spur-of-the-moment thing," she mumbles. "You like this, though, right? Or do you not like this with me?"

I'm at a loss for words because this feels like a trap.

No, I don't like this with you because you're mine. And I don't want to share you. I don't want anyone else, man or woman, touching you, kissing you, looking at you. I want your pleasure to come from me and me alone.

I want that part of Avery all to myself, but I promised her I wouldn't keep her in the box. Not like Mason did. I'm supposed to be helping her learn to be brave and confident and ask for what she wants.

"I only like it if you do. So do *you* want to do this?"

Our stares are locked as I tighten my arm around her, and it seems like we're both hoping the other will call uncle. But for some reason, we don't, so I don't fight it when Avery says, "No harm in trying, right?"

"Okay."

She rubs my cock through my jeans, and I put my lips on hers and kiss her sweetly.

"Mmm," she says. "Much better."

"What?" I ask against her lips.

"Nothing." She pulls away to give me a small smile. "Your lips are starting to feel like home."

"Mm," I moan. I couldn't have said it better myself. "Well, come home, then, Queen."

I hook my hand under her thigh and pull her astride my lap. Our hips lock together as she rests her weight on me. I love when she does that. It's the ultimate trust. She used to awkwardly hover over me, embarrassed of her weight. It took almost a whole damn summer, but it seems like she's finally trusting me when I tell her I love every smooth curve and bump on her body. She can get bigger, smaller, or stay exactly the same, and I will be obsessed with every single version of this woman I've fallen for.

"Oh gag. You guys are so sweet. Stop it with the sugary talk before you accidentally make me catch feelings," Cass says as she joins us on the couch.

"It's just sex, Cass. I'm not—"

"Calm down, lover boy," she teases. "I didn't mean I'd catch feelings *for you*." She winks at me. This is Cass's default. She knows how important it is in these situations for my girlfriend not to feel jealous or competitive, so we have an unspoken agreement about keeping most of our attention on our guest. It works better that way. "Avery, may I take this off?" Cass taps the tie behind Avery's back holding her bra in place.

"Um..."

And *there*. I see it. I wasn't imagining it. She's hesitating. There's a flicker of panic in her eyes. "Baby, you don't have to—"

"Yes," Avery says, looking over her shoulder at Cass. "Go ahead."

Without another word, Cass pulls the tie free, and Avery's heavy breasts drop right into my face. *Good God.* As it always goes when I'm anywhere near these flawless tits, I get instantly hard. *Fine, if we're doing this...*let's go. I engulf one nipple and pinch the other between my fingers. She squirms under the pressure but doesn't recoil, so I pinch harder. She groans but leans into my grip.

"Such a good girl," I coo. "I love how you can take that."

She grinds against me eagerly, like it's just us two and we're up to our usual antics, but the moment Cass's hand is on her back, she's a statue. *Goddammit.* If Avery doesn't want to do this, *why are we doing this?*

"Finn, it's not going to work like this. Can you pull the couch out?" Cass asks.

Yeah, good idea. Maybe Avery just needs to lie down. She'll be more comfortable. "Hop up, baby. This couch can go completely flat." She does as I ask, and I pull the sofa from the wall and flatten the cushions so we have a bed to lie on. At this point, my cock is angry and hard, and as much as I want to pull it out, I need Avery to set the pace here.

"Where do you want to start, hon?" Cass asks patiently.

Avery covers her tits with her forearm and manages to shrug. "I don't know. What do you guys usually do first?"

Cass winks at me, and I roll my eyes. She's being too playful. It's not her relationship that's on the line right now. It's mine.

"Do you want Finn and me to take the lead? Will that be easier?" Cass asks.

Avery nods in relief. "Yes, good. I'll just ease in."

"Okay," Cass says. "You got it."

She flattens her hand against my chest and rises to her tippy toes to kiss me. Cass is even shorter than Avery, so I have to duck down far for her to reach my lips. Instead, I grab her by the waist and set her feet on top of the sofa so we're at eye level. *Much easier.* Eventually, she's tugging at my belt. She traces my length through my jeans with her hand before she unzips me and teases me through my briefs. She slips her tongue into my mouth, and I almost fall back into the familiar comfort of our old routine until I hear something like a wince from behind me.

"Shit. Oh no," Cass says, looking over my shoulder. I release Cass and spin around to see Avery in tears with her bra retied around her neck. She's hysterical, covering as much of her face as she can with both hands. She's been watching us, crying, putting herself through the torture of seeing me with another woman.

"Fuck," I mumble. "Avery—"

She holds up both her hands to stop me from advancing, and I see her wet cheeks and smeared makeup. "I am...so...sorry," she says, completely in disarray. She's gasping for air, trying to control her frenzy. She pats her chest. "My fault...it's my fault. I thought I could...I just can't do this...I'm sorry."

"Baby—" I reach for her, but she steps away. *Dammit.* She's going to run. I know it.

"I'm so embarrassed," she murmurs.

In tandem, I take a step closer and she takes one back, toward the door. She's looking at me like she's scared of me.

"Avery, please calm down. Come here. We can stop."

She glances down to make sure her breasts are fully covered and glances at the door.

I hold out my hand. "Just come here, please." I feel like I'm coaxing a stray dog out of the street. Like if I move too fast, it's going to go running straight into traffic.

She finally takes my hand, and I breathe out in relief.

"Finn, we're fine. I'm sorry. I'll be okay." Then she rips her hand away. "But I need some space. Don't follow me." She darts from the room, shutting the door behind her.

Falling backward, I slump onto the edge of the sofa. Cass sits down next to me but knows better than to touch me right now. First, I zip up my jeans and refasten my belt, and then I growl in frustration into my hands.

"Fuck this," I mumble. "I'm going after her."

"Finn, she asked you not to," Cass says. "Just give her the night, and then go talk to her tomorrow."

"How's she supposed to get home? She's running around half-naked, crying. Something could—"

"*Finn.* She's not drunk, and she's a smart girl. She knows how to call for a ride. If you treat her like an idiot right now, she's going to be even more embarrassed. There's a fine line between protective and patronizing, okay? Don't make this worse."

I nod. "Okay."

"I'm sorry. I have no idea what happened. I kissed her first but then backed off. She's the one who wanted to—"

"I know. It's not your fault. She's been trying to prove all summer that she can handle sex with me. She's trying to be more daring so she fits into this scene. This city. She thinks that's what I want from her."

"Do you?"

"Not at all," I reply. "Look, Cass, we're not doing this anymore. You and I are going to keep our clothes on from now on." I look around the room. "And I'm not coming here anymore. Gramps can donate Ruby's for all I care. I don't want anything in my life that comes between Avery and me."

Avery

I burst through the exit doors of Ruby's and scour the long row of vehicles parked in front of the club. There is a fleet of limos waiting to take drunk partygoers home, but I'm looking for a red Escalade—my ride share.

By now my breathing has calmed and my tears have mostly dried. I made a quick stop into the bathroom to somewhat compose myself.

What the fuck was I thinking? I pull my phone from my clutch again and check the rideshare app. I had to share the ride, and I'm the second passenger to be picked up. I am not in the mood to drive around Las Vegas with a stranger, but it's all that's available right now. I'm sure I'm lucky to even have booked a ride. From the looks of it, my driver is stuck at a red light and attempting to make a U-turn, so I make a call to kill the time.

She answers in a groggy slur.

"Aves?"

"Palmer," I say through a sniffle. She hears the strain in my voice and is immediately on high alert.

"What's wrong?" For a moment, I just breathe and cry into the phone, so she asks again. "Where are you? It's past midnight."

"Outside of the birthday party, waiting on a ride."

"Where's Finn?"

My heart drops. He's going to be upset that I ran out on him, but I'm so overwhelmed at the moment. I don't want him to make it okay. I know he will, and right now I need to feel the overwhelming magnitude of my decisions. I've been reckless this entire summer, and I need to recognize that.

"I watched him kiss another woman—"

Her voice drops. "I will seriously murder a motherfucker—"

"No, Palmer. Not like that. I tried to have a threesome, and I couldn't do it. We talked about it. It was just...sex. But watching him with someone else..." *It hurt.* I trail off and try to calm my rising hysteria. "I think I'm already in love with him."

This all happened way too fast. It didn't even hurt this bad when Mason dumped me, and that was after four years. Yes, I could've told Finn and Cass that I was uncomfortable and that we should stop. Finn would've gallantly walked me out of this club, taken me home, held me in bed, and everything would have been okay.

That's the problem.

Finn makes me feel so secure that I haven't seen the mess I've been creating all summer. I've been running from my home, my problems, and getting whisked up into a situation that I am not equipped to handle. This isn't the life I want, and now I'm wildly attached. I'm probably going to spend the next four years changing my identity and personality to accommodate yet another man... and lose myself all over again.

"You tried to have a threesome?" Palmer doesn't hide the shock in her voice. "And you're in love?"

"I miss you, Palmer. I miss home. I miss me." The real version of me who isn't exhausted from trying to be something she's not. I'm mundane. I'm vanilla... And I'm okay with that.

"Did you book your flight?"

I suck in a little breath again. "Not yet. I'm going to go home right now and pack a few things. I'll get on standby. It's easier to catch a redeye anyway. Send me your hotel details. I'll catch a ride from the airport."

"Don't be silly. Call me and wake me up. I'll pick you up whenever your flight lands... Aves, it's going to be okay. I'm here, babe. This summer has been a mess for both of us. We're going to go home and pick up the pieces. We'll get through this like we always do—together."

I nod into the phone. "Okay," I whisper.

"I love you, Aves."

"I know. Me too." Looking up, I see a large red SUV pulling up in front of Ruby's neon red sign. "My ride is here. I'll see you tomorrow."

I hang up, and as I approach the vehicle, the driver rolls down the window. He looks me up and down in my mermaid costume. "Ms. Avery?" he asks.

Wiping under my eyes and trying to mop up the fresh batch of tears, I nod. "Yes, that's me."

"Left side, ma'am," he responds before rolling the window back up.

I walk to the other side of the car and pull open the door to see my rideshare buddy already seated and buckled. *Holy shit.* She's startlingly gorgeous. Forget Maura, Palmer, all these mean girls at the restaurants, Lennox, Cass, and every woman in Las Vegas whose looks I've secretly envied. This woman puts them all to shame. Her petite frame is sheathed in a skin-tight leather minidress. She looks like she's dressed as a sexy character from the *Matrix*. And her stick-straight, long black hair is pulled to the side.

She looks up at me with her big, light-brown eyes as I settle into my seat and buckle in.

"I love your costume. Mermaids are *so* in." Even her voice is melodic. She must notice my red eyes because she suddenly cocks her head to the side. "You okay?"

"Long night."

"Same," she says with a small smile. She calls out to the driver, "You can take her first. I'm in no hurry to go home."

"Were you at the birthday party?" I have no idea why I'm trying to make conversation at the moment. Maybe as a distraction to avoid more crying.

"For about five minutes. My exes got into a fight," she grumbles. "I've been hiding out ever since."

Oh, fuck me. It dawns on me instantly. I'd hop right out of this vehicle, had it not already pulled into traffic. Maybe I can still open the door and just tuck and roll. Of course this is how my night would end. I know exactly who this is. The question is...

Does she know who I am?

I hold out my hand. "I'm Avery. I'm a friend of Finn's. It's nice to meet you."

Her ears perk up at his name, and it's clear she realizes what I'm saying. She takes my hand, somewhat reluctantly.

"Nice to meet you." Her pretty eyes narrow. "I'm Nora."

Chapter 36

Finn

The morning after Cass's party, I walk into my kitchen to see Lennox making coffee. She's in baggy sweatpants, with no makeup.

I yank on the shirt I'm holding and let my groggy eyes catch up with me. I had a hard time falling asleep. I called Avery about ten times before her phone either died or she shut it off. It took all my self-control not to go banging her door down. I'm still not sure if I made the right decision. Doesn't a woman want a man willing to move mountains for her? Or is that controlling? *Fuck.* My favorite thing about Avery is that we can talk, and now, after one stupid party, I'm second-guessing everything I say.

"Lennox, why are you here when you're sick? Oh, shit. Did I forget about an appointment?" It's Sunday... I never book clients on Sundays.

"No," she says, grabbing the cream from the fridge. "No clients today."

"Then why are you here spreading germs in my kitchen instead of resting in bed? I could've dropped off food today."

"I'm fever-free, Finny. I'm just still tired. But I needed to get out of the house today. How was the party? Is Avery still sleeping?" She nods down the hall toward the bedroom.

"She's not here," I mutter. I stare at the coffee pot dripping, letting the look of pain on Avery's face last night flash through my mind.

"Did something happen?" Lennox asks, leaning back against the counter and studying my face.

"Last night was a dumpster fire floating down shit's creek. That's the only way I can describe it."

"You and Avery fought?" she asks, raising her eyebrows, clearly accusing me.

I shake my head. "Not really."

"Jesus, Finn. Save the dramatic build-up, please. What happened?"

I breathe out and shrug. "Let's see... I went down on Avery in the limo, then Morgan bought her a drink and tried to tell her I'm cheating on her with Nora, so I clocked him, and I would've done much worse, but Avery ran off scared right into the champagne room with Cass. I caught them making out, and everything was fine until I joined in, but the minute I touched Cass, Avery must've come to her senses and ran out of the room crying, ditched me at the club, and now she won't take my calls. So...yeah. Dumpster fire."

Lennox is gawking at me.

Yup. Just let all that soak in.

"I miss *one* party," she mumbles. "And I really didn't need to know about the limo part."

"I realize. I just wanted to mention it because it was the only enjoyable part of the evening," I snark.

The coffeemaker beeps, and I proceed to fill a cup. I don't bother with cream and sugar. I let the hot brew burn my tongue.

"So Avery is sexually curious—"

"No, I think Avery is confused because of her ex. And it's my fault."

"I'm going to get some coffee, and then I need you to be a little less cryptic." Lennox silently fills a cup, douses it with my oat milk creamer, and takes an exaggerated sip. *"Ah, much better.* Now, explain."

"Remember the thing you used to tell me about Nora? The tire patch thing?"

Lennox tolerated Nora for years, for me. But she always warned me that we wouldn't work out because I was patching a tire instead of replacing it.

Nora had so much damage from her prior relationship that she probably needed therapy. She needed to move to a new city and get away from Morgan entirely. A real fresh start. Instead, for a long time, I just did my best to patch all the tiny holes in her heart, thinking if I worked hard enough, I could save her. But at the end of the day, I was patching the tire Morgan punctured over and over again. We should've started fresh, but she just couldn't do that with me. It was too messy. Too many lines were blurred. We never stood a chance.

"What if I'm doing the same thing with Avery?" I ask.

She cocks her head to the side. "I didn't get the impression that Avery's in love with her ex."

I shake my head. "Me neither, but she's loyal to him. She's not willing to walk away from the business. Maybe I shouldn't push her to pick me. That's exactly what I did with Nora."

"How can you compare them? Avery's nothing like Nora."

I shrug. "She's just as insecure, but unlike Nora, she doesn't punish other people for it. Avery's graceful, sweet, strong, and considerate. And don't get me wrong, I think being vulnerable is a good thing, but I think she needs time to work on herself. Whether or not she admits it, she's still hurting over her jackass ex. Neglect is just another form of abuse, and he strung her along for years. That would fuck with any woman's head."

Lennox takes another sip of her coffee, carefully considering her words. "I don't understand, Finn. Everybody has a past. Why are you blaming yourself for this?"

I set down my cup and rub my hands over my face. "Because I've spent all summer trying to show her how to have a hot sex life like it's the only answer to a happy relationship." I tap my temple. "I planted that right here in her head. It wasn't what I meant to do, but I didn't know I was going to have such strong feelings for her."

She turns down her lips and nods slowly. "You're right. You're a pig." She shrugs. "Summer's almost over. She'll move back home. Let her go. You can go back to fucking like a man whore."

"Excuse me?"

"I mean, it was pretty inconsiderate of you to just give her exactly what she asked for. You should be ashamed of yourself."

I purse my lips at her. "Really? You're going to try to reverse psychology me?"

She pokes out her tongue. "Not at all. I'm just saying Avery deserves a guy who is willing to fight for her and make it work no matter what. Ups and downs. Grow together. Change together. Communicate. If you were the real deal, you wouldn't be here moping and giving her space. You'd be on both of your knees at her doorstep, begging her to be with you. Obviously, that's not you."

I deadpan, "You're annoying in the mornings."

Lennox flashes me a toothy grin.

"And I told you, Avery doesn't want to move here. How can we be together? I can't just pick up the studio and move it. I have more ties to Vegas than she has to L.A."

"So what, Finn? She's not ready to move her entire life after knowing you for what? Nine weeks? *Deal with it.* If you think she's something special, make it work. Do long distance and take the time to prove yourself. You're not your dad. She's not your mom. Stop boxing everybody into good guys and bad guys. That's not how life works. People are messy. People make mistakes. Some people are worth just going through shitty dumpster fires with because there's something great on the other side."

Lennox disappears down the hallway into my bedroom and returns with my phone in her hand. She hands it to me. "Look, you have a missed call from Avery."

I look at my phone and see she called ten minutes ago. Long after I gave up on trying to contact her last night. Maybe Cass was right. She just needed some time to think. I suck in a deep breath. "What do I say?" I ask Lennox. As much as I think I understand women, it's hard to think straight when I feel like this. Caught up, nervous, scared to lose her, but scared to let her get too close and repeat history.

"Just tell her you guys can start fresh. No sex deals. No conditions. No ultimatums. Ask her what she needs from a relationship. And tell her what you need too. Then find a compromise."

"Were you always this wise?"

She clicks her jaw and winks. "Yes. Just thank God you're finally listening."

"All right," I say. "Carry on." I shoo her away with both hands. "I'll call her right now."

"Uh, no, my friend." Lennox makes a face like I'm ridiculous. "I'm staying right here so you don't fuck this up. I'm invested now. Put it on speaker."

I place my phone on speaker and call Avery back. It barely rings once.

"Hey, Finn? Is that you?"

Lennox's mouth gapes open and my heart sinks ten floors. I know that voice so well, but it's not Avery's.

"Nora?"

"Yeah. Hey."

"Why are you answering Avery's phone?"

"She forgot it in the car last night when we left the club."

"She left with you?"

"Yeah. I just got it charged. Can you believe her passcode is one-one-one-one?"

"Nora, don't go through her phone—"

"Calm down, Finn. I'm just trying to return it. Yours was the only number I knew. Do you want to meet me and come pick it up for her?"

Lennox scoffs. "Uh, no. *I'll* come get it," she interrupts.

"I'll stop by Avery's to let her know," I mutter.

"She's not home," Nora responds. My jaw twitches in agitation. I'm trying not to jump to conclusions, but all of this seems very calculated at the moment. "We stopped at Dex's and then took her to the airport. She caught a flight last night."

"A flight where?" I ask. "What did she say to you?"

"Finn, I'll come by with the phone in just a bit. Okay? I'm on my way. We can talk...about everything."

Nora ends the call, and I look at Lennox in disbelief.

Lennox waits for me to say something, but I don't. Mostly because I'm having a mild panic attack. What the hell could Nora have told Avery that made her book a last-minute flight?

I thought we were okay...

Fuck.

* * *

Lennox wanted to stay, but I told her it wasn't necessary. I'm not sure what Nora thinks is going to transpire, but I can almost guarantee it's incorrect. She's sitting at my kitchen island with a hopeful smile on her face.

"Nothing happened, Finn. And I didn't throw you under the bus."

I give Nora a once-over. She looks a little thinner. She always loses weight when she's around Morgan. *It's stress.*

"Do you want water?" I ask, pulling two bottles from the fridge. I slide one her way. "Out of curiosity, what the hell would you have to throw me under the bus for?"

She drops her eyes to the counter. "That's not what I meant. I just told her that Morgan has a long history of poking your buttons. And you're not the violent type. Thank you, by the way."

"For what?"

"Not putting him in the hospital," she replies. "I know you wanted to. I like to think you refrained for me."

"No, I refrained for *me*." I have two choices right now. I can blow up at her and be an asshole for manipulating me and the circumstances like this, but all that would do is prove I'm not over us. And believe me, *I'm over it.*

"May I have Avery's phone?" I ask.

"Oh, yeah," she says, reaching into her purse and sliding it over. "It's fully charged. Someone named Mason keeps blowing her up about some big meeting that got bumped up."

I quirk one brow. "You went through her messages?" I feel a twang of guilt, wondering if Nora saw all the flirtatious, dirty messages Avery and I have been sending each other for months, but why do I need to hide it? Avery is my good thing. She's not a secret. I'm not a two-timer. Despite how determined Nora was to make me one.

"No, I didn't. Just the notifications have been popping up like crazy. I thought someone died."

I flip the phone over, facedown, so it's not a distraction, because I'm tempted myself. I want to know that Mason is only texting Avery about business, but I can't violate her privacy like that. That's the worst way to start a relationship; I know firsthand. And now that I have what she came for, I want her to leave.

"I know you've wanted to meet up and talk for a while. But I don't have anything new to say, Nora."

"Finn, look, I know it'll take a long time to build up trust again. I get that. But I really am sorry about everything. I'm here—whenever you're ready. I can be patient. Morgan and I are done for good this time. That's why we fought at Cass's birthday. I saw you, and I just knew...I'm never going to stop loving you."

"I'm glad—"

"Me too—"

"No, I'm glad you're done with Morgan, and I hope you mean it this time because he doesn't deserve you. But neither do I—"

"Yes, you do, Finn. You've always been good to me, and I know I didn't appreciate it at the time." She reaches over the kitchen island separating us. The gold bangles on her hand jingle as she holds out her hand. But I don't take it.

"What I mean is I deserve *better*."

Her eyes instantly fill with tears, and I'll admit that it hurts to see her cry. I'm not a dick. I loved this woman for a long time, and I don't like seeing her pain. I hate that I'm causing it. But for once I have to put myself first.

"Things with you and Avery are going to fizzle out, Finn,"

Nora says with a new tone. "You freaked her out."

She's baiting me. "What did she say to you? Where is she?"

I went over to Dex's house to make sure Nora wasn't lying to me. Avery is indeed gone. Even the back door is locked, which is the smart move if she's leaving Dex's house unattended. But I also know Avery would never let a job go unfinished. Dex won't be home for a few more weeks. I know she's coming back.

"She said Las Vegas is overwhelming and she doesn't like it here. She went to go get her best friend who just lost her job...Polly something—"

"Palmer," I correct.

"Yeah, she's just flying out to Albuquerque to meet her, and then they are driving back to Vegas together. They'll stay here for a few weeks, and then she's going home, Finn. She wants to go home. She didn't tell you any of this?"

I'm not sure what hurts more. To officially hear this news from Nora, or the fact that Avery told Nora all this in the first place.

"No, she didn't."

"I can wait until things settle down, after summer so you and Avery can have a clean break, and then we can pick up where we left off." She looks around and chuckles. "I can fix this place back up because you've turned it into a man cave. Where are the curtains I picked out?"

"Nora, whether or not Avery and I work things out—which, let me be clear, I really want to work it out with her—you and I are done. It's not that we can't fix what we broke. It's that I don't want to. I know what it feels like to connect with someone in a new way now, and I can't go back."

"No." She sniffs as she wipes her nose with the back of her hand. "I'm not giving up on us."

I tap the counter with my fingers as I watch her tears drip from her face to her lap. Tears that have controlled me for too long. "I'm about to go on a run, so I think we need to wrap this up."

It's a lame excuse, but it's better than get the *fuck out of my house.*

I grab Avery's phone from the kitchen counter and slide it into my pocket just as a safety precaution. I know I just hurt Nora's feelings. Who knows what she's capable of? It'd take one picture of her in my home while Avery is away to give the very wrong impression of what this is.

I don't even bother grabbing my headphones. I don't need them. I just need a brutal run in this heatstroke weather to melt away my frustration at the moment. I pause at the entry closet after retrieving my running shoes.

"Nora," I say as she passes me while I'm lacing up my shoes, "I promise you, the minute you let the idea of us go, I mean *really let it go*, someone so much better for you is going to come your way. You're going to be happy again. I know it. Take care, okay?"

She walks out the door without a response, likely shocked that she didn't get her way.

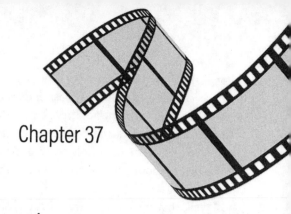

Chapter 37

Avery

"We have to make a pit stop," I say to Palmer as I scour my email. We're making the most out of the continental breakfast at her extended-stay hotel. There's nothing like mass-produced hotel biscuits and gravy. This I can actually make. Gravy isn't *that* far off from dip.

"Pit stop where?"

"Cancun," I mumble as I read Mason's panic-ridden email about how the presentation got bumped up and why the hell I haven't been answering my phone. I quickly email him back, letting him know I lost it and that I will meet him at Legacy Resorts by tomorrow. I don't bother telling him Palmer will be with me. There's no need for him to freak out even more.

"How the hell is that going to work?"

I force out a breath in frustration. I am so exhausted. It's been the longest twenty-four hours of my life, not to mention not having my phone threw a real monkey wrench into things. I must've left it in the rideshare or dropped it at the Las Vegas airport. I'm not sure. All I know is when I got through airport security, I couldn't find it anywhere. Luckily, I had my laptop with me, meaning I was able to effectively message Palmer with the airport's Wi-Fi to tell her when and where to pick me up.

To my great shock and surprise, my Jeep is still perfectly intact. I was expecting at least a broken taillight, judging by Palmer's reckless driving.

"I'm going to have to call in a favor with Royalty Airlines, yet again." It's a perk from Dr. Ruth, my mentor, that I try not to abuse, but desperate times, desperate measures. She's still able to fly anywhere, anytime for free, courtesy of her prior position with the company, and she extends this privilege to me whenever I want. "We park the Jeep in long-term parking at the airport, fly five hours to Cancun, do the presentation, fly back to Albuquerque, and drive back to Las Vegas."

"Well, that sounds fucking miserable."

"Yeah, it will be. Ready? Go check out at the front desk. We have to go."

Palmer's phone chirps in her annoying ringtone, and she screws up her face when she snatches it off the table and checks the caller ID. "Hey, you're calling me."

She holds up her phone, and clear as day, Aves with a heart is displayed on the screen.

"Finally!" I've tried calling my phone a few times, but it went straight to voicemail. Luckily, someone found it. I take the phone from Palmer's hand and shoo her to the front desk. "Hurry," I say before I answer the phone.

"Hello, this is Avery Scott. You have my phone."

"Well, hello, Avery Scott. I do have your phone."

I smile at the sound of his voice. "Finn. Where'd you find it?"

"Nora," he replies. "I heard you're in New Mexico."

My heart knocks like I'm in trouble. It doesn't look great. I ran out on Finn, then spilled my guts to his ex in a ride-share. But it was bizarre. She was so nice to me. Based on Palmer's reaction to the whole situation, Nora was being a cunning bitch, but I was just pleasantly surprised she wasn't openly cruel or snarky just because I was with Finn. I've had enough mean girls this summer tell me I'm not good enough for him. I was expecting the same from Nora, but it seemed like she understood the insecurity of being on Finn's arm. The constant worry that someone was going to try to take what's yours right from under you. I know she still loves him, but I'm glad she could be civil to me despite that.

"I have a lot of explaining to do," I say simply.

"That you do, Queen." But he chuckles, letting me know we're okay. "Can we start with whether or not you're upset with me?"

"*With you?* Finn, I screwed up. I should apologize. I, um...I think I found my limit." I lower my voice. I know I didn't say the word threesome out loud, but I'm still in a small breakfast crowd in a hotel dining room. And I don't have time to explain my sexual exploration summer to this crowd of senior citizens.

"I'd say. We can talk about everything when you get back. But I wanted you to know that Nora told me you don't want to move to Las Vegas after last night."

"It's not what you're thinking—"

"Ah, ah. Let me finish before you say anything else."

My heart thumps with nerves as I lean into the phone. Can Finn technically dump me if we aren't officially together?

"Lennox gave me some advice. She told me to sit down and make a list of all of my deal breakers for a relationship with you. So I tried, and I couldn't come up with any."

"What do you mean?"

"There's nothing I wouldn't endure to be with you. Because"— he clears his throat—"you told me in the champagne room that my lips feel like home."

I blush a little at my heat-of-the-moment declaration of affection. I meant it, though.

"Well, your heart feels like home to me. What I wanted you to understand is that the reason our sex is so good, Avery, isn't because of what we're doing; it's because of *us*. And it's going to change. We won't always be going at it daily, but that doesn't mean I'm not going to be head-over-heels crazy about you. Whether you're in sweatpants or a mermaid costume, you're still a queen to me. The hot moments are great, but so are the quiet ones. I don't need dirty talk, threesomes, or any other kink you think you need to fulfill for me. I just want you to be exactly who you are."

I suck in a breath. "Finn, please don't make me cry in the middle of a continental breakfast."

He chuckles. "Sorry I'm saying this over the phone, but you

needed to know. If you have to be in L.A. for a while, that's okay. We'll make it work."

"Are you serious?"

"Yes."

How is it possible he's this amazing?

"But I want to say all of this to your face, so when are you coming back?"

"The Legacy meeting got moved up. I'm going straight to Cancun, then back to Albuquerque, and then driving back to Vegas. So, a few days? Actually, can I ask you a huge favor?"

"Let me guess. Feed the fish?"

"You're the only other person who knows how. The fish guy will be there sometime this week, but can you just make sure—"

"Is the spare key still under that ugly toad statue by the back gate?"

"Yes, sir."

"All right, baby, I got you. I'll feed the fish, and you go knock your presentation out of the park. You just enjoy your last few days."

"Enjoy my last few days of what?"

"Being single. Because the minute you get home, I'm making you mine officially. No more gray area. No more questions about what we're doing. And definitely no more kissing other people."

"Good, okay, that sounds—"

The call waiting beeps, so I pull the phone from my ear to check who's calling. I'm mistaken. It's just a text message, but the notifications make me catch my breath.

> **Mason: I'm coming clean to Avery after the Legacy deal is secured.**

> **Mason: We're over, Palmer. For good this time. I want her back.**

"Avery?" I hear Finn ask through the phone, but my head goes fuzzy. My heart is tingling with nervous anticipation. The same sick feeling of dread you get at the top of a roller coaster when you know you're about to take a plunge.

"Finn, that sounds perfect, but I have to go. We'll talk soon."

I hang up and open the message thread. Palmer and Mason were friends while we were dating, and Palmer has stepped in as my intermediary through the worst part of our breakup, so I'm not surprised that they text.

What surprises me are all the naked pictures.

All the dirty text messages.

The *I love yous* and *I want yous*.

My heart has collapsed, but my investigative brain doesn't fail me. I know what's going on, but I want details. I need more facts. This is my best friend and my ex-boyfriend. Of all the people to rebound with. *How they hell could they do this to me?*

I run across a familiar message and can confirm Mason's first lie to me. Rumble app, my ass. He must've accidentally duplicated the message and sent it to me because he was talking to Palmer and me at the same time. What a snake.

> **Mason: I want to see you tonight. It's been over a month. I need that sweet pussy in my mouth again.**

> **Palmer: Come get it. You know where I'm staying.**

> **Mason: It's either a flight or a twelve-hour drive to Albuquerque.**

> **Palmer: I'll make it worth your while.**

It takes me another minute of scrolling before I realize the damage runs so much deeper.

This was no rebound.

> **Mason: I'm giving her the ring tonight.**

> **Palmer: Why are you going to propose if you don't love her?**

> **Mason: Stop. It's over. We can't do this anymore.**

> **Palmer: How can you choose her after years of telling me you love me?**

> **Mason: Because I love her, too.**

The messages are constant, and I scroll as far as I can before I've seen enough. It's been a back-and-forth saga of betrayal, guilt, and jealousy, and I see clearly for the first time in my life why Palmer loves me so much...why she needs me close.

She loves a competition that she knows she can win.

I take a couple of screenshots of the messages and text them to myself, praying Finn isn't going through my texts. If Mason getting pissy over the Legacy deal was enough to cause Finn to puff up like a bear and threaten him, imagine his reaction when he finds out Mason committed the ultimate crime in Finn's eyes.

I watch her finish at the check-out desk and return to our table. In a single moment, Palmer's entire appearance has changed. She's wearing the same blue jean shorts and baggie crop top hoodie. Her blond hair is pulled back in the same wispy ponytail that it was ten minutes ago, but the person who joins me at the table has an entirely different identity.

She slumps into a chair across from me. "Fuckers are trying to charge me for incidentals over some stupid cheap lamp." She groans. "I am so excited not to live in a hotel anymore." She examines my face, and her lips fall into a hard line. "Are you okay?"

"I need my keys," I force out.

She yanks her purse from her shoulder and fishes out my keys. "Of course. I assumed you'd drive." Handing them over, she asks again, "What's wrong?"

I grip my keys so hard my knuckles turn white. "Do you have any idea how much I love you?" I ask.

"What? Yeah..."

"No, I don't think you do, Palmer. See, I think you were the first person outside of my parents who I ever really loved with my whole heart."

She holds her hand to her heart but squints. I realize my message and my tone don't match, so she's confused about how to respond. "Are you okay? Who called from your phone?" She points to her phone in front of me.

"Everything I know about how to be in a relationship of any kind came from you. It was symbiotic. You're a taker, so naturally, I became a giver. I became a giver to everybody. Including Mason. He wanted a nice girl, a homebody, no drama, hard worker..."

"Okay...Avery, you're freaking me out."

"But he wanted a *skank,* too, didn't he? And I couldn't be that, so you were happy to step in."

Her face freezes. "Don't—"

"I know. *I know everything.* Don't insult me by playing stupid. Are you really in love with him, or was it just entertaining to play me for the fool?"

Her eyes start to well. "No...no. I'm sor—I'm so, so—sorry."

She can barely get her words out as she breathes in short heaves and fear fills her eyes. I don't know why she's hyperventilating like that. I've never struck a person in my life. I'm not about to start now. Maybe she's afraid because she knows the only damn person in this world who's been loyal to her...

Is about to leave her in the dust.

"Just be honest. How long? I at least know you tried to talk him out of proposing to me. That's all I needed for our friendship to be over. So tell me the truth. You've got nothing to lose. You've got *no one* left to lose."

Her face goes ghost white and red splotchy patches form on her cheeks as her eyes fill with tears. "Since your first date," she says through cries. "I've loved him as long as you have."

I scoff at the ridiculous sentiment. "That's not love, Palmer. You helped turn Mason into a cheating, spineless excuse of a man. I brought out the good parts of him. You brought out the worst. Maybe that's why he kept me around... Because he didn't like what he was with you. But at the end of the day, guess which version of himself he chose?"

She sobs harder. "You don't understand—"

"Stop. You could've talked to me," I murmur, my anger cooling, just for a moment, as I watch her all but collapse in front of me. "You could've been honest about your feelings. I would've let you have him, Palmer. I've only ever wanted you to be happy. I used to think Mason was a good guy, and I wanted a good guy for you."

"I know. I should've talked to you, Avery, *please*. I'm so sorry." She tents her hands over her face.

"It's good you didn't, though."

Her brows quirk upward. "What?"

"I needed this to happen in order to see what you really are. I've made so many excuses for you for so long. But I can't excuse this."

She hangs her head again. If she had hope for forgiveness, she must know that's gone now.

"You know what the shitty part is?"

She won't meet my eyes. Instead, she shrivels in her seat and merely shrugs.

"I want to tell you that you're a slutty, conniving bitch. I want to hate you so much, but I'm just sad. That's what happens when you really love someone, Palmer. They have the power to cut you to the core." My voice grows cold once more, and the tears I've held back for so long, from hating myself in pictures, from all the crushes who picked Palmer, from getting dumped, from all the mean girls who hated seeing me with Finn, from the feelings of inadequacy as a woman...

I let them flow...

So I can finally let them go.

Because now I know the source of all this insecurity in my heart. It was because I wasn't just ignoring the red flags. I was wrapped in the warning flag for twenty goddamn years in the form of my best friend.

"Getting dumped by Mason with a fucking ring on my hand is laughable compared to how I feel right now. *Why?* Why did you do this? I was such a good friend to you."

"I know," she whispers. "I don't deserve you."

"Agreed." For the first time ever, I change the narrative. "*And you no longer have me.*"

"Aves, please forgive—"

"No. Don't even ask. This is unforgivable, Palmer." I brush at my tears, but it's useless. We're both openly sobbing and have attracted the attention of every single person in the room. I rise from my chair, my keys still clutched in my fist. "But I'm going to be okay because once I cut the dead weight, I'm going to feel free and happy. For you, however, I hope the anchor of shame, guilt, and loneliness drags you to the bottom of the ocean so you can drown in how pathetic you are."

She mumbles something into her hands, but it's incomprehensible through her open bawling.

"I never want to see you or hear from you again. From now on, figure out your own shit. Starting with your own way back home."

With that, I rise and head through the sliding doors of the hotel. I find my Jeep and unlock the trunk. I'm immediately annoyed that the smell of Palmer's perfume has saturated it, and I get a giant whiff of betrayal as the trunk door lifts. No matter. I'll roll the windows down going seventy on the highway, and the stench will eventually dissipate.

I yank Palmer's luggage, which we loaded this morning, out of the trunk and place it on the curb. Without another moment of hesitation, I start the engine and peel out of the parking lot.

I drive away...

Changed.

No more pacifying. No more placating. No more Band-Aids for bullet wounds.

I'm ready for a true fresh start.

Chapter 38

Avery

About two exits shy of the airport, I remember a conversation I had with Dr. Ruth Donovon. After her big win with consulting for Royalty Airlines, they of course offered her a board advisory position. Dr. Donovon has done very well for herself, but she could've owned the entire block she lives on in Key Largo if she wanted to. What stopped her?

When I was debating switching my major from science to business and was scared to lose all the credit hours, she told me to *reverse* dissect my life. Don't think about my goals and what it takes to get there. She told me to picture my day-to-day life and think about what I wanted to fill my moments with. Dr. Donovon told me to let happiness build my goals. She loved to teach...so that's what she continued to do until retirement.

When I think about what makes me happy in my day-to-day, I think about Dex and his scuba diving company. I remember all the random fish facts I know—even before this summer and my obsessive deep dive into Cherry Barbs—all because of Dex's enthusiasm.

I think about Finn's photography business and how nervous he is to take risks. How he needs me to hold his hand through some of the riskier aspects of small business ownership. He's such a manly man, it's quite endearing to see him nervous about something. He has a gap that I can actually help fill, and it feeds my soul.

I never strived to be rich. Endless travel and luxury resorts are not what I'm picturing for my life. I want relationships...real friendships... I want to try new things, to learn new facts, and I want to be as immersed and passionate about my projects as Dex is about scuba diving and as Finn is about boudoir photography.

I no longer need Palmer to talk me out of a sound decision, and I certainly am not going to consult with Mason about anything, so I pull off shy of the exit and into a Walmart.

After purchasing a prepaid phone, two blueberry Red Bulls, and enough Chex Mix, protein drinks, powdered donuts, and waters to fuel a ten-hour drive back to Las Vegas, I make a difficult call to leave a complicated voicemail.

"Hello, this is Hunter."

Shit. "Oh, hi!" I shoot up in the driver's seat and brush the powdered sugar off my shirt like he can see me through the phone. "Mr. Mahan, it's Avery Scott."

"Avery. Hi. We've been trying to call you—"

"I'm so sorry. I lost my phone back at home." I pause. *Home.* It just flowed right out of me. *Home is Las Vegas.* Home is now Finn. "May I ask why you're answering an unknown number?"

"Good timing, I guess," he says through a half-laugh. "I'm actually getting ready to board my flight as well. I'm assuming Mason told you the meeting got bumped up? Did you get everything squared away with travel? Is there anything you need in the meeting room for tomorrow?"

I let out an exaggerated exhale. "Mr. Mahan—"

"Hunter, please. Oh shit...you're not coming, are you?"

"No. I'm not."

"Fuck. Sorry, that was unprofessional, but...*fuck.* We're screwed, aren't we? Even you think we should dissolve?"

"No." I make sure I'm as emphatic as possible, and then I clear my throat. "Hunter, do not dissolve Legacy Resorts or any of its subsidiaries, *please.* The company is in fantastic shape, and you guys have the potential to blow your competition out of the water."

"*Great.* Fly to Cancun and tell that to the board, *please.*"

I laugh. "Listen, you have a board member, Wallace Frank—"

"Yeah, Mr. Frank is our most senior advisor."

"He's a snake in the garden, my friend. I did some digging, and he just invested over sixteen million dollars into Legacy's biggest competitor. He's not rallying the board members to do what's best for the company... He's bought and paid for, Hunter."

"You're shitting me."

"No, I'm not. This is as close to insider trading as you can get, so you could go to the authorities, or you could invite Mr. Frank to remove himself from the board in exchange for your oversight of the matter. Then you need a few little tweaks to your branding strategy."

"Such as?"

"Legacy Resorts should stay luxury. It just also needs to be kid friendly. Parents want to enjoy adult time, knowing their kids are safe. You should take a page from Royalty Airline's book. Invest in high-end childcare with actual teachers with security cameras, rotating daily activities, and a little curriculum. Parents love when their kids have fun learning. And get the kids involved in the luxury aspect. Mommy and me spa days, Daddy and son mini-golf. Make sure all the restaurants have kid-friendly menus and have family versus adult dining times. You don't need to exclude anyone from the resorts; just segment out the experiences. The possibilities are endless. Family luxury—that's the only hook you need."

"Avery, it's a great idea. We could really use you. And I got your email about Arrow exclusively consulting for Legacy Resorts and bringing Mason on board, and we're willing to play ball. Whatever the cost to get you to sign with us."

I am not a saint. I am not perfect. I am a human being, and an opportunity has presented itself. Sue me.

"Hunter, if I'm being honest, Mason is subpar at best. He gets his work done, but truthfully, a chimp might be more productive. The bottom line is he is replaceable and is absolutely not worth a seven-figure salary. I am the backbone of Arrow Consulting... which is no more. Mason and I are splitting the business and parting ways."

"Oh, I spoke to him this morning and he didn't tell me that."

He doesn't know...yet. "He was probably trying to be professional. But the bottom line is, I'm no longer available. I am so flattered and appreciative of the opportunity, but I think my heart is in small business, so I'm going to focus my attention there for a while. But I can give you some stellar recommendations, and you have my number. Call anytime, and I'll be happy to bounce around ideas with you."

"How about another fifty thousand?"

"Hunter—"

"Sixty-k and a company car?"

"Hunter—"

"Seventy-k, a company car, and I turn a blind eye if you use the company black card every now and then. There is literally no limit on that card... You could buy Tahiti."

I laugh out loud. "That's tempting." *Not really, though.*

I don't want Tahiti. I want pajamas. I want thrift shopping girls' days with a friend like Lennox. I want a cuddly man who will watch a movie with me...and then bend me over the side of the couch and spank me a little. I just want to laugh, breathe, learn, and relax. I don't want to work sixty hours a week anymore. It's not worth the prestige. I just want to enjoy my life and build a family.

"There's nothing I can do to convince you?"

"No, I'm sorry."

He grumbles. "All right, well, expect a few follow-up emails from me that will involve a little more begging."

I laugh. "Fair enough."

"Thanks for the call, Avery, and for the information about Frank. I'm going to go talk to our CEO, and we're going to take out the trash."

"Good. I recently did the same. Feels good."

"Take care. Get home safe."

Home. "I will."

* * *

I thought my anger and angst would fuel me through the drive, but I couldn't swing it. I had to stop at a hotel and sleep a bit before I drove myself right off the road. Let the record show, Red Bulls are good for nothing except their tastiness.

When I pull into Dex's driveway the next morning, I see the fish guy's van parked on the side of the road. *Great.* I just want to go to sleep. I have a crying hangover. My eyes are puffy, my head hurts, and my back aches from this long drive. I'm not an idiot. I don't care how angry I am at Palmer. I just lost the longest, most significant relationship of my life.

Friendships don't have to end. They aren't exclusive. I was always taught to *keep the old and make the new.* The dynamics can change. You can go from talking daily to yearly. Sometimes friends can drift apart and then snap back together. They need each other in different ways at different stages of their lives. Love doesn't have to fade due to distance. Friendships can endure...

Unless someone sabotages the relationship.

Palmer could've prevented this. She could've kept it in her pants. She could've talked to me. She could've found a way to love me, almost as much as she loved herself. But she didn't. And it's going to hurt for a very long time.

I'm going to heal...

But first, it's going to hurt. And that's okay.

Leaving my bag in the car and only bringing in my purse, I trudge through the front door. I have no energy to immediately unpack like I normally do. "Hey, Fish Guy," I call out.

"Hey, Fish Lady," he calls back with a chuckle at our little inside joke. All kidding aside, I don't know his real name. It's been over two months... I can't ask now. It's too awkward.

I see my phone sitting on the kitchen counter next to a sealed white box with a note on top:

You're beautiful. You're worthy.
-Finn
P.S. I promise I didn't look.

Not right now. I want to look, but I'm a little too fragile at the moment. I can't take any more hits right now in case I don't like what my boudoir photographs look like. It's not until I grab a bottle of water from the fridge and head to my phone do I see the travesty in the sink.

Cherry...

Out of water, dead in a small dish.

I squeal in shock as I drop my bottle of water.

"What the fuck?" I squelch. My reaction causes the fish guy to stop tinkering with the living room tank and head in my direction. He dodges the spilled water with his sock-covered feet and scoops up the water bottle from the ground. "When did she die?"

I know she's a fish...

But damn.

My head starts to pound as I hold back a fresh wave of tears that hits me. Goddammit. Treachery and tragedy are just fucking exhausting.

"I found her belly up when I got here an hour ago. I'm sorry. I shouldn't have left her in the sink. I didn't know you'd be here. But I don't flush fish. It's not good for plumbing or the ecosystem."

"What're you going to do with her?" I'm not going to be a child and suggest we have a service and proper burial...but if he offers, I will go put on a black T-shirt right now.

He raises his brows at me. "Chum."

"Oh, God." I pout. "Please don't tell me that. I really liked this little fish."

"You're a fan of Cherry Barbs, huh?"

"Yeah, she used to be super active, but she slowed down. The stripe along her belly, I'm assuming it was cancer. I just hope she went peacefully."

Fish Guy bags Cherry and the dish up and sets her by his

black supply bag with the blue stripe, which matches his uniform. "It's not cancer. Some Cherry Barbs have those markings. They can even get translucent."

"She didn't have a stripe when I first got here," I say. "It developed as she slowed down. I'm pretty sure she was sick."

"What?" He looks at me like I'm crazy as he runs his hands through his curly hair. "No, it died because these are social fish. I keep telling Dex he needs to either get a separate tank or move some of these fish to make room for multiple Cherry Barbs because they like to live in clusters of their own. I've gone through three since you've been here. They are dying because of shock and isolation."

There's a brief knock at the front door before it opens and in walks the shirtless Adonis of a man who still takes my breath away after almost an entire summer of seeing his naked body.

"Hey, Queen, what are you doing home? I thought you were still in Mexico." He preemptively spins his baseball cap around, because even though he's sweaty and was clearly just on a run, I know exactly what's on his mind. I'm smashed against his sweaty, hard abs in an instant, and his lips find mine briefly. "Can a man get a call, for goodness' sake?" He points to my phone on the counter. "I left it here for that reason."

"I literally just got home." I press my finger against his lips and lean away to look back at Fish Guy. "I'm sorry, can you finish what you were saying?"

"About the Cherry Barbs? They are school fish, so they need to—"

I hold up my hand. "No, no, the part where you said *they* are dying? What do you mean by *they*?"

He squints at me. "Fish Lady, I've replaced that Cherry Barb three times since you've been here. You didn't notice? The twitchy one you're talking about died weeks ago."

I cover my mouth and gasp into my hand as I wiggle out of Finn's arms.

He looks shocked at my downpour of tears. "*Whoa, baby.*

Over a fish?"

I can't stop myself. I openly sob. *"Yes."* I point at Fish Guy. "That was so fucking sneaky. You can't just replace people's fish without telling them... *That's a lie.* I thought one thing...and...it was *all a fucking lie.* It's going behind someone's back and changing their perception of reality and making them doubt their sanity. I thought I knew her...we were so close. I saw her every day...how did I not know?"

There's an awkward lull as the two men in the room watch me weep over my dead fish friend. Only one of them realizes I'm not completely insane and there's obviously so much more behind my reaction to this news.

"Um...I brought another Cherry Barb. Do you want me to put it in the tank, or... I mean, is this legitimately upsetting you? Or is this a *lady time of the month* thing?"

Finn's expression fills with annoyance, and he glances at Fish Guy from the corner of his eyes. "Can you give us some privacy? Maybe you forgot something in your van. Go check," Finn says in a gruff command. "Now, please."

Finn waits until the front door clicks closed before he wipes my tears away with his thumbs. "What's going on?" he asks softly. "This can't just be about a fish."

I sniffle. "I almost gave you up for her. I almost picked her over you." Finn's so patient. He just nods as I babble nonsensically. "That's why I wasn't going to move. Palmer needed me, so I had to go back to L.A. to be there for her. I promised. I keep my promises."

"I understand," Finn says. "That's your best friend. It's okay, Avery. I told you, we're going to make it work—"

"She's been sleeping with Mason for four years, behind my back. *Years, Finn.* I am so fucking stupid and clueless. I had no idea. Maybe the signs were there and I didn't want to see it. I've just been working and working, completely blind to the fact that everyone was living their life except me."

"The fuck?" he whispers. "Palmer and Mason? You're not serious."

I nod as I continue to ugly cry. "I've been missing out on so much, worried about everybody else, but now, I'm worried about me. I said no to the Legacy Resorts job. I'm done with Arrow Consulting. There's nothing for me in L.A. I don't have anything to go back to...*and* my fish is dead."

He pulls me against his chest, and I breathe in his salty, musky skin. I feel Finn's lips on the top of my head. He lets me sob against him, my tears running down his chest and abs. Stroking my back, he shushes me sweetly and tells me it's okay. When I've settled and we can hear ourselves over my open weeping, Finn says, "How about we don't go back? Either of us. How about we try forward? Together."

"Forward is good, but..." I kiss his pec and then step out of his embrace. Taking a deep, calming breath, I continue, "I have to do this differently this time. So, Finn, I think you're way out of my league—"

"Avery," he interrupts, rolling his eyes.

"Let me finish. But just because you might be the sexiest man on the planet doesn't mean you don't have to earn me."

He grins wide. "Okay. How do I earn you, Queen?"

"I want a date night more than once a year. In fact, I'd like an official date night once a week, and at least once a month we put on nice clothes and leave the house and *flirt,* in public."

"Done."

"Wait, I'm not finished."

He smiles again. "Needy girl."

"I want you to teach me how to cook."

"You can finish your demands in my arms, baby." He reaches back out and grabs me by the hips. "I will happily teach you how to cook, if we can have a dip buffet for dinner every now and then, too."

"Fair enough."

"What else?"

"I want to walk with you. And I do mean *walk*, not run. But I want a relationship where we do outside stuff sometimes. I don't want to stay behind a computer screen for twelve hours a day. I want to be healthier all around."

He squeezes my hips. "Okay, we can do outside stuff together."

"And I don't ever want another woman in bed with us. I don't like it."

He nods solemnly. "Me neither. Never again."

"And the big one..."

Finn widens his beautiful baby blue eyes. "Go for it."

I inhale and hold it for a moment before I exhale. "I'm not waiting four years to get married. We don't have to rush, but I'm not going to ignore my needs for yours. We can always compromise, but if it is going to take you half a decade to decide whether you want to spend your life with me, I will walk away. I want a family. I want a home."

"Okay," Finn says. "I hear you loud and clear, Queen."

"And I don't ever want you to stop calling me Queen."

"Fine with me." He tries to kiss me again, but I lean back. He raises his brows, his patience running a little thin. I think he's ready to start our happily ever after. "Anything else?"

"No, that's everything from my end... But what about you? What do you need?"

Finn touches his smooth lips against mine. It's not a kiss, just a touch. He rubs his nose against the tip of mine. "Just this. I need you to never stop telling me what you need. I want you to cry in front of me so I know how you're feeling and I can try and fix it. No more running out on me when you're upset and making me worry."

"I can do that."

"Good."

"All right, Finn Harvey. Well, now that that's all settled, I think I'm ready to fall in love with you."

Chapter 39

Avery

I stop in front of Finn on the couch and smile at him like a lunatic with a bowl of buffalo chicken dip in my hand.

"What?" he asks with a concerned smirk. His face is lit up with the slight glow of Dex's aquarium behind me.

"Nothing. I'm happy."

"Are you sure? You can cry some more if you need to. You won't scare me off."

"No...I'm okay today." I'm cried out, honestly. It comes in waves. I don't miss Mason, but I do miss Palmer. It's bizarre. Losing your best friend is like taking off a security blanket and feeling a chill. At first it's uncomfortable, but soon after, you realize you were burning up the entire time. The cold becomes welcome.

I set the dip down and crawl on top of his lap, resting my thighs on his, letting myself be comfortable in his powerful embrace.

"Damn, you smell nice, baby," Finn mumbles.

I chuckle. "Because I smell like your favorite dip."

He chuckles into my neck and says, "No, it's your perfume." He breathes me in and then tucks my long hair away from my shoulder. "You look really nice tonight."

I think I'm learning my balance. The truth is I don't want to be prancing around in revealing lingerie and mermaid glitter...*at least not in public.* Finn has insisted we keep my mermaid costume for role-playing night. I agreed, but only if he gets an eye patch and he wraps his hand around my throat. But for every day, I've decided, I like being comfortable but with a little effort. So for tonight, I'm wearing the cute flowy bohemian shorts Lennox found for me with a form-fitting, white, baby T-shirt that hugs the bulge of my chest and the slight dip in my waist. My hair is down in natural waves, and I have on a hint of makeup—a soft blush, a little lip tint, and a touch of mascara.

This is nice. *This*, I like. This feels like me.

"It's our first official date," I say before pressing my lips against his.

"What? I've taken you out before."

"True, but tonight, I have no questions about how you feel about me, where we're headed, or what you think about me."

I run my hands all over his gray workout shirt, which is the same silky-smooth material as his black athletic pants. He looks like such a jock tonight. *Ha! Me...with a jock.* I invited Finn to our first official date night. I made all his favorite dips. I have every intention of making it up to him tonight because all we've done for the past few nights is cuddle.

Sex isn't going anywhere. After the most dramatic twenty-four hours of my life, I needed to recuperate and feel comfort in a different way. So Finn pals around and cuddles me. He's patient through my sporadic little meltdowns. When I think of Palmer, I cry. I cry even harder when I think about the fact that she hasn't bothered to call and beg me for forgiveness. I told her not to contact me, but a part of me wished she would have at least tried. Her cowardly behavior only solidifies what I know in my heart; this friendship isn't just over—it's been over for a long time.

It's okay to mourn. It's okay for my heart to hurt. And it does... Immensely. But it also feels like relief. Like the shadow that's been chasing me my entire life finally stepped into the light, and the monster... It was just a mouse. The monster of my insecurity was just a teeny, tiny, sad mouse.

Finn is letting me process patiently. He even cuddled me last night on the couch as I fell asleep watching *Finding Nemo* in his arms, my personal memorial to Cherry. I cried as we watched it, and he didn't ask me if it was about Palmer or Cherry. He just stroked my hair and let me quietly sob. In a weird way, Finn likes my tears. He says my tears, unlike Nora's, are honest. *And he wants honesty.*

I couldn't have dreamed up a better man.

"What do you think I think about you?" Finn asks. There's a sultry smile on his face, and I feel a swell growing where I'm rubbing against his crotch. He shifts his hips to subtly adjust himself with ease like I'm weightless on top of him. I love how strong he is. It's how I know I can really lean on him.

"I think you think—"

Ring, ring.

My phone sounds from the kitchen counter, the loud ringtone carrying from Dex's open-concept main floor with the tall ceilings. I'm actually going to miss this place when he returns in a couple of weeks. Then again, I'm only moving next door. I bet I can pop by to visit.

The phone grows quiet for a brief moment before it picks right back up.

"Goddammit. Let *me* talk to that fucker. I'll let him know he's lost the privilege of speaking to my girlfriend ever again. And if he has a hard time understanding, I can pay him a visit and say it to his face."

"It's really hot when you get all protective," I say with a seductive smile, placing my hands on his cheeks. I rub my thumbs against his stubble. "Say that again, but kind of growl it." I try to snarl at him, but he's not returning my playfulness. "*What, Finn?* Don't be upset. You know I'm not answering his calls."

Mason panicked when he found out I blew off the Legacy Resorts deal.

He spiraled when Palmer must've told him I knew everything about their affair. That's when he started blowing up my phone— messages and voicemails toggling between begging, explaining, and then demanding I talk to him.

He damn near had a heart attack when he was copied on the

email I sent to all of our clients, letting them know that Arrow Consulting was splitting ways and that I would be offering long-term services as a brand strategist and marketing consultant under a new boutique name: Queen Consulting, which would be based out of Las Vegas. I asked my clients to reach out if they were interested in receiving more information when I returned to work in a few weeks *after* my summer vacation concluded.

The response was overwhelming. Mason can keep Arrow and all its assets. It's nothing but an empty shell now.

My more vindictive side has enjoyed watching him spiral as I keep his messages on read and let the phone line ring. I plan on giving it a few more days before I block his number completely.

"I'm not upset if you talk to him. I am just so angry for you. But you've got an edge, baby. Maybe you should rip him to fucking pieces while I listen on speakerphone."

Not that I'd say this to Finn, but I'm eternally grateful for Mason. It was a tough lesson to learn, but I needed him to string me along for four years. I needed him to make me doubt myself so I felt low enough to ask for Finn's help. I was desperate enough to approach a man I never would've unless I had absolutely nothing to lose.

"I don't need to. I did what I needed to do, and now I'm not going to dwell on this any longer. I deserve better, and Mason deserves...*Palmer.* There's no greater punishment than that." I laugh to myself. "And I don't need to tell Mason what a huge mistake he made. His consequence is not getting to experience the best version of me." I kiss Finn's forehead. "I'm saving all that for you, babe."

"You're a queen," Finn says, guiding my lips to his. "Such a fucking queen." Our kiss deepens, and this time he reaches between us to adjust his erection, which has grown to mammoth proportions. He groans against my ear. "Are you feeling better? Can we fuck—"

"Wait."

He exhales. "Sure, why not," he grumbles bitterly. "That's all

I've been doing. I'm getting really good at it."

"Are you actually pouting?" I burst out in a chuckle. "I just want to show you something, and then you can fuck me like a madman, right on this couch."

I dart to the kitchen and return to the living room with my box of photographs.

"You saw them?" Finn asks.

I shake my head. "Nope, not yet," I say as I break the sticker seal on the box. "I want to look together."

I'm nervous, but not for the reason I thought I would be. There's one thing I desperately needed to get out of the summer, and it lies within these pictures. It was never about Finn liking these...

It's about me.

I open the box and dare myself to love what I see.

The pictures are stacked strategically so they tell a story. I see the studio first, black roses scattered on the ground. I see the disturbed sheets and just my hand gripping them tightly like I'm in the throes of passion. And the first time I see my body—my legs, covered in the black stockings that rose a few inches over my knees, I gasp.

I hand the picture over to Finn, my eyes wide as I soak in picture after picture of my naked body, my most intimate parts half covered by my hands, my hair, a rose. The look on my face in every picture is hauntingly erotic. Finn captured something I've never seen in myself.

Confidence.

"Finn..." I trail off as I hand him image after image after I look at them. My cheeks are burning, and my heart is thumping angrily. "Is this what you see when you look at me?"

He watches my eyes carefully as his brows furrow. "Yes. Avery, these are—"

"Amazing," I finish for him. I want to be the one to say it. I laugh in joy and relief, proving myself to the one person who matters. "I look really, *really* good."

Finn nods, examining the picture. "You look beautiful. So sexy."

I nod in agreement. "Thank you."

He sets the pictures I handed him on a neat stack on the coffee table. "Come on, I've seen enough. We can finish looking at these later."

Actually, I want to keep going. The feeling of loving myself and appreciating the way I look is exhilarating. It's my new addiction. But I take his hand and let him drag me up the stairs, knowing what these images have stirred up in him—a primal, lusty urge. This feels just as good...being the wanted girl.

"Closet?" I ask as we head to the master bedroom. "The big mirror?"

I watch his head shake from behind. He wordlessly pulls me *through* the bedroom, through the master closet, and into Dex's bathroom. He lets go of my hand, opens the shower door, and turns on the water.

The energy between us is electrically charged. It's like lightning struck and lingered. I stay still and revel in his masculine angst as he strips me down like I'm a doll to play with. He yanks down my shorts and panties in one pull. I step out of my bottoms obediently as he maneuvers his hands underneath my form-fitting shirt and unhooks my bra. He pulls the straps free of my arms and slides my bra out under my top but leaves it on. Then he drags me under the stream of the shower head, letting it soak me from head to toe.

He watches my shirt glue to my body, my breasts completely on display through my drenched white shirt. He peels off his own and tosses it onto the bathroom floor, shutting the glass door behind him so we're boxed into a different kind of wet dream.

He cups my chest delicately. "Before I met you, I swear I was an ass man. But these have converted me." He pinches my nipples one by one before he spins me around, bends me over, and secures my hands on the built-in bench. He smacks my ass, hard. The sound is exaggerated by the echo of the shower.

"Then again," he growls as he rubs his palm over the spot he swatted, "this gets me just as hard." I groan when he sinks his thickest finger into my crease. "I bet this pussy missed me."

"Yes," I mumble.

Finn bends over me, his chest lining my back as his free hand wraps around my throat. His lips tickle my earlobe, and he speaks right into my ear so I can hear him over the shower. "First I'm going to fuck you like I own you. Then I'm going to pull you into the bedroom and make love to you. How's that sound?"

"Mmm, good. *Yes.*"

He slowly pumps his finger in and out, and I spread my legs a little wider, inviting him to get deeper.

"But tomorrow, when you wake up in my arms and I kiss you good morning, I'm going to enjoy that just as much."

"Me too," I mumble.

He curls his finger inside me as he tugs on my earlobe with his teeth. "Why did I bring you into the shower, Queen? What do you think I want you do to for me?"

"Come," I whimper. "You want me to come."

He pulls his fingers out and rapidly flicks against my clit before he plunges back in, with two fingers this time. "No, baby. That's not enough. I don't want you to just come for me. I want you to explode for me."

My body goes weak and my legs start to shake as he drives his fingers into me furiously and the familiar pressure brews from the forbidden spot that I rarely allow him to touch.

"Oh my God," I cry out as the pressure blows past the point of tolerance. I completely let go and burst as Finn roars in appreciation.

"That's it, baby. *Good girl.* I fucking love how you can do that." He spins me around, pulls his fingers out, and yanks his soaked shorts down, his erection springing free and bouncing in place. My breath is still ragged from my orgasm, and the tension in my chest only tightens as I study the perfection that is his dick.

"Finn, I want it to always feel like this. Whenever we're

together, whether we're fucking or cuddling, I want to feel like you want me *this much* every single day."

His demeanor changes. He pauses to kiss me sweetly, pulling me against him so his dick is sandwiched between our bodies, stirring an ache from deep inside me. "It will and I do. Just tell me what you need, and I'll take such good care of you. I promise. I love you, Avery."

I nod. "I love you too, Finn Harvey. And thanks to you, I think I love me too."

A part of me wants to stop here. I want to spend the rest of this evening under the warm rain from the shower with Finn's burly arms wrapped around me, making me feel safe. But his erection is twitching on my stomach, and now I need to take care of my man.

I smirk into his chest. "Now pull my hair and tell me to get on my knees and swallow the whole load. Boss me around. Pirate-style."

He lets out a short laugh. "Dirty girl with a dirty mouth."

Obediently, he weaves his hand in my hair and clenches his fist. I'm at his mercy as he guides me to my knees and the tip of his dick nudges against my lips.

"Look up at me," Finn says.

He shoots me a playful wink before he wipes the smile from his face, getting fully into character.

"Open your mouth...*wider*...good girl." He groans in delight. "Just like that, *Queen*."

THE END

Bonus Epilogue

Finn

9 months later

"You know what we do in limos...spread 'em."

Avery's lips turn white as she presses them together as hard as she can to prevent herself from bursting out in laughter.

"Did you just steal my line?" I ask, unable to control my own smile. I watch my beautiful girl sit across from me in our fancy ride. She's been the only VIP in my world for a year now, and she glows brighter in my eyes daily.

By now Avery has several date night dresses. I made sure of it. The seafoam green dress with the exaggerated slits that she's wearing tonight is my favorite. It's the only dress I've seen that almost matches the color of her eyes.

"It's called role reversal. How about tonight, I'm the boss?" She pumps her brows at me twice. "It is my birthday. Well, the night before my birthday, but still."

Avery only agreed to this fancy dinner party at Rue 52 where Senior shut down the entire restaurant this evening in her honor. For Avery's actual birthday, she insisted on an entire day where we shut off our phones, wear pajamas all day, watch movies, and order takeout from the Mediterranean place she loves. I think it tastes like grazing in a field—but hey, my baby gets what she wants on her birthday. Tomorrow we'll only leave the house to pick up another aquarium we don't need for yet another batch of Cherry Barbs that I'm really over taking care of.

I blame Dex for Avery's fish obsession. I now own nearly as many tanks as he does. He's constantly talking her into new exotic species to collect. If it makes her happy, fine, but I draw the line at the little fuckers that require feedings with live bait.

She crosses the minimal space between us with a playful grin and lines her thigh against mine. I let her soft, warm lips linger on my neck. Her hand crawls up my crotch for a moment before I pull away. "You're no fun," she huffs.

"Queen, please don't get me all worked up right before your birthday dinner with our parents." I cringe. "Sorry, *my parents.*"

Avery rolls her eyes at my apologetic expression. "Finn, get over it. It's only a birthday dinner. Surely you didn't expect them to drive five hours just to have a meal with us. I'm turning thirty-one. That's not even a milestone birthday."

I squeeze her knee tenderly. "They *wanted* to be here. I promise you. Your dad got called away for a last-minute work thing and we know your stepmom won't travel alone."

Avery curls her lip. "Susan. Just call her Susan. My dad married her when I was twenty-seven. *Stepmom* sounds weird."

I blow out a breath, unconcerned with the technicalities. The point is I've been planning this big birthday dinner for Avery for a month now, and quite frankly it's shocking that *my* family pulled through, whereas Avery's parents are dropping like flies. It's their daughter I'm proposing to for god sakes.

"Fine. Susan won't travel without your dad. And your mom's foot is much worse than they thought. She thinks she broke it."

Avery quirks her brow at me. "I know that. She's in a lot of pain right now."

"Right. Exactly." I match her puzzled stare. "What?"

"*I know that,*" Avery emphasizes. "Now why do *you*? In fact, how do you know about my dad's work trip? That just happened yesterday."

"Daryl called me this morning and explained everything." Daryl has been my accomplice in this surprise proposal. He's easier to talk to than Avery's dad. Mr. Scott was pleasant and polite enough when I snuck away a few weekends ago to ask his permission, but it was Daryl who jumped up from the couch and pulled me into a hug, welcoming me into a family that he was a latecomer to himself.

"My stepdad called you?"

"Yeah, Daryl and I talk sometimes."

"About?" Now she's staring at me like I have two heads.

"Ships. We both like ships and sailing, and wait," I say trying to ease her suspicion. "Why is Daryl your stepdad but Susan isn't your stepmom?"

Avery lifts and drops her shoulders before she snuggles against me. "Timing. Mom remarried when I was seventeen so Daryl was there during my formative years."

"Formative years? *Oh, please,*" I say with a chuckle. "Just admit it, you think Susan is an uppity bitch." *She is.* I tolerate her to be polite, but I will excuse myself immediately if I'm stuck in a room with Susan alone. She has the eyes of an owl that peer into your soul while she silently picks out everything she thinks is wrong with you.

"*What? Nooo,*" Avery says, but she nods fervently against my shoulder.

I laugh as I extend my arm and pull her against me before my lips find the top of her head. I breathe in the minty ginger smell that has become the most familiar scent in my world. I swear my side has molded to the curves of Avery's body. She's been nestled right against me for almost a year. An entire, blissful, fulfilling year.

There was no doubt where we were headed.

But I wanted to catch her off guard if I could. Avery's always ten steps ahead of me. Every time I ask if a bill got paid for the home we share, she's already handled it. When I make a mental note to add more orange juice to the grocery list, I open the fridge and see a full jug because she's already been shopping. When I broke my phone one evening, I woke up to a brand new device, my sim card already installed, with a heavy-duty screen protector already secured on it.

All Avery's been doing is taking care of me for as long as we've been together. When I ask her why she's so good to me, she always playfully says the sex is just *that* hot, so she's trying to keep me around. But personally, I think it's because she's happy. Happy people are good to each other. Caring. Kind. Thoughtful. And I like knowing that now, I'm a big part of what makes her...*her*.

"Are you nervous about your mom and dad being in the same room tonight?" Avery says, lifting her chin to meet my eyes.

I tap her nose. "Nope." *They were warned to be on their best behavior.* After the last dinner Avery and I attended with Dad, I didn't speak to him for six full months. It took him that long to understand I didn't need him to apologize to me. He needed to apologize to my mother. *For everything.* I would've settled for a quick phone call, hell, even a text message admitting his fault in the demise of their relationship. But Dad went a step further and wrote a four-page, heartfelt letter explaining to my mother that she deserved true happiness and that he was sorry he wasn't a better man to her.

That letter earned him back a relationship with his son.

"I'm a little nervous." Avery scrunches her nose playfully.

"Why?"

"Because the last time I saw your father, I'm pretty sure he called me juicy...which I'm still not sure of whether it was a compliment or insult."

"Most definitely a compliment." I drop my hand from her shoulder and grab a fistful of her ass. "But still wildly inappropriate. He'll be on his best behavior around Senior though, who by the way is very much looking forward to meeting you."

Avery's eyes bulge as she wiggles out of my embrace and shifts her hips in the seat to face me. "I'm *a lot* nervous to meet your grandpa."

"Really?" Avery's talked to Gramps twice on the phone, once through FaceTime. I don't want to make her even more nervous, but it's a huge gesture that he flew in for her birthday dinner.

Although little does she know, it's so much more than a birthday dinner. He flew in early to give me my grandmother's ring. No one supports my relationship as much as Gramps does. I think he's just relieved to see I followed in his footsteps, versus Dad's. "Why are you nervous, baby?"

"Because I want him to like me. I get the feeling that if Senior were to tell you we shouldn't be together...well, he might be the only person in the world you'd listen to."

I immediately hook my finger under her chin and lock my eyes on hers. "There's not a goddamn person on this planet I'd let come between us. Hell, even *you* could tell me we shouldn't be together, and that still wouldn't be enough to convince me. You, Avery Scott, are my destiny. I have the most beautiful woman in the world—inside and out—and I'm never letting you go. It's as simple as that."

A year ago, Avery would've leaned away, her eyes would've dropped to her feet. But after all this time together, she's not only come to accept my praise, I think she's starting to believe it. *I did that.* It's my proudest accomplishment. Avery Scott might actually see herself the way I do by now.

"I must've been an incredible person in a past life to deserve you in this one," Avery whispers, her chin bobbing against my finger as she speaks. "I love you, Finn." She clasps her hand around mine and pulls my finger from her chin to my lips, kissing the tip tenderly.

A relaxing, soothing flood of warmth fills my veins. It happens every time Avery tells me she loves me. It's not the words. It's how she says it, like every time she looks at me she's falling in love with me all over again. That's my praise kink. My *job well done.* Look at how bright, alive, and happy she is. My worst nightmare is averted; I grew up to be a man who knows how to treat his lady. And I swear if home is a feeling...it's this. Dependability countered with nervous excitement. I know she's always going to smile at me like this, but it still makes my heart pound.

"You really don't know what tonight is?" I ask. "Are you just being sweet and pretending for my benefit?"

The puzzled look on Avery's face tells me everything. "It's my birthday dinner...but that's too obvious so I'm assuming you mean something else?"

So much for my big surprise. I can't even help myself. "You're not expecting anything tonight?" I pump my eyebrows at her.

Looking baffled, she glances across the limo as if someone might be in here with us. "No?"

"Nothing extra special for your birthday?"

She glowers at me. "Finn Harvey, if you bought me another car—"

"Nope." I learned that lesson the hard way. Avery is perfectly fine with me ordering for her at restaurants. She is *not* fine with me asking Gramps for my inheritance early so I can buy her a fancy little sports car to celebrate the successful launch of her business. She's far more attached to her Jeep than I realized. "Never again. My queen picks her own cars."

"Damn straight."

"Nothing else?"

"Okay, babe? This started out cute, but I'm confused, and a little hungry. So..." She nods her head to the limo door, indicating we should go.

We've been parked for fifteen minutes at least. I'm stalling because Lennox texted me and said they need a little more time to set up. They decorated Rue 52 to look like the inside of a pirate ship, a little inside joke that no one needs to understand except me and Avery. But it's Lennox in charge tonight. So when I told her it'd be fun to have a couple of ships in a bottle on the table and maybe have some nautical-themed napkins, of course, she took advantage of Gramp's black card and redecorated the entire restaurant.

I tsk my tongue. "Usually so keen. My baby's losing her touch."

She scrunches her face at me, pretending to be offended. "Losing my touch? What could you possibly be hinting at that I'd be expecting? I *know* for a fact you didn't buy us a puppy because we still can't decide on a breed. My passport has expired, so there's no way you booked us a surprise trip to Greece like we've been talking about. Other than a proposal—which would be crazy tonight of all nights—what in the world could you be hinting at?"

I freeze. "Why would tonight be crazy for a proposal?"

Avery shrugs at me like it's obvious. "Why the hell would you try and recreate one of the worst nights of my life and drag me right back down memory lane of the dipshit I wasted almost half a decade on?" Avery snorts in laughter, clearly missing my mortified expression. "If you're ever going to propose to me, Finn Harvey, please for the love of God, don't do it on my birthday."

She's still chuckling until she registers my pained expression. Avery covers her nose and mouth with both hands. "Oh, fuck."

"Mhm," I grumble.

"Oh, Finn...you were going to—"

"Yup."

"Oh shit. *Oh no.* I'm so sorry." Her light green eyes widen as she shakes her head. "I didn't mean—"

"What if your dumbass boyfriend didn't see it as recreating the worst night of your life, and instead saw it as righting a wrong?"

She drops her hands and gasps. "*I ruined it.* I can't believe I ruined it."

"Apparently *I* ruined it," I mutter. "But at least it would've been a surprise...so there's that."

"Would've been?" she asks as she grimaces. "You're really not going to ask me now?"

"Of course not. I'm not having my proposal going down as a recreation of the worst night of your life. I just wanted to surprise you."

"Oh, come on, Finn." She puckers her bottom lip. "Forget I said anything. Your version is so much better. It's absolutely righting a wrong. Tonight is perfect for a proposal. And I promise I'll play along and act surprised."

I raise one brow. "Really?" I ask, my tone full of skepticism. Avery is a terrible actress. It's probably because she's so sincere. It's hard for her to hide her emotions.

"Yes." She nods once, confidently. "I'll even give you real tears. That's how committed I am." Then, she laughs playfully. "Unless you planned on something over-the-top cheesy like sticking the ring in my birthday cake, then I'll be laughing more than crying—"

She stops midsentence when she sees my blank expression and lips pressed in a flat line.

Her open palm finds her forehead. "Oh shit. Finn, I'm sorry. You put it in the cake, didn't you?"

"I was going to put it in your champagne glass. Which I'm hoping is a touch less cheesy. My birthday toast to you was going to be the proposal."

Avery blinks at me, her long lashes fluttering up and down as she contemplates her reply.

"Thoughts?" I ask, smirking.

"Oh, I think it's best I stop talking now," she says seriously, trying to stifle a giggle.

"All right, you know what?" I ask, shoving my hand into my pants pocket before I drop to my knee in front of her. "I'm going to do this right here, right now. When it's just you and me, and I can say everything on my mind, clearly."

She nods, her big eyes starting to get watery. "Perfect. Okay." I know she must be itching to look at the ring in my hand, but she keeps her beautiful, soft green eyes right on mine.

"Avery Leigh, it's not just that I love you, it's that I learned what love is because of you."

"Damn," she whispers, her bottom lip trembling now. "Really good opening, babe."

"Shush," I say. When she presses her lips together obediently, I continue, "When I met you, I knew you needed me. I knew I wanted to protect you and show you how incredible you are. That part came easy. But this past year, you've taught me it's okay to receive love too. You take care of me as much as I take care of you, and I think love is knowing that in some things, I'll take the lead. But in others, you'll carry me. Avery, I don't just love you, I'm in awe of you. No matter what we go through, no matter what changes, I'll change with you. If we break, we'll fix it. I'm not just promising to give you the life you deserve, I'm promising to forever appreciate all the ways you make me feel whole. If you'll be my wife, you will never go a day in your life without knowing your worth to me."

I hold up the ring and for the first time, her teary eyes leave mine and land on the center ruby, surrounded by little diamonds. Her lips part slightly as she takes it in.

"I know we can afford something more extravagant, but this is the most valuable thing my family owns. This is my grandmother's ring. I don't know if you know this but Gramps gave this ring to my grandma when she was eighteen. It was just a promise ring. It was all he could afford at the time. He emptied his pockets to buy her that ring, and then he left."

"What?" Avery's eyes widen, completely transfixed on the story.

"Yeah. He sat my grandma down, told her and her father that he was going to make something of himself and then come back for her because he couldn't stand the idea of her ending up with a man who gave her any less than what she deserved."

"Wow. *Just wow*. What happened?"

I wiggle the ring in front of her. "She wore this for three years. They only wrote letters to each other as Gramps started building his empire from scratch."

"She didn't see anyone else?"

I shake my head. "Nope. Apparently, he was worth the wait. He came back as a business owner, homeowner, and with a much bigger diamond and officially asked her to marry him."

Avery laughs into her hand. "That is the most romantic thing I've ever heard. What did your grandma say?"

"Well, she refused the new diamond and kept the promise ring on her hand. I only got the story secondhand but I think she said something along the lines of she would've rather been poor and happy, called my dad an old fool, and sarcastically thanked him for wasting three years of their lives that could've been together."

Avery bursts out in a chuckle as a tear falls from her right eye. She sniffles. "I think I would've liked your grandma."

"Me too. I wish I would've gotten to meet her, but Gramps tells all of us a lot of stories. You know she died over thirty years ago, but he never remarried. He always says his heart is still full from Grandma so he doesn't have room for another woman."

Avery sighs as she presses her palm against her chest, above her heart. "Oh...I get it now," she muses, almost to herself.

"Get what?" I ask. But she moves past my question.

"First, Finn Harvey, I love you. The kind of love that's going to last us a lifetime. Second," she says holding out her left hand, "it'd be my absolute honor to be your wife. *Yes, I'll marry you.*" She wiggles her hand, silently instructing me to slide the ring on. To my great surprise, it fits perfectly. This ring is so delicate, it can't be resized too many times, so I wanted Avery to tell me if it's too loose or too snug before making any judgment calls. But she wears it like it was made for her.

"It's so beautiful on you." I watch Avery admiring her hand, the tears fully flowing now.

"I would've loved to find this ring in a cake, or in a champagne flute, or in whatever way you wanted to gift it to me. Finn—I would've picked this ring over any diamond more expensive. It is so perfect. *Thank you.*"

I dab her face with the back of my hand, trying to mop up her tears without smudging all her pretty makeup. "Thank you, Queen, for being the kind of woman who deserves everything that this ring means."

She leans down to press her lips against mine, as I'm still on my knee, hunched over in the limo, but a small knock on the door interrupts her. Our stolen moment is over.

"Griffin? Are you in there?"

I sigh and hang my head. "Ready? That's Gramps."

Avery laces her hand in mine, and we scoot to the passenger door. She waits in her seat for me to straighten up and greet Gramps who looks far more casual than I expected. I don't think I've ever seen him not in a suit. But tonight, he's wearing dark denim jeans of all things with a crisp button-down shirt.

"Jeans? Really?"

He clears his throat and smirks. "I'm...with the times."

I laugh. "Okay, sure Gramps."

"Don't be rude to your lady and keep her waiting," he instructs, nodding to the open door. I hold out my hand and Avery wraps her fingers around mine, hoisting herself out of the seat while trying not to make any sudden movements in her form-fitting satin dress.

"My God, you are an absolute gem," Gramps says, reaching out to shake Avery's hand. "It's so lovely to meet you in person, honey."

"Thank you. It's so nice to meet you too, Mr. Senior."

Mr. Senior? I have to hold back my chuckle. I know she's nervous, but that was next-level awkward and adorable.

Avery eagerly reaches for his handshake, but Gramps stills and drops his hand when he sees Grandma's ring secured around Avery's finger.

"Oh, I asked already," I mumble, sensing the tension. "Sorry, I should've—"

"Beautiful," Gramps mutters, cutting me off. He's suddenly overcome with emotion and turns his back to Avery, no doubt to compose himself, because we all know men from his generation don't cry.

Avery widens her eyes at me in panic, but I ease her worry with a wink. Gramps spins around with a small sniffle and says, "Since we're family now, how about a hug? And please, none of this Senior mumbo-jumbo. Call me Gramps."

To my great surprise, Avery wraps her arms around Senior unshyly, holding him in a big bear hug. "Thank you for being here. It's *really* nice to see you."

Gramps kisses the top of her head. "You too, honey. Such a

pleasure. I wish Margot was here to meet you. She'd say you wear that ring better than she did."

Grandpa sucks in another little sniffle. I never met Grandma, but it's clear as day that something about Avery reminds him of her. In some sweet, poetic justice, he knows I found the same true love that he did.

"Now," Gramps continues, "I believe appetizers are already making their rounds. Shall we head in? I'll announce you at the door as the newest soon-to-be Mrs. Harvey."

Gramps releases Avery and turns on his heel, leading us to the front of the restaurant. We trail two paces behind, and Avery laces her fingers in mine once more. She looks up at me, giving me the strangest smile.

"What is it?"

"It's so funny," she mumbles.

"What's funny?" I stop to face her, studying her bemused expression.

"You look just like your dad, but you act just like your grandpa. The way you walk, the way you hug, the way you speak... it's like having a mirror into the future." She squeezes my fingers and beams at me. "And the future looks damn good."

Coming September 2024

Snapshot
by Kay Cove

Acknowledgements

To my husband—thank you for sending me warrior quotes when I needed them most. You are forever my rock. When I lose sight of my big "why", you always remind me of the vision. I'm lucky to share your name.

To Ashley and Sara—this book would not be possible without you. Thank you for being my inspiration and my encouragement. Thank you for laughing with me and for sitting in silence with me as you patiently waited for me to get unstuck. Finn and Avery would not exist without you. No one deserves this HEA more than you guys.

To my editor, Emily—thank you so much for your hard work in helping me polish this story and telling the best version of Finn and Avery's happily ever after.

To K.B.—thank you for reenergizing me in the final quarter, right before the buzzer. Your beautiful art recharged my passion for this story and I am incredibly grateful.

To Rachel—thank you for helping me launch my first standalone story. Through your incredible vision and creativity, I know I've reached more new readers than I ever could've on my own.

To my influencer squad and hype team—thank you all for supporting me and cheering me on as I took my writing one step further than I had before. You've been there for the sweet moments, the sassy ones, and now the steamiest to date, and I will always pour my heart and soul into my writing for you guys!

To the Page & Vine family for welcoming Camera Shy into their home and helping spread my heart story to bookstores around the world. I am forever grateful.

To all of my return readers and new readers—thank you for taking a chance on me and supporting this lil ol' author dream of mine. I am finally becoming the best version of myself as I pursue my passion, and it would not be possible without you. From the bottom of my heart, thank you for being part of my dream.

About the Author

Kay Cove is a contemporary romance author, committed to crafting plot focused stories with sassy heroines and dirty-talking MMCs, full of witty banter and situations that force flawed characters to grow. She likes to challenge herself by writing in a variety of sub-genres.

After a successful career in corporate HR, she ultimately decided to pursue her dream of becoming a published author. Her current works include, the *Real Life, Real Love* series, *Camera Shy,* and the *PALADIN* Series.

Born in Colorado, Kay currently resides in Georgia with her husband and two sweet and rambunctious little boys.